MYSTERY GIRL

A NOVEL

David Gordon

NEW HARVEST
HOUGHTON MIFFLIN HARCOURT
BOSTON   NEW YORK
2013

This edition published by special arrangement with Thomas & Mercer

For information about permission to reproduce selections from this book,
write to Permissions, Houghton Mifflin Harcourt Publishing Company,
215 Park Avenue South, New York, New York 10003.

www.hmhbooks.com

Library of Congress Cataloging-in-Publication Data
Gordon, David, date.
Mystery girl : a novel / David Gordon.
pages cm
"New Harvest."
ISBN 978-0-544-02858-6
1. Authors—Fiction. I. Title.
PS3607.O5935M97 2013
813'.6 — dc23
2013001726

Book design by Brian Moore

Printed in the United States of America
DOC 10 9 8 7 6 5 4 3 2 1

To the girls who mystified me

PART I

IN SEARCH OF LOST MINDS

1

I BECAME AN ASSISTANT detective, and solved my first murder, right after my wife left me, when I went a little mad. Never as crazy as the
master detective himself, of course; he was completely nuts. Certi-
fiable with the papers to prove it. Madder than a shithouse rat. He
was (and you'll pardon the bad pun, but I'm a frustrated writer and
we're the worst, with our brittle, bitter brilliance now confined to
the Scrabble board) mentally detective in every possible sense. And
trust me, I know from crazy, being, as I admit right here at the out-
set, no poster child for emotional health myself.

But in truth, I knew I wasn't really nuts, just angry and scared
and lonely and so, so very sad. The disease wasn't in my head, but
in my heart. My heart was terribly sick. I could feel it carrying on in
there all night: feverish, mumbling, tossing in its sleep, waking up in
shivers from sweat-drenched nightmares, unable to keep anything
down. I felt like an ambulance carting it around, siren moaning, expecting traffic to part and cops to clear my way. But there was no
trauma center for me to come screeching up to. No winged nurses
awaiting me in white. I just drove around in circles, wailing, Emergency, Emergency!

In the end, I diagnosed myself. The sickness I had was just life.
And the only known cure for the malady of existence—although
deeply tempting on certain endless white nights and empty black
hole mornings—was too radical, too uncertain, too irrevocable to
try until all other means had been exhausted.

2

AS I SAID, THIS all began the day Lala, my wife, walked into my office and said the scariest, most stomach-curdling words in the language: "We have to talk." (It's never good news. Never: "We have to talk. I'm horny, but let's hurry because there's pizza on the way.") She was leaving, she told me, and we were going into couple's therapy, and I was getting a job.

Now I don't want you to think I'm lazy, although that's obviously what she thought. I'd always had jobs, in fact, far too many. My primary job, of course, was novelist. But it's hard to make a good living as a novelist. After twenty years at it, my total earnings to date were $0, and I'd been forced to set my latest unfinished experimental fiasco, *Perineum,* aside in a drawer atop my other ill born unnovels, *Toilet* and *Slow Motion Holocaust,* and become a screenwriter for hire, since if there's anything in this world I love as much as, or sometimes even more than, books, it's movies. (And my wife of course.) Screenwriting proved to be far more lucrative than novelizing, as I was quickly recruited to polish a low-budget foreign-produced horror-sci-fi-softcore feature working-titled *Dark Probings,* for a small upfront sum and a larger share of the profits. The producer explained it all to me after he arrived in his Porsche at our lunch meeting when I turned in my work. His English wasn't great, and I didn't quite follow the math, and anyway he forgot his checkbook, but at least he bought me lunch ($13.25). Otherwise, my total film-career intake up till that fateful morning amounted to $180.00 net, which my friend Milo paid me, in twenty-dollar increments, for writing up the monthly New Releases and News To Us! notices at the video store where he worked.

So, while I went on "being" a novelist in my head if not on paper, and developing screenplays in my darkened bedroom by night, over the years I supplemented this base income with many, many other jobs: messenger, delivery boy, survey taker, phone answerer, photocopier, assistant file clerk, assistant painter, assistant/driver, assistant copy editor, assistant office manager at a temp agency, temporary office assistant at an ad agency, office temp at an assisted living agency, assistant to the assistant of a motivator, (I'm not even sure what that was), and finally, the pinnacle of my assistancy: assistant manager of Bartleby's Scrivenings, a secondhand bookshop managed and owned by the sole other employee, Mary Jane Rutherford, and located near my house in the beautiful and trendy Silver Lake neighborhood of LA. The job didn't pay much, but then again I didn't have to do much besides sit at the counter, dust desultorily, argue with my boss about literary theory, and chitchat with Milo, who knew more about movies than I knew about anything and assistant-managed Videolatry next door. Both shops were going under, it being a race to the bottom between our respective industries, and MJ (she started using her initials in college when she started dating women and her real name only appeared on her checks), who had retired from a long career as a graduate student in early modernist poetry to open this shop with the last of her student loan money, retired still further, into her tiny back office, and left me out front, alone at the foremast, holding the tattered flag of Literature.

At first I assumed she was just watching porn or googling back there, which was what I did when I retired to my own office at home, and which I referred to as "thinking." Then I heard strange mutterings and saw her slinking around in dark glasses, clutching 100 percent biodegradable recycled paper bags to her chest, and I understood: she was on a self-destructive poetry binge, drinking Trader Joe's wine and reading Stevens and Yeats, aloud, to herself. Sometimes she declaimed so boldly that it scared the rare customer who'd wandered in out of the sun to kill time waiting for a bus. She even alarmed Peaches, the toy poodle that lived upstairs with Jerry, Milo's boss.

Though both stores were sinking, ours drowned first, as our

lease ran out and we could no longer afford the rent in a neighbor-hood like Silver Lake, which had become highly popular because it was full of quaint, neighborhoody features like secondhand book-shops and cinephile video stores. Jerry, who'd arrived with the early gay pioneers in the '70s, had a long-term lease at preboom, barrio prices. He'd first hired Milo as a projectionist at The Alleycat, a gay porn theater he owned, while Milo worked on his MA in queer cin-ema studies. (He still claimed that his thesis project, *Undergrowth: Body Hair and Gay Avant-Garde Cinema*, would shift the whole field, if he ever finished it.) The communal movie theater gave way to lonely video booths, and then to the rental shop, as the Internet and gen-trification drove the hairy and scary away. Now Videolatry was de-clining in turn, but Jerry's own health was failing even faster, and he cared less about the future of cinema than about having Milo on hand to plump his pillows and bring up his soup.

First MJ sold online the few really valuable books we had: a nearly fine first American edition of *Naked Lunch* (the Paris edition, published by Olympia was worth much more); a nice if slightly too-loved set of Narnia firsts; several good-to-fair Jim Thompson paper-backs (*The Alcoholics, A Hell of A Woman, Savage Night*), which I had spotted in someone's dead uncle's carton and acquired for the shop but couldn't afford for myself); the less rare 1935 edition of *Seven Pil-lars of Wisdom* by T. E. Lawrence; Casanova's *Memoirs* in six water-stained volumes; a paperback original, in fair condition, of *Flow My Tears, The Policeman Said* by Philip K. Dick. Then she tried to unload the rest of her stock wholesale to another dealer but got nowhere. Then she tried donating them to the library for a write-off, but even they wouldn't take the paperbacks. Finally, we snuck over to our lo-cal branch in the dead of night, MJ driving her wagon and Milo and I riding along, dressed in dark clothing. We abandoned the thou-sands of orphaned books on the library's back steps and raced off, as if dumping a murder victim, wine bottles and salvaged poetry roll-ing around in the back.

3

YOU SEE, MY WIFE had me all wrong: I wasn't lazy. Lazy bums don't give a damn. They relax. They enjoy life. They kick back in a quiet shady alley all day, sprawled in a heap of old clothes and snoozing dogs, whittling and whistling and guzzling hooch from a jug. I'm not a bum. I've slaved away desperately my whole life. What I am is a failure.

And I suppose I had her all wrong too, because I was utterly shocked, astounded really, when, after nearly five years of couple-dom, she walked into my "office" that day, where I was busy "thinking," to tell me she was leaving. Up till that moment, I'd thought everything was fine, if by fine you mean barely talking, rarely fucking, occasionally yelling, and mostly just lying listlessly side by side, watching TV and eating Nestlé chocolate chip cookies that we sliced up and baked from a tube. But I didn't mind, not really. This, I'd been told, was marriage. I'd been warned what to expect. And those in-stant cookies are actually pretty amazing when they're hot and soft and melty. Not gourmet chocolate truffles, or exotic rare-fruit sor-bets, or even homemade pie, but they hit the spot. And if our mar-riage was no longer a Valentine's box full of rich, dark, 99 percent pure happiness, it still seemed like the kind of warm, sweet, chewy nonhappiness I could settle for. Plus I loved her. I really did. And she loved me, or at least that's what she said, declaring it passionately, re-peatedly, as she knelt on the carpet, tears streaming down her face, and dumped me.

"I love you," she kept saying, "I fucking love you, but things have to change. And they're not changing. You're not hearing me. I love you so much it tears my heart out, but this is the only way to make you understand."

It's true. I didn't understand. But I heard. At least I thought I did. Maybe I didn't.

"I hear you," I said. "I do. And I'll find a job. I'm already looking, but I'll look harder. And the therapy, fine. No problem. Just tell me when and I'll be there. But don't leave me. Please. I don't deserve it." I dropped to the floor beside her, tried to make her look me in the eyes, her green eyes, always greener when polished with tears. "You promised you'd never leave me," I told her. "You promised me, no matter what. Remember?" She nodded, weeping now. "Please. Don't do this. Don't."

But she did it, she walked away, dragging the good luggage down the steps, getting into the good car. I guess she wanted to leave me in style. Then I shut the light and curled into a ball on the bed, cradling my heart as if it were a sick baby. How did I feel? I don't know what to say. Alone. As if in one moment, she had turned herself into a stranger and me into an exile. But I didn't cry. Why not? Because the only person in the world I trusted to hold me while I cried was gone.

4

THE NEXT MORNING, I woke up blank, expecting her warm, lumpy form beside me, and had to remember all over again. This kept happening, like an emotional amnesia, forgetting and then remembering: she's gone. Then I started job-hunting like a madman. I felt a desperate need to show up at our first therapy appointment on Friday holding a job like a bouquet. I scoured the Internet and fired off a dozen résumés. I posted my CV on a local job-hunting search engine site. I called the couple of old employers I could remember and let them know I was available, on the odd chance they'd been up all night wondering. Then, when I couldn't think of anything else to do, I cleaned the house, just in case she came back.

It was amazing, the mess I'd made. In only twenty-four hours I'd reduced our lovely home to such a state of cluttered, dingy, smelly bachelordom that even I was appalled. Newspapers were everywhere. The sheets were pulled off the mattress. I'd somehow managed to drink out of a dozen glasses and coffee cups and leave them scattered around. I began to clean in a panic, knowing I couldn't let myself fall so far so fast, especially since under normal circumstances I'm not really that bad of a slob. She was neater, sure—she's a girl. But I held down my end. I did the cooking and took out the trash. I did laundry regularly and ran the dishwasher when it was full. But I would never do it on my own. When she left, even just for a night, I fell into a shambles, the very same shambles I'd lived in before she came along, the shambles of single straight guyhood. Because the world of straight men without women, frankly, is a sad, brutal place. It's a place where breakfast is canned peanuts, and dinner is eaten straight from the frying pan, so you don't have to wash a plate. It's a place where everyone has one sheet and one towel forever. Nothing matches. We don't even know what matching means. To get two socks the same shade of black is a miracle. When you're sick, nobody cares, even your best friends don't think to make you tea, you just lie there, febrily sweating and seething, and you have to blow your nose into a T-shirt because there are no tissues, ever, and the only toilet paper is napkins you stole from McDonald's. You don't want to live there? Of course not. No one does. Not even us. But, like dogs in the pound or enchanted toads, we can't escape on our own.

That was where she'd first found me, cast adrift on a salvaged futon in an empty room with a cardboard box as a table, wearing the same clothes I'd been wearing since, well, since the last girlfriend, the one I broke up with when I moved out here to not-write screenplays. Now, as half of a married couple, my hair looked good and my clothes fit. I smelled sweet. Thanks to marriage, I was finally dateable. And we lived in amazing luxury. We had a whole closet full of just towels and linens and extra quilts. We woke up in a sunny house and all our furniture came from the same period. Modern, I think. We'd painted the walls, something that had never crossed my mind before. We owned a vacuum cleaner and had organic stuff in the fridge, and I don't mean growing in there. We had all kinds of nice things in the bathroom, too, that I'd rub lovingly on my face and hair and feet. I'd never even considered that my feet, so far away, so lonesome, might deserve to be loved, until she taught me. And I appreciated it, I really did. We all do, believe me, I can speak for the assembly of heterosexual mankind on this. We're grateful. We know it's a better life, a more beautiful, sweeter, gentler life. We just can't help ourselves. Without you we're brutal, even the best of us, we're brutal, even if only to ourselves, because to care for yourself, you have to care about yourself, even love yourself a little. And in our land there is no love but you.

5

I GOT HIS EMAIL on the fifth day, when I was getting a little desperate. The big therapy session was that afternoon, and I'd been on only two job interviews. They didn't go well. I wanted to ask, in my follow-up email: Can't we just forget this ever happened? Please delete. It had taken an enormous amount of effort merely to make myself presentable in the first place. I had to find a clean shirt and unwrinkled pants and do the buttons up right and tuck it in. I had to shave, which was awful. My hands shook from all the coffee, and I accidentally slashed my throat, but the hardest part was facing myself in the mirror. I'd lost weight, burning off my happy husband paunch in a marathon of distress, so I actually looked pretty trim, and my spouse-supervised haircut was top-notch, but there was something terribly wrong with my eyes. I couldn't blame my interviewers for wanting me gone: these people are trained to give you a firm handshake and a straight look. But when they grasped my clammy, shaky fingers and gazed into my bloody blues, they saw something even I didn't want to know.

So as I said, by day five, things were getting rough. I sat up, abruptly, at dawn. I didn't sleep much during this period, or slept only in snatches, during which I had nightmares that were identical to my waking life: I dreamed that what was happening to me was actually happening, and woke up every hour or so, exhausted.

First I rose and checked my empty email. Next I made coffee. Then, exhausted already, I took a self-pity break on the couch, face down, nose in the crack between cushions, as if sniffing for lost change. What job did I (or she, really) think I could get? By training and nature, I was equipped to do nothing but lie thusly and think deep thoughts. I blamed my hardworking parents for encouraging me to obtain a useless, outrageously expensive, and still unpaid-for education best suited to a minor nineteenth-century aristocrat. I could read philosophy and discuss paintings. Not that I ever did, but I could, if I had to, in an emergency. I could charm elegant dinner parties with witty patter, if anyone ever invited me to one. I could articulate my misery with great precision. If only I had learned to cut hair, or cook, or fix something! The mailman startled me, and I jumped to my feet as a clutch of bills shot through the slot and splattered onto the floor. Rent. Power. Student loans. How much was left in our joint account anyway? Would Lala continue to pay her share? How much did this therapy cost? What was today's date, anyway?

Spying on the mailman through the curtains, I entertained a brief reverie about his lot: strolling along, out in the air in all weather, with no one watching, making his simple rounds, then returning home to a well-earned, hearty meal served by a loving, buxom wife. How sweet, I mused, to walk around and get paid for it. Yet, as we know, there was something about the mail that drove men to slaughter. Maybe all that endless paper, piling up, like novels no one wanted. All that bad news. I sat back at my desk and rested my aching head on the keyboard.

That's when I saw it, close up, alongside my nose, an email that had slipped quietly into my box. The search engine had ground up my résumé and spat back a paltry response, one "position" in the known world that I was theoretically qualified to assume. It said only "Private Detective Requires Assistance," followed by a phone number. Assist? I could do that, I exulted. Anyone could. I called. It picked up after half a ring.

"Yeah?" the voice of an older woman asked.

"Good morning," I said in my most chipper and business-ready tone. "I'm calling regarding the ad for an assistant."

"Wrong number," she said and hung up. I checked the number and tried again, figuring I'd misdialed. As I mentioned, my hands were a bit shaky. Again the phone was snatched up almost before I pressed the last button.

"Yeah?" It was the same woman.

"Hello, I'm sorry if this the wrong number, but there's an ad for a private investigator who needs an assistant."

"Look, fella, I'm a busy woman, all right? I don't know what you're trying to pull but I ain't got time for this." I could hear other phones ringing in the background and a television's blare.

"So you didn't place the ad for a private investigator?"

"Private what?" she yelled over the din. "No. We don't need no private investigator."

"No!" I shouted back. "You're the investigator. I want to be the assistant."

"You want to be my assistant. Well you can start assisting me right now by shoving the phone up your own ass instead of waiting for me to come do it for you. What?" she shouted suddenly. "What? I can't hear you. Come in here." There was a moment of silence while I wondered whether to hang up. "Hold on," she said, reluctantly, and then covered the phone. I heard a muffled exchange. Finally, someone else got on, a man this time.

"Yes," he said. "I believe you're calling to inquire about the position of assistant?"

"Yes, sir," I said, throwing in the "sir" because this guy's voice sounded a lot more refined than the lady's had, not English exactly, but like someone who really knew English.

"Very good. I am interviewing this afternoon. Perhaps it would be convenient for you to come at four?"

"That would be great," I said, and he gave me the address. He asked my name and I told him.

"Excellent, Mr. Kornberg. I'll look forward to meeting you then. My name," he said, "is Solar Lonsky."

6

THE ADDRESS WAS IN Koreatown. I found it without too much trouble. On a jumbled street of beaten old homes and newly renovated oddities, their once quaintly shingled walls now slathered with stucco and studded with satellite dishes, the squat bungalow I parked before was distinguished by an air of benign neglect. The white fence was peeling but the trees were old and shady. Their roots broke the curved concrete walk into chunks like thawing ice. On a deep porch, under the shadowing eaves, a diamond of yellowed glass was set in a dark wood door.

I waited until after I parked to put on my jacket and tie, since my wife took the car with working AC and it was getting hot. (Autumn in LA, season of fires and earthquakes and apocalyptic winds, growing only hotter as the real world cools.) I grabbed my leather briefcase, which contained my résumé, a protein bar, and a couple of books that I'd dropped in there to make it look full, (*Portrait of a Lady, Thief's Journal,* and a volume of Proust). There was a special-delivery copy of the *New York Times* on the walk, so I picked that up and rang the bell. After a moment a slot opened and a very small, very round Korean lady peered out.

"Hello," she said in a thick accent.

"Good afternoon," I said. I was planning to continue by saying I had an appointment with Mr. Lonsky, but she shut the peephole. Then she opened it again.

"Warren?" she asked.

"No, I'm not Warren. I'm Samuel. Sam really. Sam Kornberg."

"You show warrant?"

"Oh, warrant," I said. "I thought you said Warren. No, no warrant. I still don't know what you mean."

"No police?"

"No."

"Okay." She smiled and shut the slot again. I checked the address to be sure I had the right house. Was this some kind of very formal, polite crack den? Then she was back.

"Norman?"

"No, not Norman either. I'm Sam."

"No." She spoke slowly, for my benefit, as if explaining a simple fact. "You are Mormon."

"A Mormon? No, I'm not a Mormon. Sorry. Jewish, I'm afraid."

"Okay," she said again, still smiling, and shut the slot. I was about ready to give up, but then I heard elaborate bolts shifting and locks being turned, and the door swung back with a sound like a drawbridge being raised. She waved me inside, with that pretty underhand wave Asian women use, and then rebolted the locks behind me, hoisting a heavy wooden crossbar that she could barely lift into place.

The living room was done in middle period old lady, with plastic covers on the white couches and runners protecting the thick, spotless white carpets. White vertical blinds kept out the sun. There were three televisions, all on, two with baseball games, one with soccer. There were also three telephones on the coffee table. In a white upholstered armchair, commanding the view, sat a tiny old white lady, even tinier than the little Korean lady and far more gnarled. She wore red polyester slacks and a pink blouse. Her white hair had a pink tinge to it and she wore giant, round red sunglasses and had very red lips. She was smoking the longest, thinnest cigarette I'd ever seen, grasping it between two red-tipped claws, playing cards clutched in her other hand. The Korean lady sat on the couch and picked up a hand that had been resting facedown, eyeing her opponent suspiciously.

"You Sol's friend?" the old white lady asked. She was the one from the phone.

"Well, I'm here to see Mr. Lonsky—"

"Solly!" she yelled, cutting me off. "Sol! Get out here! Sorry about Mrs. Moon," she went on, addressing me again. "White men in suits make her nervous."

"Me too," I said, trying to smile agreeably, although I was starting to wonder about this whole setup. "They rarely bring good news."

Then another white man in a suit emerged from the interior of the house. At first he was just a shadow, a looming presence in the dark hall, and the sonorous voice I recognized from the phone.

"Is the door fastened?"

The old lady rolled her eyes at Mrs. Moon and yelled, "Yeah, Solly, it's shut."

"I can see that, Mother," the shadow boomed, like Moses on the mountain. "Is it made fast?"

"Jesus, yes, it's locked for crying out loud."

"Very well," he said, and came into the light. He was, to put it mildly, enormous. He was hugely, extravagantly, preposterously obese, with fingers like hot dogs and cheeks like rosy balloons and swaying, trembling, juggling triple-G breasts that wrestled like puppies in his shirt as he walked. But he was not one of those people who should, if they were healthy, be average size. He was huge on every level, in every dimension. He was very tall, over six feet, with shoulders wider than the door, and another four inches of black-and-gray hair rising from his high, wide carapace of forehead. Each massive hand was like a whole Easter ham. His head alone must have weighed fifty pounds, archaic and regal, like an unearthed chunk of marble. He was very pale, with a sharp chieftain's nose, a prominent, densely planted eyebrow ridge, thick, tender lips like slices of rare roast beef, and huge wet black eyes that blinked and floated like sharks in their bowl of a head before retreating behind the heavy lids. His ears were like conch shells, full of pink swirls and depths, and his neck was thicker and stronger than my leg. He was dressed in a cream-colored three-piece linen suit with pleated pants, a four-button jacket, a mauve shirt, a chocolate brown tie, and highly polished brown shoes. I was taken aback, but the shoes struck a plaintive note: they were pointy, bright, thin-soled, and delicate, and he moved toward me quickly, with surprising grace and lightness, as if instead of burdening him, his greatness uplifted, buoying him aloft, while my own spindly legs clung cravenly to the earth in their clunky boots.

"Mr. Kornberg, I presume," he intoned.

"Mr. Lonsky, it's a pleasure to meet you. I found this on the sidewalk."

"Ah yes. The paper," he said, tucking it under his arm and then taking my hand gently in his soft paw while looking me frankly in the eyes. Unlike the others, he didn't flinch. He smiled. "I'm unable to retrieve it myself, you see. Allergies."

Mrs. Lonsky snorted derisively at this but kept her eyes on her cards. She laid one down and Mrs. Moon drew it, impassively. Lonsky frowned.

"I see you've met my mother and our housekeeper. Let's retire to my study for a chat. Tea, please, Mrs. Moon. I find green tea less nervous-making than coffee."

Mrs. Moon smiled and started to stand, but the old lady waved her down. "Screw the tea. We're playing here. Besides" — she looked up at me and winked — "Solly's got an assistant now." She started laughing richly, the long, tiny cigarette bouncing in her mouth. Mrs. Moon tittered behind her fan of cards. Lonsky gave them a dignified sneer.

"Follow me," he said.

He led me down a hall full of old photos and into another room. Here there were floor-to-ceiling bookshelves crammed with old books and a huge leather-topped desk. I couldn't look closely, but my scavenger's eye caught a complete Freud, a complete Shakespeare, a complete Sherlock Holmes, a complete Rousseau's *Confessions,* and all twenty volumes of the Oxford English Dictionary. A completist. There was also a chessboard in mid-game, an upright piano stacked with sheet music, and a dusty violin, as well as assorted bones, rocks, animal skulls, small carved statues, and antique ceramic bowls. Lonsky sank into his chair, wide and deep like a leather throne. He went through the *Times,* pulled out a section and unfolded it, then folded it back again, revealing the crossword puzzle. He picked up a gold-and-onyx fountain pen.

"Time?" he asked me.

"Pardon? Oh" — I glanced at my watch — "a little after four."

"Please be precise if you can."

I looked at my watch again. Was this part of the interview? Had we started yet? I waited for the number to change.

"It is now exactly . . . 4:02."

Lonsky began rapidly filling in the crossword puzzle, moving ceaselessly from left to right as if jotting down a grocery list. While he wrote, he spoke, without lifting his eyes from the page.

"So, you'd like to be a private investigator."

"Yes, very much so," I said, a little relieved now that the interview proper was under way, but still distracted by his writing. It looked as if he was doing all the across questions in order, one after the other. "I brought you a copy of my résumé." I snapped open the briefcase and searched through the jumble.

"That won't be necessary," he said without looking up. "You're from New Jersey. You attended a good college, probably in New York. You worked with books, perhaps in publishing, but more likely in a used bookshop, although business has fallen off. Someone close to you, a woman, works in the fashion industry. You're married. But, I'm afraid, you're currently having some difficulties in that area as well."

I laughed nervously. I admit I was even a little frightened.

"How did you know all that? The Internet?"

He laughed, still scribbling away. Now he was filling in the down clues.

"I merely observed you, Mr. Kornberg. That you're from the garden state I gathered from your accent. However, the more nasal features of the dialect have been smoothed over, indicating some advanced education. Also, the books in your briefcase are of a varied and refined nature, suggesting a much larger collection. I assume you grabbed them at random to fill the case?"

I nodded guiltily. He went on: "Hence, you are clearly a serious reader and perhaps professionally involved with literature. But the books themselves are old, well-worn editions, and I observed too that you immediately noted some of the better items in my own collection, suggesting perhaps a used bookshop. You're wearing a Dries Van Noten suit from last year's fall collection. Although I wear only bespoke suits myself, residing outside the commercially available dimensions, I know that Mr. Van Noten is both an expensive and somewhat rarified designer, far too sophisticated a choice for an average bookish fellow to make without guidance. That indicates some rather esoteric knowledge of clothes. Nevertheless, it is last year's and not a summer suit at all, which suggests you purchased it at a discount, perhaps at one of the private sales to which industry insiders are invited. Also, your watch is inexpensive, your shoes are unpolished, and the sunglasses in your shirt pocket are repaired with tape, all suggesting that you are frugal and not generally given to outlandish personal spending. That you are married is obvious from the ring. I assume therefore it was your wife who bought you the suit. But you missed a spot under your nose shaving this morning and there's also a coffee stain on your tie, both things that a loving wife, especially one who favors Dries, would have most certainly noticed. Of course, it's possible that your wife is simply out of town. But I regret to say that I believe the trouble to be more serious than that."

"How can you tell?" I asked, trying for a casual smile.

"From your eyes," he said. He slammed down the paper and pen. "Time!"

I blinked at him, in shock.

"Time," he said again, louder. I looked at my watch.

"4:05."

"Not bad for a Friday," he said, then pointed a heavy finger at me. "And you hesitated a bit on the timekeeping."

"Sorry."

He rose majestically, straightening his pleats. "Well, I'm satisfied, and if you are as well then I'd like you to start straight off. The case, which for reference purposes I call The Case of the Mystery Girl, is under way and mounting toward its crisis." He stopped and stared at me. "Shouldn't you be writing this down?"

"Oh, sorry," I blurted, patting my pockets as if there might be a notebook in one of them. I hadn't even realized I'd been hired. I found an old pen in the lining of my suit coat and, while Lonsky watched, wrote "Mystery Girl" on the back of my résumé. Satisfied, he went on.

"Her name is Ramona Doon. She resides at the Coconut Court Apartments on Spaulding. Number five. She should be back there by six. At that time of day, take Fountain. I want you to wait outside, follow her if she leaves, keep detailed notes, and report back to me in person once you are convinced that she is home safe for the night. Don't worry about the hour."

"Right," I said, still a little shocked that I actually had the job, and not entirely sure that I wanted it.

"And please make sure you are not observed by the lady or anyone else." He gazed down at me like a statue of a general on a horse. "This is important."

"Right." I nodded and wrote "NOT observed," then underlined it.

He nodded approvingly. "Unfortunately the state of my health won't allow me to take this in hand myself. Therefore I am taking the risk of trusting you instead. Trusting your bravery, your fidelity, and your discretion."

"Is it your allergies?" I asked.

"What? Oh yes, among other things." He gazed at me thoughtfully. "Perhaps it would be prudent for you to don a disguise."

"Disguise?"

"Can you walk in heels? Speak any foreign tongues?"

"No, I don't think so."

"Well, at least try to keep your wits about you. Lives may depend on it." Before I could take this in, he pulled a hundred dollar bill from his pocket and pressed it into my palm. "Take this as an advance, since you're short of funds." He steered me rapidly out of the room and down the hall, where his mother and Mrs. Moon were now side by side, poring over a long adding machine tape. "Don't forget to keep track of your mileage," Lonsky continued. "Mrs. Moon, please. My tea."

She went to stand but Mrs. Lonsky stopped her.

"We're busy, Sol. She's helping me add up the day's tally."

Impatient, he leaned over them and ran his eyes along the tape.

"Ten thousand six hundred and forty two," he announced.

Mrs. Moon tapped a calculator and smiled.

"Wow," I said, barely able to keep from bursting into applause. But Mrs. Lonsky scowled.

"Solar," she said. "I need to speak to you alone in the kitchen."

"In a moment, Mother," Lonsky declared, turning to me. "Go, Kornberg, go. And do your best."

"Sure," I said. "But how did you do that trick?"

"Trick?" he asked.

"You know, with the numbers."

Lonsky smiled.

"Why, Kornberg," he said, "it's called addition."

I left the Lonsky home confused but exhilarated. A job! True, the job was perhaps the oddest in an odd-job life, resulting in a CV that looked like the résumé of a maniac with ADD, unless you added, in invisible ink, *Secret Novelist*. But it was a job, at least, a nonwriting job with a paycheck, just what the wife had ordered. I decided to hang on to it for now, so I had something to bring to the table at therapy. I could always call later and back out, if a better offer came in. And then there was that fresh hundred, sharply folded in my pocket.

Still, as I headed toward the couple's therapist in West Hollywood, swerving and stalling through the traffic on Beverly Boulevard, occasionally racing a few feet forward to the next red light, I could feel my sore heart begin to throb anew: I was meeting my wife in an office to renegotiate our love, pledged to last forever. It seemed that eternity was up for renewal, today.

7

I ARRIVED EARLY, PATROLLED the sector in widening circles until I found free legal parking five blocks away, and then entered the building at a flustered jog. Sweating through my thick wool suit (Lonsky had been right), I wiped my face with my tie and opened the office door. Lala was waiting. My wife is Mexican—she has that fierce beauty, half native, half Spanish, long black hair and green eyes set in an oval face, her little body, narrow shoulders, tiny hands and feet that make her round breasts and ass seem almost overripe, bubbling and bouncing as she moves, her soft, smooth, coyly curved belly peeking between jeans and top, showing a deep navel still slightly scarred from a misguided piercing that got infected and, if you peer very closely, a few tiny golden hairs—and her real name is Eulalia Natalia Santoya de Marías de Montes. That sounds like she stole it off the tomb of an ancient nun, so she generally goes by Natalia Montes, or even less musical but more married, Natalie Kornberg. But once I learned her real name, I began calling her Eulalia and its many diminutives—Lali, Lalia, Yuli—until the perfect pet name stuck: my little Lala.

Lala works in a high-fashion clothing shop (displaying artifacts that to me are either too complicated to be wearable or too simple to be buyable at that shocking price) and she always looks elaborately right. Today she had on high leather boots, tight tucked jeans, a thin lacey blouse, a clingy cashmere cardigan, and a woolen shawl. Her bracelets and earrings jingled. Her red lips smiled. Her eyes gleamed. She looked infuriatingly beautiful.

"Wow, you look great," she said.

"Thanks." I scowled. "How are you?" I sat on the couch beside her. We were in a miniaturized waiting room, really a foyer between inner and outer doors, containing the couch, a chair, and a table with magazines.

"I'm excellent, thank you," she said. "Actually I'm going on a buying trip to New York tomorrow for the weekend. Isn't that exciting?"

"Definitely." I tried to smile back.

"I'm very excited." She leaned forward, solicitously. "How are you doing?" This was the Lala I'd grown to hate. The phony. Of course, even in my state, I understood she probably wasn't really all that excellent. She was nervous and that was a defense. Still, her choice of defense was an offense to me: a bullshit Hollywood warmth and smarmy positivity that enabled her to speak to me, the man she'd slept with (almost) every night for (almost) five years, as if I were an acquaintance. Not to mention the patronizing question, asking how I felt, as if I were an invalid she had come here to visit, and not the man whose heart she had skewered.

"Pretty good," I said. "I found free parking. On the other hand, my wife left me." Lala made a sour face and glared at her red nails, baby gems on her stubby childlike fingers. Now I felt bad. This was not the way to win her back. "Sorry," I said. "I'm just sad and upset." That cheered her up.

"Don't worry," she said. "This is all for the best. I think we press this when we're ready." There was a button on the door, with a red light beside it, as in some high-security facility. A small sign said PLEASE PRESS UPON ARRIVAL. She hesitated before pushing, as if she were launching our fate. "I'm nervous," she said, frowning, and I almost giggled, seeing my old Lala peek through. Then I remembered that she was the one who had brought us here and got mad again. She pushed the button. The light turned red.

How did we get here? I wondered, at a total, sudden loss, like a man who went out for milk and woke up in traction at a hospital. I was, I saw, unable to even begin hypothesizing the reasons we were in therapy because I was unable to grasp that we were actually the sort of married couple who might find themselves in therapy, because deep down I barely grasped that we were really married: to me Lala was unique, she superseded the categories of girlfriend, lover, wife. I remember, soon after we'd wed, when bankers and bakers first began saying, "your wife called in an order," or "your wife mentioned this . . ." I would be nonplussed, and on the verge of asking "Who?" She's not my wife. She's my Lala. But I held that belief at my peril. We were not unique. We were in fact an ordinary married couple, with ordinary heartbreaking problems, and an ordinary inextinguishable love that might flicker out or be smothered in our sleep. Our tragedy was like every other tragedy that I had witnessed playing itself out in supermarkets and parking lots and bars. Now, on the couch, her right hand crab-walked to mine and we squeezed, once, before she put it in her lap and covered it with her left. My heart swelled like a flood, cresting my chest, and retreated back into its depths. The inner door opened. A kindly old woman blinked at us, in round glasses, a pink sweater, pleated slacks. "You must be Natalia and Sam," she said and smiled warmly. "I'm Gladys. Please come in."

8

THE OFFICE WAS SORT OF new age grandma—printed fabrics, upholstered pinks and creams, mixed with candles, Buddhas, and sunset posters exhorting us to Aspire and Accept. We sat as on a seesaw, at opposing ends of the couch. Gladys perched on a chair at our apex. "Well," she asked, leaning forward eagerly, hands pressing together, as if we were getting ready to open presents, "why are we here? Who'd like to begin?" I noticed she had a diamond ring and a gold band together on one long, knobby finger.

I looked at my wife, who looked back at me, eyebrows urging me to speak, like in a restaurant when she was too embarrassed to ask for more bread.

"I don't know," I said. "It was Lala's idea. I mean Natalie." I blinked and micronodded at her. "You tell her."

"OK, fine, I'll begin," she said, as if doing me a favor, and pulled out a legal pad. I glimpsed a long list, similar to the lists of gift ideas (for herself) that she generously provided in advance of Christmas and her birthdays. Her frank and childlike lust for things used to stun me, but there was something fetching about it back then. I was the cosseted middle-class child who could never think of anything he wanted, who didn't see why he needed new jeans when he had a pair. She was the poor girl from beat-rural Mexico whose wish lists, along with wild hopes for cameras and watches, also asked for "socks," "good books," and "nice stationery and envelopes (different colors)." The idea of her covering those rainbow pages with her small, clear hand, sealing them, and sending them off to her friends, all of whom lived within a few miles, made me want to hug her so hard that the poor little girl she once was could feel my squeeze.

This current list, however, did not make me want to hug her, exactly. From what I could see it was longer than the ones she sent to Santa.

"Jesus," I muttered. "That's some list." I turned to Gladys apologetically. "I didn't even know there was homework."

She giggled and blinked brightly. "That's OK," she said. "Let's let Natalia begin with her top five and maybe you'll think of something later."

"Well, number one," Lala read. "Sam finds a job. Number two, does more chores around the house. Also, number three, you can do more errands, like for example, when I'm working you could do the grocery shopping and get dinner started. Or instead of sitting in your room all day you could be cleaning the garage or doing the yard."

"Hey," I said. "I have an idea. Why do I waste time sleeping when I could be polishing your shoes?"

Gladys chuckled, but Lala wasn't amused. She spoke in her new, icy businesslady's voice. "I'm just not getting my needs met in this marriage anymore."

"Your needs met? What am I, a needs provider? It sounds like you're changing banks, not husbands."

Gladys laughed again and Lala glared at her. Gladys shrugged. "You've got to admit, he's funny . . ."

"Very," Lala said.

"I'm sorry," I said, though secretly I was thrilled that the therapist seemed to like me, as if pleasing her were the point, as if she would pick a winner and decide our fate. "I just don't see why that's my job. I don't remember agreeing to any of this when we got married. I just promised to love you. And I have." I reached around, gazing at the affirmative posters for a hint. "Unconditionally."

Gladys held up her hands. "Let's take a breath. All of us." We did. "Good. Now, there are three areas in which healthy couples have reasonable expectations: first, money and chores, and who contributes what, then emotional support, and lastly sex. We've touched on the first two. How is your sex life?"

Embarrassed to be asked this by a grandma type with lipstick on her teeth and reading glasses on her head, I shrugged.

"Normal," I said.

Lala snorted. "What sex life?"

"Well now," Gladys said, "keeping that spark alive can be tough in a long-term relationship or when the stresses of life intrude. But it's very important. For example, my husband, Myron, and I go to spouse-swap events on the weekend and take our vacations at nudist ranches in the desert. It recharges our batteries. Last year we went to a swingers' retreat in Mexico. It was wonderfully refreshing."

I nodded, hoping the horror I felt wasn't clear on my face. Where did Lala find this shrink? Craigslist? She seemed unperturbed. "For me the problem is that I just can't feel attracted to a man I don't respect. Someone I can admire and look up to."

"How can you respect someone naked?" I said. "I'll wear a tie next time. Or a yarmulke."

"I just want a breadwinner," she said. "You're not a breadwinner."

"What is this, the fifties? Who did you think you were marrying? This is me. You want such a traditional husband all of a sudden, I don't see you home cooking my dinner, ironing my shirts, and taking care of my babies." She looked away, out the window, where the half-raised curtain revealed a length of telephone wire, the trembling top of a tree, and some pieces of blue sky. That was an unintentional low blow. Or maybe not. Lala and I had tried getting pregnant for most of the previous year, and she'd been unable to conceive. Was that when things began to really unravel? Or had it been the last attempt to stitch them up?

"Anyway," I said, changing the subject. "I got a job."

"What?" The tears seemed to recede from her eyes, and the twitchy stiffness left her smile. "You're kidding? When?"

"Just now. I came from the interview." I tapped the pad. "So you can cross that off your list."

Granny Gladys smiled broadly and clasped her hands. She seemed immensely relieved. "Well that sure is fast progress, right?"

Lala slapped my arm. "Is that why you're wearing the suit?" She seemed tickled that I might have a job that required a suit, as if I'd suddenly become head of a law firm. "What kind of job is it?" She turned toward me on the couch, lips parted, knees slightly agape, which was, I think I read somewhere, a welcoming sign. Gladys leaned forward eagerly, squeezing her hands together as if in fervent prayer.

"I'm going to be a detective."

Gladys cooed in gleeful surprise, clapping once, as if at a Mother's Day card that I'd made all by myself. Lala just stared.

"Detective?" she asked, waiting for a punch line.

"Well, assistant detective," I said, turning to Gladys for support. "I mean, I'm just starting out."

She nodded. "He is trying."

"Try harder," Lala said flatly. "You know, some men take pride in providing for their wives. They want them to have everything. They treat them like princesses."

Who were these men, I wondered? Had I ever met any? Were these perhaps the very same "assholes" who had once pursued her in their BMWs, waving gaudy watches and ski trips as bait, the "douchebags" and "jockstraps" whom she had been so glad to leave behind for me? Had she turned into one of their wives? I remembered her stories about the wealthy older lover she'd left when she came to America. "You had your chance to marry a rich man," I said. "Remember? You picked me."

I took a breath. I didn't want to sound angry. I didn't really feel mad anymore. What did I feel? "I do think you are a princess," I said. "Of course you are. My princess."

She glanced down softly at her list, as if ready to remove a few items. Gladys nodded. I probably should have shut up there, but I didn't. I never do. "But don't forget," I added. "I'm a prince."

Lala's shoulders bit and her features closed up. "I have to tell you that I am really considering divorce," she announced and gave me a dead look. I looked back in shock, hearing her actually say the word. Then she put her hands together and seemed to be begging, but for what? Compliance? Forgiveness? For what she had done or what she was going to do?

"I don't know what else to do," she said to Gladys. "I don't know how to change things. We fight all the time. It's just too hard." She turned to me, desperately. "You can't tell me you're happy," she pleaded.

"No," I said, quietly. "You're right. I can't. I'm miserable."

Her face seemed at once relieved and mournful, relieved to be mournful perhaps, or mournful at feeling relief.

"Well," Gladys said, checking at her watch with a sigh. "We have to stop."

9

I DROVE TO THE MYSTERY GIRL'S place and parked beneath a tree. It was a Hollywood bungalow colony, set on a quiet block off of Sunset, the sort of phony beach cottages they built in the '20s or '30s as offices or sets, with peeling blue shutters and curving paths around the browning rosebushes. I got out, pretending to be looking for an address, which I suppose I really was doing, and found her cottage, number five, a quaint one-bedroom, flimsy yet chic, with cacti in little pots on the tile steps and an old-fashioned lamp beside the door. I loitered about until I noticed movement beyond the thin lacey curtains, then retreated to my car, which I rolled forward a few feet until I had a view of her door.

I pulled out the canvas bag stuffed with some of the items Lonsky recommended I keep in my "kit" and which I'd grabbed when I stopped home to change from my suit into a less conspicuous T-shirt and jeans. I couldn't complete his list — I didn't own a camera, for instance, or any theatrical makeup, or a "selection" of fake mustaches — but I did have an old blond wig that Lala had worn when she'd dressed as a cheerleader one Halloween.

For now, I just took out the notebook, in which I wrote the time of my arrival, and "Subject Observed at Home," and grabbed the bag of nuts and raisins that I'd brought along in case the stakeout lasted all night, along with the water bottle, a designer model Lala used for yoga class. Fifteen minutes later my emergency supplies were gone. Half an hour after that I had to pee. I considered running to the gas station on the corner, but didn't want to risk losing the subject, so I put on NPR and listened to the news while I watched the traffic on Sunset slide by. Another half hour slowly passed. Unable to stand it any longer, I walked to the corner as casually fast as I could. They said they had no bathroom, though I'm not sure I believed them. I raced back to the car, hoping my subject was still there. I was now in acute distress and worried about permanent kidney damage. Precisely seventeen minutes later, I surrendered and relieved myself into my wife's fancy water bottle. I was about to discard it, but remembering that it cost fifteen dollars, and the ridiculous fight that this fact had triggered, I resealed it and tucked it in my bag, planning to sterilize it with boiling water later. I chuckled ruefully, imagining the fury that would be unleashed if she ever found out. Then I felt sad, imagining the jolly laughter we would have shared a couple of years before, if I'd told her the same tale. What had happened? Why did she give a shit about a purple water bottle? Why wasn't it fun being married to her anymore? Or to me?

I reached into my bag and got my Proust (book one of *Remembrance of Things Past,* the three-part Moncrieff-Rafferty version, that silver-and-black paperback that's everywhere, and which, like all true lovers, I'd learned to call by its secret pet name: *In Search of Lost Time*). This was the one detail that Lonsky hadn't gotten completely right: the inclusion of the Proust was not random. That volume, a fat block of thin paper, soft and heavy and yet somehow feathery, like pound cake, had been snoozing on the pillow beside me, in the spot where Lala used to dream. I'd always loved Proust, but now I read him both obsessively and haphazardly, the way other folks, I suppose, read the Bible, for comfort and wisdom in my time of pain. I had developed the irrational belief that almost any section, dipped up by chance, would answer my moment's dilemma. Proust himself would only laugh: no one had less faith in God or man or woman, or in the prospect of those parties working things out. I opened the book and read

He was jealous now of that other self whom she had loved.

10

THE SUN WENT DOWN, though from where I sat, I couldn't see it set. Evening, like groundwater, just seemed to seep up from the earth. The shadows of the palm trees lengthened. The pools under cars and porches deepened, then grew, scaling the walls, covering the hills and sidewalks, rising like smoke into the air. A slow parade of cars rolled by, some with their lights on, anticipating darkness, as if heading toward a funeral in the east. A star appeared, high and sharp above the mountains I knew had to be there, invisible now in the gloom. Then in Bungalow Five, behind the lacey curtains, a warm yellow lamp went on.

I got out of the car and scurried in a crouch across the street, like a Marine taking a position. This felt ridiculous as well as conspicuous, so I straightened up and walked as if I belonged there, strolling among the palms. I knew Lonsky wanted details, and in the dimness I would be able to sneak up on her place, but being on the job didn't make it any less creepy or illegal. Was I a private dick or a Peeping Tom? Now I could hear music coming from number five. It was Prince. Ramona Doon's curtains were still over the open windows. There was no breeze. No one was looking. I ducked into the shrubs.

Dogshit. That smell was the first thing I noticed as I crept through the bushes, or beneath them really, they had a sparse set of gnarled branches below a canopy of wilted leaves and blossoms. I don't know what kind, just bushes, with plenty of stale crap under them. I squatted there, listening to Prince (that song about how you don't have to be a star to rule his world. Kiss?), working up the courage to peek. Holding my breath, I raised my head above the sill. And saw nothing. Or no people anyway. There were objects of course, and to Lonsky they would no doubt reveal a biography's worth of choice tidbits, but to me it was just stuff: a rust-colored couch, a rocking chair, two wooden café-type chairs next to a little round table. On the table, a vase holding a sunflower. A TV, a few books, mostly paperbacks, I couldn't see titles from this distance, and an Indian blanket on the wall. A desk in the corner with a glowing computer and beside that a coffee cup, a spoon. The door to the back room was partly open. The music was coming from in there.

Steeling myself, I crouched back down—this detective business was hard on the back—and stole along the wall to the bedroom window. It was open as well, shrouded with another lacey curtain. Again, I held my breath, as if that might give me away and, easing up, peered over the edge.

She was dancing. What's more, she was dancing just like Prince, or a pretty close approximation of what I remembered from the video. She wasn't dressed like him, she wore pink underpants and a white T-shirt. She was barefoot, with pink-painted toes, and her breasts jumped as she popped her hips to the bass pulse. Her skin was a perfect shade of tan. Her black hair swung and scattered in a cloud around her head and her lips formed Prince's words. Her eyes were closed tight, which made me feel better. Amazingly, when the guitar kicked in, she shivered like a wire, leapt high in the air and landed in a James Brown split. Then she hopped right up and, on the drumbeat, spun around and did it all again, this time with her back to me. Her round bottom twitched. I couldn't help nodding along.

Then the song switched, perhaps her iPod shuffled, and a slow number came on. I knew this song, too. It was "Dark End of the Street," sung by the incomparable Percy Sledge. Lala and I had danced to it. Or she had, really. I was a clumsy oaf, of course, but she knew all the old dances, the cha-cha, the foxtrot, the waltz. And she loved the oldies, anything soul from the '60s and '70s especially, as well as Mexican oldies, the cholo music that the folks in the barrio still played and that I found for her on CD collections like *Brown-Eyed Soul* or *East Side Story*. Of course I was way too shy to dance in public, and too awkward to move much at all, but she taught me to dance cholo-style, the one step even I could do. You slung one arm around your girl's waist, while she hung both of hers from your shoulders, and you swayed together, barely moving, so cool and so slow. Some guys even hooked their loose hand into their pocket. We'd cling like that in our kitchen, alone where no one could see, and dance standing still, holding each other up, eyes closed.

Just then I heard footsteps on the path and a barking dog, like in a POW escape movie. I ducked down lower and peered through the shrubs. I couldn't see anything but long, creepy shadows. The barking grew near. I reheld my breath.

"OK Sparkle, good girl!" I heard a male voice cheering. "Go get it, girl!"

To my horror, I heard the dog come sniffling through the branches, barking louder, tracking my scent. I wanted to flee but there was nowhere to go except back out to where the beast's master waited. I braced myself for attack. Then a scrawny little creature, a terrier of some kind, a fuzzy rodent, popped from the undergrowth, demon eyes shining, baring its needle teeth.

"*Psst! Psst!*" I hissed, afraid to raise my voice. The little bitch barked at me. Her owner called.

"Whatcha smell there, Spark? A mouse?"

Ducking even lower under the window, afraid to so much as move, I picked up a pebble and threw it at my tormentor. I missed. The dog barked louder. Then Ramona appeared. She leaned out the window, right above me, like Juliet. I froze in terror against the side of her house. Her hair, the cotton of her shirt, I could have brushed them with my face or tickled her nose with my breath. Her fingers curled over the sill, inches from my head. The polish on the nails was red.

"Shush, go away!" she yelled at the barking mutt. "Be quiet!" Then she shut the window. The dog was unfazed, but stopped barking, as if used to this routine. It squatted and, fixing me with a quizzical expression, took a corkscrew dump by the roots of the shrub.

"Come on, girl. Do your business," the owner called. Sparkle finished up, and, as if to show her contempt, turned and back-kicked some dirt at me before trotting away. "Good girl!"

Their steps faded. My heart slowly resumed beating and I realized that the song had ended. Silence reigned. I took a few breaths, not too deep on account of the fresh crap near my feet, and then checked on Ms. Doon. She was in the front room, in the little kitchenette, chopping chicken and broccoli, dropping the pieces into a pan of crackling oil, adding onions and soy sauce. The food smelled good and I realized I was hungry. What had I eaten that day, besides nuts and raisins? Just some peanut butter and jelly on pita chips I'd gobbled before meeting Lonsky, sometime in the early afternoon. Food, like laundry, sex, and sleep, no longer figured into my domestic life.

While Ramona cooked and ate her dinner, I crouched in the dust and listened to the palms. Perhaps you're unfamiliar with the sound. As a low wind gathers, the long, slender trunks of the coconut palms shift, and the fronds at their heads knock and scratch dryly together. It is like lying awake on a ship, far out to sea, hearing the hull sway and the rigging creak. You remember, tasting the dry wind, hearing the trees whisper, that LA is not a beach. It's a desert.

My mind wandered back to my own life, over a few hills, in another empty house. The image stabbed at my throat. That's how it goes for a dog like me, on the short leash of love, pulled back every time, with a choke, to the same driven stake. That's why almost all books about obsession are to some degree artful lies: real obsession, thinking that one thought over and over forever, is so boring it would be unreadable. In this regard, all of literature's great maniacs of love, Stendhal, Miller, Hamsun, Nabokov, even Proust (although he pushes it furthest for sure), distort the endlessness of true fixation, the monotony of pain and desire, as they transform it into pleasure, into art. The one exception is Sade, who makes everything, incestuous rape, eating poop, skinning people alive, exquisitely, transcendently, hypnotically boring. Only he, locked alone in the Bastille, produced a work whose monstrousness, by every measure, truly mirrors the monster of obsessive desire.

Now, my wife can't cook for shit, and in our home I always played chef and she washed dishes, but that night, smelling the Dark Lady's caramelized onions and her soy sauce reducing sweetly in her pan, I yearned, not for my own really pretty OK cooking, but for the horrible food that Lala prepared for me on one of our very first dates. In her apartment, by candlelight, she served: a dry, over-cooked steak like a scorched flat tire, rice that was somehow both mushy and hard, and limp, lifeless vegetables, all of it blanketed in so much salt that I had to refill my water glass twice to get it down. But I ate it. I ate it all and asked for seconds, and squatting under that window I remembered it, with a pang, as one of the great meals of my life, because I knew, when she cooked me that disgusting slop, that she was in love. And when I managed to get it down without gagging, she knew that I was in love, too.

The music came back on, the soul, and I checked my watch. It was ten. Ramona was back in her bedroom, no doubt dancing with herself. With less trepidation, and more stiff-jointedness, than before (how quickly fear leaves us, how quickly it returns), I hoisted myself up and peeked.

I was wrong. She was not dancing. She was, to put it bluntly, masturbating. She was on the bed. Her legs were far apart. She sat up straight, shoulders back, one arm behind, propping her up, her other hand in her underpants, fingers playing rapidly under the cotton. Her breasts trembled as her breathing grew faster. This was all rather shocking, but it was not what frightened me most. The scary part was that she was staring right at me.

I gasped, but luckily she couldn't hear me with Al Green praying so loudly. My brain issued a command to start running, but I was paralyzed. I couldn't stop staring, as though I'd been struck by a miracle. I'd probably go down in a burning ship with a naked lady. Meanwhile, she worked by touch, facing straight ahead while her nimble fingers operated, expertly, precisely, like she was dialing in a distant station, head up to listen, tuning a far-off signal. Like a fool, I thought: she wants me to watch, she's putting on a show for me! But then I realized: light inside, dark without. She wasn't seeing me at all, was blind to everything beyond her own reflection in the window glass. She was looking at herself.

11

I DROVE BACK TO LONSKY'S and made my report around eleven. One window in the house was aglow. The rest of the block was dark with a few blue licks of TV light here and there. As instructed, I tapped the pane, then went to the door, which I found unlocked. Lonsky loomed in the hallway. He still wore a tie beneath his silk robe, the belt tight across the equator of his belly, and there were slippers on his feet. He put a finger to his lips and I followed, through the dark living room to the study. Impressive snoring roared from above, as if a small sawmill were in operation. Was it his mother? Mrs. Moon? Neither of the little women seemed capable of summoning such a sound. Perhaps they were both snoring in tandem, stoking the furnace of their dreams.

In silence, Lonsky led me into the study, shut the door, and settled his bulk behind the desk, like a ship listing against a dock. He leaned back and shut his eyes. Then he said, "Begin."

"Well." I cleared my throat. "She put on some music and danced by herself, then went in the kitchen and cooked . . ."

"Wait." He held up a hand, like a crossing guard. "Go back. Begin again. Tell me everything."

"OK, right, sorry." I peered at my notes. I'd been scribbling in the dark, crouched under the dogshit tree, and my already slanted lefty scrawl had wandered all over the page, at times crossing its own tracks. "Um, OK, it was the oldies. *Al Green Is Love,* I think." I was proud of this, naming the record, how many detectives could pull that off? But Lonsky stopped me again.

"No." He opened one eye, like a whale peering over the waterline. "Put the notes away."

Confused, I did so. Did this mean I was fired? Didn't he want to hear my exact list of what she ate for dinner?

"Now," he said, "shut your eyes."

"What? Why?" I felt a little panicked. "She fried vegetables with chicken."

"Please, just do it," he said calmly, like a doctor about to sting a patient. "Just sit back, relax, and shut your eyes. I will shut mine too," he added reassuringly.

I lowered my eyelids gingerly, sneaking a shuttered glimpse through the lashes. I settled into the chair and pretended to relax, like the reluctant birthday boy at a magic show.

"Now then," he went on, in that deep, rolling tone, "tell me everything you see. Don't worry about remembering. It doesn't matter. Don't worry if it seems pointless. Just tell me what you see now as you recall it. Tell me the story of tonight."

So I did. I closed my eyes, and let myself drift, forgetting the details of where I was at the moment, and seeing what came back of that distant time, an hour or two ago, which now seemed no closer or further away than my childhood or the brief, bright flickers that remained from last night's dreams. In recollection, time is no longer a line. It is a circle and you are at the center, with all of your memories playing around you, rotating in and out of reach. As if tucked in bed, I told him a story, about the house, the light, the smell of dogshit, the curtains, the song. I told him about the palm trees scratching themselves like insects in the dry wind. I told him about watching her cook and how the smell made me think of another warm night long ago with my wife, before she was my wife. I told him about the strange freedom of loneliness I'd found without her, about the lonely freedom of estrangement. How long had it been since I went out, alone, at night, like a stray, with no one at home to know or ask where I had been? I told him about the shut window, the hand moving between her legs, the shock, the fear, the staring eyes.

"Are you sure?" he asked me suddenly, breaking my trance. My own eyes popped open. He was leaning forward, hands on the arms of his chair. "Are you sure her eyes were closed when she was dancing but open when she masturbated?"

"Um . . ." I hesitated, while he waited, staring at me intently, as if a great deal depended on this point. Was this a vital clue?

"Yes," I said, seeing it all again, clear as day. "Yes, I'm certain."

He smiled and leaned back, nodding. "Very good. See, I told you. You see everything, whether you know it or not. It's all there." He retied his belt and folded his hands across the meridian. "Now I wonder, did she want to escape into darkness when she danced but expose herself to the light of her own eyes when she masturbated? Or, on the contrary, was she hoping to connect with herself, to shut her eyes in order to turn within and inhabit her own moving body while she was dancing and then to see herself as an image, a reflection, an erotic object, when she arrived at her orgasm?"

Did it matter? I wondered. Was this what he sent me to learn? What mystery could it solve, what crime? Where was the victim, and who the criminal, besides me?

12

LONSKY PAID ME, ANOTHER FRESH hundred-dollar bill in an envelope, and instructed me to be back at my post, outside the cottage, by nine the next morning. I left with a strange sense of accomplishment, but by the time my car had taken me a few blocks, my mood began to sink. Sailing past the other travelers, arm's distance in their cars, swimming through the lights and depths of streets and stores and bars while traffic signals flashed above, I dreaded going home to my haunted house, to await the ghost of my dearly departed wife who was off living it up in New York. So I called Milo, who was my dream date at that moment—an insomniac cinephile with no regard for marriage or books. He said to come over. He was about to watch a movie.

The question of what film to watch when in distress can be a complex one, and by the time I arrived Milo had given it some thought. (Although, I suppose, if you are Milo or me, the question of what movie to watch is fairly complex no matter what.) Milo is, of course, an utter snob about movies, precisely the languorous know-it-all who might annoy you when you stop by his shop, like the lady who held up the recent megahit *Fritz* ("Who Says a Robot Can't Be All Heart?") and asked if it was good. Milo shrugged. "It's no worse than any of that other Hollywood crap."

Awful, and yet I have a soft spot for such characters. Losers in all of society's big games, they (we) are totally powerless by any measure except this one, which no one else even cares about, and which serves only as a means of recognizing one another, like fallen aristocrats from some other realm, whose fortunes, minted in a defunct currency, count for nothing here. Milo brushing off a billion-dollar hit was like some threadbare duke turning his nose up at an insufficiently stinky cheese or spitting out a Bordeaux that only he could tell was youngish or rather too muscle-bound, while crass hedge-fund millionaires lapped it up. In the eyes of the world, we are bums. Yet in a dusty shop, a ratty theater, a parent's basement den, there we rule. But unlike the person with exquisite taste in painting or perfume, the movie nerd is classless as well. Grasping the genius of Russ Meyer or George Romero or Herschell Gordon Lewis carries no cultural cachet and gets no one laid, believe me.

"How about I spit on your grave?" Milo asked by way of greeting as he opened the door.

"I told you I'm freaking out about Lala," I said. "The last thing I need is a movie featuring castration."

"Don't be so touchy," he said. "I got a new Italian DVD copy and thought it might relax you." He was referring of course to *I Spit on Your Grave,* the infamous splatter film (Meir Zarchi, 1978), a classic of the rape-revenge genre, in which a girl, seeking woody seclusion in order to finish her novel, gets assaulted by a gang of men and then goes on a bloody rampage.

"So what do you want to see?" he asked, following me into the living room, where an entire wall was covered in a bewildering array of DVDs, VHS cassettes, and homemade CDs. An enormous TV blocked the fireplace. Milo shared this house with two people, but since neither of them was ever around, he'd commandeered the communal living space as his screening room. The house was a vaguely Spanish, vaguely modern stucco box off Sunset in Echo Park. One rainy season, it had begun to slide down the hill and was now propped up, half off its foundation, with a dubious jack, some two-by-fours, and a couple of cinder blocks, for which its inhabitants received a reduction in rent. Tonight, however, it was just Milo and I, and the discussion got very deep very fast. "OK, Mr. Lonely," he told me, waving at the movie wall. "What kind of heartbreak flick are you pining for? *Sleepless in Madison County? How The English Patient Got His Groove Back?* We're all out of *Eat Pray Love,* I'm afraid. How about *Shit Fuck Kill?*"

"Actually, speaking of fucking and killing, I was thinking of something cozy and soothing like *Goodfellas* or *The Godfather.*"

How could a movie that features a guy getting stabbed to death in a trunk cheer me up? It is, I think, the combination of a certain kind of formal perfection, a calming flawlessness, combined with the warmth of long familiarity. These are movies I had seen countless times. I've worn out both a tape and a disc of *Goodfellas,* and when I couldn't sleep, I could lie in bed and follow just the dialogue of *The Godfather* or its sequel from behind my drooping lids.

"I know what you mean but I can't see them right now," Milo said, running his hands over his face. "I just can't." (This is the other side of such intimacy. There were many beloved films, like *Manhattan* or *Taxi Driver,* that I saw so many times, I had to declare a moratorium, the way some bakers have to temporarily swear off chocolate cake.)

"A Satyajit Ray?" he asked. "*Apu?*"

"Jesus, I'm already suicidal here. Are you trying to kill me? How about *Shoah?*"

"OK, OK. Point taken. *Rules of the Game?*"

"Hmm . . . maybe."

"What do you mean, maybe? It's a masterpiece, a serious contender for best movie ever."

"I know, I know. Shoulder to shoulder with *Kane*, you told me."

"Plus, as a worldly, wise Frenchman, Renoir makes your petty love problems seem like a joke."

"OK," I said, settling on the couch. "Let's do it. Though I actually think it's his warmth, his Shakespearian compassion for human frailty, that can help me now."

"Shit," Milo muttered, scanning the shelves. "It's at the store."

"Fuck," I said. "This could take forever."

"Look, why argue? You want perfection crossed with familiarity? How about your lovable but perverted uncle?"

"Hitchcock."

"Hitchcock. Exactly. *Marnie?*"

"Too troubling. *North By Northwest?*"

"Too charming. *Dial M?*"

"Really, you know what the most perfect movie ever is?"

"*Vertigo.*"

"Exactly. *Vertigo.*" This is what I generally answered when asked those ridiculous questions, favorite, best, ever. Of course there are hundreds of best movies, but *Vertigo* to me was the one that most truly fulfilled itself: story and song, form and content, manifest and latent—like the two sides of the tapestry, every image and gesture, every moment and glance, was both the plot and the dream. It was what life would be if we were all geniuses—complete.

Milo shrugged. "Yeah, but I don't feel like seeing it tonight."

I slumped deeper into the couch. "I don't either, really."

"You know what I could watch though?" he asked.

"Yeah, muscle porn, but wait till I go home."

"Fair enough, but you know what else I could go for first, dude?"

"You're right."

"It will cheer you up. The perfect thing for when you're down and out."

"Let's do it."

So he put on *The Big Lebowski*.

Everyone loves the Dude of course, and his renown has only grown over the years, but for those of us who have drifted, effortlessly, to the bottom of the shark pool in Los Angeles, The Big L touches an especially deep place in our drowned hearts. As soon as I saw the opening shots of Jeff Bridges at a Ralph's supermarket, seemingly in a bathrobe, paying for half-and-half by check, I began to laugh. I knew that guy. Let's face it, I *was* that guy, more or less, though younger and less stoned and correspondingly far less at peace with myself. It is a comedy of course, a light film compared to the Coen bros darkies, like *Fargo* or their great masterpiece, *Miller's Crossing*, but it is a sad movie too, sad in the way only comedy is sad, and brimming with the tender love we save for life's losers, here where the evil always win and the worst never cease to be victorious.

PART II

THE MAN WITHOUT QUALIFICATIONS

13

I WAS WAITING OUTSIDE Ramona Doon's bungalow when she emerged the next day. She was in a sundress, light blue with thin straps over her tan shoulders, and red strappy heels with bare legs. She had sunglasses on, and her dark hair swung across her back as she walked to her car, a creamy old Mercedes convertible with a yellow frosted roof folded back and chocolate leather seats. We were off.

She led me westward through Hollywood and swung down to Sunset and the Strip. When you are not in any rush, when the traffic is rolling and the air is flowing and KXLU is playing and your time is paid, it can actually be a very pleasant ride. There were the billboards and the hotels and the shuttered nightclubs. There was the former health food restaurant were Woody freaks out in *Annie Hall*, and the long-ago strip club that Ben Gazarra runs in *Killing of a Chinese Bookie*. There was the rest of humanity washing past you—the ugly, the pretty, the angry, the bored, the sweaty tourist, the smoking Mexican gardener, the junior executive yelling into his headset —each one bobbing to the surface for a second before fate carried them away. Perhaps it was being here in the city of movies, or perhaps it was just the automatic magic of movement, music, and cars, but I felt comforted, as if my own stupid drama were part of some larger show, some movie set against the sweep of this landscape that scrolled by me as I drove into the wind. To give our lives a form, however fleeting, and lend our losses a name, these too are among the consolations of art.

We left West Hollywood and sailed through Beverly Hills, passing the green lawns, olive canyons, and pink hotels, the cartoon mansions of every style and period—a ten-bedroom thatched English cottage beside a Tudor mansion with five cars in the drive, next to Monticello, the Pantheon, and the Doge—like a miniature golf course blown up bigger than life. Then came Brentwood, the Palisades, those other, lower-keyed neighborhoods, somehow even more unreal. While Beverly Hills, in its exuberant overkill and luxury, is utterly itself, these further lands of fabulous wealth, poised on the western edge of the country, are more like fake hometowns, with ranch-style spreads, shingles and shutters and cute shopping pockets, except that everything, from a house to a house salad, is ten, or a hundred, or maybe even a thousand times what it costs back home, and despite the warm, folksy aura, you know, as soon as you see the ideally gorgeous moms, brutally rich dads, and the junior millionaires on their bikes: you don't belong.

But it's worth every penny, for those who can spare the change. The warm light is rubbed with sage and rosemary. The breeze smells like organic cough drops and artisanal focaccia. You can feel the unseen sea on your skin. You dip and rise, shadow to sun, through tree-lined glades of eucalyptus that shed their bark in long soft curls, and hillsides glowing gray-green and deep red. And then, beyond that last hill, dazzling you always no matter how much you expect it, the ocean is there again. Ms. Doon took a right onto the PCH, and, as if I were the one leading her, we rode right past all the tourist spots, past Malibu and Zuma Beach, past waving paragliders and sliding surfers and detoxing movie stars, way up by the county line, to El Matador, my favorite beach.

El Matador is cut like cake from the cliffside, eaten out by the ocean from beneath into caves and crumbs and columns, while sugared waves lay down in thick ruffles on the satin sand. The beach is slick and narrow, mirror-bright in the shallows. In the surf, a spindly tower of rock stands alone, like a bad tooth, severed from the cliffs by the lick of waves relentlessly swirling around it. Its top forms a tiny plateau, a little garden covered with bright clinging plants and grasses lying down in the wind. Perhaps this lone, thin rock is the matador whom those first Spanish warriors named when they too came and prayed, knee-deep in the surf, facing the bleeding sun.

I recalled my drives up here with Lala, hiking along the ridges and ravines of Topanga Canyon, walking on the beach, kissing in the caves, sucking back clams in Neptune's Net, then napping on a blanket on the sand, sea-cooled breezes chilling my arms, sunshine baking my face. Those were good days, and as I trailed my subject along the coast, longing shot through me again. It was a physical pain, this loss of a former happiness, and a possible future joy, a sharp ache across my forehead, behind my eyes, and down into the hollow of my chest. A physical pain from a metaphysical wound: It was almost enough to make me question my life-long conviction that there was nothing outside the facts of flesh and the noises of the brain. This throb, this wasting misery, this cry, what could it be, dying inside me now, but a soul?

Ramona Doon pulled into the lot, where you had to slide your money in a slot and leave the receipt on your dashboard. I parked along the road for free, cleverly swinging my car around so that, when she left, I'd already be behind her. As she began descending the long, twisted staircase to the beach, I sauntered along casually, sporting sunglasses, hands resting in my pockets. I smelled water and tasted salt as the wind came over the cliff. Her heels echoed weirdly on the wooden steps. To stay hidden, I bypassed the stairs, and took a steeper path down through the scrub.

She had betrayed me. My wife had betrayed my trust. I could still hear her promising to love me forever. To stay with me. Forever. Gasping, sweating as I humped it down the cliff, I bit down on my pain and tasted anger. That was what rushed in to fill the empty space where her love had been. I'm not saying she'd lied deliberately when she made her pledge. But what difference did that make to me?

I saw it now: love was just a feeling like any other, and when she said she would love me forever, what she meant was, right now I feel like I will love you forever, but perhaps, tomorrow, that will change.

And why not? I told myself, as the sea rose back into view. Mountains, beaches, planets all change. Everything passes away. Why not us?

Then, since I was too busy brooding on the cosmos to look where I was going, I tripped and fell on my face. I stumbled on a root and lost my footing in a small avalanche of sand. Unable to pull my hands from my pockets in time, I tipped over, headfirst, pitching forward into the dirt, and skidded and tumbled down the slope. At first I struggled, eating sand and kicking my legs helplessly, with my sunglasses jammed into my skull. Then I gave up and just rolled with it, luging to the bottom, where I landed with a grunt in a pile of rotten seaweed. Spitting sand, I looked up to see my lady reaching the last landing of the staircase. In a panic, I flattened myself against the ground, hiding my face in the stinky greens.

"Are you OK?"

I opened one eye and saw a red heel sunk into the sand beside me. Desperate to hide my identity, I pressed my face deeper into the mulch, and faked a deeper, more guttural voice.

"Uh-huh."

Her own voice was soft and smart, well educated. Burrowing into the sand and sludge, trying to appear comfortably homeless, I adopted a kind of conceptual disguise, trying as hard as I could to look like a drunken derelict without actually moving.

"Are you sure you don't need help?" She touched my shoulder gently. I felt nails on my skin.

"Uh-uh," I grunted back.

"You mean you don't need help or you're not sure you don't?"

That stumped me. I couldn't think of any response expressible within my phonetic limits. Meanwhile that hand sat lightly on my shoulder, like a bird about to lift. Then — quite cleverly I thought — I grunted, "No need help," in the manner of an old movie Injun.

"OK, then, I won't bother you," she said, one nail tracing a soft line that lingered, tingling for a moment after she left. I remained motionless, breathing dead sea, until my heart stopped pounding. Then, like a stranded sea monster, I opened one sandy eye, and watched her walk the beach, shoes in her hand, not doing anything. The wind sifted her hair. Her dress shivered close to her body.

When at last she left, I took the stairs too, a flight behind her, slopping along in my wet shoes and seaweed-scented clothes. I jogged to my car and had the engine started by the time her Mercedes rolled out. She put the roof up as we headed back to town. It was growing colder, and I could feel the damp wind slap against my face.

The truth, if I admitted it to myself, was that Lala's betrayal also set me free. It broke my heart, but also cut the cord I'd never even noticed around my neck. Suddenly everything that, for better or worse, had been a given, a certainty, was a question once again. Turned loose, against my own desperate wishes, I suddenly couldn't help wondering—what would it be like to live alone? For years every decision, from what to eat for dinner to what to do with my future had revolved around her. Even this job I was on. Alone, I could rededicate myself to my own work, write, travel, do anything I wanted, at least in theory. I could theoretically fuck somebody else! The very idea made the blood pound in my veins. If I ever wanted out, this was my chance. But did I want out or back in? And all at once, it occurred to me: everything is possible again, now that she is gone.

14

THE RIDE HOME WAS a lot less cinematic in my clammy clothes, sand grinding into my skin and the smell of old sea scum hanging around me in a cloud. She made a right on La Cienega, swung a quick U-turn and vanished into one of the drives or lots. I found a meter and paralleled in, just in time to glimpse my quarry disappearing into a shop somewhere in the rearview. I stripped off my beach clothes and pulled my sweats and a T-shirt from my detective's kit. I didn't want to lose her trail now. But could I risk following her on foot, after my fiasco at the beach? Recalling my new employer's policy on disguises, and figuring I had little dignity to lose, I yanked out Lala's thrift store blond wig and pulled it on, fitting the mangy yellow curls over my own damp rug in the mirror. I looked preposterous. Still, this was Hollywood, home of the preposterous. That gave me an idea: I took out the little makeup kit Lonsky had pressed on me and smeared red goop on my lips, instantly transforming myself into a shopworn drag queen. In any other town this might stand out, but here it was as good as camouflage.

Strolling up the block in my new getup, I was so distracted by my reflection in the car windows, it took me a second to realize I was headed for Trashy Lingerie. Had Ramona gone in there? What the hell, I decided, take a peek. I felt weirdly liberated. My very oddness made me feel invisible, and no doubt all of the other low-end trannies in the hood were regulars already. I'd fade into the background. I opened the door.

"Welcome to Trashy!" A buxom young lady in a logoed T-shirt greeted me loudly. "Have you been here before?"

I froze. I didn't even know what sort of voice to use. Male? Female? She-male? I shook my head, No. The wig jiggled. I tried to back out but she blocked me, smiling broadly.

"If you like I can show you our larger sizes for more statuesque ladies. Though you're actually very slim-waisted." She touched my shoulders appraisingly, as if measuring me for a strapless gown. I cleared my throat and spoke in a voice that, to my surprise, was actually deeper than my own.

"Thanks but . . ." To my horror, I spotted Her, Ramona, heading our way with a few hangers clutched in her hand. The shopgirl was oblivious.

"Still, your shoulders will be a problem for smaller pieces," she went on. "What's your shoe size?"

As Ramona stepped up, I shook my head and turned away, pretending to be fascinated with the makeup on the counter.

"Excuse me," she asked the salesgirl. "Do you have these in crotchless?" She dangled slinky bits of black and pink. They didn't look anything like underwear to me. More like trims she was thinking of adding to underwear.

"Only in the lavender," the girl said.

"And where can I try them on?"

"Straight in the back."

"Thank you." Ramona smiled warmly at us and swiveled away. The shopgirl watched her go, perhaps, like me, imagining how she'd look decorated in those frills. But before I could slink off, she snapped back to my harsher reality.

"I see you're looking at Azure Galaxy."

"Um, who?" I had no idea what she meant. A fellow drag queen? She snatched a bottle off the counter. "I love that one too. Let me show you."

Too afraid to move, I stood like a statue while she drew on my face. "The sky tones bring out your eyes. And the glitter stands up to your strong features. There." She squinted at me doubtfully and held up a mirror. "Perfect. Take a look?"

I looked. A very frightened, very ugly, old prostitute looked back. Then I spotted Ramona, swinging over again with her dainties. "Sorry," I blurted. "I'm late. Got to go."

"Come again," the girl called after me. "You look really pretty!"

I jogged to my car, head down, and drew only a few stares and one honk from a passing trucker. I removed the wig and tried to find some kind of wipe or napkin. Of course there was none. Why would there be? This was my car. I tried to rub the blue glitter off my eyelids with spit but only smeared it. Now the whole area around my eyes sparkled. I looked like a raccoon on ecstasy. Then I saw the Mercedes heading south.

This time it was a pleasant surprise. My lady turned onto Beverly Boulevard and led me to the New Beverly Cinema, a rerun house where I'd spent untold hours. Back on home turf, I parked leisurely and watched the mystery woman saunter up to the theater. I put my broken sunglasses back on to hide the glitter and followed. She went in, tossing a shopping bag with the Trashy logo into the garbage. Why would she dump her new items? the detective in me wondered. That place wasn't cheap, added the husband. I waited a beat then bought a ticket, hoping the teenaged clerk wasn't watching as I snuck her Trashy trash from the garbage on my way in.

15

THE DARK THEATER WAS nearly empty, with featureless silhouettes scattered among the rows. I spotted a shapely shadow taking a seat in front and slid into my preferred spot, the center of the middle row. I hadn't noticed the name of the film when I came in but I recognized it quickly: *They Live by Night* (1948), Nicholas Ray's first film, the original doomed-lovers-on-the-run movie. Its story has been repeated so often, and is so stripped down to the core here, that the film came back to me, filtered by cinematic memory, as collage, a poem of images and gestures: depression-era gas station attendants who wore suits, long black cars jittering down narrow roads on skinny tires, Cathy O'Donnell's sad eyes and pixie face and her body in those sweaters and skirts, Farley Granger's creased hair and nervous hands molding emptiness.

Why do these old black-and-white movies feel so good to me? So rich, so creamy, so dreamy? It can't be nostalgia. Color was in full command before I was born. I first saw these movies on late-night TV or video, and began only later to seek true prints. But somehow this realm of silver stars and gray shadows, black nights and slivered moons, seems closer to movie heaven, preserved in that house of secular worship where we few still go to sit silently in the dark.

By the dim light of a bright scene, I checked Ramona's bag. The contents were fabric of some sort, but not the little nothings I expected and for a moment, drunk on the movie, I imagined a bloody scarf or something noir. I held the items up to catch the screen light and saw a bra in one hand, panties in the other. Both seemed quite nice, plain cotton and of reasonable sizes (big enough and small enough respectively) but nothing scandalous. Nothing Trashy. As I pondered this, the lights came up. The movie had ended. One fellow turned around in his seat, staring at me blankly and sucking soda through his straw. Scowling, I stuffed the underthings back into the bag and stood, remembering too late that my glasses were off and I looked like Ziggy Stardust's older sister. And then I realized: the curvaceous form in the front row I thought was Ramona was really a corpulent man in Lennon glasses and a ponytail. A film nerd like me. The Mystery Lady had vanished.

I rushed from the dim movie theater into the brightly lit night. Darkness had fallen, and as always after a late matinee, reality seemed insubstantial, as if it had been soaking in sleep while I was gone. I peered up and down the boulevard, hoping to spot the suspect's vehicle, to decipher the blinking sets of lights. I hustled across the lanes to my car, digging for keys, and the LA drivers, unused to an East Coaster diving into traffic midstream, swerved and honked, the sound of their horns bending around my ears. As I fumbled at my lock, still craning my head for Ramona, from the corner of my eye, I saw, or thought I saw, my own wife drive by. I spun around. She was headed east and I was on the wrong side. I took off running after her, the wrong way, on foot, for a block to the corner, and now drivers were honking and yelling and I was out of air, out of shape, my breath ablaze in my chest. And then I saw it, the Jesus fish on the back. It wasn't Lala. Embarrassed, if only before myself and Jesus, I walked back to my car, the warm desert wind drying the sweat on my face.

I drove to Ramona Doon's house and snooped around. It was

dark and silent. The curtains were drawn. I camped outside for a while, and then, accepting defeat, I called Lonsky to report. I'd lost both of our girls.

"Kornberg! Where have you been? I need an update on the case."

"Yes, well, Mr. Lonsky, I'm sorry to have to tell you this, but I lost the girl at the movies. I followed her in but she must have slipped out."

He rumbled under his breath. "That was amateurish. Damned amateurish."

"Sorry. But I guess I am an amateur, aren't I?"

"Anything else? Anything that can help?"

"Well, actually, she left some things behind." I hesitated. "Some underwear in a bag. Does that help?"

"Underwear?" He perked up. "Of course it does. She left it at the movies?"

"Not right on the seat. She went into a shop, bought some very expensive lingerie and I guess changed into it, then discarded her regular stuff in the trash."

"You retrieved her soiled undergarments from the garbage?" he asked in his stentorian tones.

I shrugged and blushed at the phone. "I guess."

"Nice work," he boomed. "Now you're thinking like a detective!"

"Really?" I couldn't help feeling a tiny bit better.

"Anything else to report?"

"Well . . ." I decided to leave the part about the wig and falling into the seaweed aside for the moment. "Not really."

"And she isn't at home. You couldn't even guess what direction she drove?"

"No, well. I guess I got distracted . . ."

"By?"

Now I regretted speaking. "My wife. I thought I saw her drive by, that's all. But it wasn't her."

"I see." There was a pause. "I think you'd better come over."

16

MRS. MOON LET ME IN, smiling and nodding this time, and gestured toward the study, where Lonsky waited, sitting in an armchair, a volume of Shakespeare in his hand. He was wearing a dark gray summer suit, pink shirt, and black tie, with black socks and black velvet slippers. He shut the book, then shook my hand gravely and gestured toward the chair that sat beside his, a chessboard on the low table between them.

"Shall we play?" he asked.

"No thanks," I said. "I barely remember the rules."

"Move a piece, Kornberg," he muttered. "It helps me think."

I shrugged and slid a pawn forward one space.

Lonsky spoke in low tones. "Firstly, my thanks. Although the denouement of the day's events was other than desired, you acquitted yourself somewhat competently for a neophyte on his maiden voyage. Nevertheless you let the quarry slip the net and we must make amends." He moved a pawn of his own, forward two spaces, to face mine. "I recommend you return to her home early tomorrow morning. When he loses a thread, the good detective returns to the last reliable point and attempts to find the trail. Your move."

"Yes, sir," I said and inched another pawn. At least this meant I wasn't fired.

"Now," he said, shifting a bishop. "As to your marital woes. I am sorry to see things are not improving."

"I didn't say anything."

"Kornberg, I said 'see' not 'hear.' You have some basic intelligence and you follow direction well but you need to develop your perspicacity. When you entered I saw immediately that one of your sideburns is considerably longer than the other, again something a loving wife or even a concerned roommate would point out. You are living alone. Also there's peanut butter on your cuff."

I quelched the urge to touch my sideburns. "It's true," I admitted, sliding my queen out to buy a moment. "She's out of town. But it's just a business trip. Nothing to do with our marriage."

Lonsky nodded. "So you agree with me then. Sadly, things are not improving."

"No." I looked him in the eye. Now he was bugging me. "That's not what I said."

"You said, and I quote, 'It's true.' Then you paused. Full stop."

"That's not what I meant."

"It's what you said and I believe it is actually what you meant, though it may not be what you intended. Then you broke eye contact and moved your queen. To say the queen represents a woman is obvious, but in your case, it is safe to say that your wife also rules."

"It's a coincidence. I moved a random piece, for fuck's sake."

"Nothing human is random. There are no such beasts as coincidences. I take your anger as confirmation that I struck the truth. In fact you could have moved any piece. You could have crossed the bishop over to protect your queen. But you moved her away from you. You sent her on a trip. A business trip, perhaps. Though you yourself don't believe it is."

"Now you're going too far." I was almost gratified to have stumped him. "That I can honestly say I haven't even thought of."

"Not consciously, no. You can't yet bring yourself to think it. But it's there. Why did you imagine seeing her if you knew she was gone? Why did you assume the car was hers instead of assuming it was not? There must be many like it in this city. Because one part of your mind, the unconscious, but also unclouded part, disbelieves her. Again, recall precisely what you said: it's just a business trip. You used the word 'just,' and felt the need to explain what sort of trip it was, although no one, at least not I, had challenged it. Whose doubts were you assuaging then? Your own."

I sat back in silence. Then I pushed my king over. "Checkmate," I said. "In two."

"Ha!" He was one of those people who really laugh like that, head back and mouth open wide as a well. His booming laugh echoed from the depths of the great belly. "Ha! Ha! Very good."

"But if you're so smart," I asked, "how come I'm the one walking out of here, and you're the one in slippers?"

He laughed even harder, holding his gut in place as it bounced and juggled. "Ha! Ha! Yes! Capital!" He wiped his eyes. "I admire your spirit, Kornberg, if not your intellect. Draw." He knocked his own king over. "Yes, it's quite true. My own emotional life is damaged, to say the least. Quite hopelessly so. And all of my intellectual or intuitive powers have granted me no insight into my own case whatsoever. They rarely do. Even the brightest mirror is dark to itself." He seemed to smile with satisfaction at this thought and continued:

"That is my point, precisely: people unconsciously reveal to the perceptive observer precisely what they wish to hide, even from themselves. Freud said, 'There is almost no such thing as a lie, for the man who has eyes to see.' But most people don't even look. Most signals go unread, including the most essential, those sent from one unconscious mind to another, messages passed in total darkness as it were, where not a soul is watching, except perhaps for a few detectives, like you and me."

17

AS INSTRUCTED, I RETURNED to Ramona Doon's cottage the next day and parked outside. Subject still nowhere in sight. But there was action in number five: a woman I'd never seen before, in sweats and plastic yellow gloves, was carrying a big bag of garbage out the door. What the hell, I decided. Time to play detective for real. I got out and strolled on over.

"Excuse me, Ma'am," I said, as if tipping an invisible hat. "Is Ramona Doon available?"

She looked me up and down. "Who's asking?"

I decided to win her over, like Bogey and the bookstore girl in *The Big Sleep*. Of course he is Bogey, and like all bookstore girls, when she lets down her up-do and takes off her glasses, she is a knockout and he offers her a drink from the bottle of rye in his glove box. My costar had a gray crew cut and bifocals on a beaded chain around her neck, so I just tried to stand like him and said, "Well, to be honest, I have some important papers for her to sign. They say it's urgent."

"Papers? Where's your briefcase then?"

"Oh." That was a good question. "In the car?"

"Debt collector or process server?" She shook her head and I thought I'd lost her. "Figures. Though she seemed more like the rich girl type. Anyway, she's gone."

"Gone?"

"Moved out last night. Called up and told me to keep the deposit. After only one month too." She shrugged. Through the open door behind her I could see the same furniture.

"But what about all her stuff?"

"That's my stuff. I rent the place furnished short term. Her personals are in this bag. Just papers and crap. Anyways. Good luck. I guess sometimes those rich kids are the worst at paying bills."

She shouldered her trash bag and swayed off. I considered sneaking in, but she didn't seem the type to trifle with, and besides, the "personals" were in the goody bag, so I walked back toward my car in slow motion and then, when I saw she was gone, I circled around to the trash Dumpster and went fishing. The landlady hadn't been lying. It was indeed crap: used coffee filters caked with brown grime, banana peels and eggshells. Old magazines and empty toilet paper tubes. A torn dirty pink sock that I could have added to the panties, but I decided I wasn't ready to move up to that level of detection quite yet.

I called Lonsky and reported in. He felt my garbage picking showed initiative, although I left out any mention of the sock, fearing he might send me back to scrounge it up like a truffle. Then he got deep on me.

"A detective finds clues," he boomed at me over the fuzzy cell connection as I bounced along Franklin Boulevard, swimming in the gray wake of a gardening truck, a rattling wooden wagon piled stories high with branches, dead grass, and leaves, and with several grinning Mexicans riding on top and no exhaust pipe. I tried not to breathe. "Sometimes those clues are around us, in the street, in the garbage. Sometimes within. Look within, Kornberg."

I thought, *Thanks, Obi-Wan*, but audibly agreed to do a top-to-bottom search within. Then, with no real job, no real wife, and no real life to distract me, I went home and wrote a novel.

18

IT WAS IN MY TEENS and twenties that I first absorbed the great works of experimental or avant-garde or whatever, advanced, modern fiction: *Ulysses* of course, which I read twice, back to back, as if unable to quite believe what had just happened; the mad Austrians, *The Man Without Qualities, The Sleepwalkers, The Demons,* and their German cousin, *Berlin Alexanderplatz;* Biely and Bulgakov, Russian time travelers from a lost future that never arrived; those witchy vitchs, Gombrowicz and Witkiewicz—mind-bending Warsaw weirdos—and Bruno Schulz, the Jewish point to the Polish Holy Trinity, his pure, clear light snuffed out by the Nazis, ungentlest of gentiles. I remember my amazement when, picking up a stained one-dollar paperback of Schulz's *Street of Crocodiles* in a sidewalk stall one chill fall day, I found all the terror and wonder of my own middle-class Jersey childhood somehow reanimated in this tiny book by a little-known small town Pole whose prose blazed out like embers under my breath as I stood and read. I remember the scene in Biely's *St. Petersburg* where the Bronze Horseman, the statue of Peter the Great, takes off into the air, and the moment in Bulgakov's *The Master and Margarita* when the devil, wandering 1930s Moscow, sits beside a bureaucrat and whispers in his ear of Pontius Pilate, transporting us, in the turn of a page, to ancient Jerusalem. I remember exactly where I was when I finished *Molloy*, in a hammock, on vacation with my family. Head deep in the postwar European wasteland while they frolicked in the sun nearby, I felt the walls in my mind collapsing as, in its final sentences, Beckett's novel of negation negates itself, disappearing up its own arse, as the Irish genius might say. Then there was Pynchon. My copy of *Gravity's Rainbow* has blood on it, nonfiguratively, from when I couldn't stop reading long enough to make a sandwich and ended up trying to decipher terminal brainfucker prose while slicing cheese. Gaddis! I summited *The Recognitions* in winter, as if on a foolish dare, but had a deeper, summery love for *JR:* 800 pages of unattributed screwball dialogue about a drippy-nosed kid who becomes a millionaire stock baron. To me, a man who would do such an absurdly noble thing with his life was mythic, half Groucho Marx, half Hercules: like flying to the moon just to plant the pirate flag for the rare voyager who might sail by and salute. As for Kafka, what can I say? He commanded that his papers be burned after his death. He was disobeyed and now his work is the eternal flame, the bonfire into which all other writers should toss their own failed efforts. I will restrain myself here to reminding the reader of the moment toward the end of *The Trial* when, just before his execution, Josef K puts up his arms and says: I have something to say!

Is it (a) weird, or (b) sad, that I remember these Great Moments in Reading better than I remember my own life? That they ring out in the mind and tingle the spine with the power of the present, and of the real, while reality seems like the poor copy, badly printed and full of typos? Don't answer. I bring up my early and perhaps deformative exposure to books here only to explain what happened next.

Much like experimental drug users, most troubled young experimental fiction readers pass through the gateway and, with late adolescence, college graduation, and the need to get a life, outgrow the dangerous phase. But some poor fool always gets hooked, and so I found one day, that I had myself a habit. I hit the hard stuff, V. Woolf, G. Stein, *F. Wake,* but soon found that merely consuming these books wasn't enough to feed my demon. I began to write them.

And now, a couple of decades later, while most men had careers, families, bank accounts, health insurance, and wives who didn't openly despise them, I had these books no one in the whole world wanted to read weighing down the bottom drawer of my soul. My disasterpieces. My monsterworks. My wastebasket of a life.

19

HOW MUCH OF MY MARITAL discord could, if I was honest, be laid on that pyre of pages? Let's see: years of unrewarded labor, hundreds upon hundreds of rejections, all "free" time, all weekends, evenings, holidays, and vacations, devoted to a private obsession no other human could share, resenting the world that ignored my efforts while despising myself most of all, raging and ranting against literature as a bad joke and then slinking away, late at night while Lala slept, to indulge my wretched vice. These things might tend to make a person difficult to live with, like being married to a junkie, without the fun of getting high. It wasn't any better when I finally left the house. In a party of any size (one or more), I was always the least successful man in the room, wincing when Lala told a friend I was a writer, changing the subject when anyone asked how it was going (or worse, telling the truth), finally denying it altogether, just saying I was a bookstore clerk or an office worker or even unemployed when someone scorched my soul by politely inquiring, What do you do?

Even my good points, I realized upon reflection, were nothing more than skills I'd developed to manage my literary disability. The self-deprecating humor, the easy jokes about what a loser I was, the graceful playing of the jester's role at table, the mildly eccentric intellectual sidekick, ready to spice the grown-ups' talk with a silly anecdote about my kooky hobby or accept a small favor from my betters, a part-time job or a pair of pants that the successful had outgrown. The compliant pal (or husband) who knew he had no grounds for complaint. Realizing intuitively that the person I really was deep down was someone no one, including me, could stand, I became, well, *nice,* as if my life depended on it. Which it did. There was no other reason to feed me. So I quit whining. I quickly learned to have the good taste not to make others uncomfortable about my lowliness, like a disfigurement they were obliged not to notice. Rather, I set people at ease, encouraging them to take my misfortunes lightly, and even enjoy them. It's fun to have a friend who is a total loser compared to you, as long as he doesn't make you guilty about it. On the contrary, I was popular. Hanging out with me made all my friends feel better about themselves.

In other words, my whole personality was nothing more than an elaborate defense against despair. Without my failure I was nothing.

20

BUT THE CRAZY THING, the punch line, the part I had a hard time admitting, even to myself, was that I myself could no longer stand to read these sorts of novels, the kind I couldn't seem to stop writing. I don't know what changed—the focus of my eyes, the span of my attention, the shape of the synapses in my brain—but my Age of Giants was over, and (except for Proust, whom I dithered and dreamed over like a rabbi snoring beard-deep in the Talmud) I now exclusively read crime novels (but never those that "transcended" the genre), newspapers (gossip and horoscope with my wake-up coffee), fashion magazines (which Lala left within reach of the toilet), comics, and porn. Only what was funny, violent, dirty, and fast held my interest and even then not for very long. It seemed I had dedicated my life to a quest whose point even I had forgotten along the way.

21

WE HAD THERAPY the next day. I arrived right on time, but Lala was with our shrink already, in that office that felt like a fairy godmother's storybook cottage fitted inside the bluntly ugly office building. There seemed to be some bonding going on. Gladys was turning before the mirror, appraising herself, while Lala expertly wound her like a mummy in a long scarf.

"Come on in!" Lala beamed at me. "I was just showing Gladys a new way to accessorize." She pecked my cheek.

"Your wife's really got the touch," Gladys said. I realized she was wearing one of the decorative spreads that had been draped on the couch before. Was this allowed, precharming the shrink, like talking to the ref before the match? It wasn't fair. Although I was the funny one, the comic relief, Lala had always been the star. Her powers of attraction were unstoppable. Her charisma lay in her ability to make her glamour contagious. It rubbed off on you, like stardust, and near her you somehow grew more beautiful and charming as well. That was part of what had made me feel so absurdly lucky to be with her, the specialness of that attention as she glittered at me over a teacup, rapt at my routine anecdotes, or we walked hand in hand through a museum and she pretended to be mesmerized by my babble. How happy she was to hear about (not read) my novels then. How wonderful she thought it was that I did what I did. So interesting! So brave! Even in failure I was noble as long as I glowed in her eyes. It somehow didn't matter so much, if my job sucked or anyone read my books. If those attributes belonged to the man she loved, then he had to be a great guy. Here is the best thing anyone ever said to me: once long ago, as I rambled and raved, no doubt about a book or movie, I looked across the table and noticed a dreamy, unfocused smile on her face.

"Are you even listening to me?" I asked.

"No," she said, happily. "I was just staring at you and thinking about how handsome you are."

Now that very same star quality was horribly annoying, for one reason: it no longer shined on me. And what was she so fucking happy about anyway? That's what I didn't like. There were no tears dimming her eyes today. She looked radiant. So did Gladys, her wrap artfully hiding the wrinkles on her neck. We all settled in for a cozy chat.

"So," Gladys said, sitting forward and pressing her hands together in her characteristic gesture. "Who wants to begin?"

"Me, I guess." I didn't really. I had no idea how to go about discussing our issues, or even what they were. But I felt the need to seize the stage. "My job is going well. I started a new case."

"Ooh," she cooed, and blinked coyly at Lala, like a happy bird.

Lala smiled. "That sounds fascinating."

"It does?" I asked. "Since when?"

She shrugged, smiling coyly at her brightly painted nails. "I don't know. I did a lot of thinking on this trip. Just walking for miles around New York."

"But you hate walking." Lala was one of those Californians who circle the block endlessly until a spot opens in front. She adored valet parking, which I disdained, figuring, I hadn't made it all the way from home to restaurant alive just to pay someone else to roll my car into a spot.

"It's different in New York," she said. "I was out all day, just wandering in the crisp fall air."

"Mmm, that really clears your head," Gladys said. "When I'm at the colony, out in the desert, I take a long nude hike every morning and watch the sunrise."

"It's so true," Lala murmured, "and I started thinking, maybe what we need is some time apart, some space to discover ourselves and see the relationship clearly."

"A trial separation," Gladys said. "That sounds promising."

It didn't sound promising to me: those two words, *trial* and *seperation,* troubling enough on their own, were utterly depressing together. Lala warbled on.

"I mean, why shouldn't you be a detective if you want? Who am I to judge? Everyone should pursue their dream."

"But it's not," I said.

"Not what?"

"Not my dream. It's just a job. I wanted to be a novelist. Remember?"

She flickered but bounced back quick. "Of course, that's what I meant, of course."

Later, at home, I looked online. The weather in New York that weekend had been awful, wind and rain. No climate for Lala, who hated cold and sidewalks and loved her very high heels. But I didn't even have to check. It was as if Lonsky had infected me with a little of his gift. I looked. I saw. I knew: Lala had not been to New York, had perhaps not even left LA. The reason she was being so nice to me was guilt. The reason for her guilt was the same as the reason for her new joy. She had the sheen of a well-fucked woman. No wonder seeing her now felt like our early days, when she was so madly in love. She was in love again now. But not with me.

22

I CALLED MILO AT THE SHOP and told him that I thought Lala was cheating on me. He said to come right over. He had an imported copy of the new box set of old Jackie Chan films from Hong Kong, unavailable here and watchable only on his hacked all-region DVD player.

Milo and I debated which one to watch, while he deigned to accept money from the occasional customer. I chose *Project A 2*, actually superior to the first. Its costumey nineteenth century setting is cheering, and Jackie's sweetheart is, as usual, played by the incomparable Maggie Cheung, and among its many miraculous feats is that part when, in an homage to Buster Keaton, Jackie walks calmly down the side of a collapsing wall, several stories high, and steps off just as it crashes. A world where this can happen can't be all bad. Vintage Jackie Chan movies are one more small reason to suspect that life might be worth living. After all, a man can do this with his body. Not me, of course. But someone, anyone. Flight and grace and joy and wonder such as this were right there all along, trapped inside mere matter.

We were about to put the movie on when MJ arrived bearing Vietnamese food. As soon as she spotted me she plopped the bag on the counter and came rushing over, arms out, making that sound that girls (even tough brainy tattooed dykes in cut-offs, a wifebeater, and boots) make when they see a bird fallen from a nest. She hugged me tight. "I heard about Lala. I'm sorry. Is there anything I can do?"

"Rubbing your boobs in his face like that is pretty good for starters," Milo said, wrapping a spring roll in lettuce and dipping it in sauce before stuffing it in his maw. "Now how about a mercy fuck to take his mind off things?"

"He's not like you," she said, patting my head like a puppy. "You'd fuck that spring roll if it had a hole. Or better yet, stick it up yours." She grabbed one and took a savage bite.

"Look who's talking. You got a spring roll down your jeans right now. I see the bulge. You could deep throat that thing easy."

Laughing, she pushed the roll in and out of her mouth.

"Actually, I think those spring rolls are mine," I said. "You guys ordered the summer rolls."

"Sorry." MJ offered me the drool-covered one.

"Keep it," I said.

"See," Milo said, opening the summer rolls. He took one and

passed them to me. "That's part of why Lala dumped you. Right, MJ? He's a sourpuss."

"Wrong." She chewed the tip. "I think your wife's crazy. After a few random fucks to get her pent-up sexual energy out of her system, she'll realize she's made a huge mistake."

"And it's not all bad news," Milo put in, his mouth now full of summer roll. "You've got a cush job there, assistant panty-sniffing for Inspector Fatso. Yes?" He turned to a customer who'd shyly approached, box in hand. Milo looked at it, vaguely affronted. "*Fritz* again," he said, sighing, and went in back.

"Don't listen to that fag," MJ said, while the customer, a wee hipster in a porkpie hat and goatee, listened politely. "They have no idea how we feel at a time like this. Totally insensitive."

We? I wanted to ask. Instead I said, "I thought gay men were hypersensitive."

"That's drag queens, and superfemme types. They're technically women. But men on their own, totally unregulated testosterone? They're just like mobile hard-ons looking to insert. I mean, two guys meeting on a bus could just be like, Hey you, want to fuck? Sure why not? Grunt, grunt. Splat. See you later. But two women, well, you can't really imagine. Love, hate, tears, blood. That's the first week. Or month. It's menstrual theater. All human relationships are more or less impossible, but when you think about it, it's heterosexuality that seems most unnatural, like trying to mate cats and dogs. Even for a very sensitive feminine man like you." She patted my knee. "So don't feel too bad."

23

MJ LEFT WHEN THE MOVIE started. She had no patience for kung fu, another pornographic form of male-on-male action, I suppose. We locked up and turned off the neon. Later, as *Drunken Master II* (not, of course, *The Legend of Drunken Master,* the butchered version released here) our second feature, headed toward its mind-blowing catharsis, there came three loud thumps on the ceiling, and Milo, who had been snoring away peacefully on the couch beside me, suddenly stood up, as if called by a distant trumpet. It was Jerry, the boss, who had been dying upstairs for as long as I could remember. I used to see him when he still descended with a cane to take a post behind the counter, a deep well of movie knowledge and LA lore, and an old photo taped up in the back room showed him young and mustachioed, nipple-ringed and chapped, back when the neighborhood was a hardcore barrio and videotape a miracle from the future. Now all of it, everything on the shelves, was part of the past.

"Going upstairs now," bleary Milo told Mr. Chan, who whirled on the screen before him.

"Can I borrow something?" I asked, still not sure I could sleep, or rather, still a bit afraid to climb into my bed alone.

"Sure." He staggered toward the back staircase to Jerry's. I grabbed another Jackie and then randomly chose *Serpico* on my way out. Seventies New York movies soothed me as well. I pulled the shop door shut and was walking to my car, when I noticed that the light was on behind the papered-over windows of MJ's now defunct bookshop. Was a new tenant in there redecorating? Was it a thief, a very desperate, unambitious thief, stealing the few remaining books too worthless even to give away? I pressed my eye to a small tear in the paper and peeked—this spying stuff is addictive once you begin—but I couldn't see anything. Then I heard, in a high sonorous voice:

This is the dead land
This is the cactus land.
Here the stone images
Are raised, here they receive
The supplication of a dead man's hand
Under the twinkle of a fading star.

It was MJ. Apparently she hadn't gone home after all. I knocked. The voice stopped abruptly, and a brown eye, bright but glazed with a wine reduction, appeared in the little tear. I waved at the eyeball and it blinked. The door opened. She looked a little off, with a crooked smile and a bottle in her hand.

"Why are you still here?"

I gathered from her mutterings that she'd been fighting with her girlfriend, which helped explain her bitter take on relationships earlier in the evening. Drawn by nostalgia, she'd remained in the empty bookstore to drink, recite poetry, and curse womankind, and we ended up moping side by side on the bookstore's back steps, where her old desk and abandoned belongings had been dumped by the painters. I found such conversations enormously rewarding, being able to rage against my wife, love, and female inconstancy, without threatening my image of myself as a liberated, prowoman type, though I was still too inhibited to refer to "bitches" with MJ's utter contempt.

In the end, however, even my anti-life-partner turned on me. "You know what your problem is? How come no one wants to read your books?" She drunkenly poked my heart with her finger. "You can't tell a fucking story." Especially when drunk, MJ cursed with the relish of the deeply uptight, savoring the juice of her sin, while a degenerate like Milo, who might ask your aunt to please pass the fucking salt, didn't even realize he might offend.

"What do you mean can't?" I asked.

"Contraction of can fucking not."

"I just told you the whole sad story of my marriage."

"That was a goddamn bummer. A boring bummer. A borner, which is the opposite of a boner."

"I agree. That's my point. I choose not to tell stories. They're borners. Traditional narrative structure seems totally irrelevant to actual experience today. I mean, what in your life has a regular beginning, middle, and end?"

She shrugged. "How about the part where I'm born, live awhile and die? With blank pages before and after."

"OK, point taken. But then what about all those poets you read? They don't make sense either."

"Poems are short. They don't have to make sense. Like a day at the beach or a quick fuck. Novels take forever. Like life or marriage or grad school. They need some kind of payoff. A reason to go on."

"Maybe you're right." I sighed. "Maybe I've just wasted the last twenty years."

"Well don't fill another novel bitching about it." She punched my arm, kind of hard. "Let's just fuck."

"What?" I was stunned.

"Sure, why not? Milo was right. I know you always wanted to."

Had I? I suppose in the harmless, hopeless, barely conscious way that married men might vaguely lust after their lesbian cohorts. I suppose, behind my own back, I yearned for a lot of things. With drunken precision, she set the wine carefully on the steps and stood, balancing as if on a skateboard.

"I held off before," she explicated, breathing sour grapes in my face, "because it might make firing you awkward. But now? Fuck it. My whole life novel is ruined. Let's write a damn poem." She dropped her shorts and leaned over the desk. "Just yank my panties down and stick it in. High Modernist–style."

"Really? Are you sure about this? What about your, um, partnership? What about mine? I mean, I said I knew she cheated but I don't like *know* know. What if I'm wrong? Then I'll be the cheater. If I just had proof!" Like all neurotics, tortured by ambivalence, I wanted sin without guilt, pleasure without price. But what if that was the essence of the pleasure itself, the savor of wrongness, its secret sugar, the truth that addicts and spree thieves and black-clad sex outlaws of Jerry's generation understood, and that morosely married shmoes like me never would? "Though you do look great, very tempting," I added, seeing her round bottom sway before me, a plum that life was dangling within reach. How many would I get? Do I dare to fuck a peach?

"You talk too much," she muttered, then pulled up her shorts. Stepping back, I kicked over her bottle, which clattered down the steps and broke.

"Shit, my wine," she said. The upstairs window opened and Milo's head poked out.

"What the fuck's going on out there?" he yelled.

MJ and I escaped through the alley and, her energy expended, she let me drive her home. As we pulled out, I glanced up at the lit window above Videolatry. A silhouette watched us. Jerry, I assume, arisen from his bed to see the fools depart. I dropped MJ off and watched while she shuffled meekly through her front door. Her girlfriend Margie waved to me from the open rectangle of warm light. Then I drove home, glad, I guess, that nothing had happened after all. Besides, Margie, MJ's senior partner, was also a junior partner in a huge talent agency who rose at dawn to kickbox, all of which made her scarier than most husbands in this town. Instead I ate three Pop-Tarts and watched part of *Serpico*. As my eyes at last surrendered, giving up their watch, my receding thoughts floated back to the images of Jerry silhouetted in his window, of Maggie outlined in her door, and as if those passages were leading me on, I saw another doorway in another time and place: low sun gleaming through a hole in a huge dark rock. A shining beach. The sea. This reminded me of something I couldn't name, but suddenly I felt happy, and I heard Lala laughing as the tide pulled me under to sleep.

24

WHEN I WOKE UP I knew where Ramona Doon had gone. That picture I'd recalled, of bright light inside a black tunnel, a dark arch glowing in the sun: it was like the image that had been on Ramona Doon's computer screen, on her desk that night when I peeked. I had instantly forgotten it, or rather, I had not even realized that I'd seen it at all, until it returned, called forth from some subbasement of the mind.

On an impulse, I called Lonsky, but grew shy once he got on the phone, explaining in a roundabout way that I had suddenly remembered an image from Ms. Doon's computer screen and that I thought she might have gone there.

"A rock?" he repeated. "With a hole in it?"

"Well a very big rock, a boulder. Picture a lit window in a dark building," I said uncomfortably. I was describing Jerry again.

"Very well, Kornberg, I am picturing it. But how did you recognize this rock in the first place?"

"I've been there, more than once. It's up north." I paused again. "My wife and I go or used to go."

"I see," he said, interested now, but no more convinced. "I concede that you know the place. But there are any number of reasons why it might have appeared on her screen."

"You're right. It's probably nothing. Just what I guess you detectives call a hunch."

"A hunch? Kornberg, please. I'm trying to instill a sense of professionalism in you, if nothing else."

"Sorry."

"Now, let's proceed rationally. You say you recovered this memory. Fine. But how and why? After all, we did a very thorough regression exercise when you were here. It's curious that this new fact should simply arise unbidden. There must have been a trigger and this is the significant factor, not your so-called gut. What exactly were you doing when the memory returned?"

Now I was sorry I'd ever mentioned anything. "I was just falling asleep," I admitted.

"I see. The hypnagogic state. Proceed."

So I proceeded, as best I could, to tell him about the figure in

the window, and who Jerry was, and MJ and Margie, and how my
wife and I used to go to Big Sur every New Year's Eve to escape the
manic-depressing party scene and cuddle instead among the redwoods and walk on that very beach before that hollowed rock in the
rain. Finally, I ran out of words and trailed off, lapsing into an awkward silence.

"Hello?" I said. "Are you still there?"

Lonsky cleared his throat. "Leave immediately," he said in his flat
tone. "Do not tarry. I will reimburse your expenses. I suggest checking the better hotels first. Report in as soon as you can."

25

IF YOU DRIVE LIKE a maniac, you can get to San Francisco in five hours
and change. Big Sur, which is about a hundred and twenty miles
closer, is six hours no matter what. The reason is that, while you
can take the 101 freeway or even the I-5 to San Francisco, to reach
Big Sur, sooner or later you have to get on Highway 1, the long, thin
road that threads up the very edge of the California coast. Highway 1 is stunning and treacherous, full of switchbacks, shared lanes,
the occasional rock- or mudslide, and, deadliest of all, dumb, clumsy
Winnebagos lumbering along roads built for leaner cars, like the
huge person jammed into the plane seat beside you, hogging half
your space. The beauty beyond your side windows — plunging cliffs,
pounding sea, towering redwoods looming in the mist — is matched
only by the fury before your windshield as you honk and yell, straining to pass one of these lard buckets as it drags itself uphill or tries to
bumble its way around a turn.

At least that's how it felt to me as I raced very slowly up the coast,
in hot pursuit of my quarry, whom, I realized as I lost the radio and
phone signal in the rocks, I still had no idea why I was following.

26

I TRIED THE NICER HOTELS first, as instructed. Big Sur is a small town, with most places strung along the highway, and I was familiar with the main spots. First Detjan's Big Sur Inn, where Lala and I always stayed, then Ventana, the fancy place where some old friends had their wedding. Working my way north, I tried Post Ranch without luck, and then went by the Cliffside Inn, a luxuriously rustic hotel perched drastically on the rim of the world. The style was haute hippy modern: exposed beams, flagstone, ferns and glass. I asked a sunny young lady at the counter if my friend had checked in. Yes, Ms. Doon was there, but not in her room at the moment. I thanked her and then, at a loss for what else to do with myself, I went to the beach.

I parked by the roadside and ambled down a pitted road to Pfeiffer Beach, past the display of a local artist whose "art" consisted of finding things that, seen from certain, stoned angles, sort of looked like other things. A stone resembled a sleeping cat. A lump of wood was an old beggar, a branch a bird. Another, pointy rock was, he suggested hopefully, a sculpture of a mountain. A clutch of dread-locked backpackers burbled admiringly, their minds blown, while their scrawny dog gave me a woebegone stare. I crossed a dry creek bed and walked out onto the sand to look at the hole in the rock.

I don't know how else to describe it. By rock I mean a house-size boulder, fallen from the mountain that stood here once, back before the wind winnowed out this beach, before the ocean ate the land and left these jagged teeth. Now, like a home that has burned away, leaving only a doorframe or a single wall, this huge chunk of stone stands alone on the beach, and through its center runs a tunnel, a passage bored by the endless fist of the endless surf pounding on its door forever. Again and again the ocean comes exploding through the hole, spraying salt and throwing itself on the sand, then sucking itself back the way it came, lacey foam rustling like a dragging dress, down the long hall to the sea. It was to this spot we came, my wife and I, each new year of our life together, off-season, a cheap time to visit, but also an escape from New Year's dreary fun, to a cabin with no clock, or TV or phone signal, and walked down to stand on this spot. With each wave, a door cracks open to reveal a hidden corridor to the sky. It is like a magic trick: everything that was always there appears, again, and is miraculous each time.

27

I REFOUND RAMONA BY ACCIDENT in the hotel bar, watching the sunset through a martini. She wore a white slip dress. Her black hair gleamed like a raven's wing. For a split second she looked like my wife, but not really: the sun was in my eyes. As I entered the room I was helpless in the sudden glare, dazzled and blinking blindly at an outline. It was just a trick of light and memory, the hovering image of my own life that floated behind my eyes and turned every small, curvy, cocoa-colored girl into Lala.

By the time my eyes adjusted, and I realized who she was, it was too late to hide. As is customary in half-empty bars on early orange evenings, where still lives pose over deep drinks, everyone looked up, mildly, to see what I would do, including Her. So I did the usual. I walked to the bar very casually and ordered a club soda with lime. I paid—too much—took up a post at the railing, and hoped (from my peripheral vision) that she didn't recognize me as the unshaven transvestite trying on eye shadow at Trashy or the lurking panty-thief from the movies or the fallen derelict face-planted in the seaweed. My glass sweated in my hand, my back sweated in my shirt, and I tried to look relaxed as I sucked on top-price ice cubes, watching another day die, irredeemably, off the American coast.

"Don't I know you from somewhere?"

It was she, speaking out loud, to me.

"Excuse me?" I tried to say, swallowing an ice cube. It jumped down my throat and stuck there a moment, more or less cutting off my air until it melted enough to drop into my belly. I smiled suavely as I fought for breath, freezing and dying slightly from within.

"Are you OK?" she asked with a smile. I coughed, gulping as the cube finally slid down my gullet.

"Sorry," I wheezed. "Wrong pipe."

She laughed. "That's all right."

I cleared my throat. "Sure, go ahead and laugh while I choke to death. Don't offer me a Heimlich or anything."

She laughed more. I was charming her! In a pathetic way, but still. "I don't know how," she said.

"Remind me never to trust you with my life."

She shrugged. "You definitely shouldn't. Didn't your mother warn you about strangers?"

"Ah," I said. "Yes, but my father warned me not to listen to my mother. And anyway, I thought you knew me from somewhere. Or was that just a pickup line?"

She blushed and laughed loudly, and play punched my gut, with the delight of the gorgeous, adored woman being teased. For a guy who hadn't been on a date in years, I wasn't doing badly, not that I had managed much witty badinage even when single.

"Yes, I admit it," she said sarcastically, but with a spark in her eyes. "I was just trying to talk to you."

"I knew it. The oldest trick in the book. And this is your lair I've stumbled into."

"Yes." She glanced at the silent drinkers watching a silent game on TV. "This is where I come to pick up men."

Across the room a red-haired, red-faced man in red golf pants laughed loudly and slapped his pal's back. An old lady of the sinewy, sun-shrunken type, decked in a visor and strung with gold, rattled the ice in her empty glass, squealing like a witch casting a spell till the ponytailed bartender brought her a fresh one. She sighed, settling back into her chair.

"I can see why," I said. "It's quite a scene."

She shrugged. Her hair kissed her shoulders. Her flesh was perfect, like coffee ice cream, smooth and rich, racially ambiguous, and without flaws or variations in tone, so unlike my own splotchy, hairy pink hide. "So what are you doing here all alone?" she asked.

"Me?" I looked around dramatically and then leaned in. "I'm a private eye on a case. Looking for a mysterious missing woman."

"I see." With a nail she drew a jagged line, like a crack, in the fog on her glass. "And who is this woman?"

"I don't know. That's why it's a mystery."

"Is she good or bad?"

"Both, probably."

"What does she look like? Maybe I've seen her?"

"She looks a bit like you."

"Ah, then she's probably bad." She finished her drink. "I have to admit, you're cleverer than most strange men in bars, although less well dressed. What do you do when you're not on a case?"

"Read. Watch too many movies. Wander around."

"That's it?"

"I try to write a little."

"Ah, a writer. That makes sense. I bet you're good at telling stories, with the private eye stuff and all."

"Actually, I write experimental fiction. I'm not really into plot-driven stuff."

"You mean more just about the characters, their psychology?"

"No, not that either. I'm not really so interested in psychology."

"So more like a poem or something, abstract ideas?"

"No, it's a novel. Definitely not abstract. I can't stand all that intellectual abstraction."

"A novel with no story or characters or ideas? It's hard to imagine."

"Yeah for me too." We both laughed. "Actually, I don't know what the fuck I'm talking about."

"I noticed."

"What about you? What do you do?"

"I don't know. Wander about, like you said. Be a woman of mystery." She tapped my glass with her empty glass. It rang lightly. "Another gin and tonic?"

"Sure," I said. "But this time hold the gin." She frowned curiously. "I'm a master of drunken kung fu," I explained. "I might lose control and kill someone."

"Okay, if you say so . . . one virgin gin and tonic coming up." She sallied off with our glasses. I settled my eyes on the ocean and considered how nicely this was working out. The perfect way to keep a private eye on someone, without them knowing you're following, is to have them hang around with you. True, Lonsky had specified a discreet distance, but an operative working a case has to improvise. I was also amazed at how well I was doing with such a knockout. But, of course, I told myself, as I had at so many smoky neighborhood barbeques and winey gallery openings: don't worry, this is just a bit of harmless flirting, you're a married man. But was I still? Standing there, where no one knew my name, where no one even knew I was, I realized how far I had drifted, in just a day, away from my own life. I felt seasick, and I clutched the railing for support.

Then she returned, without the drinks, looking pale and unsteady herself, as if the whole deck had tilted on a rising wave. She leaned into me, muttering swiftly under her breath, "I have to go. Right now."

"Sorry?"

She gripped my wrist and whispered in my ear. I smelled perfume and shampoo and behind that something sharper, sweet and sour—late afternoon cocktails and sweat. But her voice was sober and serious. "I have to leave right now. Walk out with me. Please."

I remembered suddenly that I really was a detective (sort of), following a mystery woman, not just a writer pretending to be one to make a mystery woman smile. Was this the danger I was here to fight? Whom was she hiding from? A husband? A stalker? A spy? I looked around, but it was just the same lame crew as before. Unless they were in disguise.

"Don't look," she hissed. "Let's just go, this way." She guided me toward the back of the deck and down a stairway that led to the parking lot. "Where is your car?"

"There," I said. "But what's wrong? Who was it?"

"Please. Not now. Let's just get out of here. Please."

She hurried ahead to my car, so I unlocked it and we got in. As I rolled toward the highway, she slid low in the seat, shielding her face.

"Where to?"

"Anywhere. It doesn't matter. Someplace quiet where I can breathe."

"OK." I made a right onto the One, headed south.

"No," she said. "Turn around. Let's go to the forest. You know, the redwoods."

"OK." Glancing quickly, I U-turned in a driveway and headed north. She relaxed after I passed the hotel, taking a lipstick from her purse and touching up her mouth in the mirror.

"So," I asked, "what was all that about?"

"Please don't," she interrupted. "Don't ask. Don't ask me anything ever. That way I won't have to lie to you. I haven't yet, well not really, not much, and it feels good for once. I'm such a dirty liar. Maybe that's why I feel close to you, even though we're strangers. I feel like you're the one person who I'm honest with. Just myself. Without any lies or masks." She gripped my knee and looked at me intently. "Don't even ask my name. Please?"

"Sure. No problem." I chuckled assuredly, like a man of the world. She was making me a little nervous. "We'll be anonymous. And don't go asking me anything either," I warned, poking her leg. "I'm very deep and troubled and I don't want to talk about it."

She giggled happily. "Go ahead. Make fun of me. I deserve it." She finished her lipstick, and sat back, gazing at the scenery. "I'm happy here, with you," she sighed. "I feel safe."

That was good enough for me. I turned into the entrance for the national forest, paid the attendant, and parked. We got out and walked up the path. We spoke not, but she touched my arm once or twice to steady herself as her red heels sank into the earth and we hiked into the broken shadows under the giant trees. They soared above us, hundreds of feet high, like cathedral pillars reaching for some vanished vault. These were the oldest living things on earth. In their history, we barely registered, our whole lives brief as a bug's. And as for our thoughts and feelings, our little victories and dramas, these were less than nothing. Yet, that odd growth, the human mind, still clung to a vain idea, that our self-consciousness, the source of so much trouble for ourselves and our fellow life-forms, had to serve some purpose, some need of nature's own. Perhaps we were flowers, brains on fragile stems, seeded here as the one creature aware of all this pointless beauty and its loss: our minds, nature's weirdest blossoms, petals that open only to see the sun, and then go dark.

"What are you thinking?" she asked me as we stood together among the waist-high roots. Our bodies were closer than I'd noticed. We nearly touched.

"I don't know," I said, afraid to say. "What were you thinking?"

"This," she said, and kissed me.

28

LATER, WHEN I THOUGHT back to that moment, it felt unreal, but at the time it seemed, if by no means normal, then natural, as if for once everything were working out just like it should. I took her face in my hands and kissed her back. Now that I held her, she seemed so much smaller. Her mouth tasted like sugared strawberries and vermouth. She pushed her body against mine, arms clutching at my neck, and I felt her heart beating in her chest. Breathing hard, we grasped and shoved, as though we were struggling. It was like a slow-motion fight. Her tooth cut my lip and I tasted blood. I pulled back and saw her eyes glitter wildly like a cat's. Then she shut them and reached her mouth for mine again. We leaned against the tree, blind and unspeaking, and my hands found her body, touched her waist and hips and thighs, her breasts and shoulders and the small of her back, feverish and alive. Then a parade of Asian tourists came around the path. I suppose I hadn't heard them approaching over the pounding of my own blood in my head. Blushing and panting, hand in hand, we stumbled back down to the car and began grappling again inside. Whispering hoarsely in my ear she told me to look at her and I looked in her eyes, but she pushed me back and pulled up her dress. She wore the things that I saw her buy in the shop, the black stockings, the garter belt, the flimsy triangle of lace split to show her shining wet and pink as her mouth was after my kisses, then red inside like her mouth was, swollen and raw. Touch me, she ordered. Hypnotized, I reached out and touched her pussy just slightly and she flinched and groaned, yelping as if I'd hurt her, and pushed my hand away. She squirmed away and said not here, no please, take me back to the hotel and I started the car and I drove, though once we were moving she grabbed my hand and thrust it between her legs again. I drove like that with one hand, fighting the curves. We went back to the Cliffside Inn and parked around back in the guests' lot, where the rooms were perched over the cliff, and I could see the sweat gluing her dress to the small of her back as I followed her upstairs to her room. The smell of her hair and perfume was in my nose, the taste of her mouth and my own blood was in my mouth, and the image of how she'd looked with her legs spread in my car was blazing in my brain so brightly I could barely see and I walked right into her as she reached her door. She dropped the key and cursed softly and I picked it up. Shaking, I opened the door and we entered the room, with its tightly made white bed and the white curtain blowing in the open balcony door and beyond that the ocean crashing far below, and I brushed the straps from her shoulders and she slid out of the dress and pulled me toward her, unhooking my belt and yanking at the buttons on my shirt till I took it off over my head, then pushed her back onto the bed while she drew me to her, guiding my hands, and I reached for that little flag of lace, that little veil, and tore it away, and she pulled my pants off and licked my cock and then pulled me toward her, pulled me down saying please and I pushed my cock, wet with her spit, against her wet pussy, and she was saying yes, saying please, saying fuck me and then I was inside her, and she was still saying yes, fuck me, fuck me please, and I pushed harder, forcing myself as deep as I could, and feeling her breath on my face and her nails in my arms and then her teeth in my shoulder, the whole time saying, more, please, fuck me, please. After we finished we laid there for a while in silence and I might have fallen asleep, for an hour or perhaps just for a second. Maybe I just blinked my eyes. But when I opened them it was dark out, the sun was finally gone, and when I turned to kiss her, she was gone too. I sat up, still confused and dim-eyed in the dark, and saw her standing on the balcony, framed in the door, a silver silhouette, still as a statue in the moonlight, looking down at the sea. And I called to her, I just said hey there you are — since I wasn't supposed to know her name — and she might have heard me, or perhaps not, since she did not look back, she just stepped over the side and I heard her scream.

For a moment I did nothing. I felt like my arms and legs had turned to marble. Then I jumped up and ran to the balcony naked. I pushed through the curtains, which wrapped around me in the wind, like a veil I had to tear through or a cloud that had come between me and the moon, and I felt myself panic for a second and it all began to feel real once more. I looked over the balcony's edge. I saw nothing. Not nothing. I saw dark water beating on dark rocks and throwing up moonlit foam. I saw white foam drooling over jagged black rocks. I saw dark cliffs black with trees. I saw the vast black ocean, starred with silver sparkles under a vast black sky. I saw waves. I saw white stars. I saw the moon.

29

I WON'T BORE YOU with the details. The cops came and at first they weren't sure they believed me. Yes a Ramona Doon had checked in, and yes she was missing, but dead? They treated me like a be-fuddled boyfriend who'd been ditched, until a body washed up with the dawn tide at which point they freaked out and held me, at a far less glamorous hotel, for the inquest. Although the corpse was too mangled by the fall, and too softened by the sea, for easy identifica-tion, a Doctor Parker, who had reported a woman missing in Pasa-dena, eventually arrived and informed the authorities that her real name was Mona Naught. He had been treating her at his psychiatric clinic for years, until she ran away. She had been, at best, depressed and troubled. At her worst she was delusional and most definitely a threat to herself. This was not her first try. The coroner returned a verdict of suicide and sent us home.

I had called Lala from a landline and left her a message canceling therapy. This time I was the one out of town on shady business. She didn't call back. I also called Lonsky. He took the news as he took everything, his oceanic calm unchanged, the depths revealed only by a long sigh, after which he instructed me, in his usual rumbling baritone, to listen sharply to what the cops said and report in as soon as I returned.

30

AT FIRST, WHEN I TURNED Lonsky's corner, I thought the flashing lights were for me. I was somehow in trouble for something. Then I saw the ambulance parked alongside the cop car and the fire truck fur-ther down the street. Maybe Lonsky's mother had suffered a heart attack. I parked and joined the loose group of spectators on the sidewalk. The neighbors watched from their own lawns and porches.

"What happened?" I asked a fellow audience member, a Korean kid in shorts and a baggy T-shirt. He shrugged.

"Somebody was saying the dude's too fat for the thing."

The dude had to be Lonsky of course, but there were any number of things he might be too fat for. Had he gotten trapped in the house somehow? Fallen through a weak floorboard? Was this a jaws-of-life situation? Against my will, I pictured his mountainous flesh floundering among the shards of a shattered toilet.

"What thing?" I asked. The kid shrugged again.

But the answer was soon revealed. A small team of firemen and EMTs emerged from the house guiding a gurney on which a foam mattress was balanced with a sheet of plywood beneath it. Atop the gurney was Lonsky, in red silk pajamas, lashed to the mattress with thick straps. A napkin was loosely knotted around his neck and he seemed to be clutching a wooden spoon in one hand. Slowly the contraption was wheeled onto the porch, carefully held in balance by men on both sides.

"Oh shit," the kid muttered respectfully, under his breath.

"What's on his face?" I wondered aloud.

"That shit's batter, yo!"

Indeed, Lonsky seemed to have chocolate frosting smeared around his mouth and cheeks. He licked his lips thoughtfully as more firemen laid planks over the steps. Madams Lonsky and Moon brought up the rear of the procession, Mrs. Moon weeping openly, Mrs. L. stoic, smoking a cigarette and scolding a fireman for stomping a flower with his boots. At one point the gurney's wheel slipped off the ramp and, as the onlookers gasped, Lonsky listed dangerously to one side. But the men heaved and, groaning together like galley slaves in a storm, they righted his lurching bulk. As they rolled down the walk, Lonsky spotted me.

"Kornberg," he called. "Kornberg!"

I approached the gurney, but was stopped by a cop.

"Hold it."

"He's calling me. He's my um . . ." I hesitated.

"Kornberg!" Lonsky yelled, and now the float halted as he waved his spoon and rolled from side to side. "Let my assistant through! He's my protégé!"

"That you?" the cop asked. "You that guy's protégé?"

"I guess," I said and crossed the lawn.

"Mr. Lonsky," I said. "What's wrong? Are you ill?"

"Kornberg," he called, and as I came closer, I saw that he was not tied down simply for balance. His face was distorted, red and wet with tears. I saw their traces in the dried frosting. "Kornberg . . ."

"Yes sir?"

He waved me closer still. His throat was ragged. He whispered. "Who killed her?" Everyone looked curiously at me.

"Who killed who, sir?" I asked.

Suddenly he howled, like a wounded beast, like a lion pierced by a spear. "My love!" He lunged at me, tearing the button from my shirt and nearly upsetting the cart as he struggled with his keepers. I gaped in shock. "Find the killer, Kornberg," he moaned. "Avenge my love!"

Four men lay across his limbs while another slid a needle into the meat of his arm. He thrashed wildly, like Prometheus bound. Then he seemed to subside into himself and, as his servants strained to slide him into the ambulance, the great man drifted into sleep. Huffing, the EMTs shut the door while the sweat-drenched firemen mopped themselves off. The ambulance slowly pulled out, a bit low on its wheels, and the onlookers wandered away.

Mrs. Lonsky looked me over, tapping ash from her smoke. "I suppose you'd better come in," she said. "Solar left your pay."

PART III

PORTRAITS OF SOME LADIES

31

THE CASE OF THE CLUELESS HUSBAND

(FROM THE FILES OF SOLAR LONSKY, DETECTIVE)

THE SUBJECT OF THESE NOTES, to whom I shall refer as K., first arrived at my office seeking employment as my assistant, though even in our first meeting, which took the form of a job interview, I was readily able to discern his true motives: he was coming to me for help, for relief from his own psychic pain. His wife had recently abandoned him. He was a failed novelist who had subsisted as a used bookstore clerk before ultimately failing at that as well. Well past the age when most men have established careers, homes, families, and positions of respect, he continued to flounder like a child, lost in his life, barely able to dress like a grown-up or seek a job without spousal prompting. Yet he seemed to have no idea why his wife might leave him. On the contrary, childish, grandiose, self-centered, and riven by hysterical fears and deep unconscious struggles that rendered him helplessly, perhaps hopelessly, neurotic, he blamed her and felt like an innocent victim. He had no glimmer of what might actually be going on, least of all within himself.

I decided to take his case. My reasons were several: First, as a student of human nature (and by nature here I mean the grand landscapes, ever-changing climates, and infinitely wondrous wildlife of the unconscious and still mainly uncharted mind), I could not pass up the opportunity to observe this extraordinary specimen at close quarters. Second, I was fond of him, despite his numerous shortcomings. He represented a rare type, a dying breed, the intellectual bohemian idler, the supposed man of "books and art and ideas," who appeared, if only by virtue of his incompetence, to remain apart from the world, untouched by the love of money, status, fame or even normal respectability, and who asked only to dream on, but who awoke in shock to find himself in the wrong century, the wrong country, the wrong world. Certainly, the wrong class. Lastly, though I am not technically speaking a doctor, nor a believer in spirits, I do try to ease the pain of my fellow humans as they pass through this plane; being of service to the sick is my code. Thus I could not turn him away, for whether he knew it or not, he came to me as a patient, crying out silently and unconsciously for my help. After all, he arrived asking to become a detective, when he had never before in his life considered doing any such thing. Why? To solve the mystery of himself. To find what had been stolen from him: his wife. And to discover by whom.

In "A Difficulty in The Path of Psycho-Analysis" (1917), Freud introduces the concept of the Third Wound to describe the repeated assaults that scientific knowledge had inflicted on human conceit: first, Copernicus discovered that the sun does not revolve around the earth and that man is not in fact the true center of the universe. The second blow was delivered by Darwin: man is not set apart from the animals, nor formed by a creator in His image, but is in fact a creature among others, a variation on a theme, and no longer the center of life on earth either. The final, vanquishing blow, was of course Freud's own: his discovery of the unconscious—that immense internal sea, full of fears and wishes, memories and fantasies, whose depths remain largely unsounded—revealed the truth, that our inner world is as alien as the universe without. "[I]ts inner nature is just as unknown to us as the reality of the external world, and it is just as imperfectly reported to us through the data of consciousness as is the external world through the indications of our sensory organs."

Man, it turns out, is not even at the center of his own mind. The greater part of our own life happens, one might say, behind our backs. "The ego is not master in its own house."

Never had this insight of Freud's seemed truer than when I met K. for our second session. I had set him the task of surveilling and observing a woman who I believed possessed the key to an important mystery, which I will not undertake to describe here (see The Case of the Mystery Girl). Arriving to make his report, I was amazed to see him struggle as he tried, somewhat desperately, to present himself as an eager professional, grasping a notebook and pen, ticking off irrelevant details as his unconscious leaked relentlessly through the cracks. While his words and tone were literate, reserved, even prudish, the dirt under his fingernails and the leaves in his hair, even the faint air of canine feces about his person, spoke of an almost savage state of regression. The partially unzipped fly and bunched underpants visible over his rear waistband were due, no doubt, to squatting for hours in the dark. But the fact that they remained uncorrected, left deliberately if unknowingly on display—what purpose could they have but to assert his sexual identity to another, more powerful male, to "present"? Then of course there was the blond lady's wig peeking from his knapsack, symbolizing the wife perhaps, the burden of a repressed Other who would not remain hidden, or else the wish for a burial, the death of the troublesome mate. Or was it his own feminine side, creeping from the darkness, the "woman within"? Of the meaning of the water bottle in his rucksack, which I found upon later inspection to contain urine, I will not even venture a guess. Suffice it to say, the man was keeping secrets, from me and from himself.

In an attempt to probe more deeply, I suggested to K. that he set aside his "notes," and try a simple relaxation exercise as an aide-mémoire. He agreed. However, he vocalized his resistance by asserting that such techniques "never work" for him, insisting that he cannot be "hypnotized" because he tried once when quitting smoking, and launching into a long and largely pointless anecdote about acupuncture and a yoga class his wife once made him attend.

Nevertheless, it was clear that the larger part of him was eager, even desperate to be heard, for no sooner had I begun to talk him through a very simple deep breathing and visualization exercise of the sort recommended to tense air passengers than he fell into a kind of trance, revealing a deep and precise memory. He also left some drool on my chair cushion.

Our next meeting was hardly conducive to analysis, the fault entirely mine. I was indisposed, suffering a recurrence of the illness that has plagued me for most of my life, and which I cannot avoid addressing here in some detail in order to proceed with this report.

Much of the exploring and learning a young person does, particularly when he or she is bright, takes the form of mystery-solving. Why is the sky blue? How does gravity work? What causes fire? Can cats fly? What is in that book I'm not allowed to read, that drawer I'm forbidden to open? Even the most primal and immortal questions of all can be seen as mysteries. Freud and the Ancients offer their famous readings, but I saw Oedipus as the first detective story and with the first, best, and now most tired twist: Oedipus Detectus searches for a killer who turns out to be himself. Although our own crimes and secrets are in general less horrific (and our punishments less severe than poor Ed's), the essential mystery we all solve is the same: Where did we come from? Where do we go? The child peeking through a keyhole at his mother taking a bath, or crawling on the floor beneath her skirt, or lying in bed hearing her parents wrestle in the next room, her father's curses, her mother's cry—each little gumshoe learns the shocking secret for himself, the truth they try to keep us from uncovering: We enter the world naked and bloody through a hidden opening in our mother's body, where our father has secretly planted a seed. And each of us will leave this world as well, disappearing one by one, as in a late night horror show, until we too vanish forever. Sex and death stand behind everything, before the beginning and after the end.

Of course, my early career as a detective in training was a bit humbler. Early cases included: Who the Hell Keeps Taking the Paper? (the next-door neighbor), Where Does the Guy Up the Block Go in the Middle of the Night? (to visit the next-door neighbor's wife while he's out of town on business), and Where Is the Cat When He's Not Here? (shockingly, it turned out that my cat, Patchy, had a whole other family, who let him in, fed him, and petted him, calling him by another completely different name, Mr. Boops.)

Although a bit disillusioning, these first ventures nevertheless inspired in my young mind a vision of the world as full of enticing secrets to be discovered. The next step, the lesson that opened up my interest in psychology, came a bit later, when I began to ponder the concept of lying. Reprimanded and severely spanked for my own mendacity, in the Case of the Vanished Chocolate Bar, I began to wonder how my mother could "tell" I was lying, she said, by the way I twitched and shifted. I remember the term she used and which fascinated me to no end: "You gave yourself away." Why, I wondered, would I do that? Why would anyone? Nevertheless, as my mother astutely observed: "Everybody has a tell."

So the man who arrived at my father's place of business, the kitchen table, promising him that his debt would be paid on Friday when his check cleared, was deliberately lying, while the next man, who confidently assured my father that he would recoup all losses on the next game, which was a "lock" was, in his own mind, really telling the truth, despite being equally "full of crap." Why? He was lying, not to us, but to himself! This was a life-changing insight: while truth and lies are opposing concepts, they are not set in their logical relationship. The honest person constantly puts forward the falsehood he believes, while the liar unknowingly reveals the truth. Within a few months, I was reading Freud, and soon I was skilled enough to see through most anyone, even my mother, the best gambler I ever saw, when she spoke the first of the only two lies she ever told me, an hour after my father, who had been yelling on the phone and smoking a Pall Mall as usual, suddenly clutched his chest and fell, crashing into the coffee table and burning the rug. I stared as his face became a mask, mouth open, eyes still. I peeked from my window as men took him away in what looked like a plastic garbage bag and loaded him into an ambulance. And when my weeping mother told me that he was now in heaven, watching over me, and could hear me when I prayed, I knew that she was bluffing. I knew she had nothing at all.

It is a truism that psychologists and therapists are first drawn to the field in order to solve their own problems. Perhaps only those of us who realize that we ourselves are unsolvable go on to be great: the powers of insight we develop are that much stronger, and, useless on ourselves, they snap into sharp focus when aimed at another.

In my own case, my difficulties did not begin to emerge until my late teens, though looking back now I wonder, did I have a premonition about my own fate? Was I somehow, unconsciously, preparing myself? If so, it was of little use. When my turn came, I believed the lies my own mind told, just like an amateur.

At first I began to suspect that someone was watching me. I wasn't sure who, of course, because I couldn't catch them. But I became convinced that "they" were lurking outside the house, ducking behind a tree when I turned or quickly pulling their shades. When I drove with my mother, I would become certain a car was following us. I would force her to drive in circles, change lanes, make sudden, aimless turns, but this proved or disproved nothing. Perhaps the reason the suspicious blue car didn't follow was that the driver knew I suspected him and so was acting like an innocent person driving a blue car to trick me. Or perhaps it had been the green car all along.

As my fears worsened, I took to wearing disguises. First I tried to hide this new obsession (my obsession with hiding) from my mother by simply donning a hat or scarf or dark glasses. Soon however, I became an expert, devising and refining elaborate characters with wigs, makeup, clothes, and prostheses: an old man, a large woman, a mailman, a blind beggar. Of course on some level I knew this was ridiculous. I am not a small person, and leaving my house in an Afro wig, my skin darkened and wearing a housedress, did not make me less conspicuous. Quite the contrary! But I could not stop.

Finally I gave up leaving the house altogether. My mother was growing deeply concerned, but I was in denial, still consulting for colleagues via the mail, reviewing case files and critiquing their reports. Still, a crash was inevitable, and as my paranoid fantasies combined with the compulsive eating that marks my acute manic phase, I would order grand feasts, instructing the deliverymen to leave the food on the porch. Finally I lost all control and ordered Indian, Chinese, pizza, Mexican, and Thai at once. The deliverymen arrived to find me in an upper window, disguised as a rabbi and ordering them to place the food in a basket that I lowered from a rope while tossing loose cash onto the lawn.

It was after this incident that I apparently blacked out and woke up in Green Haven, a well-regarded hospital for the mentally ill. I was medicated, stabilized, and returned to a coherent, if shaken state. They say that doctors make the worst patients. I certainly had as little interest in my psychiatrist's attempts to fix me as I had regard for my hosts' ideas of quality in food, books, or housekeeping. My only concern was to get out as soon as possible, first by arguing with my keepers and demonstrating my intellectual superiority (this rarely wins people over, I've found), and later by acceding to their demands—interpreting their splotches, solving their puzzles, coughing up their preformed epiphanies, and, most important, swallowing their pills.

The pills! That chemical rainbow, those little time bombs of sanity, were to define the next era of my life. The cycle was always the same. For a while, I eat the brain candy, and life is placid as a suburban kiddy pool: chlorinated, clear, depthless, and dull. Sluggish and sheepish but technically sane, I paddle along, until something, a case, a clue, a crisis, or sheer boredom, restarts my mind. Inevitably I forget to take the pills or I "forget" to take the pills, or I misremember that I did take them or I just decide I don't need them anymore. I'm better. I'm fine. Actually, I feel great. Greater! Really, I've never felt so good. The air is fresh and the sunshine sparkles and I savor every moment of the day. Food tastes wonderful (uh-oh) and music sounds divine (really this is the only medicine anyone needs) and I am grateful to be alive. I find myself deeply engrossed in my work, my mind blooming with new ideas, and frankly I am more brilliant than ever (though of course I am never brilliant enough to recognize that this happens every time, that this very brilliance is a symptom of the coming crash). Finally, I become so brilliant that I can barely keep up with my own amazing brain as it races ahead, without sleep, without cease, seeing more and more, understanding more and more, reading the world like a foreign text that suddenly makes sense, like a closed book that suddenly falls open.

It is at this point that some small part of me, some inner librarian, taps my shoulder or whispers in my ear and asks, "Isn't this merely a fiction? Don't we remember how it ends?" But I don't listen, my ears are plugged and I am racing ahead to the climactic chapters: paranoia, delusions, epic binge eating, intellectual ecstasy, and suicidal despair. And then I turn the blank page.

I wake up in Green Haven with a tube in my arm and Doctor smiling kindly down at me and I know it has happened again. And again. And again. For it is a circular story, an eternal return, with minor variations (an escape, in my underwear, from dwarf-commandos who turn out to be girlscouts, a taxi trip to Sacremento chasing a cloud) and one major development: as the years passed, I ceased to be a troublemaker. I was too much humbled. What good was my supposedly great brain if it could not help me, if in fact it was my own worst enemy, the nemesis that beat me every time? (For those who are keeping score, this was the occasion of my mother's second and last lie to me: her assurance that I was going to be fine. Once again her poker face revealed exactly what was on the cards she pressed lovingly to her maternal bosom. I will never be fine. She was, as she'd say, full of crap.)

Besides illness, the other great force that humbled me was love. As Freud so beautifully writes: "Whoever loves becomes humble. Those who love have, so to speak, pawned a part of their narcissism." However, he also notes: "One is very crazy when in love."

Her name was Mona Naught.

Today Green Haven is like a second home to me. It is in a sense my alma mater. Instead of going to college (I was Harvard bound) I left home for the hospital, and there I have returned for further studies, albeit as subject and not student. Nevertheless, I learned a great deal. Just as a botanist, unable to visit the jungle, might become an expert on tropical flowers in his greenhouse, so I too have gained much from close observation of the rare species, the wild orchids and dark nightshades, the delicate violets, rank weeds, and bursting sunflowers that thrive in Green Haven's eternal and protective spring.

After a week's recuperation and stabilization in my room, I was able to descend to the common areas, and gravitated to the "library." I place the term in quotes because this room was hardly well stocked with either books or silence, but still it was much my favorite room in the house, free of the television and admirably proportioned, with high ceilings, wide chairs, and french windows open to the breeze that whispered in so alluringly that, though I might not, after a crash course of Haldol and electroshock, know my own name, I knew with one deep breath and the vague touch of soft air on my face— it was spring. Well enough to be bored, but still weak enough to be dazed, I shuffled in, failed to find either a new book or a worthwhile chess opponent, and drifted off into the land of nod with what, for all I knew, was a week-old newspaper on my knee. As is often the case when wading in that murky river between waking and sleep, my mind began to float downstream and a scene from memory appeared along the shore: I was on my back, on the stretcher, rolling down a hall, returning to my bed from the ECT room, where the mechanics had rebooted my mind with electricity, that torture which like so many things — whiskey, morphine, love — is medicine to some and poison to others. For me, frankly, it was a relief, the calm after the electrical storm, my brain washed clean after a long rain, or better yet, wrung out after a good scrubbing. At last I knew the fuzzy befuddlement that the healthy and stupid call "peace of mind." The electrical staff generally endeavor to avoid interpatient encounters, but there was some delay by the elevator as my wheel stuck (my bulk is not easy to transport, and in fact my room at the clinic is fitted with a special bed), and I heard another stretchered patient roll raving down the hall. It was a woman and she was howling. I could not see her face beyond the white-coated backs fighting to hold her down, but as she screamed in a ragged, schizoid voice, I saw a hand, long, slender, delicate, with narrow tapered fingers, a violinist's hand, drop over the edge of the gurney. The nails were done in red.

"It's not true," she was screeching. "It's all a plot. I'm not Mona Naught. Zed's alive. Please, someone believe me. It's not real."

Suddenly I awoke, or revived, or resurfaced, in the "library." My eyes popped open and I caught a thief filching my paper. Instinctively, I grabbed the intruding hand by the wrist. It was slender, fine-boned, red-tipped, and the thin wrist was circled with a pink ID band. It was the hand from my dream.

"Pardon me," the attached body said in a voice that was surely not the voice from my dream. That one had been a raging, raw, decidedly psychotic screech. This voice on the contrary was smart, amused, musical and refined. "I was just hoping to borrow the crossword. If you're finished snoring through it, I mean."

"Yes. I mean, no," I said. "I'm not using it." My mind was still foggy.

"Then unhand me, sir."

"Sorry." I released her reluctantly. "It's the afterglow of all the electricity they ran through my brain. I apologize."

"Don't." The fingers fluttered off lightly, like a butterfly bearing away the paper. "I know what it's like. That's why I want to try the puzzle. To see how many brain cells I have left."

"By all means then, proceed."

She smiled her thanks, I think, though I can't be sure. The spring sun was shining whitely behind her, frankly her face was a diamond, but she gave a little witty curtsey, then retired to a table with, I was pleased to see, a proper pen, not a pen-cil. She did it in ink. While she bent to her task, biting her lip and brushing her long black hair behind her ear, I observed and surreptitiously timed her, leaning back, lids low, one eye on the grandfather clock. She was beautiful. She had a small face, large eyes that seemed sad although she was quick to smile, even to herself, as she filled in a word, then gnawed the pen with her little white teeth. She finished in ten minutes. Not bad really for a young person recovering from electroshock, though I can't say what day of the week's puzzle it was.

"So," she said, standing and smoothing her hospital robe as if it were a skirt. "How did I do?" She handed me the completed puzzle.

I laughed. She'd caught me. "Just about ten minutes," I said. "Quite impressive."

She beamed like a child. "Thanks."

I held out my hand. "I'm Solar Lonsky, by the way."

Fearlessly, she placed that pretty hand inside my ridiculous beastly paw. "Pleased to meet you. I am Mona Naught."

What can I say? (Dear Reader, gentle doctor, fellow detective, alien scholar, reading this archive perhaps in the far future, long after my molecules return to carbon following their brief adventure in consciousness, after my case studies are unearthed and published, perhaps on a tiny chip that you will read through the tip of your tongue while floating in a gelatinous blob through space) I fell in love. Preposterous, I know: an enormous (enormously obese) socially retarded, hermitic (hermetic), certifiably demented old fool with a heart like a scalpel falling for a demure little cocotte. But then again, isn't love preposterous on the face of it? Isn't it by definition a ridiculous enterprise? We have come up with only two modes to describe it: the tragic, about which I need say no more, and the happy version, the comedy, which suggests that even in its joyful, lucky, wedding-dance form, it is somehow absurd, and unable to be taken seriously, leastwise by the audience, frantically cheering for their own wishful thinking. Being happy in love means getting the big joke about humans, and I was the biggest, fattest joke of all.

And my beloved, what did she think of me? Well, she certainly did not love me as I her: rapturously, exclusively, carnivorously. I am not an attractive specimen, and physical love is impractical for a medicated man of my proportions, heavily stuffed as I am with both blubber and libido-killing pills. And the great love of her own short life was her husband, deceased.

But she was my love nevertheless, and if she did not love me back at least she did not despise me or if she did she hid it well. She was kind, and no doubt in that place, she was lonely. She needed a friend. She did not discuss her past or why she was there, and I did not inquire, though rumors swirled: she had a mysterious birth, a notorious husband who met a tragic death, she'd been living abroad in glamorous exile, and then, inevitably, after the flight, came the crash, the slash, the naked crying, the nightmare ambulance, the candied smile of happy pills. But that all belonged to another Mona. Our friendship was a little oasis, an island in the center of the day-room at Green Haven, where I taught her chess and she described the paintings and buildings and plays she had seen in London and Paris and Rome. She drew my portrait in crayon.

Then the day came when the keepers released me, and for the first time I was unhappy to go back home, to my study, my work, my books, my mother. Back to me.

Time passed, memory faded: hers, I mean, not mine. As Dr. Freud notes, time does not pass in the unconscious, and everything that has ever happened is happening now. So too in my affective life, the clock had stopped. It was midnight in the museum of my heart. I kept watch and walked the empty chambers, guarding the precious exhibits: Here is the smell of her hair. Here are her eyes, green stones flecked with black. Here are the tiny bird bones moving in her hands. Here is her laughter, that sudden flight, that wild flutter folding into a smile. Here is that one crooked little tooth tucked behind another. Her narrow shoulders poking the thin cardigan. The pimples bursting, a five-point constellation, across her smooth forehead when her period is about to arrive. Her voice in the evening playing cards. Her long dry hand shaking goodnight. Her soft lips on my cheek the day I left. All this I preserved for posterity, in a vault whose only key I hid with her. Then one night, the doorbell rang.

I was the only one up so I answered, something I generally avoid. I peeked through the portal. It was she, messy and distraught, her hair wild, her cheeks streaked with black tears that trickled from her eyes to the corners of her mouth. I opened the door.

"Mona?"

"I'm not Mona. Don't call me that," she whispered in another voice. It was the voice I'd heard in the hospital corridor, the voice from my dream, raspy, raw, and crazed.

"What do you mean? What's wrong? Come in, please."

She wouldn't come in. As I fear the outdoors, so Mona, or "Mona" in her crisis, loathed the inside. She refused to cross my threshold. She shook her head in horror but clutched at my hands. I admit this thrilled me: aside from that first handshake and the brief farewell kiss on my cheek, we had never touched.

But if her warm, clammy hands on mine made my sore heart soar, her story broke its wings. Clearly, my darling had been driven out of her mind. She chattered out a frantic tale between clattering teeth. She claimed that she was not Mona, that she was being forced to play her, by some elaborate and complex conspiracy involving her husband, her doctor (who was my doctor too, Dr. Parker), and, of all people, a famous motion picture director called, absurdly, Buck Norman, providing her scenario with the classic paranoid's pathetic signature, the love or enmity of the famous. She also claimed that her husband, dead for years, was hiding on a mountain with a fabulous treasure. (She was hyperventilating by this point, and her clutch on my hands, once delightful, was beginning to numb. I could feel her nails digging in.)

She had escaped from the hospital. Her plan was to discard her false identity and thereby win her freedom. Would I therefore proceed immediately to Vegas and make her my wife, Mrs. Lonsky? (Never mind that she had just unwidowed herself by declaring her husband extant.) She knew, she said, that I had loved her once. Perhaps I did still. She did not love me, she admitted, but she respected me, trusted me, admired me above all men. She would be a good wife . . .

She was on her knees now, weeping into my crotch. She kissed my hands and bent to my slippered feet. That was unbearable. I lifted her into my arms. She weighed nothing. I kissed her cheek. Nothing like that was necessary, I told her. She owed me nothing, not even gratitude, for since my heart was hers, by rights everything else I possessed was hers too. She had only to ask and she would have it, especially as cheap a gift as my name. I told her we would leave at once.

I returned to the interior of the house and called for a taxi since I do not drive. (Nor had I ever flown on a plane or been to Las Vegas.) Then, while she hid on the porch from Buck Norman, ducked down low behind the railing and some bushes, I quickly prepared to go out: overcoat, scarf, hat, umbrella, gloves. I was tempted to disguise myself but fought the urge. I returned to "Mona," cowering by the door as headlights approached. And then, summoning the courage that only love can inspire, I shut the door to my house behind me, took my bride by the hand, and stepped into the dark new world.

Alas it was not the taxi. It was the police. Dr. Parker may not have my insight when it comes to psychological analysis and interpretation, but he is no fool. When the nurse found Mona missing, he searched her things, found my unanswered letters, recalled our friendship, and dispatched the authorities. There was a bit of a melee I'm afraid. For a small woman Mona put up an impressive fight, biting and scratching. I rushed to her defense, plowing into the fray, powerful but useless, like a furious bull walrus flummoxed on land. I thumped two policemen to the ground with my padded blows before a swift crack at my knees with a nightstick toppled me to the pavement, where I floundered hopelessly in my cloak and gloves and extra-long scarf. My umbrella opened accidentally and I couldn't see. More officers came and an ambulance. In the end they took her away and, after my mother proved I was insane with some official paperwork, dragged me back in the house.

What can I say? After this, to use the technical term, I decompensated. First, I went off my meds. I needed my full powers to help my ladylove. In reality I stopped sleeping and started eating, glutting myself with fried chicken, ice cream sundaes, and pâté on toast, while I tried to untangle her story. In the end, after a few accusatory letters turned over by Buck Norman's security consultants, and a number of wild late night phone calls to Dr. Parker's home number, it was decided for the safety and sanity of everyone involved, and with my mother's consent, to swear out some restraining orders keeping me from approaching Mona, among others.

So it was with great surprise that I received a phone call last week regarding a new case. It was my old friend, colleague, caretaker, and foe, Dr. Parker. Mona was missing again. Had she contacted me? No, she had not. Could I then use my skills to find her, since he believed she might harm herself?

Frankly, I was of two minds. Nothing in Mona's behavior or statements led me to believe she was suicidal. On the contrary, she wanted desperately to live. However deflected or defective, however bent, her impulse was a drive toward life. She was, in her own mind at least, fleeing for her survival. It was "they" who wanted her dead and/or buried. Nor was I especially eager to send her back to Green

Haven, a place she loathed and saw as her doom. Still, even as a fake "doctor" and a fake "fiancé," I had a duty to ensure her safety in any way I could. She was clearly not capable of living unassisted. I agreed to take the case, but also resolved to investigate more deeply, to try for once and for all to discover the truth. Who was the woman I loved?

32

I WAS APPLYING for temp jobs when Roz Lonsky called. It had been nearly a week since the incident in Koreatown. I'd spent it hunting for work and waiting on my wife, both with middling efforts and poor results. I had no idea where Lala had gone, or with whom, and I was beginning to wonder if I was better off not knowing.

Roz told me that Solar was doing better, somewhat. He was still in the hospital, but stable enough for visitors, and he'd asked for me. I was hesitant but she insisted. I was the only person he'd asked to see. At last, with nothing else pressing on my agenda, and with a mixture of morbid curiosity and guilty sympathy, I agreed.

Green Haven was in Pasadena. True to its name, it retired sedately behind a white fence and a deep lawn, with a long drive leading to a mansion in pseudo-slave-plantation-style, columns beside the door, and capitals over the windows. Tastefully screened by Italian cypress were a newer, more hospitalish building and a large parking lot. All in all, it didn't seem like a bad place. The nurse at the desk was plumply pretty and polite, patients wandered freely over the lawn, and the room where they sent me to meet Lonsky was full of books and board games, with a nice breeze drifting through the screens. I was tempted to check in myself, but I couldn't afford it.

I was also relieved to see Lonsky looking fine. He entered jauntily, nodding to the nurse, who was reading a gossip magazine by the door, and smiled when he saw me. He was wearing a plain linen suit, a white shirt, and a cream bow tie, with cream socks and soft brown leather slippers. He shook my hand gravely and gestured toward a pair of armchairs, waiting for me to descend before hitching his creased trousers and taking a seat. I noticed that the chess set from his house was there on the end table between us.

"Yes, my mother was kind enough to bring my set from home," he said and smiled at me. "I've been dying for a game, old foe. It's good of you to come."

"What? You know I can't—"

"Perhaps this time, I'll take you," he said loudly, cutting me off, and then leaned in, sotto voce. "These rooms have ears, Kornberg. Keep your voice down and move any piece."

I looked back at the nurse. She scratched her head and sighed as she turned a page.

"Fine," I said and slid a pawn forward a square.

Solar smiled sadly. "A small move. Don't feel inadequate. You tried your best. Her death is not your fault." Then he shrugged. "Unless the pawn represents the penis, defeated by your wife's defection."

"My penis is fine, thanks. Solid as a rook," I said. "But it's true my wife and I are taking a break."

"Then we are both alone," Solar said. His knight leapt over his pawns and took its place on the field. "Work is a detective's only salvation."

"I'm not a detective . . ."

"Shhh . . ." Solar wiggled his finger. "Your move."

Defiantly, I moved my penis pawn forward. "I'm not a detective. And the case is officially closed."

"Wrong on both counts. True, you are an amateur. And you failed in your first assignment. Tragically so. But you are still my only hope. So what other choice do I have?" He moved his other knight out, jumping the pawn line, to join his brother on the field.

"You just said it wasn't my fault. I didn't know she was suicidal."

"To be precise, I said you failed. Tragically so. But it's not your fault. It's mine." He looked me in the eye. "I am probably the greatest detective of my generation and yet I did nothing to save the love of my life. Your move."

"Love? I — I didn't know you even knew her." I saw myself clutching her by the tree, pulling her panties off in the dark hotel room, staring out at the empty ocean. "She was your girlfriend?"

"Not in the carnal sense. But I loved her nevertheless."

I fingered a bishop, then changed my mind and pushed out a knight instead. "I'm sorry. I had no idea. But you can't protect people from themselves. And the coroner closed the case."

"I suppose that is true, Kornberg, however platitudinous. It is also irrelevant. She did not commit suicide. Ergo, the case is not closed. Rather, it has become a case of murder."

"What? But I was right there. I saw . . ." I realized I was speaking loudly and crouched toward him. "I saw her jump with my own eyes."

"No offense, but I would hardly describe your eyes as reliable."

"You wouldn't? Well, no offense to you either, but have you opened yours lately and looked around? You're in the loony bin. That's a place for people who don't know what the hell they're talking about."

Lonsky chuckled. "Humor can be refreshing in this dour setting. I consider it salubrious and generally welcome in an assistant, but only in judicious proportions. Now see if you can follow: certainly she was deranged, as am I. But that's precisely how I know she could never have jumped. Just as I was unable to help her in part due to my own agoraphobia, so she too was deeply acrophobic."

"Is that spiders?"

"She was desperately afraid of heights, Kornberg. A hotel balcony atop a cliff over a crashing sea? She could not have set foot on it. Not even to gaze at the moon."

He gripped the arms of his chair and pushed himself to his feet. "You will have to excuse me. It's time for my meds. My mother can arrange your pay. Our first step is to build a dossier on the victim. A biography if you like, in your writerly terms. The background." He waved a finger like a baton. "The reason for her murder lies buried in her past, Kornberg. Thus must we dig."

He held out his gigantic hand, cracked and creased and stained as a catcher's mitt. I gave him mine. As he squeezed it softly, I felt like a girl accepting her first dance.

"It's true," he said, "my personal feelings were engaged. That, along with my psychosis, may indeed have clouded my judgment. But now that she's gone, this is just like any other case." He laid the heavy hand on my shoulder. "A woman was murdered on our watch, Kornberg. We can't have that. It's bad for business."

33

I WAS ON MY WAY back out when the pretty front desk nurse stopped me and said Dr. Parker wanted a moment, if I didn't mind. I followed her down a hushed hall to a white wooden door. She knocked reverently before showing me in. It was a big room, book lined and high ceilinged, with a marble mantelpiece and a large Oriental rug. Dr. Parker, whom I dimly recognized from the inquest, stood at the other end, behind a big desk, staring out french doors at the garden and surveying his domain. He turned.

"Ah, yes, Mr. . . . ." He put on glasses and glanced down at file on his desk. "Cronenberg."

"Kornberg, actually." I held out my hand and began the long march as the nurse shut the door behind me. I had plenty of time to look him over on the way. He had wavy gray hair combed back from a distinguished forehead and the smooth good looks of a tan tennis player. White teeth and a white doctor's coat over his suit and tie. He leaned forward and gripped my hand, revealing the thick gold Rolex on his wrist, then sank back into the depths of his leather command chair while I plopped into one of a smaller uphol-stered pair.

"Thanks for stopping in," he said.

"Sure."

"It's unusual, of course, for me to meet with a patient's visitor," he went on, "but Solar is hardly the usual patient."

"I understand," I said, though I didn't. What did this guy want?

He took his glasses off and sighed. "The death of a patient is al-ways terrible. Mona's was tragic. In many ways I feel I failed her. Her loss will be with me always. And I know how much she meant to So-lar as well. Don't forget, I'm his doctor too, although he sometimes forgets it. He is quite brilliant, but he is a sick man and in this case utterly without objective judgment." He looked me in the eye, half pleading, half accusing. "She committed suicide. You know that bet-ter than anyone."

"Yes," I said. "I do."

"She was young, beautiful, bright, but she was deeply wounded. She swung from manic highs to suicidal lows. She'd made other at-tempts, which I doubt Solar knows."

"Then why are you telling me?"

"Because if he persists in believing her delusions, if he takes them as his own and allows himself to become unhinged by grief, the con-sequences could be severe, another breakdown, perhaps a real psy-chotic break. I'm asking you as his friend, to try to calm him down, rather than, let's say, aggravate the condition. He knows she wasn't killed. It's just his guilt driving this. Something we can all under-stand, I think." He peered at me, this time with a look more like sad-ness. "The fact is, between her childhood, her husband, and her own demons, there was nothing anyone could have done. Do you under-stand?"

"Yes," I said. "I understand completely." I stood and put out my hand, which he took warmly in both of his. "Just curious," I said. "You mentioned a husband. I didn't know she was married. Is he still in the picture?"

"You haven't heard? Her husband was an obscure avant-garde filmmaker. He blew his brains out, right in front of her."

34

I TOOK THE CASE. Why? Guilt, I suppose. And curiosity. I felt as though I'd failed her, but how? What had she wanted from me? I'd failed Lonsky too, in my first and only mission, and betrayed him, however unknowingly. I knew their ideas were total nonsense, the love song of two loons. But I felt an obligation to help, if only by playing along a little more.

And then I suppose there were all the things I couldn't help, my own unsolvable case. My life had suddenly become such a complete and total mess that fleeing into someone else's fantasy world seemed like a relief.

Besides, I needed a job. Clearly, no one sane was going to hire me.

35

THE FIRST STOP in my investigation was the video store. I wanted to consult Milo.

"Zed Naught?" He thoughtfully scratched an armpit, where his finger found a small tear in his T-shirt's seam. The video monitors played *Sullivan's Travels*. A customer wandered up with a stack of Pixar movies and a little kid in tow.

"Be right with you," Milo said, sniffing his finger meditatively. "Hmm, Zed Naught . . ." The kid knocked over a stack of used DVDs and Dad bent, sighing, to retrieve them.

"He shot himself," I offered.

Milo snapped his fingers. "Zed Naught!"

"That sounds familiar," I said.

"*Ladbroke Grove*," he said, and dashed into the back.

"Excuse me," the aggrieved customer called. "I'm trying to rent these?"

"I'm helping someone, sir," Milo answered. Giggling, the child knocked the stack of videos over again and the father looked at me beseechingly, begging me either to help him or kill him. I knelt to gather discs until Milo reemerged.

"Not there. It's off the market. We only have this." He handed me a VHS tape with a torn cover depicting a cartoon woman with large breasts, demon eyes, a serpent tongue, and blond beach hair. *Succubi!* The credits listed Zed Naught as director and the screenplay by Zed and Mona Naught. The unpromising tagline read, "They're Hot, They're Bi, and They'll Suck Your Soul Dry!"

"If you want to know anything else," Milo said, nodding upward while the dad listened in confusion, "you'll have to ask the man upstairs."

Although his video store was my second home, I had never been up to Jerry's apartment, but his long reign as the ailing king banging his cane on the floor to summon soup had given him an aura of wonder, and I was excited when Milo told me that an audience had been granted for later that afternoon.

His place was tastefully threadbare and cluttered in a manner keeping with an old, gay upper-middle-class intellectual with good taste and poor health who had lived in the same place for thirty years. The walls crawled with culture: books, records, DVDs and CDs, even a metal cabinet full of film reels and a 16mm projector standing like a shrouded Futurist sculpture in the corner. Underneath the rows of paintings, drawings, and framed photos, the walls were painted bold colors, now mellowed, chipped, and faded, crimson, gold, sky blue. The once blond and modern furniture was old and worn. The curtains were drawn against the sun.

Milo said, "Just a minute," then left me on the couch for what seemed like a very long time. I heard barking from beyond the walls. Then, in the distance, I heard the clop of a cane, a sound I knew from below. The knocks grew louder, like the stately gait of a stallion approaching, and a high steady wheeze reached me, a whistling that rose louder and higher. At last, the door opened and Milo emerged, wheeling a small oxygen tank, followed soon after by Jerry, the master of the house, leaning on two canes and breathing through a clear plastic mask, trailed by the trotting pooch.

I stood and put my hand out, but he ignored me, focused on reaching the recliner across the room. I had expected older and thinner, but he somehow looked shorter too, littler all over, as if time had melted him down to an ancient child. His skull floated in a cloud of white hair. His teeth and eyes jutted out, white and blue. His hands shook, ribbed with blue veins. The fingers bristled with rings. He didn't acknowledge me but it was clear he'd dressed carefully for my visit in a blue shirt and white slacks with a black scarf knotted around his neck. As he lowered himself deliberately into the chair, I noticed a bottle of water, an inhaler, and a pair of glasses ready on the table. The dog leapt into his lap.

Milo bent over him and spoke loudly, pointing at me: "Sam is curious about Zed Naught. Zed Naught!"

Jerry lifted a withered hand and I jumped up to shake but he ignored me again, and pointed at the inhaler, his arm wavering like a twig in a storm. Milo removed the mask and handed it to him. He drew deeply and released a long sigh, then took a tiny sip of water, slid the glasses on, and finally aimed his bright, wide eyes at me as if surprised to find me there on his couch. He smiled a deathly grin and spoke, in a pleasant, even tone:

"Actually, he was born Johannes Zachary Naughton, in 1950 to an English military officer stationed in Bavaria and a local woman of the minor aristocracy. He attended the Slade in London and studied painting, but also acquired a used sixteen millimeter camera and made some early shorts, like music videos really, with some obscure rock bands, which he then scratched, painted, drew on, and burned. Since the films were silent, he had to play the records alongside the screen. His first feature was ambitious. Known as *Ladbroke Grove,* it was a four-hour black-and-white opus featuring two women and a man, all small-time players in the music and art scene at the time, and set in a rambling dilapidated house in London. Financed by drug dealers, the film's original negative was seized in a tax case following the producer's arrest, but its notoriety grew after one of the female stars, a well-known punk hair stylist named Maxi Paddington, died from an overdose. The other one is Daemonica Uta-Floss, the former model, who you might remember as the singer from Sküm, who later married Dick Fungus of Putrid Corpse."

"Huh," I said, realizing my notebook was in the car.

"*Ladbroke Grove* was never shown commercially but Zed was still considered a key figure in the late seventies, early eighties London post-punk pre-industrial-house scene and moved in highly fashionable circles in Paris and Berlin, where he made his next major film *6X4*. Seen as a response to Warhol, the film is shot in various stocks, including grainy black-and-white, Super Eight color, and surveillance video, and documents life in a Berlin after-hours club from midnight to six a.m. The footage is then slowed down four times for a running time of twenty-four hours. Intended as an installation, it was projected on four walls of a dark room at once with viewers sitting on cushions in the center. One wall would show hours one to six, while at the same time, the next wall to the right would show hours six to twelve, then twelve to eighteen, and the fourth wall eighteen to twenty-four. As the first segment ends the films rotate one wall and restart, so that over twenty-four hours a complete circuit is made."

Jerry stopped, abruptly pausing the monologue, and his eyes drooped shut, hands clutched around the snoozing dog. Worried that something was wrong, I looked to Milo, but he gave me a confident nod and sat back. We waited. I listened carefully for breathing, and was just about to panic when Peaches yipped. Jerry's eyes popped opened, and he resumed speaking as if unaware he'd ever stopped.

"This film, as far we know, was screened three times. First in Berlin, at the after-hours club where it was made. However, the club was illegal, and the extra publicity surrounding the screening drew the police who raided the show after just a couple of hours. All the tables and chairs had been removed and replaced with mattresses and big pillows, and when the police turned on the lights, several people were found having sex, or sleeping, or passed out from booze or drugs. Naught himself was not present. He was in Morocco, drinking tea with the Bowleses.

"The second screening was at the Venice Biennale, in 1980, when, to ensure the integrity of his vision, Naught insisted that a select audience agree to remain sealed in the room for the entirety of the performance. Nevertheless, Italian security was lax and in the morning, the only remaining viewers were some vagabonds who had no place else to sleep and their dog. The last time it was shown was in the home of a collector who had purchased the only known print of the complete work. He screened it once, at a private showing, projecting the film on the four walls of a locked and empty room for no one before sealing it forever. It was however written up by several critics as a triumph of negativity.

"With this success under his belt, and an international reputation, Naught was courted by several famous fans in Hollywood, including Jack Nicholson, Francis Coppola, and Warren Beatty, and he moved to LA, where he undertook a number of projects, few of which reached fruition. Scripts and ideas started out strong and became derailed somehow, including a psychedelic Western version of *The Tempest,* a live-action version of the Pogo comics involving puppets and costumes, and a multimedia rock opera based on Sade, involving live on-stage sex and called *The 120 Minutes of Sodom.* Interestingly enough, all three projects foundered in part because he refused to cut or alter the original texts. He was also, at points, attached to *The French Connection III* and *The Odder Couple.*

"In the end, the only feature he made here was the low-budget horror flick *Succubi!* He later undertook a series of shorts, which drew inspiration from his growing fascination with the occult. An intended trilogy, only the first two parts were ever made. They were shot mainly at his home, a run-down mansion on a road off Laurel Canyon, and apparently detailed some of the odd goings-on — orgies, rituals and what have you. The whereabouts of these films are unknown. They have never been publicly shown."

He subsided again, eyelids slipping, only this time his head fell forward to his chest and I thought perhaps he had fainted. Again I looked quizzically at Milo, who shrugged. I sat back. Several minutes passed in silence. Finally, I stood, waved my thanks to Milo, and took a step toward the door, but Peaches barked at me and Jerry's eyes opened again. I hopped back into my seat like a student caught passing notes in class. He cleared his throat.

"Lastly we arrive at his final and most notorious work. A depressive gun lover, Naught had long insisted that he would die at his own hand and film it. The last years of his life were difficult: The final cut of *Succubi!* was taken from him, slashed to bits, and dumped on the home video market. He owed a fortune to bankers and tax collectors in several countries, and apparently also to gangsters. Finally, he was indicted for embezzlement and tax fraud. His health, after decades of abuse, was poor. One night, he shot himself in the head. Legend has it the camera was running, and that this film is actually the last third of the Infernal Trilogy, but no one can even prove it exists."

"What can you tell me about his wife?" I asked.

"Mona? She was a Hollywood kid who met Naught when she was fifteen. At sixteen they married. He was forty-five. It was scandalous but it seems they were really very deeply in love. Apparently she was watching when he killed himself, some say running the camera, and she was never the same. She took off, to New York, Paris, Bangkok, Tokyo, further and further, living in exile as a kind of underground celebrity. She came home, broken, and I'm told, still lives in an institution."

"She killed herself a week ago, in Big Sur," I said.

"Ah, well. Poor girl." He took a rattling breath, drank some water, and went on. "As I said, the films are hard to find. *Succubi!* you have. *6X4* is still in a private collection. As for *Ladbroke Grove*, there are three copies. One in the vault of the Kulchurbunker in Zurich. One at MOMA in New York, where an injunction prevents it from being shown until the litigation, which has been going on for decades, is resolved." He paused to draw another long, creaky breath. There was silence.

"And the third?" I asked.

He gasped. His hand quivered in the air, one finger pointing at the corner. Milo jumped up and offered him the inhaler. The dog barked and howled.

"Should I call for an ambulance?" I asked.

Jerry shook his head fervently and pushed the inhaler away. He drew in a long, rattling breath and pointed again. Milo grabbed the water, but Jerry brushed it off, shook his head, tried to speak.

"Um, should I leave?" I wondered aloud.

"Light," Jerry whispered. "Off."

"OK." Milo nodded. While I watched awkwardly, he lowered Jerry's recliner into relax position and fitted the mask. The oxygen sighed peacefully. Then Milo strode purposely out of the room. I smiled uncomfortably at Jerry, who stared back from beyond his mask, blue eyes like twin moons. The poodle bared its little fangs.

"Thanks," I said. "For telling me all this."

He waved a finger.

Milo returned with a bowl of popcorn and two Cokes and set them on the table before me. Then he turned out the light and started up the projector.

36

LADBROKE GROVE IS SET in an old creaky house in a private walled garden on a small street in a then broken-down part of London. It's a dingy gray London, resting between up times, no longer the swinging scene of *Blow-Up,* but with the yuppie-trashy "cool Britannia" of hip nineties bankers still far off. This is a London of smoky pubs, council flats, and skinheads, of wankers and kebabs and chips. Of skies the color of overdone meat, old rain that barely fell, shoulder-high clouds, and ancient libraries where wind groaned through the shelves. Of lamplights on cracked wet cement, bad teeth, warm beer, ten-packs of fags, and the dole. Of taking the piss. Pissing down. Pissing off. Every sort of piss.

In the film's opening scene, Garreth Barke, a scruffy young artistic type, accidentally brains a cop in a demonstration and goes on the run with a mournfully beautiful dark-eyed commie-waif who hides him in a squat (the doomed Maxine). When the cops show, they hop the garden wall and are taken in by the neighbor, a glamorous blond who lives in a mansion owned by her husband, whom we've seen pull away in his Bentley on a business trip. Most of the movie takes place in this house, which was in fact owned by a baroness or marquise, an art supporter Naught knew, and actually located miles from the neighborhood that gives the film its name.

It is, I suppose, my kind of movie, an artsy talkfest where pretty people blab about big ideas, then strip down to roll around in bed or argue, the edges singed here and there with random beauty: grim sun through dusty windows, cracked plaster walls, bed heads brooding over chipped cups of tea, nimble fingers rolling cigarettes in fascinated close-up, pale asses by moonlight in rumpled sheets, eyes in smoke, the scene where they play records and dance. I won't soon forget the part where the two girls bathe, dousing each other with that handheld hose thing, the blond's white legs rising from the suds and dipping over the rim like twin swans, or the brunette's miraculous, twenty-year-old tits, perfectly round and aloft, as she stares into the camera and delivers a passionate diatribe on American imperialism, while lucky Garreth, lean and naked with a bad tooth and itchy pubes, broods and blows smoke across the screen.

In the end, what climax there is gets generated by the imminent return of the industrialist husband and a vague plot to hold him for ransom and smuggle Garreth to freedom. Police surround the house and Garreth is shot. Then, either there is an avant-garde twist that went over my head (it had been hours now, in the close heat of Jerry's apartment, and I hadn't eaten anything but popcorn all day), or maybe Milo jumbled the reels, or else Jerry, who was fading in and out of a snooze or coma, had mislabeled them decades ago: now the brunette is the one living with the rich husband, looking moody in a lot of eye makeup and a superchic gown, staring out the window of the chauffeured Bentley, while Garreth and the blond sneak through the garden naked and back into the squat. Or perhaps she is imagining this as she stares into the rainy twinkling night traffic. It's hard to say. Then we pull back and see that in fact it is Garreth in the Bentley with her. She pulls out a small pistol and shoots him. Next we see the two women burying Garreth in the garden. They climb into the Bentley together and we see them kiss through the rainy windshield before driving off under the credits.

37

DID I MISS MY WIFE? I was too angry to miss her. And yet the old wiring remained, the neural paths that lit up at the sound her name, the sight of her vitamins forgotten in the fridge, her scent afloat in a sweater hung in the closet. I didn't miss her, but I ached in the places she once touched me, like a fresh blister rising still tingles with the kiss of the flame: I remembered. I remembered her that last day at the therapist, her green eyes aglitter with mean joy. I remembered her narrow shoulders in my arms when we hugged awkwardly on the street after, and how easy it might have been then to break her lovely neck. I remembered when she left me, cheekbones crossed with tears like that Indian who hates pollution, banging her Louis Vuitton case down the stairs, baby feet sweet as always in high heels, each toe dipped in pink like a perfect pebble. I remembered our first nights together when, after we fucked, I realized she was crying there in the dark, and I was frightened that something was wrong, until she told me she was crying because it was all so beautiful. I remembered when her nails bit my chest during sex and I'd have to pin her hands. I remembered her ass in a thousand ways, in thongs and panties and frills and ribbons. I remembered the impressions her tight jeans left on her hips. I remembered the pimples on her back that she hated, from her salty sweat and hair grease in the summer. I remembered how to save time in the mornings we'd just shower together and fuck while we were in there, before heading out for the day, since we were both too tired at night. I remembered when she started peeing in front of me (the first night actually, she wasn't shy) and when she gave me permission to fart in her presence and then tried to retract it, since she felt I abused the right. I remembered in the winter when she got in bed in long underwear, a knit wool hat, her thick nerd glasses, and the retainer that was supposed to stop her from grinding her teeth. She looked retarded, but I couldn't wait to wrap her in my arms and squeeze. I remembered how she talked in her sleep, and sat up one night while I read beside her, eyes shut, and in her dream announced: I'm so sleepy. Lie down then honey, I told her, go to sleep, and she did. I remembered that I loved her and then I remembered how she'd stopped loving me and how that made our whole life and love together and everything I remembered a lie. And then I remembered to hate her again.

38

THANKS TO JERRY, I got in touch with Daemonica, the blond actress from the film. (Much married and divorced, she was currently known in full as Daemonica Angelika Uta-Floss-MacTeague-Goiter-Goldstein.) She lived in Brentwood, in a big house with a Ford Navigator out front and many large, mostly nude photos of herself all over the walls. A round-faced Mexican housekeeper opened the door and with a sweet smile told me: "She on the deck."

I passed through a room displaying a number of gold records, a few framed and signed guitars, and a large naked oil of the mistress supine over the mantel, and stepped onto a deck overlooking an oval pool, still and blue as an opal. There I encountered a woman, Madam Whatever I assumed, folded over in a yoga pose, her body encased in a black unitard, while a nimble young man in white karate pants helped hold her in place.

"Does my enormous ass look absurd?" The woman's voice rose, thick and throaty, from the upside-down face between the legs.

"Sorry," I said. "I could come back later."

"But I've been waiting for you, darling. You're one of the few men alive who've seen it in its heyday and have the brain cells left to remember." She shook her bottom a little.

"It looks great, actually," I said, and it did. The skin tone was different, a tobacco brown now instead of that crème fraîche white, but it nevertheless remained a top bottom.

"Thank you, my dear." She exhaled heavily, and the man helped turn her right side up. Her face was flushed, and her cleavage, squeezed tight in the spandex, was sheened with sweat. Her nipples declared themselves, pressing out through damp rings of moisture, like thirsty little kitten tongues. Her hair, up in a bun, was still white-blond as in the film, and the rest of her body, though stained darker as I said, was still impressively close to that ideal. Her face was a different story: heavily lined, overly tanned, saggy jowled, slashed with lipstick. She laughed wetly, showing teeth nearly as brown as her face.

"Hear that, Reg?" she croaked at her yogi. "Says my bum's still buggerable."

He smiled and nodded rapidly. She winked at me and picked up a bottle of Evian. "Guess I can hold off on the lipo for a bit. The third round, I mean." She laughed her juicy laugh again and guzzled from the bottle. Sweat coursed down her breasts, which heaved and trembled as she drank. She shook her hair out and it fell down her back. "Fucking hell, I'm sweating like a horse!" she shouted, and Reg handed her a towel. She swabbed her pits and wiped under her boobs, lifting each and letting it fall, then sawed the towel between her thighs, still eyeing me all the while, before handing it back, soaked, to Reg.

"Miss me," she said, more as a command than a question.

"Um . . . a little?" I tried, thinking maybe she had me confused with someone else, but Reg produced a spray bottle and moistened her face and chest, then his own. He aimed it toward me with a querulous expression.

"No, thanks. I'm fine."

"Let's have a drink," Daemonica said, "before I bloody faint."

Her accent was Bride of Dracula goes to Carnaby Street, just what you'd expect from a part-Hungarian, part-Romanian, part-Ukrainian ex-model raised in Madrid and Monaco, who married and divorced a few Brit rockers and sang for a couple of deathcore sludge-rock bands. I followed her back inside, where the housekeeper met her with some kind of thick green shake in a glass. She handed one to me as well.

"Oh," I said, "thanks, but . . ."

She quaffed deeply. "It's organic kelp. With protein powder, spirulina, parsley, ginseng—" I took a polite taste. It wasn't too bad. Kind of like a malted with no ice cream or syrup or malt. I drank more.

"—and whale semen," she added, smacking her lips.

"What?" I coughed.

"Very expensive. Good for the blood, organs, skin, and stamina. I have it flown from Japan."

"Hmm . . ." I managed to nod, holding a rich swallow in my mouth.

"Drink that once a day and you'll be hard as a rock," she said. "Right, Reg?" He giggled as she chugged, leaving a thick mustache over her lip.

I discreetly spit into my glass while pretending to sip. "Mmmm," I said. "Filling. Too bad I ate such a big breakfast."

"I live on it. Haven't touched alcohol or sugar in twenty years." She lit a Marlboro and then, while the housekeeper and Reg both stood by, she stripped off the uni. Her body was impressive, if you like blond goddesses. Her nipples stood triumphant. The hair between her legs was a wild mane, white as snow.

"I hope you are not one of those men who are terrified by the female bush," she announced, exhaling smoke through her nose.

"Not so far," I said.

"Good, then the sight of my cunt shan't disturb you." She drew smoke and released it through dilated nostrils, while frankly sizing me up. "But don't get the wrong idea, darling. I only like them young, hung, and dumb, like Reg here." She laughed hard, gargling with her head back, as Reg blushed and blinked his big brown eyes at me.

"Now I need a soak," she went on. "Reg wrings me out like a dishrag." Reg giggled as we followed her down a few steps to the pool, where a Jacuzzi bubbled and steamed. She stepped in carefully, drink in one hand, cigarette in the other, and descended till she was covered up to her shoulders. "Sit," she demanded. I sat on a beach chair nearby.

"Now then." The Marlboro dangled from her red mouth. Ashes dropped into the bubbling froth that seethed around her boobs. "You are writing a book about Zed?"

"Kind of." I supposed that was a convenient lie of Jerry's, or Milo's maybe. "I'm doing some background for now."

"Well I knew him as long as anyone, I guess," she said. "Anyone alive. He was a pretty boy then, so funny and charming, with his scarves and tight pants, and these gigantic sloppy paintings he made in his awful garret, they looked rather like great wet nightmarish vaginas to me. Now I can't imagine getting nude in a cold dirty place like that but then believe me the girls were lined up around the block. They quite liked it I suppose, being ravished on a chaise among the rags."

"Yourself included?"

"Of course, darling. It was the seventies. It wasn't polite to decline a shag or a drug, from boy or girl. And like I said, he was quite the dish. He slept with everyone." Her fangs bent her U's and W's into V's and sharpened *the* into *zee*. "But of course I was married to the Baron, and the other girl in the film, Maxi, was more his type. He liked the dark meat. But don't we all? *Grrr.*" She growled at Reg, who giggled. His slender form was nut-brown and hairless.

"Can you tell me about the movie?"

"Making the film was rather like posing for him, I'd say. One felt him seducing one, manipulating one, dominating one, but also beseeching one. One felt needed. It was damp and cold in that house and he kept us all there, Maxi, Garreth, and me and his crew members, who were all really artists and musicians he'd picked up someplace. All living together and shooting for several months. That was his idea, this experiment. He'd cook big meals. Wonderful earthy stews. We'd play music and sing and dance. And of course everyone slept with everybody. But he would also rage and yell or make us sit and wait in strict silence while he just stared into space, you know, deep thinking. We were so besotted, we didn't mind. Plus he locked the door to keep us from leaving. It was my husband's aunt's house and he took the keys and locked me in it. Extraordinary! You couldn't do that now, could you? Just the insurance is unthinkable." She sipped her drink and her long, pointy tongue flicked extra whale sauce from her chin.

"After that we lost touch for awhile. He was in Paris or somewhere and I was mainly on tour in South America, where we were always a smash for some reason, they couldn't even understand the lyrics, or else we were staying up at my husband's castle."

"The Baron?"

"No, darling the Baron was quite penniless. This was my second husband, Manfred. His record went quintuple platinum or something absurd like this and he bought a small island off the coast of Scotland. Technically he was the king of it I suppose. Quite fun really. We had our own money printed that we'd hand out to visitors, though of course you couldn't do much with it but buy a pint at the pub we set up in the basement. Zed came once to visit, brought along these two Chinese girls, I believe. The rumor was they were sisters but I don't think so. Cousins, maybe. Anyway, he was the perfect guest, the only one there who could actually ride and shoot and all that. Giant feasts at that long table, a boar stuffed with pigeons and wine in five-hundred-year-old goblets. Terribly decadent. Though far too chilly for a proper orgy. We played cards mostly. And drank Scotch of course. This was ages before I got sober. Then, much later, I met his wife, the widow, in Cannes. I was there with my husband, a different one, a record producer, and she was just there I suppose. Bit of a mess, I'm afraid. Always drunk or high on something and crying for no reason in the loo. But a lovely girl. Just his sort, I saw immediately. Small, dark, with spooky eyes. She reminded me of poor Maxi. He always had marvelous taste in girls."

39

DAEMONICA PUT ME IN TOUCH with Garreth Barke, the male lead from *Ladbroke Grove,* and we met at the Slug & Sword, a pub in Santa Monica that catered to the UK expat community. That afternoon, there was a knot of angry red-faced men in shorts and one scary drunk woman crowded at the end of the bar, watching rugby from some former colony. I found Garreth in the back as he'd said, but I wouldn't have known him. The slender, pretty lad from Ladbroke had grown into a head-butting barroom baritone, slow-roasted into mellow middle age. His hands were scarred lumps. His nose bore a delicate filigree of fine red tendrils, blooming over his cheeks. His faded blond glory receded over a sun-scorched dome. His eyes were small and icy blue.

"He was a clever old bastard, I'll give him that. Saw that right off when I met him, back in London, in another age. Had a way with the ladies, too. Of course, back then we thought it was grand to prance about like Tinkerbell in a scarf, pink trousers, and pointy boots. I'd see him round the pubs. A great drinker and great talker, so he was all right by me. A lot of real talkers don't like anyone else to share the limelight, but I say, a man's got to drink sometime, hasn't he? Plus he was the type to spend his last quid on a pint for himself and a friend, then put the change in the fruit machine and let it spin. I saw him pull that trick and win in the Drowned Fox, a scalawag's pub in Earl's Court, catering to the finest pimps, pushers, and pickpockets. He spent the whole takings right then, standing the house to drinks. Every villain in the place loved him. Pure class! He was untouchable from then on, safe anywhere in London.

"He was a painter when we met and I hung about more in the music world, played a bit of guitar and sang, but we chased the same girls, and so when he asked me to be in his movie, I said, why the fuck not? I had the idea I was playing a secret assassin like, and it turned into I know not what, but no bother, I had a grand time. Free rent and whiskey in a house with two pretty, mostly nude girls, right? Still, the movie never came out, some trouble with the taxman I recall, and it all came to dust in the end. Then I heard he left town, and the next time our paths crossed was when fortune brought me to this sunny shore, where a poor lad with a golden voice and the gift of gab could eke out a pittance playing gangsters and drunks on cop shows and in the movies."

He hoisted his glass and gazed through the amber into the distance. "LA, you're a bitch goddess. Half slut, half princess, and all whore." I wanted to ask about the finer differences between the various terms, but you don't stop a true bullshit artist on a roll. "Mate, I've played paupers, princes, pirates, and poets. I tangled wits with Columbo and got kicked in the nuts by Rockford. In my sweetest memory, the one I'll savor on me deathbed, Angie Dickinson herself kissed me and slapped me, the first on camera, the second later on in her trailer. But still, even the golden calf's tits run out of milk and honey sometimes, and around nineteen hundred and ninety-five, I found myself on the bum, trying to buy a sandwich at Mrs. Gooch's, that overpriced bloody grocery in Beverly Hills. Now, old Zed was a cocksman of note, and . . ." He smacked his lips, as if tasting his own spicy tale, and thirsty at the memory of his dry days, raised his glass, only to find it empty. He looked at in surprise, then at me.

"Please, allow me," I said. On cue, the waiter brought him a lager and took my money. "God bless," he said and took a deep swallow. "Now where was I?"

"You were telling me about Zed in LA."

"Ah, yes. Exactly. O cruel bandit time! First it takes your friends, then your enemies, and at last your memories of them all." He drank again. "As I was saying, old Zed was a cocksman of note, and just as I was scraping up my last pennies, along he comes swooping like Errol Flynn in a jeep, dressed in khakis like the great white hunter himself, and on each arm a dark young beauty. I tell you the girls were finer, and younger, than some bottles of Scotch I've known."

"'Zed,' I said, 'me long lost brother!' Well, he recognized me right off, gave me a great hug. I told him my troubles and, Bob's your uncle, I was in that contraption of his, bouncing up the hill. Now in those days old Zed had a big place up Laurel Canyon, built by who knows, some porn merchant, a real plaster castle with the works, grand dining hall, black-bottom pool, snooker parlor. He'd acquired it cheaply because a mudslide took the road out and the land was too steep for city pipes. But what does a man want with civilization when he's got a sweet young Mrs. and a concubine to boot? He had his own water tank and septic, a generator for light. And you needed a four-wheel drive. I felt like Indy Jones heading around those turns or over the plank bridge. Now and again a drunk visitor would roll into the woods and they'd haul him out with a winch." He poured most of the glass down his gullet and blinked at me as if he'd just woken up. "Where was I?"

"You were going to tell me about his wife," I prompted, worried he'd get too drunk to remember.

"Ah yes, sweet Mona. The child bride, Princess of Castle Naught! A soul like a wishing well, over which one longed to yearn, casting one's heart into the deeps of those eyes. Her mother was a great courtesan. An actress-singer-dancer, scorchingly sexy but without a drop of talent. Lucky for her, she got pregnant by a famous man, and in exchange for not bugging him, he set her up with a house and enough to get by."

"Who was the father?"

"Good question. As far as I know, Mother kept shtum, even with her daughter. Meanwhile, she was determined to make a star of little Mona, music lessons, dance, elocution. She was smart as whip, too smart, actually. By fourteen she'd had it. Told mom to stuff it and went on a tear with the other Hollywood brats of the day. That's when Zed met her. She moved into the castle with Mum's blessing, I heard. She could've done worse. Zed made her read, at least, since she dropped school, serious books he piled up by the pool. He took her to museums and showed films in the house. I remember, he made both girls study, and quizzed them over dinner. It was rather sweet really, in a depraved sort of way."

"What was the deal with this other girl?"

"Ah, well, there we have to dig a bit deeper into old Zed's skull. The man was a great aficionado of the ménage à trois. I mean, we've all done it of course, after a few too many, or just enough, eh?"

I nodded and barked out a laugh.

"But for Zed it was more. Some kind of primal drama. He and the wife were always on the hunt, bringing girls back to the castle. I was living there too, you see, for a few months, as a kind of court jester. So I got used to seeing them come and go. But this one girl stayed. She was different, special. Her name escapes me. She was Mexican, they'd met her working a club, coat check or go-go dancer or something. She'd come up rough as I recall, beatings, booze, the lot. She was the same age as Mona but already hustling, working as a taxi-dancer downtown, waltzing and fox-trotting with the Asian suits, no doubt giving hand jobs round back as well."

"What happened to her, do you know?"

He shrugged. "Who knows? When poor old Zed punched his ticket, she disappeared, maybe back to Mexico. I was well out of it by then. Got a bit dark for me. I like a drink now and again, and a toke as well, and I did plenty of acid back in the day, and I've been known to sniff a bit of coke if you're offering, but still, I'm a creature of the light, and Zed was a dark prince up on his hill. I got a job touring with a revival of *My Fair Lady* and was in Miami when I heard. I never saw sweet Mona again. And the other girl, poof! But I remember she was a beauty, too. Funny, they looked a bit alike. People used to mistake them for sisters, which gave Zed a thrill. Still, it was more than fun and games for her. It was love."

"With Zed?"

"Perhaps in fatherly way. But I think it was Mona she truly loved."

40

I CALLED SOLAR LATE at night. He'd been released into his mother's care, on condition that he agree to drop our "case," and wanted to hear my reports when he could sit on the phone without disturbance or suspicious ears. It was hard to imagine many eager spies: my evidence consisted of rambling anecdotes gleaned from vague sources and a few obscure, forgotten movies. And my dreams. He insisted on detailed reports of my dreams along with any associations I might have to aid in interpretation. This, he assured me, was where the really choice nuggets were hidden, the clues I discovered without knowing I had found them, which my interlocutors had revealed without intending to, or withheld without even knowing they knew.

In the meantime, my place had become a clubhouse, with empty beers marshaled on the coffee table and dishes stacked in the sink. The idea was that Milo and MJ were looking after me, but in practice it was a holiday for them, eating my ice cream, sprawled in front of *Come Drink with Me* (1966), King Hu's kung fu masterpiece. Milo brought over his ancient, dusty VCR to watch *Succubi!,* but after we plugged it in and made popcorn, we found another tape already jammed inside. So it remained there, blinking 12:00 forever, while we poked it occasionally with a butter knife. If Lala came back now, she'd divorce me immediately.

"How's Detective Whacko?" Milo said as I hung up the phone. MJ snoozed as the movie played lushly, swift bodies in the bamboo forest at night. I reached for the ice cream and he handed me the empty container.

"The whole quart?" I asked.

"It was about to melt. MJ ate most of it, anyway."

"Right." I flopped down on the couch with her between us. "He's fine. He's not so whacko."

"They lock him in at night."

"He's home at his mom's now."

"That's sweet. How old is he, fifty?" He opened a beer and tossed the cap toward the empty ice cream quart. It ricocheted across the room. "Hey, don't misunderstand me. This is the best job you ever had. I'm jealous."

"Well, we can't all handle the life-and-death pressures you deal with. Speaking of which, did you fix the VCR?"

Looking deeply hurt, Milo made a show of pushing the buttons a few times. He banged the top with a beer bottle. Then he gave up.

"The thing is," I told him, "I am kind of fascinated with these people, Mona and Zed. I feel like that's the life I originally set out for,

artists wandering the earth and all. Somehow I ended up like this instead, a boring, pathetic loser."

"The only thing pathetic and boring about your life is you."

"Thanks. I feel a lot better."

"Seriously. It's like the deadly art of Zen. You see the glass as half
empty," he said, setting his bottle on the table before us.

"It's totally empty."

"Ah, but that's your perception, my child." With a flourish, he in-
verted the bottle. A few drops fell on my rug. "I see it as full . . . of
air."

"Or shit. What's your point?"

"Yes, that chick and her old man were cool, interesting, fascinating people who had wild, kinky sex, traveled everywhere, and made
awesome art while you've done none of those things. But they're
dead. Because that's what happens. The cool die off. The boring and
pathetic go on forever. Now get the bong. We've got a movie to finish."

As it happens, Milo snored through the end of *Come Drink with
Me*. I too slept deep that night, and woke up late, confused by dreams
in which Lala and Mona, both dead, were sending me annoying
emails from the beyond. Although I felt foolish, I couldn't help going
to my dusty office to see. There was nothing besides a message from
Dr. Parker that had arrived early that morning. It said he had something urgent to discuss with me and would be grateful if I could stop
by and see him as soon as possible. He'd be in his office at Green Haven.

"What do you think he wants?" I asked Milo, who was in the
same spot on the couch as the prior evening only now he was sipping coffee instead of beer. MJ, I dimly recalled, had woken up and
left in the night after an angry text from the wife.

"The Doc? He's probably pissed. He found out you were helping
Inspector Coo-Coo stir up trouble like he warned you not to, going
around and talking to all those weirdos and playing investigator."

"You're probably right." I poured coffee and looked for milk in the fridge, foolishly. "But he will have to wait. I'm having tea with a warlock today."

41

ANYWAY, THAT'S WHAT JERRY called him, I didn't actually address him as such. I called him Kevin. He had designed the costumes and sets for Zed Naught's last, Satanically inspired films and had been a witness to the antics up at the haunted house. He lived now in a cottage in West Hollywood, a little gingerbread confection—crooked porch, paned elvish windows, lumpy, shingled roof—tucked, on its patch of green, between a newly ugly apartment building and a pet supply megastore. He answered the door in a kimono. His longish gray hair was cut straight across the brow in a kind of Klingon do and his fingers were ringed in large stones. A hunk of amber hung on a chain around his neck.

"Hello," he said. "You must be Samuel." I shook the long, elegant hand, and the rocks rolled between our fingers. "Come in. Come in out of that terrible sun."

"Thanks." The tiny room was crammed with a lifetime of clutter, an amazing profusion of framed photos, tarnished mirrors, sculptures, collages, and other wondrous objects: a bearskin rug, a gold leaf table, a grandfather clock with a doll head on a skeleton inside its belly, an antique chest of drawers painted pink and covered with glitter, an upright piano topped by a deer antler candelabra. Against one wall leaned a giant timber cross, upside down and strung with Christmas lights. It was like an art installation designed by a team of moody thirteen-year-old girls.

"Sit, sit," he called, waving at a low white couch heaped with silk pillows. I squatted. A tray of tea things and cookies was already set on a coffee table that consisted of a crawling marble boy with a glass plate on his back. He sat, legs crossed, in a high-backed chair and made the tea, my eyes level with his knees. "Now then. Jerry tells me you are writing a book about Zed Naught?"

"Possibly. Did you know him well?"

"Indeed. We were quite close at one time. Quite close. As I recall, he first came to a series of lectures I copresented on Aleister Crowley. Then he asked me to work on a film he was planning. I design costumes and scenery." He swept his ringed hand over the room like a magician's assistant. "I also do interiors. I feel they are sets for the drama of life."

"I see. Was he serious about the occult?"

"Mmm. As you can imagine, there are always dilettantes about, particularly in Hollywood. Yet I suppose only a somewhat jaded sensibility would seek to slake its spiritual thirst in these extremes, these high mountain streams and deep dark wells. It is the glare of the spotlight that drives us to explore the shadows. Don't you agree?"

"Yes."

"I'm so very glad," he said and, leaning across the table, touched the back of my hand with a long, bony finger before pouring the tea. That one nail alone was painted black.

"Sugar? Cream?" He smiled expectantly.

"No thanks."

He leaned back, recrossing his long, oddly hairless white thighs, flashing a subliminal glimpse of what I thought were lace panties. He sipped his tea and I sniffed mine. It had an odd perfume.

He smiled warmly. "Do you like it? It's my own blend. I find it soothing." I didn't. He was a warlock after all. I didn't want to turn into a toad. I set the cup down.

"You were saying, about Zed's interest in the occult?"

"Yes. He proposed a series of films drawing their inspiration from the Black Mass. He'd done a lot of reading. Crowley and LaVey of course, but also Fraser, Bodin, Huysmans. He'd even studied very early parodies of the Catholic Mass, dating from the Middle Ages. They called them the Feasts of Asses."

"I think I've been to a few of those."

He smiled thinly, unamused, and I tried to redeem myself. "I'm familiar with Huysmans," I said, dimly recalling his nineteenth-century novels.

"Ah so. We are familiar with *À Rebours?*"

"I've read it."

"I discovered Huysmans and Baudelaire when I was just a farm boy, believe it or not, hiding in my attic, strangely obsessed for reasons I could not myself comprehend by Poe, Wilde, and the withered lace in my grandmother's trunk. Of course it was Huysmans's *À Rebours* that inspired Wilde in the first place. In *The Picture of Dorian Grey,* his book is the poisonous French novel that is said to twist Grey's mind toward decadence and nihilistic hedonism. The effect on me was similar: I found the book in the library—no one in Plainsview, Nebraska, was well read enough to ban it—and ran away to Paris immediately. Things had changed of course, but not as much as you might think. I met a theatrical designer and became his apprentice, in many things."

À Rebours or *Against Nature* was a kind of rebellion against Naturalism and the realistic style captained by Zola and which, like so much nineteenth-century European bourgeois culture, continues to more or less rule today. Huysmans's hero disdains accepted reality and the conventional culture that surrounds him, and out of disgust, desire, boredom—infinite desire, infinite boredom—turns to a world of decadent, brooding artifice which, taken up as an aesthetic manifesto, formed an important basis for Symbolism in poetry and art.

It is also essentially plotless, more an argument than a story, and a particularly intraliterary argument at that, a fictional character railing at great length against other books. A 1925 translation actually announces, in proud type on the cover, "A Novel Without a Plot." This happened to be a pretty good description of my own literary endeavors, as well as the prime reason given for their rejection. Was there really a time when publishers considered this a plus, the selling point that would inflame the public frenzy? No plot! I could hear the electric buzz along the line outside the bookstore.

The warlock opened a lacquered Chinese box. "Cigarette? They're Egyptian."

"No thank you."

He screwed one into an ivory holder, lit it with a glass table lighter, and blew a long stream of smoke at me while he narrowed his eyes, as if I were a chair he was thinking of redoing. I tried to look jaded and blasé. "I read that Huysmans modeled his main character on Robert de Montesquiou," I said. "I happen to be a big Proust reader as well."

"Ah oui, Proust . . ." he muttered and flicked ashes toward a standing art nouveau ashtray. They fluttered down like a tiny drift of decadent snow. "Yes, Montesquiou, we believe, was the main model for both Huysmans's hero and Proust's immortal Baron de Charlus." He tossed this off as if he and the other foremost authorities had just been weighing the matter before my arrival. The real Montesquieu was a wealthy eccentric who lived in a dream world of his own making. According to the poet Mallarmé, whom Montesquieu reluctantly admitted to his home for a brief visit, there was a room done up like a monk's cell, another like a yacht, and a hall that held an altar and cathedral pews. A fake snowscape contained a sled set on a snow-white bearskin. One can only imagine what or who was hidden, locked away in the dungeon when the poet came knocking.

Looking around again, I realized the extent to which my host's own chamber, with its ratty furs and paper-mache skulls, was a small, sad attempt to cast his life in that heroic mold. This then was the final decadence, the darkest, smallest, sickliest flower at the far reach of the thinnest stem. First come the great originals, then their many descendents, on down through camp, drag, glam, goth, and metal, each one raising a spiked fist with nails of black and red. And finally it all ends here, with Kevin, whose own fragile playhouse was an artifice of their artifice, a third-hand thrift store copy. But wasn't this the fate of all artists? Wasn't it all a desperate fight against reality? And didn't reality always win? Wilde in prison, then exile, raging against the drapes in his cheap hotel, Baudelaire, wasted on opium and ill health, Poe mad and drunk in the streets of Baltimore. Proust coughing all night alone under his blanket of pages. Even the greatest writers were losers. Those who triumph in real life don't have time for poems. The only difference between the giants and peons, such as Kevin and I, was the depth of the crack each of our defiant blows would leave in reality's mirror. Against nature, indeed.

The doorbell rang shrilly. "Who can that be?" Kevin demanded, turning on me. "I'm expecting no one!"

The buzzer sounded again, loud enough to wake drunken firemen. "Yes!" he thundered, opening the door. A hefty old woman with a clown's worth of bright red hair peered through the screen door.

"Kevin? Kevin?"

"Yes, Mrs. Greenstein, what is it? Can't you see I've a guest?"

"Is Tora here? She didn't come home last night and I'm worried."

"No she is not, thank you!"

"Well I'm worried because she didn't come home last night."

"Yes, I believe you mentioned that. But rest assured, that randy, mangy alley cat is not in my home. Though last night she was as usual screeching in heat outside my window. I'm sure she'll come home when she's hungry, and pregnant no doubt."

"You don't have to be nasty. I own this house. And your rent is late. Again."

"Please," he groaned. "Mrs. Greenstein, if you insist on humiliating me before my guest, I will explain that I am expecting payment, momentarily, for some royalties due."

"What guest?" The landlady pressed her nose to the screen. I waved.

"This is Mr. Samuel Kornberg, an author."

"Hi," I said.

"He is interviewing me about the strange life and tragic death of a dear friend with whom I once collaborated intimately, the illustrious filmmaker . . ."

"Nice to meet you, I'm sure," she said, and curtsied slightly. "I didn't see you there. I'm worried about my Tora. She didn't come home last night."

"That's too bad," I said. "I'm sure she's fine."

"Yes, yes, she's fine. Thank you, Mrs. Greenstein, I will be in touch."

"OK, well as soon as that royal payment comes . . ."

He shut the door. "Forgive me. My neighbor is losing her senses, poor thing, and I don't like to be cruel."

"Not at all," I said.

"Now where were we?" He retied his robe. "Zed *avec* Huysmans. Zed proposed a series based on the Black Mass, a kind of nonnarrative exploration, a dark pilgrim's progress of the soul one might say. We conceived it in three parts: *Invitation, Consummation,* and *Ascension.* He used Huysmans's other novel, *Là-Bas,* or *Down There* in English, which describes the Black Mass rather accurately."

"Zed wrote a script about it?"

"Yes, well." He shrugged and lit another cigarette. "I use the term 'wrote' loosely. I rarely saw him sitting down unless he was eating dinner. He was more of a pacer and a talker than a writer. He had vision though, and passion to the end. He was ablaze. But his wife did most of the actual writing. I did sets and costumes and someone else the camera."

"Who? I'd love to interview him as well."

"Funny, I don't recall. Just this kid from somewhere, you know."

"Can you tell me more about Mona?" I asked. "I'm particularly interested in her, as background you know. You say she wrote? She acted in the films too, I heard."

"It was no act, believe me. The rituals were quite real, and as far as I know the only ones on film. I even procured the host from a wayward priest of my acquaintance."

"The host?"

"The desecration of the host, the consecrated wafer, is key to the ceremony, my dear. The priest inserts it in the vagina of a priestess, then has sex with her atop an altar, ejaculating onto the wafer. This defiled wafer is removed and used in the mass. The priest in our film was Zed and the priestess was played by Mona."

"Really?" I saw her in my arms again, then in the billowing cloud of the curtains, and then gone. "And she did this by choice? She was . . . she liked it?"

"She was no victim, if that's what you mean, not like some of the women back then. Like this Mexican girl, their pet. She had that born-to-be-used look. One felt a bit sorry for her. But not Mona. She was right in the very thick of it. I saw her getting whipped and spun on the wheel, hot wax dripped on her loins. I saw her take on a half dozen men, women whatever, but she always seemed I don't know, victorious."

A dreamy look came over him, as odd emotions welled up in my chest. I felt hurt, jealous, angry, but at whom? A dead woman I barely knew? Her suicided husband? I dreaded telling Lonsky and sullying the image of his dream girl. My dream girl too.

"This Mexican girl, do you recall her name?" I asked, changing the subject. "It would be helpful if I could track her down."

"No, sorry. Her name didn't seem to matter if you know what I mean. I think she went back to Mexico after Zed died. Everything dispersed."

"But you shot those three films before he died?"

"Three? No," he corrected me. "There were only two."

"You named three, *Invitation, Consummation . . .*"

"Yes, three were proposed, originally. But we only ever made two. There was no *Ascension.*"

"Why not?"

Kevin smiled. "Are you a religious man, Mr. Kornberg?"

"No, not at all."

"Then you probably won't understand. But once you invite forces such as these into your life, or offer yourself as an instrument, as Zed did, in the Black Mass . . ." He shrugged theatrically.

"You're saying the devil appeared and took him?"

His smile widened and he tapped my hand again. "I'm saying be careful what doors you open . . . Bitch!" He jumped to his feet, startling me as his robe fell open and revealed a vanilla body, old now and withered, covered with melted tattoos. He pointed at a small black kitten regarding us from the kitchen doorway, head cocked adorably, with big green eyes and oversized ears.

"Meow?"

"There's the little slut!" he shouted. "I'll get help. Don't let her out of your sight!" He gathered his robe and ran out. "Mrs. Greenstein!"

Smiling, I turned to the cat, speaking as I might to a madman on a ledge.

"Hi, Tora. Good kitty." I put my hand out and she split, fleeing into a closet. "Fuck." How did I end up in this spot? Cautiously, I pulled back the door.

It was a linen closet, shallow shelves lined with flowered paper and stacked with sheets and towels. The floor held cleaning supplies, rolls of toilet paper, a pile of shoes. Then I noticed a furry tail, wavering slightly as it curved between a pair of blue rain boots. It slithered away like a snake and disappeared, seemingly into the wall.

I looked over my shoulder. Kevin was still nowhere in sight. Curious, I moved the Lysol and Bounty and found a gap. I pushed and the wall of shelves folded back, revealing a small hidden chamber, no more than an archway really, that had been cleverly disguised by an expert set designer.

The inside of the space was painted red, and there was a pentagram in black on the floor. On the wall hung an upside-down cross, silver this time, and atop that an animal skull, some kind of ram, with two great horns, curling like shells into spirals. On the floor were melted candles, red and black, along with a few books, bound in black leather, and two large Betamax videocassettes. Faded labels, written in a fine, sloping hand read *Invitation* and *Consummation*. The cat regarded me from the center of the star. It hissed and darted past me in a blur.

Shaken, I quickly shut the panel and the closet door. I grabbed my bag and hurried outside, where I saw Kevin on the front path, tugging Mrs. Greenstein, who pushed along on a walker. He waved in alarm.

"Wait! Don't go! I haven't told you about my work in the musical theater! I have a scrapbook!"

"That's OK. You've been too kind already. I'm afraid I'm late. I'll call you."

I hustled to my car and got in. The warlock watched me from his front lawn, robe fluttering about him in the hot wind, while the old woman crept toward the door.

42

NEXT I RELUCTANTLY DROVE back out to Green Haven to endure a scolding by Dr. Parker, but this time, when I walked into the lobby, the reception desk was abandoned. I waited a few minutes before I noticed the buzzer, which I pushed. There was no sound, but the cute nurse emerged from a door.

"I'm sorry," she said. "It's been crazy here today."

"Isn't that usually the case?" I said lightly, trying for charm. She blinked. She wasn't listening. I gave her my name. "Dr. Parker is expecting me."

Now her eyes widened and focused on me. "Do you have an appointment?"

"He wrote me this morning and asked me to come in."

"He wrote you? Dr. Parker?"

"Right. Just ask him, I'm sure he'll tell you."

"Ask him?" she repeated, dumbly.

"Listen, will you just . . ."

"Please," she said, her voice cracking, and put up a protective hand, although I hadn't moved. "Just please wait here one second." I stepped back as she rushed out. I waited, and waited, and resisted the urge to buzz again. Then she reappeared, poking her head through the door.

"Sir?" she called. "Will you please follow me?"

I did. She led me down the familiar hall that reminded me (I imagined) of the White House (blue carpet, white walls, high moldings) and into the doctor's office. He wasn't there. Instead, I found a different, younger man in a black fashionable suit, and a cop, in a not at all fashionable Pasadena PD uniform. Two other men, in coveralls, were unpacking equipment in the back, as if they were there to repair the air conditioner.

"Good morning," the suit said. "Mr. Kornberg?"

"Yes."

"Hi. I'm Russ Fowler." He was a well formed, evenly tanned man with dark eyes, white teeth, shapely eyebrows, and handsome hair and hands. He gripped my hand and gave it a firm, dry pump. "I'm told you had an appointment with Dr. Parker?"

"Yes, that's right. He wrote me . . ."

"Well. I'm afraid I have some bad news. Dr. Parker passed away today."

"What? When?"

The cop spoke from behind his sunglasses. "There was an accident at approximately eight thirty a.m. this morning. Single car. Apparently, the deceased had a blowout driving at high speed and lost control of the vehicle. He was alone. Responding officers found him dead on the scene."

"That's fucking terrible," I said. "Jesus fucking Christ."

"Sir, I will thank you not to blaspheme," the cop said.

"What?" For a second I didn't realize what he meant. "Oh, sorry. I didn't mean anything. I'm just in shock."

"I understand that, sir. But I am a Christian as well as an officer of the law of the City of Pasadena."

Russ intervened. "Thank you, Officer Clemento." He winked at me. "I'm sure Mr. Kornberg meant no offense." Clemento gave me a hard look as Russ led me to the couch. He sat beside me. In the rear, the workmen removed a large painting of a landscape from the wall and revealed a safe.

"So, Sam," Russ went on, patting my knee. "What were you here to see the doctor about today? Are you a patient?"

"Me? No. He wanted to discuss something." I tried not to stare at his hand on my leg. "Why do you ask?"

"Sorry to seem intrusive. I'm here on behalf of the board of directors actually, to help clear the doctor's desk, so to speak. You can imagine what a terrible time this is for all of us. Dr. Parker was the heart of Green Haven, not just the brains."

He smiled warmly as, behind him, the workmen put on masks. They lit a blowtorch and, as the orange finger touched the safe, sparks began to jump. My phone buzzed in my pocket. I stood abruptly.

"Nothing like that," I said. "It wasn't a professional visit. Thank you both for your time though."

Officer Clemento nodded his shades. "You drive careful now."

"Thanks," I said, heading for the hall as the steel began to sizzle under the flame. "And God bless!"

It was Milo on the phone. He'd unjammed the VCR. "Guess what was in there? John Waters. *Desperate Living.* I was wondering where it was. It's shredded. But *Succubi!* is good to go."

Walking to my car, I told him about my visit with Kevin and the Beta tapes.

"What did you do with them?"

"Do? Nothing. I got out of there."

"Are you fucking kidding me? Do realize what you had there? That's like King Tut's Tomb. No human eyes have been cast upon them in forever."

"Yeah, yeah."

"Not to mention what a copy is worth on the collector's market."

"How was I going to take them? He'd know it was me."

"Whatever. Remember what you said about being a pathetic pussy?"

"I think 'boring loser' was my term."

"We're both right."

43

SUCCUBI! (A.K.A. SUCK-YOU-BI a.k.a. *The Demon Bitches* a.k.a. *Der Lesbosuckers*) tells the tale of two mismatched college roommates, Cassandra, a blond cheerleading type, and Val, a brainy, bespectacled brunette. Forced to do an anthropology project together for their sleazy, mean professor, the two roomies unearth a moldering old volume entitled Magick that contains a section on succubi, female demons who seduce men and drain their life force. Next, a series of horrible traumas seals their friendship. First, the anthro professor molests Val and threatens her with expulsion if she tells. Running home in tears, her T-shirt ripped, she is accosted by the troll janitor and his drunken white trash pals. Meanwhile, a bunch of jocks attempt to rape Cassie in the locker room. That night, in their underwear, the girls bond and, half kidding, they perform the forbidden ritual they find in the back of the book, the one that says Do Not Speak These Words: they light candles, prick their fingers, get naked and hold hands, boobs just barely touching. They speak the spell. A storm rises, lights flicker, Moogs moan, lightning spiders the night. They end up in each other's arms, first in panic, then in lust, twisting in a fit of ecstatic torment before collapsing into sleep.

In the morning, embarrassed, they laugh the whole thing off as a drunken escapade and agree to forget it ever happened. Needless to say, it's not that easy. In fact they have invited two evil succubi,

Lillith and Nahemah, to take possession of their bodies. Unaware of what they are doing, our heroines wreak vengeance on their tormentors one by one. Val, dressed in a schoolgirl outfit, goes to see the professor. She flirts and goads him into spanking her and "teaching her an anthropological lesson" with several obscene fertility artifacts in the office. Imbued with monstrous strength, however, Val turns the tables. She overpowers the professor, whips him, and sodomizes him with a gigantic African phallus. Ironically, he loves it and admits it is just what he needed. But at the moment of truth, as he is attaining orgasm, Val plants a passionate kiss on his mouth and, via some cheesy effects, sucks his soul from his body in the form of a purple cloud. She then decapitates him with a Persian scimitar, circa 2500 BC. (Of note, for the true cinephile, were the samurai-style blood spray, covering a shelf of ivory artifacts; the sick thud of the head landing; the wisp of purple smoke Val breathes out after inhaling his soul and the purple stain on her lips.) Meanwhile, Cassie, in a cheerleading uniform, is gruesomely dispatching Brad, the date-raping quarterback: Offering to perform fellatio in the locker room shower, Cassie instead castrates Brad with her teeth, spits the offending organ (clearly a hot dog) into a urinal and then sucks his (green) soul from his screaming mouth before he croaks, burping up a little green puff afterward, as if she'd overindulged. Purists might argue that real succubi (whatever "real" means) come to men in their sleep and drain their potency, but the filmmakers understandably chose to alter that rather simple and reductive equation, and earn an R rating by minimizing the sex, shielding the viewer from any actual genitalia, and yet still providing the colorful violence that modern audiences demand.

The rest of the film is pretty much a continuation of the above, with the chicks knocking off the dudes, separately and together, in an increasingly baroque manner. Plot support is provided by Mark, an anthro major with a crush on Val, and Jim, a cop investigating the killings who likes Cassie, as they first pursue the girls as dates, leading to some nice comic relief, then as suspects, and finally as supernatural victims. Meanwhile Val and Cass are researching their own plight and the whole thing comes together, somehow, in a crazy battle in the library involving flying books, their pages flapping like bat wings, fire-breathing devils, decapitated bodies trying to rape cheerleaders, and a naked battle to the death between Val and Cassie and Nenemah and Lillith, with each actress playing her own double, in purple or green body paint.

In the end, the living triumph, and the two couples (the expected, hetero-human couples, that is) get together for a well-deserved vacation. As Val and Mark, Cassie and Jim cozy up in adjoining hotel rooms, all is well. Or is it? A certain demonic expression in their lovemaking (curled lips, wild eyes, gelled hair, moaning), some aggressive cross-cutting, (boob, tooth, painted nail, boob, tongue, boob), the (rising, throbbing, groaning) music, and the passive happiness of the men, all suggest that the succubi have not been entirely banished to hell.

PART IV

ANXIETY'S RAINBOW

44

WHEN I OPENED MY EYES, Mona, the dead girl, was looking down at me.

The last thing I remembered, I'd left Milo and MJ wasted on the couch, and stumbled into my room after *Succubi!,* too wiped out to brush my teeth. Now I was in bed, flat on my back in the morning light, with the face of Mona, the girl I'd seen leap to her death, peering in my bedroom window. She was frowning, but otherwise looked pretty good for someone whose body had been splattered on the rocks and then beaten to froth by the sea.

"Mona?" She looked me in the face, eyes wide in alarm, and ducked down out of sight.

"Mona!" I threw back the covers and jumped to my feet. On the mattress beside me was Milo, utterly nude and curled into a fetal pose. I gasped again, momentarily thrown, and checked myself. I had boxers and socks on. A small mercy. Mona, meanwhile, had vanished. I made a dash for the door, slid on my socks and landed hard on my assbone. I scrambled up, ran to the front door, tried to unlock it, realized it had been unlocked already, unlocked it again, and ran outside.

It was a beautiful morning. At this hour, which I rarely saw, the sky was still transparent and the street was clean. The world smelled fresh for a change, as if newly baked overnight. I scampered around the house in my underwear, hoping the neighbors didn't see, and dashed into the flowerbed that lay outside my window. She was gone. I crept around in the bushes, checked the backyard, and peeked like a spy into my own garage, where my car innocently slept. I went back to the spot beneath the window, looking for footprints or bent leaves. There were plenty, probably all mine. I looked through my window at my now empty and too, too sullied bed. I ran out front and stood on the lawn for a moment, hoping to catch a trace: a car light, a flash of hair, a tiny breath of perfume. Then my lawn sprinklers went on, drenching me and my undies. They were set to go off at seven every other morning but I'd never actually witnessed it before. I squealed like a child and ran inside. I could hear Milo singing in the kitchen as I dashed into my bedroom and grabbed a towel. I dried off and, unable to find my robe, wrapped the towel around my waist as I hobbled back out.

Milo was in my robe, and no doubt nothing else, frying something on the stove. "Nice jog?" he asked.

"Did you see her?"

"Who? MJ? She's here somewhere."

"No . . ."

"You mean Lala? She's back?"

"No. Another girl. Looking in the window at me. This morning. I tried to catch her but she's gone."

"Like a female Peeping Tom? Do they even have those? A Peeping Tonya?"

"Yes, exactly. Did you see her?"

"Get out of here. A girl was spying on you naked? You wish."

"Actually you're the one who was naked, but let's leave that for now. I was asleep, and when I woke up I saw her . . ." I took a breath and said it: "She was the girl I was following, Mona."

"I can't sleep with clothes on, OK? It's not natural. I can't breathe."

"Do you get what I'm saying? Mona. The girl who killed herself. She was here. Just now."

"You mean like a ghost?"

"No, for real."

"Dead people don't come back to peep in your window for real. Only ghosts or zombies. Hey, maybe she's a succubus now. She probably would have blown you if you'd pretended to be asleep. Here's your breakfast." He peeled two burned lumps from the pan and plopped them on a plate.

"What is that?"

"French toast."

"I didn't think we had eggs."

"You don't. I used oil. And you didn't have any syrup or cinnamon or anything, so I had to substitute Swiss Miss cocoa powder and strawberry Jell-O mix."

"Hmmm." It looked, and smelled, like a meth lab gone wrong. "Where's MJ anyway? I'm worried. Her car's out front."

Milo held the greasy spatula aloft. "Hold on, listen." We listened. Muffled snoring filtered through. "I hear another demonic succubus."

We found her on the couch. She was on her back, fully dressed but with her shirt pulled up over her head, exposing her very shapely breasts. A strangled snoring reached us from inside.

"I bet that's her," Milo said. "Nicer tits than I expected." He prodded one with his finger.

MJ wriggled and groaned. "Stop! Help! You fucking asshole. Get me out of here. Rape!" We yanked her shirt down and revealed her sweaty red face, plastered with damp hair. "That was awful," she gasped. "I dreamed a giant was sitting on my face."

"You're not the only one who had bad dreams last night," Milo said as we trailed MJ back into the kitchen. She grabbed the pot and poured coffee. "Sherlock here dreamed that a dead girl came back and winked at him."

"It wasn't a dream. I was awake. I saw it." Or I thought I did. Now I wondered.

"How do you know?" He waved the spatula for emphasis, sending a spray of grease across the kitchen. "How do you know you're not dreaming right now?"

"Let's test it." I grabbed a big cleaver. "Hold out your hand." He laughed.

MJ took the knife from me and chopped a piece of French toast, then took a bite. "As much as I hate to, I have to agree with Milo on this one. The dead don't walk the earth. Not till the rapture any-way." She looked meaningfully at Milo, who shrugged.

"Go ahead," he said.

"You," she answered.

"It's your idea."

"What?" I said. "Just tell me. It's not like I can't hear you."

MJ sighed. She took my hand.

"Sam, Milo and I are concerned, as friends."

Milo took my other hand and then grabbed MJ's, forming a trian-gle.

"We love you, bro," Milo said.

"What the fuck?" I pulled loose.

"It's this obsession with that dead girl," MJ said. "It's unhealthy."

"It's not an obsession. It's a job. I'm investigating."

"Investigating what?" she asked. "She killed herself. You saw it."

"Don't get me wrong. It's a sweet deal." Milo chimed in. "I mean if Inspector Giggles will pay, who cares? But you're taking it too far."

"Look," MJ said. "It's not just a job anymore, is it?"

I shrugged. She went on.

"At first I went along with it. Why not? Your wife left. You're in a tailspin. I understand. Most guys would get drunk and bang a hooker. You follow a dead girl. Fine."

"I did bang her."

"Once!" Milo interjected. "And she jumped."

"Don't you see?" MJ took my hand again. Milo reached for the other, but I smacked him away. "You replaced Lala with her. Instead of thinking about your wife, missing your wife, talking about your wife, it's this dead girl. In real life, Lala just left you for some dude. Sorry, but that's it. But in your dreams, your wife is dead, and this new girl, who you idealize, who you feel guilty over, her you see, alive." Her phone rang. "Sorry." She went to it.

Milo patted my shoulder. "Are you masturbating enough? I can lend you some cool seventies porn from the shop. I know when the sperm backs up on me, I get crazy ideas."

"I'm fine."

MJ came rushing back with a shriek. "Oh my God! That was Margie, calling about your work."

"Your Margie?" I asked her. "About what work?"

"Your novels, silly. What else? Remember when I asked you if I could show them to Margie?"

I remembered. It was a year ago, during a particularly low swing of despair when, as I prepared to douse both my work and my hair in kerosene, MJ had agreed to ask Margie about finding me an agent. Nothing had happened.

"To be honest," I said. "I didn't think she even read them."

"Well, she didn't. She doesn't really have time for traditional reading. But I told her about them."

"So?"

"She wasn't interested."

"OK then."

"But!"—she paused dramatically—"I made her promise to keep you in mind. And guess whose office called asking for your work? And now wants to meet you about a writing job, a big one? This afternoon?"

45

THE BUCK NORMAN SPREAD, set in the high country north of the city, looked more like a quaint village, or the set of a quaint village, than the luxury compound and high-tech multimedia fortress it really was. Like Disneyland, the gears and wires, guards and guns were hidden behind a happy, folksy façade: a wooden ranch-style fence, piney trees, a gravel drive, a big shingled house surrounded by barnish looking outbuildings, stables, and corrals. Two horses ran in synch, noble manes aflutter. Carefully curated wildflowers bloomed and grasses bent in a fresh breeze that never reached my part of town, yet there was no smell of horseshit or sound of labor. My car was greeted by three friendly folks who approached in a loose triangle, smiling from different angles of fire. At point was a happy blond in her twenties, dressed in tight jeans and a pristine white T-shirt, hair up under a Dodgers cap. She looked sweet and homemade as cherry pie but her accent was from beyond the old Iron Curtain.

"Hi, how are you?" she said, though her eyes asked, Who are you and how are you armed? One of two extremely buff dudes in jeans and Abercrombie T-shirts smiled from behind her like a well-trained guard dog, while the other sniffed around my car.

"Hi, I'm Sam Kornberg. I'm here to see Mr. Norman. I'm a writer?"

"Oh the writer! Great. He's a writer," she told her pals, who smiled, clearly charmed. "In our country people admire very much writers. I am Joan," she chirped cheerfully, pronouncing it slightly off, like "John." "It is American diminutive for Russian name you can't say." I shook her hand. "This is Billy and Joel." They waved.

"Hi guys. Is Joel a Russian name?"

"Americanization of Yoel," she explained. "Now Buck expects you. Come in!"

I followed her into the house (her boys stayed outside). We passed through wide-open spaces floored in wood and flagstone, with Navajo rugs, African masks and modern abstractions on the walls. There was a buzz of happy business being done. Two bearded geniuses in knee-length cutoffs and skate sneaks looked up from a computer bay and waved. Hi! Smiling Mexican women chased squealing white babies among a wonderland of toys. Hi! A tall, bald German man in kitchen whites chopped brightly colored veggies with a huge gleaming blade. Hi, Joan! Lunch is almost ready!

Down a few hand-hewn stone steps, we entered a large sunny room, walled in books on two sides, with a huge stone fireplace and glass doors open on a garden, a pool and, down a little path, the beach. Buck Norman stood and took off his glasses. He was a nice-looking teacher type, with a trim salt-and-pepper beard, smart eyes, and thinning hair, barefoot in a T-shirt and jeans. We shook hands warmly, full pumps.

"Sam! Come on in. Thanks for making the drive on such short notice. I'm Bucky. Have a seat. You thirsty? Want a water or anything? Joan, please tell Marcus we'd love two waters when he gets a chance."

"Hi," I said and sank into a leather couch. It was the kind where you had to lean back almost supine or sit on the rim. Buck perched on the edge of an armchair, but then stood right back up.

"So, you're a novelist. Man! I have to admit I really admire that. I mean I'm a creator, I suppose, in my own humble way, but I could never do what you do. The focus. Day after day. Year after year. I can't sit still long enough. Or shut up! Just between us, that's why I direct, it allows for a lot of standing around and talking. Those are the main tasks, really. Sure you have to be quiet during a shot but how long is that? Five minutes sitting in silence? That's your whole life. Just sitting there. And you love it. You wouldn't change it for anything. I respect that. Thanks Marcus, that's great."

"No problem." A grinning black fellow with long dreads handed us each a bottle of water.

"Thanks," I said, trying to cross my legs without sliding backward.

"He's a great guy, really talented," Buck said, as Marcus loped out, then went on: "But as different as our jobs seem, me walking and talking, you sitting and thinking, aren't we both the same in the end? Really, when you really think about it? What are we, Sam? What are you? And what am I?"

"People?" I guessed. "Just people?"

"Storytellers. Yes, people, true, good point, but people who are storytellers. I use images and sounds and action and dialogue to tell the story of say, a little league team of orphans who rob a bank to save their town in *Stealing Home* or two mixed-up people like you or me just looking for love, except one is a Nobel Prize–winning cripple and the other's an Olympic gymnast with Alzheimer's, in *Thirty Days Hath September.* Or just a simple little tale about a boy who thinks he's a robot meeting a robot who longs to be a boy in *Fritz.*"

"That's a top pick at my friend's video store," I chimed in.

"I'm grateful to him. But you know why? Storytelling. Now, you on the other hand use words, and ideas and paper, to tell similar stories, like, for instance" — he tapped the stack of manuscripts on the table between us— "in *Toilet,* remember the part when the men's room attendant rescues the hooker who's OD'd and choking on her puke in the stall, and he has to give her mouth-to-mouth, but when they kiss he has a vision of her as Jesus and starts crying?"

"Right," I said, although actually that was all a dream sequence, cleverly inserted inside another dream sequence, built around passages from the *Tibetan Book of the Dead.*

Buck snapped his fingers. "And then, right at that moment, wham, the pipes burst and the whole place floods and everything we've flushed away for the whole book returns. Now that, my friend, is storytelling!"

"Really? It is?" I myself had been afraid to look at the book for years, as if it were evidence of a crime I'd committed in a blackout. "Thanks. Thanks so much."

"Don't thank me. Thank your talent. The intern who read it for me went to Harvard and she was really excited. Though she says you have second act problems."

"She's right."

"And it's a little dark for the megaplex." He laughed, a high, fast chuckle. "But hey dark is good sometimes. I can go dark too. Like with 9-11. Maybe you saw *Another Sunrise?*"

He was being disingenuous. Everyone on the planet had seen it, except for me. I stayed home in a silent protest that no one heard but Lala, who went with a friend. It wasn't very good, she agreed, it was cheesy and fake, but she cried, like everyone in the theater, so what was the harm? That was! Crying at a bad movie, just because it skillfully manipulated real suffering, was both to distort and deny what really happened while perversely and complacently enjoying our own emotions. It was middlebrow high art, an intellectual exercise for those who didn't want to actually think about it, the feel-bad hit of the season.

"Of course I saw *Another Sunrise*," I told Buck. "It was great."

"Thank you, Sam, but I wasn't the one who was great. That's my point. Just like in *Toilet*, it was the story, and the characters, they were great. Well, not the terrorists of course. Though they were great villains."

"Right," I said. "Exactly." He'd lost me, but it didn't seem to matter. He sat down, finally, and cracked his water. I drank some of mine.

"I get so dry out here," he said. "Even though it's by the beach. It's this wind I think. Anyway, tell me your story, Sam. What are you working on now?"

I froze. I drank more water. I realized too late that I should have come up with something. It was the sort of thing one discussed at these meetings, or so I'd heard. With no time for a lie, I was stuck telling the truth.

"Well, Buck, I am in fact working on a novel, like you said."

He smiled and nodded.

"This one's called *Perineum*."

"Nice. I like it. Sounds, I don't know, sort of Latinate. What's it about?"

"Well, that's hard to say. I've just started really. It started as a cycle of love poems just focused on that one . . . word, and now it's evolving. It's about themes of betweeness really, of being in some way between two points, two places, between life and death for example, pleasure and horror, birth and I don't know, waste." I exhaled, exhausted by my own bullshit.

"Great theme. But what happens?"

"Well, I don't quite know yet, Buck. You see, I start with the voice."

"Yes! Your voice."

"Not exactly."

"The character's voice."

"More the book's voice. I'm trying to hear the book talking, the voice of consciousness talking, to itself, in a void, while no one listens." I wanted to cry. As I rambled on, digging my grave deeper, I wanted to think my ideas were beyond this guy's understanding, but the truth was I didn't understand them either. No one did. Not really. I'd been working on this new novel for a year. I'd written ten pages of nonsense. I was done. I was an unnovelist. My grand experiment was over, the results were in, and the conclusion was: I suck.

Buck sat back. He looked at me, hard. I expected him to laugh or tell me to fuck off and get a real job, like private detective. He nodded. "OK," he said. "I'm in."

"What?"

"I don't know. Call me crazy but I love it. Look, I've heard a lot of pitches. A lot. And what are we always saying we want? Originality. Something we never heard before. Something that knocks our socks off. Well, I never heard anything like *Palladium* before, and believe me, my socks are off!"

"Really? Thanks. I can't believe it." I wasn't sorry to hear he'd changed the name, in case he looked it up later, but I couldn't picture myself delivering ten inscrutable pages. "What exactly do you want me to do?"

"You're a writer, Sam. I want you to write. Write *Pandemonium*, here, with me. Let's tell that story, together."

"Wow."

"Now." Buck stood again and started pacing. "I'm not going to bullshit around with you, this idea is great but it needs a lot of, I don't know, a lot of meat on its bones. Are you committed to anything else? Writing for anyone else?"

"No." As a storyteller I was unemployed, but I thought of the fictional crime I was investigating and the obese madman who was waiting for me to report my latest dream. "No, nothing. Well, I kind of have this day job."

"Fuck it." Buck toasted me with his water. "Sorry but really. A day job is to support the writing. The night job, that was your real life, right? Well, from now on it's going to be all night."

Buck said he'd have someone call "my agent," Margie, and work out the details, but essentially I'd get a weekly salary plus various tasty "pieces" of "development" as well as a nice fat slice off the "back end." Although it all seemed sure to fail, I couldn't help but float back out to my car in a delirium of affluence. I could get a new car stereo. Or a new car. I could get a new wife. Or buy the lost one back. I was finally the man she'd meant to marry all along.

At the exit of the drive I met a new Prius coming in the narrow gate and stopped to let it pass. It paused beside me. Russ, the handsome hunk from Dr. Parker's office, was behind the wheel.

"Yo, Sam. Great to see you!"

"Hey, what brings you here?" I asked.

"I work here, with Buck. That's what brought me to Green Haven. Buck's on the board. He's a huge supporter of mental health issues. Usually I work in development though, so I'll be seeing you around. We all love your stuff." He winked, as though I were a young starlet in a bikini. "Welcome to the winning team."

46

BACK ON THE ROAD, my euphoria dissipated as I joined the endless creep of cars, their owners staring out at each other like captives sealed in glass. I checked my phone and found an urgent summons from my still current employer. So I rushed, very slowly, to the Lonsky headquarters, mentally composing what I figured would be my final report. Bucky's job was almost as odd as Lonsky's, but I had to consider seriously an eccentric billionaire who won Oscars over an eccentric hermit who lost competency hearings.

I arrived to find the big man in an agitated state. Where had I been? A roast was in the oven, and he was worried my traffic problems might delay feeding time. I apologized and, without explaining, dove into my review of *Succubi!* He sank in his chair, low like a hippo in muddy water, eyes shut. The giant hands were chapeled before his lips, propping up the flying buttress of his nose. Then I told him about Mona's appearance at my window that morning. As I began reasoning aloud, "I know what you're thinking, horror movie plus beef jerky after midnight equals bad dream," he raised a hand.

"I find little profit in wondering over that small difference," he said.

"Life and death? It's a big difference," I said.

"A very important one yes, but perhaps not so big. In any case, what I intended to say is that there is no way for us to objectively establish the fact here and now, since you were the sleeper. Let's say it was a dream? What of it? It is often in dreams that we perceive the truth. She will come again, I suspect, and then you can ask. Please continue." His eyes slid shut.

I told him about Kevin. He remained impassive until I was done. Then his chins lifted, one by one, and his eyes opened on me. "One thing is certain. It was shortsighted of you not to take the tapes. You will have to return and obtain them."

"What? How?"

"There are any number of ways. Perhaps if you disguise yourself as a census taker or, better yet, a worker from the public utilities company come to investigate a gas leak. I have a nice collection of mustaches and eyebrows . . ."

"Huh . . ." I tried to change the subject by mentioning Doctor Parker's sad demise, but he was even more vexed. He sat almost nearly upright.

"You should have called me immediately as soon as you found out he'd been killed."

"I didn't think it was urgent. It was an accident."

"When will you learn, Kornberg? There are no accidents. In The Case of Dora, Freud's patient spurns an amorous advance from a young man. Distraught, the fellow dashes into the street without looking and is nearly run down by a carriage. Freud interprets this as an unconscious suicide attempt. Genius!"

"Yes, well, the cops say Dr. Parker had a blowout. Your unconscious can't burst a tire, can it? On the other hand, Mona, who everyone says did commit suicide, you interpret as murder. Know how Freud would interpret that? Meshuggeneh."

"Perhaps. But unlike your scientific speculation as to whether you are dreaming or not, my meshuggeneh ideas are based on evidence." He drew a letter from his desk drawer. "I received this in today's mail. It's a letter Mona left for me, to be delivered after her death. Her final testament. I believe it is what Dr. Parker was hiding in his safe, and what, fearing for his own life, he meant to give you. When you didn't respond in a timely manner, he mailed it, perhaps on his way to work that fateful morn." He unfolded the letter and cleared his throat. "My Darling Solar . . ."

47

WHEN WE FIRST MET, you reminded me of my father, though I know that's a cliché. And I only met him once, my real father, assuming he even really was. I was seven. I remember because it was my birthday. I was having cake with my mom. We were about to light the candles, and she said to wait, that someone was coming. I didn't know who she meant. It was just she and I, like always. I didn't have many friends, and we had no family. For some reason, I got this crazy idea it was Big Bird. I was in love with him then and watched that show obsessively and I'd heard at school other kids talking about the amazing figures who came to their parties, parties I was not invited to, and I guess it occurred to me that maybe my mother had arranged for Big Bird to come as a surprise. Imagine my disappointment when it was a human man, though I had to admit he was very large. And despite his lack of feathers, I was also impressed with his general hairiness. Of course he brought a gift, a big box wrapped in pink paper with a red bow. It contained a My Pretty Pony, which is what I wanted most of all. I was shy but the Pony won me over, and I consented to sit on his lap and blow out the candles. I recall he ate two huge pieces of cake, which also impressed me enormously. After he left, my mother told me that he was my father, but that he was a very famous and important man who was too busy working to come visit and that for the same mysterious reasons we had to keep it a secret. Though I wonder if it was at all true. Maybe he thought it was. Unfortunately, just because my mother tells you something is no reason to believe it. I'm afraid I have inherited this trait, though often I'm the one that I lie to. In fact, now that I think about it, I am not even sure that this incident ever occurred. It's quite likely that my mother merely told me about this mythical meeting much later. Or maybe I dreamed it up myself, high on my medications, after seeing a movie here in the hospital on TV. So you see my dear how it is when you are lost. Even your memories are not your own. Where are they? Where did they go? Who took them? My doctors, my lovers, my captors, my enemies, my friends? I sometimes imagine that late at night, they come into my room and erase my mind, like a disk or a sheet of paper, and imprint the clean white surface with the image they want to project, the image of Mona. I imagine that I do not even look like I think I do, that the face I see in the mirror is not really mine. Is this other face the one you see and love? Or are we both caught in this same delusion? I imagine when Dr. Parker takes me in his office for a session, that he is hypnotizing me into believing who and what I am and that he does the same to you. Maybe we are both really asleep, and dreaming all this. That is my sweetest fantasy, that I am napping in the library right now, close to you.

Sometimes I dream that I am the widow of a famous artist, a great filmmaker. I'm a glamorous and beautiful woman, being taken to parties at nightclubs and grand dinners in castles, seduced by men and women, given the finest wines and drugs, then rushed off to a yacht at midnight to sail into the middle of the sea, and drink champagne at sunrise. I imagine that is my life and that I just got a bit too drunk and high, a bit too tired to lift my eyes, but when I do, in a moment, this hospital room will be gone and I will see the sun, the empty blue sky, and smell the clean ocean air. This is Fabricio's yacht, or his father's, some sort of count who owns a shoe factory and a vineyard. The son does nothing but collect motorcycles, gamble, and chase girls, while he waits to inherit the title and the money. Does this make him a viscount or is that different? He takes me riding on his Ducati and we go so fast I think we will lift off into flight. I feel the engine pulling up, up, like a winged stallion, while we lean over the neck, holding it down. I am so terrified I leave claw marks in Fab's sides where I clutch his rib cage, but the vibration of that machine, that power beneath is almost unbearably exciting. Like all of the men I meet, he is fascinated with my husband, with his work, with our life together, my young marriage, his suicide. I refuse to discuss it, which they love. It makes it even more mysterious. Some propose but I refuse them. I consider myself still married and in the end, after five years abroad, I return to Los Angeles, to Hollywood.

I never should have come home. I thought it would save me, ground me, pull me out of my dreams, but it only buried me alive in them. Hollywood is my graveyard, and this hospital, this bed, my grave. It all began that summer, my summer of Fabricio, troubling dreams I couldn't shake and worse, little cracks in the daytime, in reality, moments when I'd forget where, or even who, I was. Sometimes I'd feel, lying with my eyes closed in the sun, that I'd open them and be by the pool in Laurel Canyon, the old house, with Zed beside me, reading out loud. Sometimes I'd think I was here, in my room at the hospital, hearing the soft step of the nurses in the hall.

Then it got to be I was wide-awake, walking down a street in Paris or stepping into a nightclub in Berlin and suddenly I'd blank out and not know my name or why I was there. It was terrifying. I'd play along, nodding at my companions, laughing at their jokes, letting them put me in a cab, but all the while I'd be screaming inside. Then just as suddenly, it would all come back, and I'd be OK again for weeks. But I lived in constant dread of an attack, and maybe that fear and anxiety even triggered them, which lead me to fear the fear, to become anxious over the anxiety, around and around, in a spiral, headed down into nothingness. Finally, I snapped. I had what the doctors called a psychotic break and ended up in a hospital in Germany. They shipped me here, old friends, people I didn't even remember, paid for it, and Dr. Parker began to teach me about myself again. I learned who I was, about my childhood, about Zed. He said the trauma of witnessing Zed's suicide had triggered a breakdown, and I'd tried to control it with drugs and alcohol and reckless sex and that had all made it worse. He said he could help me remember. And I suppose he did, he had the evidence, the passports and newspaper clippings. But I always suspected there was something more to my story. I should have hired you then, my darling Solar, to solve my case. For a crime had been committed. A missing person case. Me. True, I am dead now, as you read my words, but do not mourn, my love. Long before my death, someone had already stolen my life. I was lost. Find me, detective. Save me. Please.

48

LONSKY SET THE PAGES down on the desk. I could see the sheets covered in a feminine scrawl.

He knit his hands over his belly and set his eyes on me. They were tearless, of course. And pitiless.

"So, now that you have heard her last words, you, the last to see her alive, now that you've received this message from beyond the grave, a letter delivered by the dead hand of another, begging for our help, now, Kornberg, what say you?"

His gaze bore down on me like Moses on the Mountain. My phone buzzed relentlessly. Milo 911. Perhaps I was out of beer or there was a Cheech & Chong marathon on TV. My friends were right. I had to seize control of my fate from everyone, including them. And him. And her. And her. Losing my wife, I had begun to lose my mind, letting Mona invade my dreams, and my dreams invade my life: madness lay ahead. Look at Lonsky, thumping his desk with a paw.

"Well, have you fallen mute or have you something to say?"

"Yes, sir," I said, with a smile of relief. "I quit."

49

WALKING OUT OF the Lonsky residence a free man, I did feel a lot better. I'd explained, as best I could, that as far as I was concerned, the background dossier on (Ra)Mona was complete. Without going into specifics, I said it was time I focused on my own career. I knew all I was ever going to about The Subject. I called Milo back from the car, preparing to fire him too, but he wasn't at my house after all. It was worse.

"Good news. I went ahead and got those movies for you."

"What movies?"

"From that old queen. I called and said I was your assistant, which she believed no problem, ha, and asked when you could come by for a follow-up interview. The witch said she was going to be out at a soiree or whatnot, probably picking toadstools all night, but you could come by for a tea again tomorrow. So I just waited till she cleared out, hopped in, and got them."

"Hopped in? How?"

"I remembered what you said about the closet and all."

"You broke in?"

"What's the big deal? I break into your house and borrow things all the time. We just watch it, dupe it, and return it before the old bag knows."

"You break into my house?"

"I have to, you won't give me a key. Anyway, I'll close the shop early and get the Beta decks set up. We'll watch downstairs. Jerry's not well. But I bet he'd be proud, if I told him. Which I probably won't."

"Jesus, Milo, I never told you to do this . . ."

"This isn't about you, man. Or me. Or who broke into whose house. This is cinema. Just be here at ten. And don't worry. No one will ever know."

50

I HEARD TROUBLE COMING before I reached the parking lot and sniffed it in the air before I touched the door. It sounded, and smelled, like Led Zeppelin, "Immigrant Song" pounding through the store's sound system, so loud I felt its galloping rumble in my belly and heard Plant's cry ring out, even as I turned into the lot, which was packed, despite the closed sign and drawn shades. I squeezed in between a black pickup on monster tires and an old primer-spotted Nova. The dark air around me was thick with roasted meat smoke and the sweet funk of good weed. Either there was a party going on or someone had run over and then incinerated a skunk.

Everything doubled when I opened the door. The music blew my brain back in a blast of reverb. Smoke billowed out. The scene resembled a combination Dungeons & Dragons convention, *High*

Times thirtieth-anniversary reunion, and summit between black metal war clans. Grim reapers lurched around with beers in their hands, talking through beards of white, black, green, and red. An albino wraith tottered by in Goth rags and Frankenstein boots, holding hands with a pink haired pinup in fishnets and a crimson corset. Through the smoke, I could make out a chubby tattooed lady, topless and bouncing up and down to the sonic thunder, her tremendous breasts atremble as she shook her fists at heaven. I put a tentative foot inside, but a hairy monster in a leather vest blocked my path with what looked like a real sword.

"Hold! Who goes there? Declare yourself!" The gristled beast faced me with red eyes like boiled beets sunk deep into blackened sockets. He showed stubbly teeth. I stepped back, eyes on the weapon, prepared to flee, but Milo emerged from the clouds.

"That's OK, Bjorn, this is the guest of honor."

Immediately, the gatekeeper stood back, his sword raised at attention. "Enter at will."

"What the fuck, Milo? What is this?" I asked as he guided me toward his command post behind the counter.

He shrugged. "Word must have slipped out about the films. They're a legend all through the community."

"What community?" A Satanic dude wandered past with a shaved head, droopy waxed mustache, heavy eyeliner, and a pentagram pendant over a black velvet tunic.

"The underground-art-rock-magic-kink-noise-film-spooky-stoner-occult-metal scene, I guess. Don't worry. Everyone here is very low profile. They mostly have criminal records."

"That's reassuring."

"And once these copies are run off, we're going to make a nice little pile. I'm already taking orders." I was about to raise several objections, but a gaunt graybeard in a pointy hat and a tie-died purple robe appeared and grabbed my hand.

"Thank you, sir, for finding what was lost. I am White Wizard.

If you ever need me, just call." He raised his furry eyebrows and gleamed. "With your thoughts, I mean. There is no phone in my van."

"Right, I will think about you. Thanks."

The topless girl I'd seen before tapped my shoulder. I jumped.

"Hi," she said, and handed me a beer. Her tattooed boobs jiggled and the creatures inked over her soft skin jumped and shivered. "I'm Bluebell. I love what you're doing for the community. Thank you so, so much."

"You're welcome."

"Ladies and gentleman, and everyone in between, your attention please!"

Distracted, I hadn't noticed that the music had stopped. Milo was standing on a chair, brandishing a remote. He went on. "Welcome, cinephiles, Satanists, metal heads, stoners, and sexual deviants of all stripes." There were scattered cheers and a confused dash of applause as the crowd appraised each other. "Tonight we have gathered for what may be the very first screening of a lost treasure, *Invitation* and *Consummation,* parts one and two of Zed Naught's legendary Infernal Trilogy." A roar went up. Bluebell hopped up and down. Her beer foamed. The White Wizard tossed some glitter in the air. I spotted MJ by the door. She waved. Then someone handed her a bottle of tequila and she took a slug. Milo went on: "But first let me introduce you to the man who made it all possible, the hero of our community . . ."

Spitting beer, I poked at Milo. "No, no that's fine . . ."

He pointed the remote at me. "My dear friend, the experimental, nonlinear novelist and junior private eye . . . Sam Kornberg!"

A roar went up. The gathered tribe shook their various weapons, pipes, and wands. MJ hooted and waved her bottle. A handful of barbarians began to chant and pump their veiny arms. "Korn-berg! Korn-berg! Korn-berg!"

"Let the films begin!" Milo shouted above them. "Lights out!"

51

INVITATION IS ONLY EIGHTEEN minutes long, and appears to be shot on 16mm. There is no synch sound, only a lurching, soaring, screaming score attributed to none other than Daemonica herself on synthesizer and church organ and her rock star then-husband on electric guitar, appearing, according to Milo's quick Internet work, under the pseudonym High Lord Assmore. The film begins with a sunset, in fact the whole thing takes place during a protracted sunset, while an orange lump of fire melts, like a child's fallen snow cone, into a neon-blue California sea. This slowed footage of the day's last drops dripping into darkness is intercut with a kind of fast-forward course in Western civilization coming to its conclusion, an apocalypse composed of stock footage, amateur theatricals, and the occasional flight of fugitive beauty snatched from thin air.

As the sun sinks, shrinking and swelling with a diseased organ's glandular grandeur, the guitars begin to howl and a whole series of creatures seems to answer the summons: An ancient Egyptian pharaoh (who looks a lot like Kevin the warlock, but much younger with black eyeliner and a shaved chest) emerges from a cardboard temple covered in crayon hieroglyphics and throws a spear into the air. A Greek oracle (garlands in her long blond curls, fake boobs under her toga) rises from the smoke of a cave and runs through the woods, pursued by a hairy Pan in plastic horns, tooting on his pipes. An Aztec goddess in gold body paint and a feather mask climbs a plywood pyramid (close shot on the peak only) holding a bloody sword. (Was this the unnamed Mexican chick, third wheel in the Naught Family Triathlon? The credits called her only Rosa Negrita.) The parade continues and some actors reappear in new guises: the milky blond returns in a white wig and a Marie Antoinette bodice with a beauty mark on her cleavage; Kevin pops up in a mustache and full Fascist ensemble. (Continuity, problematic throughout, gets especially shoddy here. Marie's beauty mark jumps from right breast to left, and Kevin, when appearing next as Manson, has a seemingly real beard in one shot and an obviously fake one in the next.) Animals leap into action as well, in nature doc footage of bounding stags, soaring bird flocks, and barking wolf packs. Things reach a sort of crescendo when we see these animals dying, falling, bleeding, intercut with zoomy flashes of knives, swords, spears, and arrows being waved around. Night falls. Total darkness fills the screen. Then, in a gorgeous bit of business, a full moon forms like a pearl on the ocean's silvered tongue. There is a meteor shower, a real one, bright traces like so many scratches raining and dying on film. A flame jumps, we think it is another, brighter comet crossing the heavens, but it is a match tossed into the darkness right before us. It lands, igniting a bonfire. As the flames flare up, apparently in Zed's backyard, we see the various characters from the film, Greek, Roman, Aztec, Nazi, and so forth kneeling around it, cleverly cut so that the doubled and tripled actors can all be seen. Even the animals seem to be there, though obviously stuffed, a stag, a wolf, a goat. Then, hazily through the flames, two figures emerge in hooded cloaks, holding hands. The assembly cheers, fists raised. The music orgasms. The end. The credits are a bit of a letdown after this, since they are poorly set in shaky letters and the musical score, a bit too short, suddenly begins again, only to end abruptly about thirty seconds later.

The audience, now sprawled on the floor or leaning against the walls, burst into ecstatic applause. "I can see why that is a legend!" Milo shouted into my ear. "Wait till I go online. I will rule the nerdosphere."

I shouted back, "Don't forget we're not supposed to have seen this! We stole it."

"Borrowed. Art belongs to the people. And I'm charging them like a hundred a copy. You want to run over to 7-Eleven before the next feature? I'm getting hungry."

"No. It's short. Let it roll. We better get these back quickly."

52

IF *INVITATION* WAS AN AMATEUR production twisted into high art, *Consummation* was homemade avant-garde porn. The film seems to begin where the first one ended, on a fire-lit night at Zed's, but the cast and props are different. Now there are torches blazing in a large ring, with the trees and ridges of Laurel Canyon outlined in black above. Now the circled participants are all in black hooded robes, with their faces variously masked (demon, gorilla, ghost) or painted (whiskered kitten, red devil, mime white). A giant pentagram is painted on the ground, and in the center of the star stands an altar draped with red velvet and a large upside-down cross that looks like the one in Kevin's closet. Then, as the music climbs and wails, a kind of royal couple emerges, a man in a purple robe with a goatish mask covering the top of his face, Batman-style, and sprouting small horns, and a woman in a white robe with a white Zorro-type mask revealing pouty red lips and bright eyes blinking through its holes. Zed and Mona. He holds a sword in one hand. Mona cuddles a white rabbit. In their other hands, each holds a chain, and crawling behind them, both bare-bottomed, are a priest and nun, the nun holding an incense burner in her mouth, the priest with a pillow on his back, on which, as a drunken zoom reveals, rests the consecrated host.

"Holy shit, here we go! Black Mass!" Milo said, opening a bag of chips.

"You mean unholy shit," I corrected him.

The onlookers hail them. The Priestess disrobes. She is completely nude except for dagger heels, and completely shaved. She lies down on the altar and a couple of worshippers chain her with cuffs that dangle from it. Then the Satanic priest, Zed, drops his robe. He is nude as well.

"Uncircumcised, interesting," Milo said, crunching a chip. He handed me the bag but I declined, as Zed begins vigorous intercourse with Mona and the worshippers chant and clap. There is some wilderness footage of wolves crying, forests burning, asteroids vaporizing into the sun. Back to Zed, who turns, tumescent, on the priestling, who worshipfully holds out the pillow. He ejaculates over the host.

"Nachos!" Milo shouted. The crowd in the shop went howling mad. Warriors high-fived. Wizards wailed. I thought I caught a glimpse of MJ hugging Bluebell, snuggled in her cleavage.

On screen, a volcano erupts. A comet crashes. A toreador slaughters a bull. An ax splinters a door while a girl screams. Lava spurts and flows, igniting the darkness. It drips into the sea and becomes glass. An island is born. Then a worshipper, with a clown mask under his hood, slits the rabbit's throat and lets it bleed into a chalice.

"What the fuck? I'm going to have nightmares," I said.

"That was unnecessary," Milo agreed.

Zed breaks the host into pieces. Still nude, he climbs onto a throne that I recalled as the chair Kevin lounged in during my visit, and the congregation lines up. Each kneels to eat a piece of defiled host, sip bunny blood, and plant a soulful kiss on Zed's hairy bottom.

"What the fuck?" I groaned again.

"That my friend, is the devil's kiss," Milo whispered.

Then the congregants gather around the altar, dropping their robes, and as the music soars and dies, they approach the masked priestess, to worship at one of her three open gates.

53

THIS TIME THE CREDITS rolled in silence. Someone turned on the lights. The community was now strangely subdued. Whether due to substance overload, moral queasiness, or just shooting their aesthetic wad, they seemed lethargic, sated, even depressed, rather than whipped into the orgiastic fever I'd feared. The White Wizard was downcast, picking sparkles from his beard. Bluebell was still topless, but she now sat on the carpet hugging herself, as if she were cold. MJ was nowhere in sight.

"Well," I said finally to Milo. "I can see why this was kept secret. It's a real buzzkiller. Thank God I don't have to explain to Lonsky how the love of his life was a nasty ho." Despite the evidence, I found it hard to believe myself: this was the real Mona, the girl I'd found and lost, studied and mourned? "I quit that job just in time."

"Here's to Buck Norman and his shitty movies," Milo announced, uncapping another beer.

"I guess. That thing still seems screwy, though. Why would he want me?"

"Who knows? Maybe he owes Margie a favor and she's doing it because MJ asked, to keep you from killing yourself."

"Did she say that to you? She thought I was that fucked up?"

"No, but I might have mentioned it."

"What? Fuck you." I shrugged. "And thanks, I guess. For caring and shit."

"I love you too." Milo pulled out the tapes. "And you can thank me by putting these back in the warlock's magical closet."

"No way. You're the one who stole them."

"If you haven't noticed I've got customers here. I've got to burn disks, get the place shut. Kevin is gone for the night but if the tapes aren't back tomorrow, who's he going to suspect?"

"Shit," I said, sighing. "I take back my thanks, you fucker."

"It's easy. The side window is open. Just creep in and split." He handed me the two cassettes. "I sure wish we had part three. *Ascension*. What the hell could top this? Maybe they actually shove live bunnies up each other's asses."

"That's why you're not a storyteller like me and Buck," I told him. "You don't see the arc. Part three is where Satan appears."

54

ON MY WAY OUT I saw MJ in the shadows. She was next to Margie's big black BMW and I started over to say hello. Then I saw: Margie was on her knees, crying, while MJ stroked her hair. I hurried past to my own car, pretending not to see.

I realized then how truly self-centered I was, too busy headlining in my own dramedy to see that she was a star too. It finally occurred to me that hanging out at my house, drinking and watching movies with Milo and me, and loitering in the bookstore, was a way of avoiding her own home and life and wife. Her relationship was in trouble and it was big-shot Margie who was the pursuer, the bereft, the wounded soul, at least for today. I felt sorry for her, stuck feeling like me.

It is one of the simplest, most difficult truths: the amazing fact that other people are real and thinking all day about their own complex lives, just like we are. In a restaurant, a store, an office, look around: each one of those random brains is a whole world, same as yours, a spinning globe of worries, desires, memories, and fears, with families and friends, enemies and half-forgotten faces, reaching back deep into time, and somehow existing right across the bus. Now multiply that by 6.7 billion. That is our reality: an endless number of endless universes, each one dancing about the others, changing and evolving, blinking out and shining on, appearing and dying, forever, an infinite darkness alive with brief little stars.

55

MILO WAS RIGHT FOR ONCE. I snuck into Kevin's without a problem, under the window and over the sill, into a crouch on the floor. I took one step in the dark and tripped over an armchair that seemed to be in a different spot than before, stumbling into a table full of doo-dads, which jiggled and rolled. I flicked on Milo's flashlight, gasp-ing as the beam fell on a mounted cow skull with a baby doll's head in its mouth. It had little glass diamonds for eyes. Then I picked my way across the room, spotting bits of set dressing from the films — a fake dagger encrusted with plastic jewels on the mantel, a dirty white wig now draped on a stone Buddha head. At last I found the linen closet and opened the door, then drew back the hidden panel. I berated myself for not remembering exactly where the tapes had been before. But it would be fine, I told myself. He had no reason to suspect anything, and how often did he even check? I set the tapes to one side of the pentagram and shut the panel. I pushed the Lysol and toilet paper back in place. As far as I could tell, it all looked the same. I shut the closet and, as I turned to go, relieved to be done with this paralegal errand, the flashlight beam swung over the dark room and landed on Kevin the warlock's face.

He didn't look happy to see me. He didn't look happy at all. For one thing, his face was upside-down. And the eyes and mouth both gaped, aghast, in horror and very clearly without life. Kevin the Sa-tanist had finally met his dark maker, and it did not seem like the re-union had gone well. I jumped, and without thinking, like a child trying to blot out a scary movie, I shut the flashlight, plunging Kevin and myself both into darkness. That was much worse, of course. Now literally in a blind panic, I ran straight into the coffee table and rammed my shin against the marble edge. I howled, then choked it off into a whimper, afraid of what might be listening. I stumbled to the door and found the light switch.

Kevin had been crucified, nailed to his upside-down cross, from which the trailing Christmas tree lights still blinked, now that I'd switched on the power. The nailing had been done with a gun, I surmised, from the many tightly grouped nail heads that lined his blood-encrusted palms like rusty rivets or clustered like thorns on his twisted feet. I also noticed, with a lurch in my stomach, that all of his fingers had been cleanly if brutally removed, sliced right off near the knuckle, as well as both of his big toes at the joint. The cause of death though, I would guess, was the handful of nails driven into his heart, and the single steel head, which I had failed to see at first glance, that was hammered, skin-deep, between his eyes.

I'd seen enough. Too much. I turned to flee by the front door, switching off the light, then froze again as the thought "finger-prints," flashed in my brain. Fingerprints, right there on the switch even. I flipped it back on and then, wishing I was the sort of fellow who carried a hanky, grabbed a stuffed bunny doll from the shelf and retraced my steps, wiping the doorknobs, closet, hidden door, tapes, windowsill, and window with a shaky hand. I stole the bunny, fearing DNA. Then I vaulted the window, stumbled, and fell with a splat into the garden. The glass window came slamming down and I heard it crackle into shards and fall, with a sickening tinkle, like a bell. A dog barked somewhere and I scurried to the car in terror, expecting a nail through the mind at any second. As I got into my car, cranked the engine, and split, I thought, or imagined, that my headlights caught Tora, the cat, watching from the shadows with a wicked grin.

56

I RACED TO LONSKY. In retrospect I find this curious. Why him and not the police? OK, not the police, I was afraid of having to explain my very dubious presence. But why not just home or to Milo and MJ even, any of who might have provided as much or more comfort, protection and sane, or sanish, advice than the Big Man? As Lonsky would say, what would Freud say? Was I running to my father fig-ure in my hour of infantile terror? Was I fleeing the madness of the real world for the far more orderly and wise world of a madman? Was this the famous "flight into illness"? Was I cracking myself and about to cross the line into crazy? Was I already gone? Was I driving through Hollywood lost in my own nightmare? Had my broken heart eaten my brain?

Or was I beginning to believe that this was in fact a real case, a real crime, and that Solar Lonsky was the only detective real enough to solve it?

57

LONSKY LISTENED AS HE always did, blank as a mirror, placid (and flaccid) as a Buddha. He was not alarmed by my alarm or frightened by my fear, though when I got to the end, the part about falling in the garden and limping off, he looked up, and when he was sure I was done, he stood, a little more quickly than usual.

"First you must undress."

"What?"

"Your clothes are no doubt saturated with soil and other evidence. Remove them all, shoes as well. And I'll take the bunny too, if you're ready." I looked down and realized I'd been strangling it in my lap. I gave it up.

"Don't worry," he continued. "The authorities have no reason to connect this with you and I shall incinerate the items in question. You may retain your underwear. I assume you managed to keep it, at least, out of contact with the crime scene."

"Can't I just throw them in the wash?" I called as he left the room, but I did what he asked and undressed. He returned with a plastic garbage bag, into which I deposited everything I had on, including some fairly new sneakers, and he gave me his own circus tent of a robe, which I wrapped around me. After this exhausting burst of action, he lowered himself with a sigh into his chair. "Now then . . . tell me about these films."

I told him. He took in everything, including the awful icky details, without reaction, then peppered me with detailed questions about setting, lighting, and who did what, with what, to whom. Then, just when he'd gotten me confused, he asked me to go through it all again from the top. The meeting with Kevin. Milo's robbery, or borrowing (borroberry), of the cassettes. Also both films again in their entirety. And then the return of the tapes and the discovery of the dead warlock. I balked briefly but knew it was impossible to move the mountain, so I told and retold until finally, exhausted, I seemed to exhaust his curiosity and even my own fear, as I sat back, drawing normal breaths. Lonsky, meanwhile, appeared to fall asleep, his chins resting softly upon his fulsome breasts. His hands clasped each other across the small world of his belly. I knew he was alive because he occasionally grunted, though I admit he did not actually snore. I sat still as long as I could. Where could I go, in that elephantine gown? Then I cleared my throat. He raised a finger to still me, so I waited another century. Then his eyelids rose, he took a deep breath, sighed, sort of sat up, and said, "I would very much like to meet this Mexican girl, the one called Rosa Negrita in the film. I would like that very much indeed." For no particular reason, at that moment, he reminded me of Gertrude Stein, though I couldn't recall reading if she was ever quite this fat. Something about his repetitiveness, his oddly formal oddity, his perfectly smooth, unruffled, ordinary bizarreness. Imagine Uncle Gertrude as a detective. Did this make me Alice B. Toklas? Did she ever try to quit?

"Yes, well, so would I," I said, "but no one seems to remember her real name, if they ever knew it, and we're going back ten years now. Apparently she headed home to Mexico after Zed died." I crossed my legs uncomfortably in the billowing garment, remembering Kevin's white thighs crossing in his. "Do you really think he was killed for those tapes?" I asked. "It seems incredible. I mean they're somewhat outrageous but nothing compared to half of what's on the Internet, or right on the shelf in the porn section of Milo's store, believe me."

"I do believe you. But he was most certainly killed for them. Or for something on them, more precisely. Perhaps some detail whose significance we don't know. Or for the missing third tape. You've told me everything?"

"Yes of course. You know I have. You ran out of questions."

"And there is most definitely a connection to Mona's murder," he pronounced, as though gazing into a crystal ball, "though I don't yet know in what it consists."

My mind returned to Kevin and his missing digits, the horror in his face, the nails. "Why do you think he refused to talk when they tortured him? I would have."

Lonsky shrugged. "Perhaps he felt strongly enough to die for whatever he was protecting. Perhaps they killed him too soon or pushed him too far. Psychopathic torturers are not known for their patience. And there is one other, unfortunate possibility."

"What's that?"

He looked me level in the eye. "Perhaps he did talk, as you say you would have, and gave up the goods. But when his tormentors went to find the tapes, they were gone."

58

NEXT I NEEDED TO DRESS. Solar conferred with Mrs. Moon, and in short order I emerged from the Lonsky home in a spare pair of Mrs. Lonsky's bright red elastic-waisted pants, which reached, culottes-style, about halfway down my shins, and one of Solar's own shirts, which swamped me in every dimension, huge cuffs and collar flapping and the bottom hanging down my thighs. It was belted with kitchen twine. (The ladies' belts were too small, and Lonsky's useless.) As for my feet, Mrs. Moon herself kindly donated a pair of yellow-and-black quilted slippers with white ankle socks.

Although I was loath to appear before Milo in this getup (I smiled masochistically, imagining his sadistic glee), duty trumped pride: I had to tell him about the killing. I tried calling but he didn't pick up. It was after one. He'd be closing the shop, so I drove east on Beverly to Silver Lake Boulevard, skirted the black reservoir, and cut back right onto Glendale Boulevard. It was as I turned the corner that I saw the flames.

I had to stop my car up the block. Fire trucks and cop cars blocked the street, and folks stood around in clusters, watching the show. Even then it took a minute to register: this furnace coughing smoke was once Milo's video shop, and MJ's old bookstore, and Jerry's apartment upstairs. Jerry! In a sudden panic I rushed forward, through the crowd, past the cops, and over the hoses. No one tried to stop me, no one even noticed, but still when I got halfway across the lot I stopped myself. What could I do?

"Kornberg!"

It was Milo, standing in the shadows. His clothes were smudged, his face was dirty. He had gauze around his hands.

"Milo! Fuck! Are you OK? What happened? How is Jerry?"

"He's all right. I had to carry the old fucker. He's at the hospital now though, to be on the safe side."

"What happened?"

"Everything was fine. The screening broke up. I was making the copies. All of a sudden I heard this like *whoosh* from the back room. Then I saw the fire. I got everybody out then ran upstairs." We both looked at the shop, a baked and cracking skull. Firemen shot hoses into a black toothless mouth, while smoke rose from the eyes.

"Poor Jerry. He must be devastated."

Milo shrugged. "The shop was doomed anyway. He knew it. He'd been trying to find someone to buy the collection, but no one would promise to take it all. Now the insurance will pay off. And I got his films out from upstairs, his personal stash, so he can sell that to collectors. Shit. He's better off. Now he can kick back and die in luxury. I didn't get the copies of Zed's films though. Sorry. Those are gone," Milo rasped, as he did after too many bong hits. He spat on the ground.

"I'm the one who's fucked," he went on. "I'm out of a job. I would have been better off the other way around, if Jerry croaked and the shop lived. I would have inherited everything. I'm the goddamn executor."

I smiled. This is why I loved and admired Milo above all my friends. He'd carried that old man out on his back, then run back and forth through a burning house to save the history of cinema. But now, with the danger passed, he insisted on being a prick just out of principle. I'd hug him, but he'd never stand for it. "What can I do?"

He reached into the plastic bag at his feet and pulled out a six-pack. "Open one of these bitches for me. And the Funyons. I can't with these fucking bandages." He looked me over, as if for the first time, and smiled. "And why are you dressed like a circus clown? Are you trying to cheer me up?"

59

I KEPT MILO COMPANY till morning, standing in the lot and then sitting on his hood, until the last flames were extinguished. While dawn broke, firemen stomped about, crunching glass, spraying foam in corners, and poking with hooked sticks, as if making sure each and every item was thoroughly trashed before ending the party. I told him about Kevin and he listened grimly. The idea that the burning of the video store might be connected seemed both blatantly there before us and totally impossible, a mirage. It represented a slide into the life of Lonsky's mind, a land where coincidence was itself proof of connection, where merely having a thought was a clue that something hid beneath it, where denial was confirmation, where the most audacious idea, the worst fear, and the worst desire were always true, and where the most intellectually advanced and logically rigorous thought approached magic and madness. Neither of us was quite ready to go there yet, at least not out loud.

That was when I noticed the biker. He was the only other spectator remaining, still astride his bike, a worn meerschaum pipe stuck into the middle of the huge fuzzy beard, from which he occasionally belched smoke. He had long dark hair under a blue bandanna, a leather jacket, dirty jeans, boots. His bike looked like a Harley, or some big American make, but it was hard for a layman like me to say since it was stripped and painted, dull black tank, chrome fittings, and no logos or marks of any kind. Had he been in the crowd at the screening? Could he be the arsonist, if there was an arsonist, enjoying the glory of his crime? It seemed a bit much. But still I got the creeps when, as if feeling my own gaze on him, he turned and caught my eye. He grinned broadly, smoke curling from that dark thatch. I remembered the devil's kiss from Zed's movie, those nude supplicants loving that other hairy orifice. My stomach turned, and I felt the predawn chill. He mounted his bike, kicked it alive, and cleared its throat in a long rumble that drew everyone's eyes before he popped the clutch and screeched away, the sound rising to a whine as he streaked up the hill and was gone.

I offered to accompany Milo elsewhere, his place or mine, but he wanted to swing by the hospital and check on Jerry, then crash. So I got in my car and drove home through the clear morning air, still lost in my internal smoke and darkness. I suppose that's why I didn't notice that the lamp beside my front steps was out, or that my shades were down, or that anything was amiss at all until I stepped inside and shut the door behind me and flipped on the light.

I'd been robbed. Or wrecked. Home-invaded. The place was trashed. Furniture was overthrown, my books unshelved and scattered. Couch cushions had been gutted and their stuffing blown, pictures pulled from the wall and smashed. I gawked stupidly, stepping through the kitchen, over broken plates and food pulled from the pantry, things from deep back that I didn't even know I'd had: canned navy beans and instant miso soup and a bag of flour, exploded in the center of the table like a white star. Then I heard movement, a rustle and a breath, like someone creeping around in my study. I picked up the cleaver.

"Who's there?" I yelled, my voice quaking and quacking more than I would have prefered. I yelled again, more assertively. "Come out of there right now! I'm calling the cops."

That's when a voice answered, small and soft: "Please don't," and the dead girl stepped from the shadows and into the room.

"Hello, Mona," I said. "Welcome back."

PART V

THE MISRECOGNITIONS

60

FIRST OF ALL, MY NAME'S not Mona. Or Ramona. I'm Veronica Flynn. I never even heard of Mona Doon or Naught or anything till a few weeks ago and I swear I had nothing to do with anybody's death. And your house was like this when I got here. The door was open so I came in and hid just to wait for you. I don't know who did it. But I suspect it was them. The people who hired me. But I don't know their names or who they are or why. I don't know anything. OK. I'll start at the beginning but you have to promise not to call the cops and you have to put down that knife. Like I said, my name's Veronica, but I never liked it so I go by Nica or my friends call me Nic. My mother named me after Veronica Lake, of course. That's my mom all over. Living in fantasy. I don't know much about my dad. He died young and drunk, car crash. Though later I heard her say on the phone he'd moved back to Albania. My mom was always busy working, mostly waiting tables, or sewing at this tailor's or working at this cracker factory, we'd have closets full of crackers, or else chasing her latest loser boyfriend, a bunch of drunks and gamblers and assholes who hit on me as I got older, but for some reason she always thought they would be good influences. She was obsessed with the movies, especially old movies. She'd convince me to stay up and watch the late show with her, even when I was a little kid on school nights, or rent a couple of videos and eat pizza. She'd see anything really, but old movies were the best. The old stars. She hung on to that fantasy, that glamour and love and beauty. I guess I loved the movies too and just being with her, like any kid would, but as I got older I realized not only was it a ridiculous fantasy but those women on the screen didn't even get to live it either. Most of them ended up no better off than my mom. Grace Kelly became a princess of course but then died in a wreck. Kate Hepburn nursing a drunk, waiting her whole life for a married man when she could have had anyone. Ava Gardner, unable to really love anyone till Sinatra, then unable to stand him. Elizabeth Taylor? Enough said. Judy Garland. Marilyn of course. Veronica Lake, my namesake, stunning, perfect, maybe even more perfect than Marilyn, dying drunk and alone from hepatitis. So they didn't even escape, did they? Anyway, I wasn't going that route. It was pathetic and early on I decided I had to get up and out for real. So I focused on school, I got A's, and I focused on being popular, cute, whatever too, because I knew that was important. I learned how to flirt and make the boys like me. I learned what the older men my mom ran around with liked. I learned what the older women liked too, how to appeal to their mothering instinct with sob stories about my mom and her nightmare boyfriends, and how to avoid making them jealous or competitive. It all came easy I guess, though I worked hard. I studied, I held down a job, I played tennis, ran track. I got a scholarship to Harvard. At first the plan was clear, medical school, surgery maybe, maybe cosmetic surgery, help desperate women like my mother who were trying to cling to their men, help desperate men buy bigger penises, whatever. The vanity business. The fear-of-death business. Those are always good. Though looking back now, I should have known I wasn't destined for medicine. I'm not the caretaker type. Sick people disgust me. All that whining. Once a guy I was seeing got the flu, what a baby. Laid in bed in his pajamas asking for soup and worrying about if he had pneumonia. I ditched him immediately. Another time this guy cried. Ridiculous. I couldn't laugh in his face, he was my professor, actually crying about how long it had been since his wife touched him. Yuck. I totally lost my hard-on for him after that, though I had to string it out till the end of the semester. Most female med students are more motherly types. They want to be GPs or OB-GYNs. My God, placating pregnant bitches all day, who could stand it? Or if they're shy they go into research, or pediatrics. Not me. I hate kids. That's why I had my tubes tied. Yes, I said, tubes, when I was eighteen. First-year biology just confirmed what I'd always known, sex is a trick. It's all just an evolutionary con game designed to ensure the survival of the species and of your own genes. So men feel driven to spread their seed and women go into heat when they're around suitable males and release pheromones, like a cloud of perfume that sucks men in, like that cookie smell they pump into the mall. Pleasure is the bait, orgasms are the trick that lures us, women especially, into slavery, motherhood, and a lifetime of servitude to men. Because in female brains, lust combines with another chemical change, another programmed instinctual response that binds us to our offspring long enough for them to mature, again ensuring the genotype continues. Same reason we have the whining gene, the ability of babies to screech in a way that forces us to wake up and feed them or keep them warm or whatever, instead of just sleeping peacefully while they die. We have the cuteness gene. Why are we programmed to adore tiny soft cuddly creatures with big eyes who goo and gaw? So that we won't just eat them or step on them or throw them in the trash. Otherwise puppies and kitties and babies wouldn't stand a chance in this world, would they? They'd be snacks. That's what binds women to their offspring and men to their families, but of course, once the women have children their brain chemistry shifts, and the primary bond is with the child now, and they lose interest in the husband, except as a provider and protector. As a sexual partner, a stud, he's served his purpose: providing sperm. Do you think that's what happened to your wife? She realized you were subpar breeding material? No offense. I don't mean sexually, we fucked and you're normal enough as far as that goes, but how are you in the providing-and-protecting department? I mean, let's face it, there's not much of a future in literature is there? She had to trade up while she could. So she moved on. Sorry. I'm not saying I feel that way, because obviously I'm not looking to breed. And I'd rather have my own money. So that's why I tied my tubes. Because I'd always been promiscuous. I liked sex. It was pleasurable, it was exciting, it relaxed me and got rid of my tension and it's good for the organism, for the blood pressure, skin, muscles. But I wasn't falling for the love trap. That's for losers. Anyway, that's how I got into porn. I liked sex, I liked money, and I wasn't looking for a boyfriend or hubby. It started at Harvard. Competition was a lot stiffer than in high school. Academically I had all the other strivers to worry about. I had the scholarship kids, the financial aid kids, the minorities, the disadvantaged, the black and Latino ghetto kids with something to prove, the Asian or Indian kids whose families worked twenty-four hours a day running a minimart so they could be doctors. It wasn't even enough to make A's. You had to win things, edit things, compete. Then there was the social status competition, which I knew mattered just as much, the style and snobbery competition with the rich white kids whose parents paid top dollar or donated something. The legacies, whose great-granddads went. They were dopes. Fools. George Bush types who could barely read. But I knew that they would still inherit all the money and privilege and I had to win them over too, fit in with them or I'd be their servant. That took money, for clothes, trips, restaurants, whatever. I couldn't be slaving at some work-study job, making minimum wage. I needed real money, like the girls who drove Beamers and took private golf lessons. I couldn't care less about these things. Those girls were just husband hunting, but if I wanted to rise in their world, I needed the equipment. So I started stripping. It was easy money. I knew how to manipulate men by then of course, I'd been doing it my whole life. But the hours were tough, late nights before early class and I was worried: how long before some frat fucks from campus wandered in and recognized me? I wore wigs, makeup, learned to disguise myself even when nude. I made the grades, in class and on laps, but by the time I graduated it was clear I wasn't going to be a doctor. Also my Mom had passed away, from breast cancer, and I needed to make a living. Plan B was B-school, an MBA. I would focus on biotech stocks. But I couldn't afford grad school, at least not the brand names that would get me in the door. So I had the idea to go into porn. I'd always watched a lot of porn. I liked the nasty stuff. Girls getting used like trash by assholes and big-dick retards. I knew I could do what they could. I was an athlete. Plus I hated the cold. I was sick of the Northeast. And I guess part of me was still drawn to Hollywood because of my mother and the old movies. Though of course it's all gone now. Just like traces remain. Like the old mansion Jayne Mansfield bought on Sunset and painted all pink, forty rooms and a heart-shaped pool, for a bad marriage to a bodybuilder that didn't last. It's still there. I think some Arab owns it now. Or the Mormons or Scientologists. Even the movies are nothing now. The actresses aren't mythic creatures, they don't have that charisma, they're just cute little operators, like me I suppose. There are no real stars. Except in porn. In porn everyone is a star, have you noticed? The trashiest, most disposable tramp is a star. Or starlet. No one is in a supporting role, except the men. They are props, literally. Tools used for performing a job. Like a wrench. So anyway, I got a couple names from the manager at my club and went west. My plan was to make a lot of money and invest in stocks online, get out in a couple years with enough to go to school debt-free, maybe even with a house or a condo. Well, the first part went OK. I was indeed a natural at the porn business. Maybe I even kind of overdid it, like fifty movies in two years. Maybe you saw me? I acted under the name Candy Apples? I won some awards. *Weapons of Ass Destruction* won Best Anal. I play like a female Rambo named Bimbo, oiled up and in torn clothes. I get captured and tortured by the enemy and forced to play Russian Roulette with their dicks. I know, right, that was *Deer Hunter,* but it kind of like jumped around to a lot of Vietnam movies for inspiration. We did a sequel *Bimbo 2: First Pud*. What about *Two and a Half Men and One Slut?* That one had two twin brothers, a dwarf, and me. *The Whorin' Identity,* where I wake up and I don't know my name but have an amazing talent to deep throat and there's a butt plug in my bottom with a bank account number on it?

What else? *Sex Toy Story* was cool, though the 3-D sucked. I did a fetish specialty picture, *Phallus in Underwearland*. A Western, *True Slit*, with Rooster Cockring. I suppose there was a certain psychological draw as well. I sort of liked the life, the attention, the adventure, the cheesy glamour, and the power in a way. I was their fantasy, the object of their desires, and there is a lot power and pleasure in that. It's an escape from yourself. But the magic wears off quick. It's tough work, believe me. And the money part didn't work out like I expected. I'm not complaining. I own my condo in Santa Monica and my car. My teeth are all fixed. But the golden age of porn is over, as a profession I mean. With the Internet flooding the whole world in free sex. Millions of clips and films. Thousands of amateurs posting themselves for free. Chat rooms. Video hookups. Live cams. The profit margin is nowhere. I was smarter than most girls. I bought stocks and ran my own website instead of buying fake tits and a junkie guitar-playing boyfriend, but I wasn't ever going to get rich. And I lost a lot in the market. We all did. And it's a short career. Like all athletes. A small window. I didn't want to be a thirty-year-old porn slut. I know it's hard to believe but after awhile having wild sex all the time with hot people in beautiful settings for money . . . it gets really depressing, actually. I'd see the women who'd been at it too long, the ones who got into drugs, the nymphos who had to top themselves, push the degradation for some reason, the biggest gang bang, whatever. I didn't want that to be me. So when the offer for private work came around, I took it. It was call girl work, basically. Super high-end. A very rich man with very elaborate fantasies. The male libido is a strange thing, the mind of a fetishistic or perhaps ritualistic fantasist is a strange thing. He'd seen my movies and was looking for a certain physical type. There were certain outfits, makeup, hair. Characters I had to play and scenarios to act out. Dialogue. I suppose I became an actress sort of. Much more than in my actual films, believe me. Maybe even closer to a real artist. But you would know more about that than me. That room where I was hid-

ing, is that where you write? You have a ton of books, almost all fiction, too, I noticed when I was crouched behind the desk. Yes, poetry, by fiction I meant poetry too. Yes OK philosophy and literary
theory but those are sort of like fiction too, right? I mean it's not real
like science is real, is it? Not like medicine or economics or even history. Yes I saw that, but that's art history. Art history is like the history of a fiction isn't it? The story of a story. That just proves my
point. Which is how you can be so learned and wise and know nothing about the actual real world. Like literally nothing. I mean facts.
Real facts. Like how much blood is in your body or how much
money is in your bank. I know both those things all the time. I bet
you don't know either, ever, do you? About 3.5 quarts. No, me. You're
bigger so like 5.5. Anyway, what I'm saying is I'm a practical girl. I've
never seen the point of art. I prefer facts, bodies, numbers, things.
Money. That's why I took the job. A lot of money. Like thousands for
a night. I saw very quickly I could pay off my debts, build my nest
egg, and go to business school if I wanted. But there was more to it
than that, I realize, now that I find myself in this mess. I was intrigued by the idea of living out my childhood fantasies, you know,
my mother's silly unfulfilled dreams that she instilled in me with
those old movies. Grace Kelly and Cary Grant in *To Catch a Thief,* Bo-
gie and Bacall. Kate Hepburn. The porn shoots are a kind of lame
fantasy, sure, but they are also a kind of realism aren't they? They're
happening. Like documentaries. This was different. This was theater. Art. I drove to a random spot and parked my car. A limo was
waiting. I climbed in. A man in the back, always the same man, my
escort or manager like, very handsome and polite. He would explain
the role and what I had to do for his boss very carefully. We'd drive
to the location, I was blindfolded, so I never knew where, but I was
led into a large bedroom with every luxury except there were no
windows behind the curtains. I was provided with a costume and
makeup. I'd practice my poses, my lines. Sometimes there were even
written scripts and photos or drawings demonstrating exactly how

to stand, sit, walk, or speak. If it was a long process there'd be food, a shower, even a nap. Then I would cross a hall or step through a sliding door and meet the man himself. The client. The boss. Sometimes I would punish him. I'd be dressed in a red silk robe, nude beneath, and I'd tie him to a cross and I'd whip him while forcing him to recite his crimes. I still remember: murderer, fornicator, liar, thief, pervert, scum. I had to call him a hack and a commercial sellout. He'd beg for mercy and kiss my feet and thank me for punishing him. Then in the end I had to forgive him and like hold him and tell him it was all right, that he was a good boy and a great artist and I loved him. I had to tell him he was a genius and that I respected his work so much. Once I had to dress like a nun, although with stockings and a garter belt under my habit and perform an exorcism on him while he was tied to the bed, sprinkling him with holy water and spanking him with a huge cross to cast out the demons. Then of course the forgiving at the end. I had to let him suck my boob a little too, which was sort of gross, but harmless. The scary nights were when he would pretend to sacrifice me. It was like a pagan ritual or Satanic I guess. There was a five-pointed star, like a pentagram drawn on the floor, with candles burning at the points and torches. Now I was in a white robe and he was in black, hooded. He tied me down and chanted over me. He had a wafer, you know the sacramental thing, and wine, and he'd make a big deal out of desecrating them, spitting on them, stepping on them, sticking them between my butt cheeks and then mumbling the Our Father while he took it out with his mouth. Silly. I know. I probably would've giggled if the whole atmosphere wasn't so spooky. Then he'd sacrifice me. The first time I was terrified, although I'd been warned and assured and really the ropes holding me down weren't too tight. I could have slipped out pretty easy. In fact, he liked me to struggle but I had to be careful or they'd fall off. Still when I saw him kneeling there above me with that huge dagger held high above him, yelling, Hail Satan! I freaked. He brought it down right between my tits. Of course it didn't hurt at all, not really. A slight pinch as the rubber blade retracted and then the fake blood squirted out. He went nuts then. He actually jerked off on my belly. I never once saw his face. He wore a mask. Ridiculous, I know, the whole thing. It just seemed like a harmless joke. A lot less work than porn for a lot more money. It seemed like a crazy dream except I woke up holding an envelope full of cash. I'd live my very normal daily life. I'm really very conservative, believe it or not, very conventional. I'd go to the gym and yoga, clean my house, look after my portfolio. I like to cook. And then, maybe once a week or once a month, I'd get a call, always from that man, telling me what time and where to meet. Anyway, I'm rambling but I guess it's sort of like an excuse or an explanation for how I ended up in this fix, how I let myself drift into it. One day the man, the agent or manager guy said they had a different kind of role for me. That's what he called it, a role or a game, like it was all make-believe and fun. I was to learn my character, my name, and back-story. I moved into the rented house they provided, complete with props, clothes. There was a man, they told me. The man was you. I let you spy on me, watch me dance and touch myself. I put on a show, like in porn. Yes of course I knew you were out there, hiding in the bushes. It was hard not to laugh when that little poodle had you cowering. And I knew it was you at the beach and in the lingerie shop. How could I not know? Your wig? I let you follow me around like they said and left the clues. I left my panties for you in the trash. Did you take them? No? Huh. I was sure you would. Then I went up to Big Sur. I waited for you in the bar and they told me what to talk about and how to act. To say my name was Ramona Doon and act all femme fatale–like. They said that was your thing. Then I was supposed to take you back to the hotel. To get you relaxed and you know, to seduce you. And then disappear. I just hopped over the balcony and the agent guy was there, waiting to help me down. He had the room below. Then we left and he paid me, a lot, and that was it. Look, I knew it wasn't really a game or a practical joke like they said,

I'm not that stupid. I knew they were conning you for some reason. I thought insurance or blackmail or something. Catching you with a girl. That's all. And I was scared by then, too. I wasn't entirely truthful before, you see. They weren't my only clients. I was performing a similar service for other men, other rich guys who I met in hotels and well one of them turned out to be a cop. I was arrested and I was out on bail and really scared of jail, of how it would affect my future, everything. Well they knew, this agent, he somehow knew all about it, which right away frightened me. How did he know? Was he involved with the cops? He said he could fix it, make it go away, and he did. As soon as I agreed to the job with you, I got a call the next day. All the charges were dropped and the whole thing was erased from my record. It was gone. So I understood then, these were powerful people, and I was even more afraid of them now than the police, but I swear I didn't know about the suicide. I didn't know about a death. I thought I, she, the character, Mona, would just disappear like a mystery for you. I thought she was make-believe, a fiction. But I was worried, so I kept an eye out, watched the news and read the local papers online and then I saw the little piece in the police blotter about a body found, a missing girl who jumped to her death, Mona Naught. And I knew it was a setup. I became terrified. I couldn't go to the cops. I was a criminal, right? A hooker. And I was involved, some kind of accomplice. I had no names to give them, no addresses, nothing. And apparently they had a lot of power with the police. I slipped into the inquest in disguise. I saw you and heard that doctor, Parker, describe the girl I'd played. I started to get paranoid and think I was being followed. That my place had been searched. Not like this, not wrecked, but things were moved, or gone. Then I read about Parker dying. And I was afraid to go home, to call anyone. Who would I even call? I have no friends, not really. No family. No one I can turn to. I was trapped. So I came here to you. For help. I'm sorry. I'm sorry I got you involved in this, whatever it is. I don't blame you for hating me, but I can help, we can help each other. I have money. Here, with me. Cash. Just don't call me Mona again or Ramona or anything like that. I hate that name now. I wish I'd never heard of that fucking girl.

61

THE DOORBELL BUZZED. It took a second to register, as Mona or, I guess Nic (or Nica?) was telling me her story in my kitchen, where we were both still standing across from each other. It wasn't a comfortable arrangement for conversation, with me gripping the cleaver, ready to spring if she ran, and her in the doorway, hands on the frame, as if awaiting permission to enter. The sun was bright now, shining in my eyes, giving her the tactical advantage in case of combat, and washing her blond hair (which was real: this gold or Mona's black?) with a blurry nimbus, suitable for a ghost visiting the fall of the house of Kornberg. The scene was hypnotic, and the drone of the doorbell seemed far off, like an alarm clock intruding upon deep sleep. Plus, no one ever used the bell. They knocked or walked in. I barely knew what it sounded like.

But Nic reacted like a hunted animal. She ducked low, as at a rifle's cock. "Who's that?" she demanded.

"I don't know," I said.

"Just ignore it."

It buzzed again.

"I'd better check," I said. "Killers don't usually ring first do they?"

"No one can see me here." She looked frantic.

"OK," I said. "Hide in that room. But don't move or touch anything. Just wait."

She nodded and vanished back through the door, then popped her head out. "The knife," she whispered.

"Right." I put it on the counter as she slipped out of sight, then cleverly moved it again and hid it under a towel. Then I went to the door. "Coming!" I yelled. As soon as I peeked through the peephole I knew. They were plainclothes cops. Two tightly groomed men in blue suits, one white in his forties with mustache and red tie, one brown in his thirties, blue tie, no mustache.

As always when authority appears, I panicked immediately. Were they looking for Nic? Or Mona? Or any of them? Would they accuse me of killing Kevin? What about the break-in and trashing of my house? Did they somehow know? I suddenly felt the need to conceal the wreckage, although it was of course my house. I was the victim and could trash it if I wanted anyhow.

"Who is it?" I asked in voice that sounded thin and strangled and not very convincing. They know I know, I thought.

"It's the police ma'am. Sorry to disturb you."

I cleared my throat and opened the door a few inches. "Hi," I said. "Good morning." I stepped out onto the landing, shutting the door behind me casually. I realized I was still dressed oddly, but these were LA cops. I could have been naked for all they cared.

"Good morning, sir," the white one said, holding out his ID. "I'm Sergeant Northing. This is Detective Dante." He pulled out a pad. "Are you Mr. Kornbrenner?"

"No," I said eagerly, hoping the guy they meant lived up the block. "I'm Kornberg."

"Yes, sorry, sir, that's what we mean." Northing made a note on his pad. Dante spoke up.

"You witnessed a crime recently. The suicide of a Mona Naught?"

Probably I should have blurted out the truth right then and run to their car for protection. She's here! Hiding in my office! Shoot! But I played it cool. "Right," I said. "That was me. But I already gave a complete statement and I don't know anything more. Nothing else has happened at all. Except normal everyday things, of course." I chuckled casually.

"Yes, sir," Dante said. "You were very cooperative, thank you. However there's been a small problem and we're liaising with the

San Louis Obispo County Police on this one, just contacting everyone connected with the case in the hopes of clearing this up."

"A problem?" I wondered lightly. Like she's not dead, perhaps?

"Yes, sir." The white one consulted his pad again. "As part of the
normal postautopsy processing, the deceased's fingerprints were
added to our federal databases. Well, it took a while but we got a hit.
From the INS actually. That's why it didn't pop right away."

"So?" I was relaxing a bit. I didn't see what this had to do with me
or the girl cowering in my house.

"Well, the match in the INS computer had no connection with
any Mona Naught. Apparently, these prints belong to a Mexican national who was reported missing by her family some years ago. Her
name was . . . Maria . . . Consuela . . ."

Dante stepped in as whitey began torturously overenunciating
the Spanish. "Maria Consuela Martinez Garcia, from Tepic, Nayarit.
Does that name ring a bell?"

"No, not at all," I said. Another girl? Another name? How many
were there?

"Seems she first entered the country back in 1990 on a student
visa."

"Sorry." I shook my head, answering honestly for once. "I have no
idea what this means."

"OK. No problem. Since her death has already been ruled a suicide, and no one else claimed the body, the coroner went ahead and
released it to the family in Mexico."

"I see," I said. To them the case was closed. It didn't matter who
the dead girl was, as long as they could file her away under something and shut the drawer.

"Hey, you know what?" I added, in a casual tone. "I didn't really
know the woman, but still, after all, I'd like to send her family a
card. Do you mind if I get that address from you?"

"Certainly, sir." Dante smiled his approval and Northing printed
carefully into his notebook and tore out the page. "Here you go. I'm
sure they'll appreciate the thought."

62

STEPPING BACK THROUGH my own door was like stepping into space. Perhaps the house would be gone completely, leaving only a green hill. It all seemed equally possible. My wife might even be back, sitting on the sofa, complaining about the mess.

Nic, it seemed, was real, so far. Or at least she hadn't changed into a cat or anything. Still, rather like a cat, she poked her head out of the kitchen as soon as I shut the door.

"Is it safe to come out?"

"Not really. But come on anyway. We have to go see someone."

She stepped away, shoulders back. "Who?"

"My boss. The one who hired me to follow you. He's a detective. He can help."

She narrowed her gaze, figuring the odds. "Why should I trust him?"

I shrugged. "Don't trust anyone. I wouldn't. Especially not you. You're the biggest liar of all. I'm just a schmuck."

She seemed to find this reassuring. She removed my meat cleaver from where she had been concealing it under her skirt and laid it on the counter. "OK. Let's go see the boss."

I opened the door and made sure the cops were gone before ushering her out. "Actually, I thought this guy was a total nut job up till a few hours ago. Now I think he might be a genius."

63

MRS. MOON LET US IN. Lonsky, regarding Nic without shock or surprise, heard our story in the study while his mother made an egg salad sandwich for "the girl," who admitted, when Lonksy asked, that she had not eaten anything but Tic Tacs for a day or more. As was his wont, he settled deep in the brown leather armchair, listening like a log until she finished her tale and then lapsed into uneasy silence, awaiting his response. He sighed. A finger twitched. She gave me a look. I nodded reassuringly. Roz came in with a sandwich and a glass of ice tea.

"Here you go, hon," she said. "I put sliced cuke and tomato on the sandwich. Hope that's OK."

"Oh yes, thank you." Nic sat up eagerly and balanced the plate on her knees.

Perhaps sniffing the food, Lonsky raised his lids. "Even with sliced fruit, that is hardly a sufficiently nutritious meal."

"I know what you're going to say, Solly," Roz said, wiping her hands on her sky blue slacks as she left, "but to me cukes and tomatoes are still veggies. Have been for as long as I've been alive. Never mind what modern science discovers."

"It's hardly a question of scientific discovery," he told Nic, who nodded, wide-eyed, and wiped a bit of egg from the corner of her mouth. "They have seeds. They grow on vines. Hence, they are indeed fruit."

"Is that all you have to say?" I blurted, losing my cool after urging calm on Nic. "Jesus fuck, Solar. This is her! The mystery girl. Someone clearly hired her to fake Mona's death. So it was murder, like you said. Now they killed Kevin. And I guess Doctor Parker too. Who's next? Me? They broke into my house. If I wasn't out, watching my friend's goddamn store burn down by the way, I might be dead too. This whole thing is a nightmare, that you got me into, and the only insight you can offer is that cucumbers are fruit? Hey genius, guess what? Fruit is fucking nutritious! Maybe you should eat more of it yourself, you crazy fat bastard!" I stopped and caught my breath. My hands were shaking. Nic stared in amazement, chewing, her eyes and cheeks wide. Lonsky considered my statement thoughtfully, as shame flowed in over my anger and fear.

"Look," I said. "I'm sorry. . . . You're not fat. I mean, well . . ."

He waved a finger. "Not at all." He spoke in his normal, even, round tones. "You are quite right. The matter of nutrition is secondary. You will eat on the way to Mexico."

"Mexico?"

"Certainly. Although you might have phrased it with greater aplomb, in essence your assessment of the case thus far is correct. As I suspected, Mona has been murdered, and you and I have been used to make it appear a suicide. Now all loose threads are being cut, I'm afraid. The questions you raise as to the underlying purpose of their enterprise are also quite valid. We must ascertain the motive. And the answer, I suggest, lies to the south."

"This is nuts. You're going to get me killed. I say we go to the cops."

"Not wise at this juncture, I'm afraid. As Miss Flynn indicates, our adversaries seem to have a great deal of influence with the police and we have little evidence on our side. We can't even offer a suspect."

"Well, I'm not going to Mexico. I quit. I'll go to Canada instead. It's a lot safer. And cooler this time of year."

He shrugged. "I believe you already quit yesterday."

Stalemate. There was a long pause while Nic swallowed her sandwich and sipped her tea. "You're a detective, right Mr. Lonsky?" she asked. "A private eye?"

"In a manner of speaking, yes."

"Very private," I muttered.

"Well I want to hire you." She reached into her bag and took out an envelope. "I have five thousand dollars cash right here. I want to hire you to figure this out, and to protect me." She put the envelope on the desk. "And I want to go to Mexico, with you," she told me. "I'm not safe here anyway. Neither are you. You know they'll find us eventually. And also, I feel . . . bad. I want the people who killed that girl to be caught."

Lonksy nodded. "I will accept your case, Miss Flynn. But I require an assistant to do the legwork."

They both looked at me. I sighed deeply and rubbed my eyes. The exhaustion of these last two days suddenly washed over me. Nightmares unfolding without sleep. I nodded. "How may I be of assistance?"

"Good," Lonsky said, lifting the envelope. "I shall take one thousand as retainer and return the rest." He removed his dough, and handed her back the envelope. "Now Kornberg, go home quickly and pack a few things. Don't tarry, it might not be safe. And if you have anything of special value, take it or bring it here."

"You might want to change too," Nic said. "No offense. I like what you have on. But they're kind of old-fashioned down there."

"Good point, Ms. Flynn." Lonsky nodded. "Do put on something more appropriate."

"Look who's talking," I said, and explained to Nic. "He dressed me in these clothes. These are his mom's pants."

She shrugged. "Hey, whatever. I don't need to know."

Lonsky went on: "Then proceed south to the border. Stop to eat, drive safely, don't be foolish, but make sure you are in Mexico by nightfall."

64

SOLAR HAD SAID TO TAKE anything of special value. I thought about that as I changed and threw some clothes in a bag. Was there anything? I couldn't take the TV or computers. Pictures? Treasured mementos? Not really. This was Lala's house, I realized, and I stayed in it like a long-term guest, though I wouldn't admit that to a divorce judge. Just that one little room was mine, the office. I lived in there with my only real possessions, my books, in a kind of fort built inside the larger home. And my own novels? To say they were personal or important was to miss the point completely: I hated them. They had ruined me. I was nothing, and it was all their fault. I loved my books like a sober alcoholic loves a case of twenty-year-old Scotch or a man in prison loves the cash he stole, but would I save them from a sinking ship? I decided to grab the copies from my bottom desk drawer, if only for symbolic value. I'd leave them in the trunk.

The office was worse than I thought. Almost every book was off the shelves, dumped in broken-spined heaps, my carefully ordered sections and subsections now split and piled like firewood, a bonfire ready to go. I waded in for my manuscripts, but the desk was tipped over and emptied, so I had to sort through the mass of papers and files and forgotten stolen office supplies and make extra sure before I gave in to the horrible surge of loss that I admit I didn't expect to feel and that almost embarrassed me in its hollow, howling intensity: My books were gone. All of them. My novels. All the drafts. The clean copies, ready to be sent to interested publishers. The backup CDs. The external hard drive. All gone.

65

"I'M SORRY ABOUT YOUR BOOKS." We were on the freeway, headed south, chewing the last cold fries from the In-N-Out Burger we'd hit on our getaway. We had the windows down, and soft air buffeted my head like a pillow fight, cushioning my ears. Cars streamed around us, four lanes each way, their forms blurred by speed and fumes, the heat from their engines cooking out and the sun blasting windshields and bumpers. Here and there a pair of running lights bled whitely in the daylight. The sky was clear but the wind smelled like poison.

"I mean," she said, her hair jumping around in a mad scribble, "sorry about your novels. Your writing." She pushed back her sunglasses and dipped an arm in the wind, letting a cigarette go skipping and sparking in my rearview before vanishing under some wheels. I hated when people did that. I gritted my teeth and faced forward. I didn't want to discuss my books. She breathed smoke at me. "That really sucks."

"Yeah," I said. "Thanks."

"Can I ask you something?"

"Maybe."

"Why did you write them?"

I sighed loudly. She couldn't take a hint. "I forget."

"No I mean, why that kind? Why not normal stories, that people like to read? Maybe you could have sold them."

"I don't know. Brain damage?"

"Seriously though. Why not write regular realistic stories?"

"Are regular stories realistic? Does your life work like that?" I glanced at her, obscurely accusing, and she looked away with a frown.

"Whatever."

I went on: "No, really. When you take a shower, do the thoughts in your head sound like a normal book? Is there a narrator saying she did this and that? What about first person? Is the I who you are now the same as the I you were at ten years old, or the I you forgot you were at three, or the I you were two minutes ago when you were thinking of something else that you can't recall now? Where did that person go?"

She shrugged. She didn't care. No doubt she was sorry she'd asked, but now that my mouth was open, I felt unable to shut it. "What about other people?" I demanded. "Do you really know them as whole characters, complete with backstory, motive, and quirky traits? Do they have arcs? Or are they just passing glimpses, bits and angles that you have to put together yourself and that keep changing? I thought I was learning Mona's backstory. She turned out to be you. What about time? Do you really experience it as a single line, a freeway moving forward? Or does it jump and skip, speed up and slow down? Does the past erupt into the present? Does the future retreat or attack? Does the present escape us? Is it ever even here? Does your life have a plot?"

"It does now. So does yours."

"Ha. True. But that's not a good thing is it? It turns out life was more pleasant as a meaningless mess. Plot is malevolence. Closure is death."

"So you just like hate any book with a story?"

"Of course not. I mean, Shakespeare has a plot. Greek tragedies. Stendahl and Balzac and Jane Austen. Homer. But there's a point where things shift, with modernism, I guess. Really a similar thing happens in painting. Attention turns away from naturalistic representation as we begin to suspect that the established version of reality isn't the whole truth. So the novel turns inward. It becomes about consciousness, language, memory, thought, and feeling. That's the twentieth century."

"And the twenty-first? What's next?"

"Nothing's next. It's over. Turns out the story of literature does have an ending. It's Facebook and reality TV. It's video games on cell phones. No one has the attention span to read *The Man Without Qualities*. No one can sit still and focus hard enough to untangle *Finnegans Wake* or develop the patience to face *Gravity's Rainbow*. Who will ever open those books again? The late great novelists. It makes sense in retrospect. They were recording the death of their own art form. As a medium disappears, there's always a final explosion of virtuosity. A kind of decadent, baroque eruption of style that no longer has any object or audience but itself. A last flower. So even if I didn't just completely suck, I was still born with a useless ability, like archery or taking shorthand. So it doesn't matter if my books were erased. No one was ever going to read them. It's like I speak a dying language, Navajo or Yiddish. And the sad truth is: I have a hard time even remembering it myself."

On that, I felt, rather plaintive note, I fell silent and stared, steely-eyed, at the vanishing point ahead. Nic said nothing. It was a lot to absorb. I let a long pause pass while my ideas sank in. Then I heard a deep breath, though definitely not a sigh of sympathy, more like a murmur of content. I glanced over. Sure enough, she was snoozing. I'd bored her unconscious. Another reader lost.

Beckett was right: after the greatness of Proust, and Joyce, and Kafka, all that was left was a voice, talking to itself about itself, alone in the void of a skull, with no one listening, until it too ran down and stopped. From his book *The Unnamable* to my own pale offerings, which I might as well have titled *The Unpublishable*, *The Unreadable*, and now *The Unwritable*. Coming soon: *The Unthinkable*. The End.

66

I DROVE IN SILENCE all the way to San Diego, while the imposter slept fitfully beside me. She snored softly and scratched herself once between the legs. Tiny drops of sweat formed on her upper lip and gathered between her breasts, like warm breath appearing on a glass. Her skirt billowed softly and fell. Her nipples stiffened and softened under the fabric of her shirt, responding to some invisible caress, a breeze or a dream. Who knows what she was struggling with, there beside me? Her hands gripped each other. She drooled.

I desired and despised her in equal measure. She made me uneasy to a degree that seemed out of proportion to the compact, soft person dribbling on herself beside me. Of course she had deceived me and drawn me into this mess, and I suppose I resented her for that. She had outwitted me, proving to be far more cunning an operative than I could ever hope to become. Tricking me was child's play for her. The hard part was pretending to fall for my own ridiculous clown show.

But then again, so what? I had never claimed to be much of a detective, and she too had been tricked and used. The deeper shame, the sore spot that made me want to argue with anything she said, about books or plans or where to stop for gas, was realizing how badly I had wanted to believe her act. How deeply had I embraced her thin lies, desperately grasping at the illusion she dangled before me—the possibility, the slender, pathetic hope, that I, a foolish, aging, almost-divorced failure, an introverted, deluded, prematurely bitter, never-was and never-would-be writer, an overall total reject, could be, even for a day and a night, the hero of a true drama, a turbulent, passionate, romantic, tragic adventure, costarring a mysterious and beautiful woman: it was a kiddy story that she herself saw through in a blink, and had never believed for one second of her young life. I was the one born yesterday, the boob off the turnip truck, the sucker. She was the wise guy, the adult. So what if I wrote novels no one could understand? She read me like an open book. That was why I couldn't stand her: just like any good writer, she told me the truth about myself.

67

WE WERE NEARLY THERE when I remembered: Buck Norman had copies of my novels. I was so happy I hit the accelerator and had to slam the brakes before I ran into the slowing cars ahead. Nic bounced forward, then jerked back, choked by her seat belt, something I secretly enjoyed.

"What's happening?" she mumbled, her tongue thick with sleep.

"Nothing." I honked. "Some nut cut me off. We're almost there. I have to make a call."

Traffic was heavy now, approaching the border, an epic slow jam of tourists, truckers, workers, and products heading endlessly back and forth. I pulled into a lot that offered long-term day rates. Nic rubbed her eyes in the mirror and sucked on her empty soda while I frantically searched for Buck Norman's number on my phone. Finally, I got through.

"Buck Norman's office, Russ speaking."

"Hey, Russ. It's Sam Kornberg."

"Sam! How's it going?"

"Good, good, listen: I wanted to tell Buck that even though I'm superpsyched to start working with you guys, I've kind of had a personal crisis come up."

"Oh no . . ."

"No big deal. I just have to leave town for a few days and I wanted to let you know."

"OK, no problem."

"I also have a favor to ask. My computer had a meltdown and I was wondering, those copies of my books that Buck had, could you maybe get those to me or make me copies? I totally lost my files. It's a nightmare."

"Don't worry. I have them right here."

"Really? Great. Thanks Russ, I appreciate it."

"Sure thing. Safe journey."

I locked the car and we joined the line of tourists filing over the border, like one big parking lot and ticket booth, all headed for the amusement park of Mexico: sex, booze, highs, greasy food, cheap prescription drugs.

"Who was that on the phone?" Nic asked.

"No one. It's about a writing job. But I remembered they have copies of my books."

The overwhelming sense of relief I felt surprised me, but I was too tired to figure it all out. Sleeplessness, stress, fear, and freeway numbness had drained my brain. My eyes burned and there was a low hum in my head like a fluorescent tube on the blink. The mob of tourists flowed around me like pink cartoon blobs, hairy legs, angry red necks, white arms speckled with prickly heat. Packs of children attacked from nowhere, nipping at our knees, brandishing tiny boxes of Chiclets and phony silver jewelry. Mariachi music lurched from open bars and tequila fumes rippled in the heat. I smelled burning grease, sweat, dogshit and suntan lotion. The sun was a white disk. This was why it was hard to think fast in Southern California. The blank brightness made me feel like I'd been hit across the head with a two-by-four. I was stunned, like a cow heading down the chute.

"I have to sleep," I told Nic. "I'm going to end up in a ditch without a kidney."

She snorted, but said, "I know a place we can crash. There's a hotel I've used before on the next block. It's safe and fairly clean."

"What do you mean 'used'?" I asked, but she ignored me and I trailed her into a doorway and up a flight of stairs. The dark, narrow hall was dubious, but as promised, once she pushed through the inner door, we were in a small lobby smelling of disinfectant, where a young man in a pressed white shirt and flat, parted black hair greeted us politely from a desk. To my amazement, Nic addressed him in rapid Spanish. He nodded quickly, *Sí señorita,* and retrieved the key.

"Did you ask for adjoining rooms? It's safer."

"I asked for one room. It's even safer."

"For you maybe."

"Don't worry." She patted my arm. "I won't jump your bones this time. If you recall I got paid to do that." With that, she led me down the narrow, tiled hall. The room was tiny, clearly partitioned with the thinnest drywall from a larger former room, with a preformed bathroomette containing a plastic toilet and a shower. The mattress was thin foam over a plywood base. I took off my shoes and lay down and was asleep. Nic poked me. I opened one eye. She was in her panties, removing her bra from under her shirt in that complex way women have.

"You know, that phone call you made reminded me of something. What was that guy's name again?"

"Buck Norman. He's a director," I told the pillow. "A storyteller really."

"What?"

"Nothing. He's hiring me to write something, supposedly. We'll see."

"No, not him. The guy you spoke to, who you said had your books."

"Russ? Russell something."

"Yeah. My client. Not the guy himself, but the one who worked for him. His procurer, I guess. The one who managed everything, told me what to do, paid me. Like I said, they were super crafty, but one time I heard a chambermaid call him Mr. Russ. I didn't remember till I heard you and it rang a bell."

My eyes opened. I blinked at the window, where a thick Mexican blanket glowed with Mexican sun. "What did he look like?"

"I don't know. Dark hair. Six foot. One-eighty maybe. Long face. Wide forehead. Narrow nose."

"Take it easy, I'm not a sketch artist. Did he have kind of a TV star look? Wavy hair, white smile, tan?"

"Yeah that's it. You think it's the same guy?"

"Maybe." Now I was awake again. I sat up and looked in my pants for my phone. "I'm going to call Lonksy and tell him."

"There's a lot of guys named Russ around, I'm sure. It's probably just a weird coincidence, don't you think?" she said, yawning.

"Probably. But Mr. Lonsky doesn't believe in weird coincidences. That's why he's a genius. My phone's not working."

"No. You're out of the country now, remember, genius?"

"Right."

"We can call him from a pay phone after we nap."

"Right." I remained sitting up, my mind swirling pointlessly, like a drain. A thought was struggling to declare itself but gravity was pulling it down.

Nic tugged my hand. "Lie down," she said.

"Right." I lay down.

"Shut your eyes," she said.

"Right." I shut them.

"Now sleep," she said.

I slept.

68

WHEN I AWOKE NIC was gone. Panicked, I jumped up and dressed, but then found the note on her pillow, "back soon—relax," so I undressed again and took a shower that was more like a lukewarm sprinkle. Still, it helped, and I was feeling halfway human by the time she walked back in, now in jeans and a fresh T-shirt, and gave me an excellent café con leche, the Styrofoam warm in my hand, a skin of brown milk over the coffee. It was perfect. She'd found a short flight to Puerto Vallarta, she told me, where we'd change for the bus to Tepic, the small provincial capital of the tiny state of Nayarit, where our now Mexican mystery lady was born and where she was to be laid to rest tomorrow.

We climbed in a cab. Hadn't my wife once warned me to never take a cab in Mexico? They were notorious kidnappers of dumb wealthy gringos. But as Nic asked for the *aeropuerto,* a word I recognized at least, I admitted that the miniature old man who nodded and stuck a smoldering brown cigarillo between brown gums looked harmless enough, except for secondhand smoke. Then, without warning, he kamikazied into traffic, leaning on the whining accelerator of his beat-to-shit Toyota and drifting laterally across a spinning circle of delirious vehicles. A Tijuana traffic circle seemed to function like a centrifuge, sending cars flying everywhere. There were no seat belts, of course. And a brain-size nest of cracks in the passenger's half of the windshield let me know what would happen if I made any false moves. Nic pulled out a fresh pack of cigarettes and lit up happily.

"It's nice to be back in Mexico," she said, leaning back and exhaling. "It's so easygoing."

We somehow got to the airport alive and, as my fear of Mexican driving segued into a fear of Mexican flying, I found an international phone and called Lonsky. I was nervous and weirdly guilty about confessing the Buck Norman connection, out of loyalty or sympathy or perhaps charity. I was sorry for the lonely nut and felt bad abandoning him.

His own interpretation differed slightly. "I see," he said after listening to my recitation. "Well, the motive for your reticence is clear. Of course you were afraid to tell me about your sudden and rather surprising success as a writer because you wanted so desperately for it to be true, and you knew I would shatter it, however unwillingly. In any case, the pieces now fit without doubt. First, you encounter this Russ person at Dr. Parker's office. Clearly the undisclosed board member he represented was this Mr. Normal."

"Norman. He's very famous . . ."

"I do not attend the cinema. I find the stories ludicrous and the seats insufficiently commodious. In any case, this Norman, famous as you say, suddenly wishes to employ you to write for him, a highly paid and urgent but vague assignment that would necessitate immediately terminating your service with me as well as being out of your house while it is ransacked. And now, thanks to Ms. Flynn's fine memory, we know the same Russ was the one who facilitated her work as a courtesan, allowing us to consider Mr. Norman as perhaps the unknown masked client and also as quite possibly the prime mover behind the plan to kill Mona and use the three of us to make it appear as a suicide." He paused for a breath.

"But why? What motive could he have?"

"That we cannot yet know. But I suspect it has something to do with the third part of the trilogy, the lost film of Zed Naught's suicide. And with Mona."

69

IN PUERTO VALLARTA WE ate smoked marlin tacos at a stand by the airport and glimpsed the marlin-blue sea before connecting for the bus inland. A Mexican bus ride is different: the danger of travel has created a system of higher-end luxury buses cruising on safer, smoother, and theoretically faster toll roads. Luxury meant doilies on the headrests and blaring Latin disco, not necessarily effective air conditioning or shocks.

It was a long ride, with many stops. We passed dusty valleys and ridges of bright rock, where at each stop men dressed like cowboys in tight Wranglers, pointy boots, and big hats came outside and looked the bus over or greeted the driver while long-haired women watched from doorways and kids peeked from behind their legs. We passed through a tunnel of jungle, green umbrella leaves sweeping the roof, and hanging vines brushing the windows. Old ladies got on with every conceivable cargo, woven plastic bags of vegetables, bananas, blankets, coffee, then got off again fifteen minutes down the road in front of another, identical little town. There was an ancient woman in men's overalls with a tiny face like an old plum, purpled and folded into hundreds of wrinkles, covered in fine white fur. There was an old man on a bench watching us go by, eating a tomato from his hand like an apple, in big bites. We passed Indians in bright clothes with embroidered bags over their shoulders, selling crafts roadside, waiting for the bus or walking along with their children. It's like a soft blow to the heart. When was the last time you saw an Indian family strolling down the sidewalk in LA, New York, Chicago, Missouri, New Jersey, Miami? Finally, shaken by the mumbling engine and lulled by the heat, Nic and I both fell asleep, sticky and leaning together. I woke with a start when she elbowed me. We were in Tepic.

The bus left us in the central square, where as if to mock me the sleepy little cinema was playing an import from up north, *Fritz: El robot con corazón — una película de Buck Norman.*

"Bastard," I muttered under my breath.

We dropped our luggage at a small hotel before taking a local bus, a van really, to where the Garcia family lived, on a quiet, run-down block.

The street was formed from stones — not cobblestones or paving stones — just plain rocks, gathered at random and dug into the dirt to form a path that was more like a riverbed than a road. Open sewers ran along the high curbs, past homes and the occasional corner shop or bar. Skinny dogs slept undisturbed. The cars rolled around them, lurching and halting over the raw rock. The house fronts were walled, whitewashed plaster or cinder block, with iron gates and shards of broken glass stuck in the cement along the tops. The waxy green wings of orange trees were visible here and there. We heard chickens and children and a faint, laughing TV.

The gate to their house was open. It was a lot nicer inside: a sheltered courtyard with a hand-set flagstone floor, fruit trees and sunflowers, a bench and a freshly washed Toyota Corolla. The house was a single story, with a small barred window in the front and a shadowy open door. A man in a black cowboy shirt, dark jeans, and black Stetson stepped out.

"*Buenas tardes,*" we said.

"*Buenas tardes,*" he responded.

Nic explained in Spanish that we were friends from America, passing through, and wanted to pay our respects. He seemed somewhat confused, Tepic was hardly a major crossroads, but he nodded politely and welcomed us in. He was a neighbor, he said, who lived a few streets away. We stepped into a dim living room, tile-floored, with cement walls and a low ceiling. There was a thick rug and a red plush couch covered in plastic with a matching recliner. There was a huge antique cabinet-style TV with another, flat screen TV on top of it. The remote was inside a plastic Ziploc bag. There was a grandfather clock in a corner, stopped at 3:10. There was a large crucifix, a picture of Mary, and a calendar from a supermarket on the wall. We could glimpse action in the kitchen, women bustling, dishes clanking, and see through to a yard out back, but in here people sat in shadowed silence. The neighbor introduced us. Two older aunts in shiny black dresses, one fat, one thin. An uncle with a thick gray mustache and dark wraparound shades. I realized, when he held his hand out to shake while facing slightly off at an angle, smiling at the space beside me, that he was blind. Another uncle, skinny in a too-big Western suit, blue with white piping, and slicked-back hair, his wide hat like a pet on the couch beside him, asked Nic in Spanish where I was from.

"Los Angeles," I said. We shook hands.

"*Mucho gusto.*"

"*Mucho gusto.*" He explained, again addressing me through Nic, ignoring and yet speaking to her, as if she were there as my translator, that he'd spent several years working in Colorado.

"*Sí.*" I nodded.

"Coffee and donuts," he told me gravely.

"Right." I smiled.

"He says that's all the English he learned to say," Nic told me. "On his way to work in the morning."

He grinned broadly, showing some gold.

"Very good," I said. "Coffee and donuts."

"Coffee and donuts," the fat aunt said, smiling and nodding at me. I shook her hand too.

"Coffee and donuts," I told her, and nodded at the skinny aunt, who smiled shyly. "Coffee and donuts to you." She seemed pleased, giggling and batting her lashes, so I gestured to the company. "Coffee and donuts for everyone."

"OK, that's enough," Nic said, and steered me toward another open door. Perhaps it was usually a dining room or bedroom. Now there was a coffin on a long table, candles burning at the head. I hesitated. The flames seemed to float and throb in the air above the wicks, pulling at the shadows on the wall like puppets. I entered, walking quickly but carefully, as if crossing a narrow bridge, and looked in the box. I saw a dead girl with long dark hair, or what appeared to be the body of one anyway: her figure was draped in a long black dress, her hands, in white gloves, held a rosary, and a black veil, woven of opaque muslin, completely covered her face.

I stared at the black cloth, as if trying to pierce it with my mind. I stared so hard that I almost convinced myself I saw it move just slightly in the faint, jumping flame light, as though lifted by a breath. I held my own breath and put out a shaky hand to peel the veil back: there was only a plastic form, a kind of white mask holding the veil in place. I felt a hand on my arm and assumed it was Nic.

"It's just a mask," I whispered over my shoulder.

"*Sí, señor.*" The voice was male and not friendly, and the hand on my shoulder was strong. "Her real face was destroyed in the accident. This is just for the funeral."

He was a big guy in his thirties maybe, in a black suit, white shirt, and thin tie. The uncles stood in the doorway, no longer smiling. One cradled a shotgun casually in his crossed arms. The hand tightened. "Now that you've mocked our grief," the man said, "I think you had better come out back and explain yourself."

70

"MY NAME IS RAMÓN. I am the cousin of Maria." I'd been led out to the backyard, a walled garden with a few trees, some plants growing tomatoes, red peppers, and cukes, or maybe zucchinis. Hens burbled in a coop. A big dog slept peacefully on the end of a thick chain. Over an open grill, women turned slices of steak and cactus. Flames hissed and jumped at the grease. Nic stood with them, nodding and smiling, but when she looked over at me her eyes were wide and anxious. I sat on a plastic chair across a table from Ramón, with the two uncles standing above us.

"You said you were friends from Los Angeles," he was saying. "OK. Friends are nice but they don't come to Tepic for a funeral. I want to know what you are doing here." He leaned in close to me and fixed his eyes on mine. "Did you really know my cousin?"

"I don't know," I said. I took another breath but couldn't think of anything more to say. "That's what I wanted to check. I'm sorry."

He took a crumpled pack of cigarettes from his pocket and shook one out, then offered the pack to me. I declined. He lit up with a Zippo and snapped it shut. "Explain."

"I'll try. I'm not sure I can. Your cousin was living under the name Mona Naught, in a hospital in California. We don't know how exactly, but she was at the center of some kind of mystery. This girl" —I nodded toward Nic— "was hired unknowingly to impersonate her. I was also tricked, into witnessing her suicide."

"And you now question this?"

"Perhaps. I was really just following the clues. I don't know what they mean but they led here."

"And you think she was murdered."

I said "Maybe," but I nodded yes.

Ramón nodded with me. "I have suspicions too. When out of nowhere, the Americans tell us that my cousin, who was missing for so many years, was found dead, we contacted the Mexican government. They say she crossed back into Mexico years ago."

"That's all they have?"

"That's it. They're sending the documents. But my question for you is, if she really came back, why didn't she tell us? Where has she been all this time? And how did she end up dead up north?"

"That's what I'm here to find out."

Ramón patted my arm, in a manner half threatening, half friendly. "You and me both. She was my cousin. We grew up together. If someone killed her, then it's my job to see justice done." He put his lighter in his inside jacket pocket and I saw the gun he wore under his arm.

"Are you a cop?" I asked. "A detective?"

"No," he said, dropping his cigarette between his feet and grinding it into the sand with a metal-tipped cowboy toe. "I'm a taxi driver. You?"

I shook my head. "Novelist."

71

WE ATE. DESPITE THE VAGUE (or not-so-vague, given that several of our coeaters were armed and that a refusal to devour and effusively praise the cooking might be the last straw) sense of menace, we were hungry, and the food was delicious: tender, slightly charred slices of steak topped with wedges of thick, white cheese, grilled cactus, and whole scallions, scooped up in a fresh tortilla. I scarfed it down. Perhaps fear, like the country air, had sharpened my appetite, my appreciation for life and its fleeting pleasures, like consuming other once living things.

It was with my wife (my ex?) that I had first eaten food like this, real Mexican food, at her favorite places all around the East Side and over in Boyle Heights, dollar taco stands and trucks that specialized in just one thing (pork carnitas, shrimp in a chilled red soup), ladies who made tamales in their home kitchens (meat or cheese with chilies, glued into the corn paste and steamed inside a leaf) and old school family-run restaurants, like La Serenada de Garibaldi, where the subtle and sophisticated dishes (the zucchini blossoms and frothed egg around the burnt pepper and cheese of a chile releno, shark soup in tomatillo sauce, the twenty-something ingredients, hand-ground in a stone mortar, that go into a basic mole) were served under the imperious hawk eyes of the boss lady, who sat at a back table, doing the books over hot chocolate and pan dulce, and occasionally calling over a waitress to excoriate.

But what truly won my heart, was what I tasted again that night, with armed men and sleeping dogs around me, mouth numbed by peppers, cooled by rice milk horchata, gobbling down what tasted like my last supper: the deep allegiance to those primal, celestial tastes, hot and sweet. So, so hot and so, so sweet. Lala put chile on oranges, melon, cucumbers, corn, eggs. She put chile on sugar, buying a baggy of chopped cane from a pushcart and shaking it full of hot sauce before digging in, the burn of the first bite followed by the soothing juice of the cane leaking onto your tongue. And don't forget, these people discovered chocolate. What contribution can a supposedly glorious European civilization offer to match that achievement? And coffee! Therein lies the ancient potency of Mexican food. Chocolate, chile, sugar, coffee: these are flavors we can feel as well taste, that enter us like drugs, through the nervous system, delivering pleasure and pain.

Ramón let us know we were expected at the funeral in the morning, after which we'd get down to crime solving. I tried to squirm out of it, but he was clear: we were now honored guests and we'd do as we were told. Mourning, then vengeance. He pushed back his plate and lit a Marlboro. "But first, tonight, we drink."

72

WE DRANK. THEY TOOK US to a place on the edge of town, more like a hut than a proper bar: just a concrete slab floor with a drain in the center and a roof of corrugated tin and thatch, with a couple of tarps lifting lightly in the breeze. There were cinder block walls on two sides, one of which had a long bar, and the rest was open. You could smell the fields out beyond the gravel parking lot, the moisture and the vegetation. A jukebox played sad Mexican cowboy tunes, and some beer posters featuring gigantic breasts and icy bottles, both beaded with sweat, provided the decor. It was empty except for a few old men nuzzling beers and staring at the TV and some truck drivers in caps laughing and playing dice at the bar. A dude with a long, droopy mustache and a big cowboy hat called for a beer, then lit a cigar and sat to read *Alarma* in a corner. No gringos and no women besides Nic. Shots of tequila and a round of Dos Equis arrived. We toasted.

"To Maria," Ramón said.

"*Que descanse en paz,*" Nic said and all the men muttered their agreement and clinked her glass and we drank. It tasted like burning piss. I forced myself to gag it down, gasping and wheezing. The others laughed.

"Wrong pipe," I said, pretending to laugh along while I wiped my tears. "Can I get a water?" Coffee and Donuts pushed across a beer.

"Thanks," I said and took a small sip. More shots arrived. These were from the bartender, in sympathy for our bereavement, and we toasted his health. The truckers saluted us too. One was fat, in a jean jacket and with a chain wallet. The other was tall and boney in tight jeans, a leather vest, and a lot of fake gold. This time I was careful to throw my head way back and fire the alcohol straight down my gullet. It still killed, but I held it together and it poisoned my stomach instead of my tongue. The cold beer helped, but I really wanted a Coke.

"El coco?" I asked. "Coca-Cola?" as more shots landed in the puddle at the center of our table. No one seemed to hear me over the music. Someone saluted something and we drank. Nic looked flushed and her voice sounded thicker.

"I like it here. It's like we're in that movie."

"What movie?" My voice sounded weird too, but I wasn't sure if the problem was my tongue or my ears.

"You know, the one where they have to get to Mexico."

"That's almost half of all movies."

"No!" She yelled a bit too loud and smacked my arm a bit too hard. "The couple. Ali McDraw and Steven Queens."

"*The Getaway.*"

"Yes!" She grabbed my wrist. "I fucking love that movie. She has this great jacket and then he shoots that guy. Doesn't it feel just like this? Who made that movie?"

"Sam Peckinpah."

"See, I knowed you'd knewed." She sneered. "You fucking nerd."

"But the movie's not in Mexico," I said. "They just cross the border at the end. Mostly it's Texas."

"I thought they crashed into the river and drowned at the end? Or you think they did but he lives?"

"You mean *Convoy?*" Ramón broke in suddenly. The blind uncle nodded in agreement.

"*Sí, está Convoy!*"

"You're right," I said. "Peckinpah made that too. During the time when he referred to himself as a whore."

"Cristo Cristo Fersoon," Coffee and Donuts put in.

"*Sí,*" I said, "Kris Kristofferson."

"Ten-four, good buddy," he declared.

"For me," Ramón said, "the best of Peckinpah is *The Wild Bunch.*"

"*Sí.*" Blind Uncle nodded emphatically. "*La pandilla salvaje.*"

"*Sí, Mapache,*" Coffee and Donuts added.

"You guys like *The Wild Bunch?*" I asked. "I thought maybe you'd think it was too harsh a view of Mexico and from a white guy too."

"We don't like gringos so much," Ramón agreed, "but we love Westerns. And you know that Mapache is acted by Emilio Fernández, a Mexican star?"

"I know," I said. "Here's another thing. He posed for the Oscar statue."

"Fernández?"

"Yes. That's him, naked."

"All those blancos," Nic said, "kissing his Mexican ass on live TV."

Ramón reported this news excitedly to the others. We joyfully toasted the fact that, for lo these many years, American superstars had in fact been worshipping a golden Mexican idol. The truckers seemed to be snickering at us, but a sense of goodwill pervaded our part of the room, so I forgot to worry.

We agreed that despite, or maybe because of, Peckinpah's macho, drunken, Romantic-nihilist vision of Mexico as a kind of combination heaven and hell where his characters went to live out their destinies, there was no denying that Peckinpah knew and loved the country. He was crude, bombastic, even insulting, but he got so many small details right, and this we know is how artists—who can have no truck with politeness or even fairness—show their love. We all adored Leone too, of course, who set his most openly political epic in Zapata's day, *A Fistful of Dynamite*, a.k.a. *Duck, You Sucker,* a.k.a. *Once Upon a Time in the Revolution,* though in his case the love was purely symbolic: the Italian film was shot in Spain with white actors. I tried to bring up Buñuel, who, exiled from Franco's Spain, ended up living in Mexico for decades and turning out dozens of pictures, including the classic harrowing tale of barrio kids, *Los Olvidados,* but Ramón and the uncles didn't know him: he never made Westerns and this was, after all, the West.

"What about *Touch of Evil,* the Orson Welles movie?" I asked. "Do you know it?"

"Of course," Ramón said. "I saw it on TV as a kid and again at a rerun house." He shrugged. "You know it's ridiculous. Charlton Heston as Mexican police."

"Yes. Though maybe not any more than as Moses or Michelangelo."

"And the other Mexicans, the gangsters, are cartoons."

"True."

"And his Mexico is not even Mexico."

"No. You're right," I said. "It's Venice Beach in LA."

Ramón shrugged. "But what can you do with a genius?"

"Right. It's a masterpiece."

"*Sí*. To Orson!" We toasted and the others joined in, the uncles and Nic equally oblivious of why they were drinking.

"I have a toast," Nic announced with drunken braggadocio. She lifted a sloppy shot. "To Mona Naught, may she rest in peace."

"To Mona!" Everyone drank.

"Who?" Ramón asked with a grimace after he swallowed.

"It's the name your cousin was using," I said.

"And me, too," Nic put in.

"OK, to you too," Ramón called, lifting another glass.

"*Si*, to you, *señorita*." We all drank. I sat back heavily, and took some deep breaths, determined to sit the next round out. My head seemed sealed in bubble wrap, my eyes and ears were blurred, and my lips had a hard time feeling each other. My thoughts also seemed to land softly from far above, like individually wrapped packages I had to open one by one.

"To my wife!" I yelled, surprising everyone, even myself. They all looked. I didn't even have a glass in my hand. Coffee and Donuts pushed one across. Everyone hoisted a shot.

"To your wife, wherever she is," Nic said.

"To your wife, whatever her name is," Ramón added.

"May she rest in peace," I said, and I drank. There was a moment of silence.

"*Ay cabrón*," Nic said, "I've got to piss so bad." I winced but no one else seemed to care. She rose unsteadily, leaning on Coffee and Donut's shoulder for support, and wandered toward the restroom. Laughing and drunk themselves, the truckers swiveled on their stools to watch her.

"Hey, gringa," they called. "Hey, puta, come here."

The skinny dude with the vest and chains got up and blocked her way. His trucker hat was on sideways now, in a B-boy-style or just from drunkenness, and he grabbed her wrist as she passed. She pulled back, trying to laugh it off and walk around him. He blocked her again. Ramón stood.

"*Oiga, amigo*," he called over, sounding reasonable if firm, but the fat trucker stood up and faced him. He was even bigger and fatter and uglier than he seemed sitting down. Bright boils throbbed like sirens on his forehead and neck.

Red alert! Things suddenly looked very bad, and with the other two males in our party old and/or blind, I realized it was incumbent upon me to get my ass kicked for Nic's dubious honor. I stood reluctantly and gripped the neck of a beer bottle, completely forgetting there was still beer in it.

"Hey, cabrón," I called out as I tried to wield the bottle barbrawler-style, and the contents splattered over me and my friends. There was a dead moment as everyone, including me, stared. Then the fat trucker burst into laughter. His friend joined in, along with Ramón and Coffee, and even Blind Uncle, though how could he get the joke? I tried to smile disarmingly. Meanwhile, Nic pulled away from the creepy trucker, but he grabbed her arm hard. The fat trucker stopped laughing.

"*Pinche cabrón*," he said to me. "I'm going to take that bottle and cut your little white balls off."

Ramón made fists, the bartender ducked, and everyone was bracing for battle, when the crack of a shot erupted, so loud and so close that I didn't understand what was happening when the skinny trucker's cap jumped off his head like a frightened bird. He looked around, eyes wide in terror, as if his own hat had betrayed him. I froze, afraid to even turn my head, afraid to blink. Everyone froze, except for Ramón—he pulled his gun, a flat automatic, and poked it into the fat one's gut. Then we all looked to see from whence the shot had come. Blind Uncle was holding a huge revolver, its mouth still steaming, aimed right at Skinny, although Blind Uncle himself was kind of staring off to the side at empty space. It was like his ear was cocked.

Ramón spoke loudly in Spanish, then threw some crumpled bills on the bar and said, "We're leaving. And you can all drink in peace. Just as soon as the señora uses the restroom."

"That's fine," Nic said. "I don't have to go anymore."

"All right then, after you," he told her. We all filed out, with Ramón and Blind Uncle in the rear. As we left, the mustachioed dude in the corner, smiling now and puffing a cigar, graciously tipped his hat.

"Holy fucking shit!" Nic yelled as we scooted to the car. "How the hell did he do that?"

"My uncle?" Ramón got the taxi going and steered us onto the road. "He's a master marksman. He doesn't need to see anymore. He can hear like a bat and sense movement and even feel the air currents and temperature with his face. Right?"

His Uncle nodded in agreement. "*Sí, sí.*"

"But he shot the hat right off his head!" I said.

"I did?" Blind Uncle asked me.

"Hell yes, you did."

He chuckled. "Lucky shot."

73

RAMÓN PARKED IN FRONT of the hotel and escorted us in, greeting the proprietor and explaining that we were his friends in a way that politely assured both our safety and our surveillance. Still, it had its plus side: when Nic requested bottled water and some extra towels they appeared immediately. Ramón gazed out our window at the desolate square with its dry fountain and the tall old church facing us like a stale wedding cake, smoking thoughtfully.

"You know you're being watched, right?" he asked us.

"I know. By you and the desk clerk. We won't leave."

"No. By the hombre in the pickup." He pointed out the window. The dark outline of a hat sat in a beat-to-shit pickup, parked in front of the movie house across the square. The last showing of *Fritz* had ended and the lights were off.

"Who is he?"

"Who knows? Police? Bandit? Maybe he followed you here from the north." He threw his cigarette at the guy, but it just dropped to the street below, bounced once, and kept burning between two cobblestones. He grinned. "You better watch your step down here, gringo." He winked conspiratorially at Nic. "Didn't anyone warn you?"

"Yeah," I said. "They especially warned me not to trust taxi drivers."

Ramón laughed and punched me in the arm. It hurt but I managed to smile instead of flinch. He bowed his head at Nic. "*Buenos noches, señora.* It was a pleasure drinking with you. I will see you in church in the morning."

Nic locked the door behind him and went to the window. She stared out at the pickup, which sat in the shadows, the cowboy silhouette unmoved.

"He's just smoking," she said.

"Uh-huh," I responded. I was sitting on the bed and my skull was spinning. It would rotate counterclockwise for a few turns, then lurch back.

"I think I know him from somewhere," she went on, peering over the sill.

"You know he can see you, right?" I asked. "It's dark out there and our light's on. You're lit up like a drive-in movie."

"Oh shit." She ducked in drunken panic and clawed the drapes. They came clattering down and she yelped as they hit her. "The light, the light," she whispered, as if suddenly he could hear us too.

"Yeah, I'll get it," I said, rising carefully. "Just don't wreck anything else." I hit the switch, and like changing the channel, our room was now black-and-white, the furniture gray, the corners shadowed, the light through the window silver. I stared at the truck across the way. Its headlights came on and it rolled off lazily, muffler burping. I lifted the curtain rod back onto the brackets and drew the thin cotton closed. Some light still filtered through and there was a line of yellow under the door.

"He's leaving," I said. "I guess you scared him after all."

"Fuck you," she said from her spot on the floor, then, "Help me up. I'm drunk."

"No kidding." I grabbed her hand and hoisted her to her wobbly feet.

"OK, I admit it," she declared. "I'm not really as tough as I seem."

"You don't really seem so tough," I said, sitting back heavily on the saggy bed. "More kind of mean. Or cold-blooded, I guess. In a smart way of course."

"Now that's mean," she said, waving a loose finger of accusation around the room. "And unfair. And now I really do have to pee. I've been holding it in since that fight." She tottered over and flicked the bathroom light on, stood in the illuminated rectangle. "You know," she said, unbuttoning her jeans, "I'm not really mean, or cold and tough like you think. Just honest."

Then as if to prove all our points she used the toilet without shutting the door, kicking off her shoes and stepping out of her jeans. She sat and I heard her little piddle. I could see her feet, the red painted toes and the little blue panties binding her ankles. She flushed and stood, leaving the panties on the floor. She wriggled out of her t-shirt and unhooked her bra.

"I think we should fuck," she said. "It's the only way I'm going to get to sleep."

"Um," I said.

"Besides," she explained, moving closer, entering the glow of the window, which touched her hair, shoulder, nipple, hip. "We're both tense and scared with a high level of adrenaline in the bloodstream. Which can actually add a real boost to the sex."

"Yeah, I've heard that."

Now she was in front of me, her smooth skin visible in the dark. "And then after we come, with all those endorphins released, we won't be so angry or frightened anymore. And we can rest."

"I've heard that too," I said, moving only my eyes. "Amazing how the human body works."

"Isn't it?"

"The thing is," I said, feeling my spine tighten as she sat on the edge of the bed across from me. "I do feel a little weird about us, you know."

"Weird about what?"

"Us. You know, not really knowing each other."

"What are you, a girl? I'm naked here, offering myself. What else do you need to know?"

"I mean being together like we were. Under false pretenses. For pay."

"Oh I see. It bothers you that I'm a whore."

"No. Shut up. It bothers me, or maybe depresses me is a better word, that I've been with two women in the last five years, you and my wife, and she dumped me and you were just doing it for money."

"Well," she said thoughtfully, sliding under the covers, "I'm not being paid now. In fact, I'm paying. Which makes me the client and you the whore."

"That's true," I admitted. "Good point."

"Does that make you feel better?"

"Yes, it does, actually. It feels great."

"Good." She patted the mattress beside her. "Now take your clothes off, whore, and get in this bed."

74

THE CHURCH BELLS WOKE US. We dressed quickly and went downstairs to the square, where we could see a small crowd of black-clad mourners gathering outside the church. We gulped a quick coffee at the counter of a café and hurried across the plaza. We hadn't brought formal clothes, but it was a rural place, a farm and ranching town, and while everyone was severely proper and all floors, hair, shoes, and children were spotlessly clean, dress codes were country and

there were a few men in stiff jeans, fancy boots, and shirts buttoned
to the neck and collar, standing around, awkwardly respectful, holding their hats in their hands. You could see the deep furrows of the
comb across their hair. We took up a post beside them, sentinels
along the back wall.

Like many poor churches, it was magnificent and overwrought,
festooned with glitter-and-marble icing, bedoodled with arches,
niches, flying angels, singing saints, and hailing Marys. It stunned us
with its space and height and cool silence, offering the people a tan-
gible vision of heaven, a working model of the miraculous to comfort them as they died facedown in the dirt and sun.

The Maria we were burying had been poor too, and she'd vanished long ago, so the church wasn't crowded. The few rows of
weeping women and frowning men and squirming kids were lost in
the deep stone canyon, and from where we stood the action on stage
was obscure and distant, like hieroglyphics or a modern dance seen
from the balcony. We left quickly when the pallbearers hoisted the
coffin and the robed priest floated toward us.

The daylight blinded us. We stood to one side, hangovers pul-
sating, while the coffin rode out on the shoulders of six men, who
eased it onto the back of a truck already thick with flowers. The
priest looked odd out here in the light and noise, like a costumed
actor who'd snuck backstage for a smoke or a wizard who'd been
caught without his magic wand. He lit a small black cigar and put on
mirrored shades. As the mourners filed out, more people joined the
crowd. A small brass band began a wandering tune and the parade
set off toward the graveyard. Nic and I tagged along with the strag-
glers, behind a wide grandma who rocked back and forth, holding
hands with a little girl in a mourning dress complete with frilled pet-
ticoat, hair ribbons, and gleaming patent leather shoes.

"Fritz! Fritz!" the girl yelled, pointing at the theater, but her
grandma dragged her after the coffin and we followed.

"Bastard," I whispered to Nic, who shrugged and lit a smoke.

The inscription over the graveyard gate read AQUI LA ETERNI-

DAD EMPIEZA Y ES POLVO VIL LA MUNDANAL GRANDEZA, which Nic translated roughly into English as, "Here eternity begins and vile dust goes to the grand world," and while the vile dust settled, on the stones and flowers and polished shoes, in our hair and throats and the lines on my hands, we followed the little troop into eternity, a city of tiny palaces that the good citizens had constructed to house their souls, like elaborate birdcages or the dollhouses of spoiled girls, far more splendid than their own mortal homes. After all, we are alive a short while, dead forever. As for this realm of dust, our grand and fallen world, only dead babies passed through untouched by sin and sorrow. That's why in some places down here they were called angels, and the music played over their tiny coffins was joyous. They'd won.

To my surprise, due to some overflow of feeling, combined no doubt with my piercing hangover and raw, postcoital emotions, saltwater filled my eyes and began to dribble out. This being a funeral, I let myself burble, as if in an emotional spa, until I saw the frown on Nic.

"You OK?" she asked. "You sick or something?"

"I'm fine," I said, abashed. "I'm just upset."

"All right, calm down. I was just concerned." She handed me a ratty napkin from her purse. "I've never seen a man just start to cry like that."

"Jesus," I said, suddenly laughing through my snot. "What a bitch."

"Fuck you," she snapped.

"Fuck you back."

"Pussy."

"Cunt."

Then we noticed Ramón waiting patiently nearby. The funeral was done. "Thank you for coming," he said. "My family appreciates the gesture of respect."

We both mumbled condolences. I blew my nose loudly in the napkin, and Nic scowled at me, but I noticed her own eyes were full now, perhaps only with anger, but my words had stung. Ramón went on.

"I have some news too. The authorities wrote back today. They say my cousin's passport was renewed at the Mexican consulate in Los Angeles in 2000."

"That makes sense," I said. We explained how that year Zed killed himself, and his wife moved to Europe and their "Mexican friend" disappeared. Perhaps she was the missing girl.

"Yes," Ramón said. "But then why nothing else, if she returned? No phone calls. No visit. And then there's this. They sent a copy of the renewed passport." He reached into his inner jacket pocket and drew out a folded sheet.

"There's a problem with it?" Nic asked.

"A big one. This photo. It's not my cousin. I have no idea who this woman is." He handed the photocopy to Nic, who shrugged.

"I don't know her either," she said and handed it to me. I looked.

"I do," I said. I held the paper hard, in both hands, as if protecting it from the wind that swept around us, raising dust. "She's my wife."

PART VI

LALALAND

75

THE TAXI MADE FOR the open road.

After the initial storm of disbelief, in which I could only agree, with everyone, that in fact it was crazy but in fact it was my wife, and after I explained that Lala was Mexican, and that she had left me, and after I told Ramón the name of her hometown, San Pancho, a small place which he knew and said was a few hours away, he finally nodded, frowned, and lit Marlboro Reds for everyone but me: "So. I will take you to your wife's village and we will see."

We then lapsed into a bumpy silence. The Blind Uncle rode up front with Ramón. Nic and I were in the back with Uncle Coffee and Donuts, grave and stately in his tall hat. There were no seat belts naturally, but there was an old portable black-and-white TV sitting on the dashboard, strapped down with a frayed cord, a soccer game flickering in and out. Who was this for? The blind man or the driver? Maybe it was to entertain paying passengers. All the windows were down, and as soon as we found the highway and began to pick up speed, fresh air swirling our hair and blowing through our minds, the mood automatically quickened. Even I, clouded with confusion, felt myself lean into the wind. My life was a smoking wreck. I had nothing. I knew nothing. I was adrift in the whirlwind, speeding into the unknown. Thinking seemed pointless, impossible. Everything just blew away.

Ramón, Blind Uncle, Coffee and Donuts, and Nic all puffed happily, smoke swirling. We raced forward, the little engine whining, bouncing over humps, flying around turns, right into the jungle, never braking for a curve or a slope. I gasped and grimaced and braced for the short stop, when that TV would decapitate the blind man and send his head spinning into my lap.

But everybody drove that way here, zooming, swerving, surging ahead in all manner of eccentric *Road Warrior* vehicles, high on spirit and speed. We hopped into the wrong lane to pass a rusty pickup full of Indians, who waved as we sped by and straight at an oncoming truck, whose driver didn't slow down at all, but winked his lights, as we swerved right to cut in front of a wood-paneled truck loaded stories high with sugarcane, a dark, barefoot boy in a headscarf sitting on top, holding a machete like a pirate. Three shirtless smoking men were in the cab, and they smiled serenely down on us as we slipped in and survived. Then a grandma on a small Japanese motorbike with a sidecar full of bananas merged from nowhere and we narrowly avoided killing her. Ramón immediately began leaning into the wrong lane, looking for a way to pass her, but more trucks were barreling toward us, and suddenly we had to duck back to avoid three flying cars that buzzed up from behind the sugar mountain and hopped in front of us. Each was more wrecked than the last: First came a Corolla with smoked-out gangster windows and mismatched parts, a yellow front quarter panel on a black car with one red door. Next was a Chevy Malibu missing a door altogether. Two skinny men and one very fat woman sat together up front. In the back a man reclined, feet up sideways, peeling a banana and grinning at us from the open doorway. I don't know what the last car was, it no longer had any particular make, covered in primer, rattling and jumping, front and back windshields crackled, dragging a muffler like a holiday sparkler and spitting black smoke. Ramón, however, didn't seem annoyed at being cut off by three cars, and in fact they right away began encouraging us to cut them back, waving and flashing. Answering the call, Ramón hit the gas and sent us hurtling into oncoming traffic. I held my breath as a bus appeared ahead. We passed two cars. Our engine droned and cried. The Death Bus loomed. I shut my eyes. At the last second, the Chevy Three-Door dropped back to let us in and we slid into our own lane again.

Yet somehow, despite the velocity and the recklessness, the anger that is ever-present in American traffic was entirely absent, replaced by an openhearted exhilaration. Road rage was road joy.

As we broke through to the shoreline and flowed along the beach, we passed a row of brand-new, mass-produced McPalaces, concrete pillars and satellite dishes, fences and four-car garages. The sun and sea shone through the gap where one house seemed to have collapsed into a drift of bricks and plaster.

"These houses belong to smugglers," Ramón shouted into the air, like a tour guide.

"What happened to that one?" Nic asked about the wreck.

"He had some trouble with the Federales, and when they came to take him he was gone, into the jungle. So they knocked down his house." We took in this monument to justice. Ramón glanced back at me over his shoulder. "We are almost at San Pancho. It is a very small town, a fishing village where some rich gringos have winter houses. We will find the church where your wife's birth was recorded and see if her family is still around."

"OK," I called back. Uncle Coffee and Donuts nodded at me manfully, and over his shoulder, the Blind Uncle gave me a thumbs-up.

76

THE SIGN SAID WE were entering San Francisco, which everyone unanimously called San Pancho, the place where Lala had mentioned, vaguely, that she was born. It was a beach town, low white buildings asleep in the sun, wavering palms, their fronds a deeper green than in LA, and the Pacific a warmer, more royal blue. Hills climbed high above the village, hung with clusters of bright bougainvillea and hibiscus, and broken here and there by the gleaming homes of the white, empty until winter.

We parked in the town plaza and stepped into the small church. Again the cooling darkness swallowed us, as if we'd descended into a cave. Ramón spoke to an old woman in black who was lighting candles. She led him, Nic, and me into the back, where the priest was in his office. The uncles took a seat in the rear pew.

We followed the little round lady as she waddled down a narrow hall and opened a door, smiling as she waved us in. After the chapels, the priest's office was antiglamorous, small and jammed with a cheap Formica desk, a pleather chair patched with duct tape, two battered seats, and a worn couch for guests. Papers were piled everywhere, and filing cabinets lined the walls. The priest, a portly gray fellow in a white shirt and black pants but without his dog collar, sipped coffee from a paper cup and flicked ashes into an overflowing tray the size of a hubcap.

"Buenos días," he said, smiling but grunting a little as he hauled himself up to shake hands. Ramón made the introductions and we all mucho gusto–ed, after which he sank back down with a sigh of relief. Ramón took out his Marlboros and offered them around. The priest lit up delightedly and leaned back in his chair, smoke blowing high like a whale's spout. He crossed his fingers behind his head, so that I was constantly distracted by the threat that he might set fire to what was left of his hair. He switched to English for my sake.

"So, señor, how can I help you? I understand you need information for your wife?"

"Thank you. You see, she's missing and I'm trying to learn about her background. She was born here in San Pancho."

"You think she'd come back here?"

"No . . ."

Ramón intervened. "You see, padre, my cousin died recently. Her funeral was this morning."

"I'm sorry, my son."

"Yes, thank you. We had not seen her for many years, and there is some question that she was connected with this man's wife, or that the two women were using the same name. You see, we could not have an open casket, due to how she died. In a fall."

Ramón glanced at us and I realized that of course they had lied to everyone about the cause of death. Catholics. Otherwise they would have had to bury her alone, far from the company of the other righteous dead. The priest nodded sadly.

"Yes, it is a hard world. Only God knows why. I suppose we will have to look her up." He stared at the filing cabinets as if having to stand and open one were the final proof of God's injustice to man. "I will need your wife's name and date of birth."

I wrote out the information out on his desk pad, and he leaned forward with a grunt, his chair cushion farting as he shifted, and found some glasses. He held them in front of his face. "The family name is a common one here but I don't remember the girl. I was not the priest in this church when she was baptized." With a further sigh, he stood, tossed some ash over his desk as a blessing, and headed for the files.

"OK, births, births . . ." he muttered, searching back through the decades. Ramón watched patiently. I could see Nic squirming.

"M, M, M . . ." He opened a drawer marked I–N and files burst out like a bouquet. Nic hopped to her feet and handed him the fallen papers. "Bless you, dear," he muttered and stuffed them in a basket on top. He continued ruffling, ashes scattering among the leaves. Ramón looked sleepy. Nic looked enraged.

"Ah, here it is!" he called out, sounding much too surprised. He read: "Eulalia Natalia Santoya de Marías de Montes." He handed the paper to me and we all gazed down. Indeed it was a birth certificate in my wife's name. Though of course to me this wasn't ever her real name. She was Lala.

"You know, let me just check something else," the priest said, buoyed by his success. He pulled another fat folder out and flipped through. "*Sí, sí,* it is as I thought. Look." He handed it to us. It had Lala's name as well. Otherwise, I didn't understand, but Ramón did.

"A death certificate," he said. "For six months after the birth."

"*Sí.*" The priest nodded sadly and returned to his desk. He lit up a fresh smoke and sat back, exhausted. "You see, it's a typical technique for acquiring false papers here. You find a child who died very young, which was still quite common in the poor towns. You request a birth certificate as if it were your own or your relative's, perhaps showing some fake ID like a student card that is easy to obtain. Of course the clerk has no reason to cross check with deaths, it's not his concern, he provides the document. Now you can use this to get a passport, driver's license, whatever." He folded his hands atop his head again so that the smoke spiraled up from his skull. "I don't know why your wife, or your cousin, needed a false name, but you did not bury this person today. Eulalia Natalia Santoya de Marías de Montes has been dead for almost thirty years."

77

WE ATE. AGAIN. It had been another long day and this time no one spoke much as we sat around the table while the sun sank, shelling shrimp grilled in garlic and sucking down raw oysters that a man on crutches shucked to order and that we dosed, of course, with chile and lime. I finally got my Coke and insisted on paying the bill for the table, which was ridiculously cheap.

They dropped us at a small hotel, Ramón checking with the clerk to be sure we knew where the bus to Puerto Vallarta would depart, across the village square, in the morning. We all hugged and smacked each other's shoulders and commended one another to God. We might be hopelessly separated by culture and language, but we'd shared a drunken adventure and that bonded us for life. We waved them off in the taxi like old pals, then went back inside, where the dude with the walrus mustache and the big hat, the one who'd been reading the paper in the bar back in Tepic, was waiting with a stink bomb cigar in his teeth.

"Señor?" He stopped me, mirror shades flashing. It was ridiculous to be wearing them at night, of course, but the effect was menacing and I stepped back, expecting more trouble. He held out a note. I took it cautiously, at arm's length, as if it were a gag. He tipped his hat and stepped back, taking up a position by the door, where he puffed his cigar and waited politely.

"What the fuck?" Nic whispered. "I've had enough for one day."

"I think that guy's been following us."

"In the truck!" she said and punched my arm. Again. I was going to have bruises. I opened the note. It was neatly typed in English: If you want to know what happened to her follow this man.

"What do you think?" I asked.

"Which 'her' does he mean?" Nic asked. "The cousin? Your wife?"

"Whichever. Do we go or not?"

She sighed. "I guess we have to. That's why we're here." She turned to the waiting stranger. *"Vámonos,"* she said.

He led us around the corner to an old Ford pickup and gestured for us to climb into the bed. It did indeed look like the one that had been following us. I gave Nic a boost and hauled myself up, barely settling on a wooden crate before we jolted into action.

"Look on the bright side," I said. "If this is a kidnapping, security's pretty lax."

We left the town and began climbing, slowly, up into the hills. Almost instantly we were in darkness. But unlike a sealed bedroom, this was jungle darkness, thick and warm, wrapping you in itself, like the hot breath and soft fur of an animal rubbing against your face and brushing your shoulders. The sky was riddled with stars. We jolted left, climbing higher, and the trees closed over us and there was nothing but the headlights breaking the blackness ahead and the chatter and chirp of the nightlife all around us. The truck turned again, onto a dirt road now, and the lights showed a white retaining wall, then a gate. The stranger punched a code and it swung back. We were on a steep driveway made of cobblestones. In the moonlight, a big white house towered up before us and we stopped. The stranger helped us out. He pointed at the open door. He tipped his hat. And while we stood and dithered, he hopped back in the truck and he left. So we went inside.

78

THE MAIN ROOM OF the house was huge, with adobe walls and thick rafters vaulting a high ceiling. There was an open kitchen with a serious stove and copper pots hanging from the crossbeam, as well as a long, thick dining table and couches and sunken armchairs around a fireplace of pig roast proportions. Sliding doors opened to a large patio and a pool. There were many books, in English, Spanish, French, and German. There were all manner of crafty and arty knickknacks around, clay figurines and stone bowls, woven blankets and torturous candelabras. But the most striking thing, aside from the amazing view of jungle, beach, and crashing sea that leapt up as you entered, was the art on the walls: large unframed canvases painted with bright, simplistic forms, whether deliberately primitivist or simply primitive I couldn't say, all depicting the same woman —Mona, or one possible Mona, anyway—her face, her nude body, in thick strokes against fields of color, sometimes covering the whole canvas in deep paint, sometimes with bald patches shining through. In some pictures the setting was clearly this house. I recognized a large leather chair and the bougainvillea pouring over the white patio wall. In others, she seemed to be involved in some mythological or ritualistic drama, holding a spear or whip or wearing a childish crown and sitting on a throne, holding hands with the devil while nude men groveled at their feet, or else hoisting a torch to awkwardly light a bonfire, while witches and demons pranced.

At one end, the main room connected to a large bedroom where the unmade bed and scattered clothes suggested very recent occupancy, but the garments, a pair of jeans, a denim shirt, and some boots, were all men's. At the other end was a studio where it seemed as though the portraits had been made. There were a great many tubes and jars and vats of paint, heaps of smeared rags, stained and battered brushes in coffee cans, overflowing ashtrays, a dish still caked with fried egg, and nearly finished on one wall, a very large mural perhaps six feet long. Here the model, or muse of the house, seemed to be copulating with a minotaur, a figure who combined the horned and bearded head of a bull and the torso and arms of a wooly man, with cleft hooves, a tail, and a rather bullish endowment as well. The actual penetration was the mural's central focus, the genitals cartoonishly enlarged, blown up junior-high-bathroom-style, a ball-and-shaft combo entering a narrow, slitted eye.

Nic peered dubiously at this final piece in the exhibit. "Wow," she pronounced, and then, in that odd, slightly autistic way she had, asked: "Would you say this painting is a good painting? I mean, would you hang it on your wall? What about a Picasso? Why is that better? I mean it's worth more, obviously, I know that, but why would I hang it up and see it every day while eating breakfast if it's ugly and doesn't look like anything?"

"It does look like something though." I pointed at the face, a plain oval with black hair in a line down each side, a tiny arrow of a nose, two big eyes, and lips like a candy heart. "It looks like you . . . or her. These paintings are of Mona, whoever that is. And the scenes remind me of those films I got from Kevin's." I touched the figure's forehead and my finger came away brown. "And this one is still wet."

"But who could have painted it?"

As if on cue, thunder cracked above our heads, as though we were standing in the hollow of a drum, while outside the window, lightning shattered the horizon, and a torrential downpour began. The lights flickered. The windows shook. The patio was instantly flooded. I remembered Lala, long ago, telling me that during certain months, in the town where she was born, it rained like this every night, as low clouds carried the ocean onto the land, pouring out short, violent storms that dried right up and were forgotten in the next morning's sun. Perhaps this really was where she was from after all. Another explosion. The lights fluttered again and, as if in a cave painting, the face on the wall seemed to waver, considering us with equipoise while the minotaur ravished her body. Gasping, Nic bolted from the room.

"Wait. It's just a storm . . ." I rushed after her, into the dark living room, as the power came on and the large TV began to glow.

"Look," Nic said, pointing. There was a typed note taped to the bottom of the screen. I removed it.

Welcome Guests, Please make yourselves at home. I'm sorry I couldn't be here to greet you in person, but I've left a disk in the player. Please listen carefully. It is programmed to erase itself after one play. Any attempt to stop or remove it will trigger the self-destruct mechanism. Just like *Mission Impossible* (the TV show and not that insipid film).

I looked over at Nic. "What do you think of this?"

She shrugged at the remote lying on the coffee table. "Press it," she said.

I pressed play. We saw a man standing in what was clearly this room. He had a cowboy hat and a beard.

"That guy looks familiar," I said. The man smiled wordlessly, and removed his hat to reveal a bandana. Long black hair tumbled out. "Holy shit!" I said. "That's the biker who was following me in LA."

"What biker?" she asked, but I didn't have time to answer, because now the man removed the bandanna and the hair with it, revealing another head of hair, also long but entirely gray. Next he peeled off the lower beard, leaving a walrus mustache. Nic clutched my wrist.

"That's the guy who drove us up here. The Mexican hombre!"

He peeled off the mustache, revealing a clean-shaven and hand-some if rather haggard face. He smiled and lit up a short black cigar.

"Hello," he said in perfect, clipped, vaguely British English that still carried a flat Germanic tone. "My name is Zed Naught."

79

GREETINGS FROM BEYOND the grave and welcome, I suppose, to purga-tory. After all, isn't this where rich old white people go to spend eternity? I know it feels like forever for me. Really, the toughest part about hiding in Mexico ten years isn't the corrupt officials, who are actually quite helpful and reasonably priced on the whole, but the need to blend in with so many dead-boring and generally horrible old Americans, Germans, Brits, and Aussies. What a bunch. Broiling in the sun, satellite dish on the roof endlessly running football and commercials for beloved cookies and toilet paper from the home-land, while they drink themselves into oblivion. Have I become one? I can only hope that if I do I have the courage to blow my head off for real this time. I've often thought that it was a mistake not to kill my-self then, when I had the chance. My existence ever since has been a kind of descent into hell, as if I were in Dante's suicide garden, trans-formed into a twisted and monstrous tree, rooted here among the vegetative tourists and slowly burning away in the heat. But some-how I felt I no longer had the right to end it myself. I was in a sense, already dead. This was the afterlife and dead people have no way out, except, I suppose, resurrection, and so I carried on like a zom-bie, eating, sleeping, talking, walking, and of course making art, which I can't help continuing, like a compulsion. I could not really make films. I had no money or resources, could not use my name or draw any public attention to my work. So I painted, sculpted, drew. I am terrible at all these things. My sculptures fell apart, the stone shattered under my clumsy chisel, and the clay collapsed because I used too much water. All are probably part of an adobe pig hut now. My paintings are ridiculous, abominations. An insult to real art. But like a stupid child drawing on the wall, I couldn't help myself. As long as I persisted, and I say "persist" not "live," as I was dead already, I had to go on making art. I have no desire for these works to last. You would be doing me a favor if you destroy them, if you simply torch this whole place, this exhibition of my wretchedness, when you leave.

I admit, it was not always quite so bad. The first years of exile were better. In fact it was a golden time for me, a kind of reprieve, a vacation, as Mexico is for all of us, but for me also a vacation from being myself and from the life in Los Angeles, which had become a prison, although I admit a very comfortable one. A pleasure prison with glass walls so you can imagine you are free, as long as you never actually try to step outside. Of course these can be the most difficult prisons from which to escape. And I did not go willingly, not at all, I fled in cowardly abject terror, but I still found, once I had absconded like a worthless scoundrel, a deep sense of relief and freedom. I could breathe. I slept, especially here by the ocean, like I had not slept in decades. The sweet sleep of the newly dead, resting in fresh earth. Not that there is anything original in that. There's a long tradition of Europeans and Americans coming to Mexico to disappear, into exile or death. Ambrose Bierce was a legend to me. I remember, as a child in my grandfather's house in Bavaria, he was obsessed with the American West like so many Germans, and we always were reading about the frontier, cowboys and Indians, the desert and the open plains. I remember learning then about Bierce, the writer of spooky tales, heading off to join Pancho Villa and fight for freedom in Mexico, the people's war for land and freedom, long mustaches, crossed bandoliers, and bare-breasted Indian maidens. He disappeared into the unknown and I longed to follow. Later as an adolescent I read D. H. Lawrence, of his great escape, crawling out of the coal mines, out of the dark, dank asshole of his fatherland, and the smothering, castrating living death of the motherland, running away later to find light and sun and sex in Mexicos old and new. Then Lowry and Greene, the atoners, who came to Mexico to drink and suffer, to confront God face-to-face and be saved or die. Then there are the successes, the lucky exiles who came and stayed and somehow thrived in the native soil. I am thinking now of Buñuel in film. A whole career in the Mexican cinema and even after he returns to Europe to make his final masterpieces, he remains a resident of Mexico to the end. It was his home. And most of all, of course, B. Traven. He stands apart. The mystery of his past. Who was he? An anarchist who escaped from prison? The Kaiser's illegitimate son? He flees Europe, from who knows what, becomes a seaman, a voyager traveling the world on cargo ships. Then to live among the Indians in the south, to work in the mines beside the peasants, to immortalize their stories in novels, and then at last to become rich, to write *The Treasure of the Sierra Madre,* to drink with Bogart and marry a great beauty. He really had his cake and ate it too. So of course to me, longing for escape from dreary, rotten Europe, Mexico was like a magic word, like the secret that could release me. It was nonsense of course. By then the beautiful new world was utterly violated, whored out and lobotomized, but as a kid I was too dumb to know it, and who wouldn't be tempted by even the scent of freedom, of life, when suffocating in a dead museum like Europe? Remember, this was after the war, the fifties, my world was a garbage heap and not only that, an abomination as well. As a child I played among the ruins of a civilization that we all knew was utterly worthless and horrific anyway. The Germans! I grew up knowing that I belonged to a cursed race, humiliated losers who deserved to be destroyed, who brought our destruction raining down upon ourselves, almost as if there were a God, but one who arrived too late to matter.

So much for my mother's side of the family, the pretty daughter of once proud Bavarian minor bullshit landowners, cultured Europeans ruined and penniless after the war of course but still stuffed full of sheet music and Goethe, though the piano and books and shelves had all been burned for fuel. Yes, you say, but my dad was English, a soldier, so this means I was half from the winning side too. Half a victor! Some victory. Do you have any idea what England, especially northern backward sodden rotten England was like in the fifties? Unbelievably bleak. A wet dirty nasty country waking up to the fact that their finest hour was over forever, they had given everything to win, to win not by conquering but by suffering, by holding out, and from here on it was all decline and despair. Their greatness had all been a dream, they were a small northern country with awful weather and disgusting food, an island off the coast of Europe, a minor character on the world stage, a sidekick tolerated by America and Russia, the big bullies, as long as it kept its mouth shut. So they clung to old glory and new bitterness, about the supposedly noble empire they once had. But what was glorious or noble about it? What is any empire but the systematic murder, rape, and subjugation of others? Colonies! Who besides nations have colonies? Vermin, pests, diseases. Cancers have colonies. Parasites. Termites. Invading and growing and sucking the life's blood out of living creatures, living cultures to feed the ancient, swollen, and depraved Queen. And yet, in those ugly brutal freezing schools they sent us to, those perverted teachers with the horrible frightening teeth taught us how these ungrateful wretches, brown, yellow, red, should thank us and kiss our arses for teaching them how to tie a necktie and brew a proper cup of tea.

Where was I? Oh, yes. This is why, from the beginning I always longed to come to America, not so much because I was interested, though I was in a way fascinated and I admired some things very much like jazz and the Ramones and the novels of Chandler, but because I knew I had to escape from home or I would die. America might be a nightmare but it was a living nightmare. And the attraction to film was I think for me the same, a way to live a bit, to breathe. The other arts were done. Painting was done. Literature, done. Music, almost done, a few last sounds to make. Theater, almost over, and the one or two good things, Beckett when I was still very young, were really just the acknowledgement of this, the last sigh before finally shutting the fuck up. Sculpture done. Really, really done. Ballet? Done after Balanchine, so now totally done. Modern dance? Well really it doesn't matter because I can't dance anyway, I am very clumsy so this is a moot point and not worth discussing. I could not become a dancer. Architecture? Architects are even bigger whores than film directors, who are tremendous, stupendous, gargantuan whores. Well, today all artists are whores of course, whores with no shame even. They used to be thieves, hustlers who took what they needed from the rich by trickery, which took some cleverness at least, but now artists are just silly foolish giggling whores sitting on billionaires' laps at parties, sucking soft limp stinky hedge fund cock under the table. Thus, I chose film as my medium.

Not because I had hope for it. I want to make that perfectly clear. I am a fool perhaps in many things I admit, but I am not a total idiot of the sort that would have hope for the art of film. No. I had no hope at all for cinema. None. But it was alive, at least, a new art, perhaps fifty years old when I discovered it, when it entered my life, my history. The other arts were over. Their stories, their journeys, were done. I don't mean of course that people stopped practicing them. Of course people will always keep making art, writing books, painting. I also don't mean that no one is making good or even great art or writing good or even great books or dancing good or even great dances too. After all, such people are real artists, born artists and poets and they do what they do because they have to, like a primitive man painting a cave or a prisoner scratching the wall of his cell. They are possessed. They have no choice. The historical predicament cannot stop them. Still, any really intelligent artist must understand his own historical situation, his predicament, and so any really good contemporary artist is in some sense a memorialist, an elegist for his own medium, because he knows he is speaking after the fact, as one who came too late. If he is good, or even great, then this is part of his greatness, the greatness of the one who fights even when the battle is lost, because he is a warrior and such is his fate. That is not me. I am not a great artist. I am not really very talented or all that smart. My films are not even very good. Anyway I don't watch them. They are not the sort of thing I care to see. I like for example Buster Keaton. I like some silent films from Europe like *Caligari*. I like Marx Brothers. Bugs Bunny. I like too some more recent films. I like Jackie Chan. John Woo. *A Better Tomorrow Part Two* I like very much. Part One as well but Part Two is even better. I find some Johnnie To very good. *Triad Election* is excellent, both parts. Really it is one large work. My point is, I am not so arrogant as to think I am a great genius of cinema or anything else. But I had to do something with my life and I understood that while I was too late in a sense for history, too late to do anything but lay a flower on the history of my culture, my family, my people, I was not exactly too late for the cinema. Cinema itself was maybe too late. This I admit readily. I admit this categorically and in advance. I acknowledge this a priori. I . . . my cigar seems to be out, one moment. There. As I was saying, we do not doubt or challenge the lateness of the cinema as such, not at all. Only a true moron would do so. Rather I suggest that it is this very awareness of lateness, which is inherent in cinema, inscribed into the very act of watching a film, that accounts for its strange beauty. Its sadness. Its sad, strange, melancholy beauty, which is I believe already there, in the very act of watching a film, any film, it is there in film as such, so I am in no way taking credit for this. It is there in a good film or a bad film. And while one might legitimately surmise that the best filmmakers, the artists of cinema (being aware of their historical predicament, of their lateness) will therefore, by my own definition be aware of this, it does not follow that this knowledge or any other technique or talent creates the feeling I'm speaking of, the sadness, the beautiful melancholic sense of loss. It only means that they know it is happening while the fools do not. It has to do with time, this sadness. This lateness. This loss. With the relationship of film to time, which I believe is unique in the arts. Music of course has a very important relationship to time, but music is said to keep time. We are on the beat, with the beat, behind the beat. So here music is making us aware of time but also moving us through time. Theater and dance I would argue have duration, just as literature has sequence, but these are art's hopeless attempt to erase time, to destroy time, to defeat time by either making us forget it, as in theater, or in literature and painting by rendering time itself powerless. The uniqueness of film, its special quality, comes from the fact that film does not hide time, nor defeat it, nor does it move us along with it, rather film makes us aware, always, of time passing us by. Film is in this sense the late art form par excellence because everything that appears on film is already the past. Even the present is instantly the past on film. A movie camera or projector is a machine for making time pass or rather for making the passage of time visible. Film is what passes. It renders time visible. Hence we feel this loss, the loss of the present, the sadness of the very moment that is always dying away.

So that's how I ended up in Hollywood. The twin pulls of America and the movies. I had an art career in London and Berlin but I had to escape. I couldn't stand those snobby, overstuffed yet pathetically desperate European art whores, although of course I was one of them myself. One of the worst. And no matter what anyone says, no matter how much you crow over Antonioni and Bergman, in the end to really engage with the cinema means American cinema, Hollywood cinema, the golden age. It is like a Catholic and the Vatican or an Englishman and the Queen, or a German and the Camps: the thing that you might hate but that still defines you, that you must acknowledge and somehow confront. Plus there was a lot of sex to be had in Hollywood with healthy happy tan American girls, and warm non-German, non-English weather and cheap rent. You like fucking outdoors? In the fresh air? I do. I love it. Or by the pool. Or just to relax and take a piss in the warm sun like an animal. I love this about LA. I love the sun and the whores and the cheap rent and the Korean barbeque and the old American cars. So what if some whores are dumb? You think everyone with an English accent is smart? They elected Thatcher and reduced their own country to a bleak, wet, gray, tired, used-up slag heap. Anyway, I'm not so smart myself. I sound smart to Americans because of my European accent and because I read a few books in school which is so rare here. If you know a little Shakespeare, one play, *Hamlet,* and two poems by anyone, Americans think you're a genius. Really I read much more later on in Mexico. One good thing about being dead is you can catch up on your reading. Though finding books in English or German is hard. My Spanish is OK now, I can read. For English and German books you have to order, or go the estate sales of dead expats, dead white whales, where the locals snatch up the clothes or furniture but no one else wants the books. Then you get to read what everyone has on their shelves but never reads, Shakespeare, Goethe, Homer, Dante. A lot had never been opened. I read the *Norton Anthology of English Poetry* cover to cover. Finally I became an educated European, a cultured man, reading the unread books found in the vacation homes of retired drunken soccer-obsessed Euros. For the first time in my life, I read the Bible, relaxing here in my tomb.

Where is my lighter? That is the problem here. You can get Cuban cigars but you can't keep them dry in this humid, fetid, rotting jungle. So. As it happens, in the end, I did not make too many films in Hollywood. Oh well. I am a lousy whore after all. I am willing. I am not proud. I will show my ass and tits. I will take the dick. Take it deep. But I cannot with a straight face tell the customer, I love you, sir, you are so handsome, your dick is so big, you make me come so good like no one else. Maybe you say I am too smart for them but honestly I think I am too stupid. A smart whore knows how to lie to the customer, to bullshit him, to tell him what he wants to hear. When they ask me what I think of their idea I always said, this is sheer stupidity but I will do what you say, it's your money. This they don't like. It's not good enough to suck it up for money. You must pretend it is for love. But then, like in a storybook, like in a lame stupid American movie, I did find love in Hollywood after all, true love and happy ever after, with the most beautiful, the most brilliant, the most courageous, the most filthy and horny whore I've ever met. My darling wife. No, I correct myself. She was not a whore. A whore does it for money like me. I am the whore. She, my friends, was a slut. A slut does it for love. She loved me. I won't say she was my soul mate since there is no such thing as a soul. That is a ridiculous fairy tale created to enslave the childish ignorant masses who fear life almost as much as death. But she was my brain mate and certainly my body mate—my cock was the partner of her cunt, my tongue was the best friend of her clitoris and yes her ass too, her lips were pals with my testicles, and my mouth became intimate buddies with her nipples. The self-help therapists and women's magazine editors say that the mind is the most erogenous zone of a man's body. This is ridiculous of course, it is the underside of the tip of the penis. But still, something in my brain lit up when I met her. Like sticking my dick in an electrical socket. I knew I had found my destiny. I felt the way real artists feel when they pick up a brush or a pen. Did I ever think she was a demon, succubus, come to suck the marrow of my mind? Of course. Many times, I called her demonchild, devil, vampiress, goddess, monster, and queen. I felt that she had enslaved me, with her cunt and her brain and her eyes. My work became about her and for her and then also with her. We were partners, cocreators, and I say without false modestly or any sort of hesitation that she was the leader, the primary creative force, not I. I am not ashamed to admit this as a man. She was superior to me. I worshipped her. I was her slave. Her dog. Yes, I know, my form of worship was not typical. I am an atypical man, and so an atypical dog as well. People thought I was exploiting her sexually, involving her in perverse fantasies, degrading acts, delirious escapades, and transforming her into an erotic object. This is all true. I was doing all of that and more. Much more. But it was all to please her. These were her fantasies, her desires, and I was her plaything, her willing, very willing, this I admit freely, her decidedly eager and willing servant. I was in heaven. But I was also dwelling in fear. Fear that she would leave me, tire of me. Fear that I would fail to satisfy her, that I could not meet her needs, sexually, creatively, even financially, so that she would leave me behind. Some part perhaps of my film *Succubi!* deals with this. We cowrote it and during the process I shared with her my fears, and, very cleverly, she suggested we make a story on this. Also my best films, our best films, the trilogy, *Invitation, Consummation,* and *Ascension,* were a long homage to her. I don't say that it was dedicated to her. That is an insult. I would not dare to say such a thing. It belonged to her. It was hers. Of course in the end my fear came true. She did leave me. But it was not because I failed to please her or to spend enough money. She simply outgrew me. She outgrew this life here. She needed to be free. She had grown up and was ready to leave home. No, the difference in our ages did not ever bother me. It excited me. Fine, I am a pervert. Good. I have never given a damn about your bourgeois morality anyway. I am an outlaw, OK, a nonviolent, intellectual, and comfortably well-off outlaw, a meek, obedient outlaw, but here I am still in Mexico, like Billy the Kid. The other reason was that when I met her I knew she was a genius, and to genius age is irrelevant. Yes, I am a pervert, I admit this fully, but I stand up and claim I am also a feminist, because when I met this girl, this young girl, I immediately recognized an equal. I don't expect you to understand, because you weren't there, you didn't know us, you didn't know her, but we were in fact a true marriage of equals, or perhaps in many ways she was the stronger, yes, she was the leader. Between a middle-aged mediocre artist and a fifteen-year-old genius there is no contest. She wins. This is why when I met her I did not hesitate. I threw myself at her. I begged. From the night I met her, at a party in the Hollywood Hills, where she was sitting in a hot tub in her bikini bottom and no top, smoking a joint with the also topless wife of the owner of the house, and their four breasts just sort of bobbing in the bubbles and the nipples gazing peacefully at me through the steam, and I climbed in beside them and the wife, her husband was a British film producer, he was out of town somewhere making a picture, and the wife said, Zed, have you met Mona? And we shook hands, which the ladies laughed at, my being so formal with a topless woman, and I said, It is a pleasure to make your acquaintance and she said, *Enchanté,* and I kissed her hand, her soft, wet little hand, and she giggled and said, Please, sir, have a seat. And I sat down in the tub with them and they handed me the joint. The water was very hot and at first the heat and smoke dazed me. It was dark too, where we were, with the main party at the other end of the estate, across the flat, still pool, glowing blue like a hole in space, and the laughter and voices and music seeming so far away, and the lights all around us, the lights of the city and sky all flowing together into one great sea, everything blinking on and off, star, car, airplane, satellite, comet. Before I knew it the producer's wife had gone, she said to get a beer, it was only us two remaining, and I had barely seen her face, it was dark, the scene just lit by the moon and the tip of the joint, and we talked and talked and laughed and laughed, then I realized we had stopped talking and stopped laughing and were just sitting, just sitting there and staring into the darkness in silence. Marry me, I said. Let's drive to Las Vegas and get married. She laughed. You're stoned, she said. I am, I said, it's true, but I mean it, let's get married. She laughed, I can't get married she said. I am fifteen. I can't legally marry for a year. OK, I said. I will wait. She laughed again. Then she kissed me. And one year later she was my wife.

I have cancer. That's why I rose from my grave. I'm dying, again, and this time, the doctors assure me, it will last. When I received this final verdict, I decided to leave my one valuable object, my only treasured possession, to the only woman I ever loved, my wife, or ex-wife, I suppose. We had not been living together for some years but it did not matter. She was still my genius and I knew she would know what to do with my gift, which has supported me all these years. I am speaking of course of the film, the one and only copy of *Ascension.* It is the desire of some very powerful people to keep unseen this film that has bankrolled my very comfortable life since my death. Now I decided to give it to her, since it was hers all along, to

profit from, to release or to destroy as she saw fit. But when I contacted her, when I told her that I was dying and wanted to meet her
one last time and deliver the film, I did not foresee the danger it
would create. My enemies were not sleeping after so many years. As
soon as I began to arise from my grave, their alarms went off. They
had been watching her and watching for me, watching everyone we
knew. As a result, my stupid actions placed her in danger, grave danger. If the film falls into their hands, then she is certainly dead. Of
course as you know by now, it does not contain my suicide. I had always promised to kill myself and film it. This was well known. I had
always assumed that was how I'd die. But as long as I had her, I found
I wanted to live after all. At least a little bit more. I'm glad I did. The
film, *Ascension,* is in a bank box, a safe deposit, number 5424, at the
Desert Savings Bank in Twentynine Palms. She is the only one left
alive who knows what it contains. I've sent the only key under a
fake name that she would know, because she used to call me by it, in
Mexico, the name I wish was mine. Go there, retrieve the key, then
get the film, and use it to help her. Go to the UPS in Twentynine
Palms and ask for—

80

AT FIRST I THOUGHT the house had been struck by lightning. I thought
the sound was more thunder, rolling from the sea, and the shattering impact on my left was the lightning strike or maybe the storm
blowing out a window. Without thinking, as though pausing to answer the phone during a movie, I hit stop on the video remote control. A red X flashed on the screen and it went blank.

"Oh shit," I blurted, realizing I'd fucked up. Then Nic gasped and
I looked where she was looking. The sliding glass door was gone
and a woman was standing in the frame, pointing a large machine

pistol at us while the rain fell in curtains around her. She wore skin-tight pink Lycra pants, red booties, and a purple sports bra. A man flanked her, pistol up, dressed in small, tight, crotch-cuddling running shorts, hiking boots, and a T-shirt slit to make room for his swollen biceps. The front door opened and another guy came in, aiming a shotgun. He was in running tights that contoured his buttocks and genitals, sneakers with neon springs under the heels, and a tight mesh top. We raised our hands, the remote still in mine, as the woman stepped through the shattered frame, glass crunching under her sneakers.

"Who the fuck are you guys?" Nic asked.

The girl ignored her and stepped up to me.

"Nice to look at you again," she said in her heavy accent.

"Hi," I said, my hands in the air. "Yes, it's funny to bump into you here." I turned to Nic. "She works for Buck Norman, the director. But I'm sorry, I don't recall your name."

"John," she said.

"You're an actress?" Nic asked, looking her over, confused and frightened but curious.

"No." She smiled. "I am not actress. But I make the action. I can say this in English?"

"You mean, you take action?" I asked.

"Take? No I give. I give action."

"Yes, but that's not how you say it. You say take."

"Why take if give?"

"Or just act. You act."

"Yes OK." She laughed. "I like." She pointed the gun at Nic. "I am not actress but I act, OK?"

Nic nodded. "Sure."

"And you are the harlot."

"I'm what?"

"The harlot. Is the right word? Perform sex acts for payment?"

"Let's just say I act, like you, OK?" Nic said.

John shrugged. "OK, keep your pants untwisted." She turned back to me. "You were watching a movie, maybe?" she asked. "We are also looking for a movie."

"We were about to," I said. "There was a disk in the player."

John took my remote. She aimed it and hit play. Static. She shrugged and turned it off.

"The movie we want is real movie. You know, not disk. Old fashionable film. Where is it?" She smiled again. "Just tell us and no problemo."

I smiled back. "We'd love that. We definitely do not want any problemos." My arms were getting tired and I could see Nic's sagging as she also smiled and shrugged her empty hands. "But unfortunately we just don't know. We have no idea. Sorry."

"Sorry," Nic chimed along.

"That's OK," John said. Then her hand flashed out and the gun hit me in the mouth. It seemed like nothing, a mere flick of the wrist, like a good tennis player catching a lob, but I stumbled back, my face ringing and my mouth full of blood. I tried to curse but I just burbled, and something hard rolled on my tongue. It felt a lot like a tooth.

"You watch her," she told one of the aerobics dudes, Billy or Joel, I forget. "You bring him with me."

The other muscle dude, (Joel?) poked me with a gun, and I followed John, afraid of another blow. As I passed Nic I heard a small whimper, whether of fear or sympathy, I don't know. Blood still dribbled down my chin, my shirt was soaked, and my tongue had definitely located an empty spot on my upper left corner.

"Don't worry," I reassured Nic, or tried to, but it sounded, well, rather worrying, like "Doonesbury." The guy behind me pushed and I coughed out my tooth. It went skittering across the tile floor. "Toof, toof!" I yelled, chasing it around. John turned back.

"What now?"

"He puffed me," I explained as I searched the floor. It was gone.

"Stop fooling around. Both of you," she said and led us into the studio. She pointed to a rattan armchair. "Tie him to that."

I tried to say it wasn't necessary, but "necessary" was too hard to say, and Joel bungee-corded my arms to the arms and my legs to the legs of the chair. I had a perfect view of the mural. I noticed how artfully the blood had been done: where the woman drove a sword into the bull, the gore seemed splashed on, as though it had actually gushed onto the painting, rather than being in the painting, if that makes sense. Also, I couldn't help observing that Naught had taken special care with the genitals. Where the bull's oversized penis met her vagina, every vein and curlicue of hair was lovingly and realistically rendered. On the other hand, the sky was stylized, with the sun dead center between the bull's horns. And the landscape, now that I stared at it, looked familiar. The long desert horizontals, the odd rocks and rounded protrusions, the witchy humanoid cacti. It was Joshua Tree, the national park right by Twentynine Palms.

The pain in my mouth had receded to a low, steady throb, like a bass line, more soul than funk, and there was less blood than before. I figured they intended to interrogate me now, and I quickly reassessed my obligation to Lonsky and the cause of justice in general. I decided to take a quick shot at lying and then talk. John calmly set her gun down and removed her fanny pack, while her sidekick languidly aimed his gun at my lap. He leaned back against the fresh mural.

"Careble," I said, lisping through my fat lips. "Baint's web!"

Joel frowned at me.

"Webaint!" I said. "Webaint!"

"You shut your face up!" The boy barked in a thick Russian brogue, waving his machine pistol at me. I flinched and ducked automatically, although of course I couldn't move. A howl came from the next room. "Whada buck is dat?" I blurted, straining against the bungee cords. "If dat Nic?"

"Let me check," John said and looked into the next room. "Yes it is." She glanced at her companion and they both giggled. "Our friend has a fetish for nipples and your lady has pleasant ones."

"Thass unef . . . You don affa do dat!" I sputtered, blood spraying through the gap where my tooth had been. John unzipped her pack, rummaging in it calmly like she was looking for her lipstick, then crossed to the table behind me.

"Liffen," I said. "I fink we got awff to a bad shtart. Maybe you hab the wong idea. I'm only here becauf I ga a note fum a shrange hombre, bery shrange . . ." I was straining to the left as I spoke, toward where I thought she was, but John appeared on my right, and before I could register what was happening, she leaned over my hand, where it was lashed to the arm of the chair, and wielding a small, sharp pair of gardening shears, the kind with a spring between the handles, she grasped my right pinky finger, and neatly chopped it off, just below the joint. My finger jumped away, like a snipped twig.

Stunned and numb, I found myself staring at the little stump for an endless second before blood and searing pain began to flow. Then I screamed, so loud and high I shocked myself. The terrible wail seemed to come from far off, perhaps from a small animal caught in a steel trap. My hand too seemed a mile away, pumping blood like a faucet someone forgot to turn off. Tears flooded my eyes and my vision burned. I was crying. Then I felt the left pinky go. I entered a new realm of pain. Both hands seemed to be like torches, blazing.

"I wuz gomma talk," I whimpered. "I wuz gomma talk . . ." I fought the urge to faint. My vision cleared slightly and she appeared before me, holding my two little pinkies in her palm.

"OK, now," she said, delicately sliding a pinky, nail first, into my right nostril. Joel snickered. She slid in the left, also up to the first knuckle so it stuck. "I want you to listen very careful. Are you listening?"

I nodded. "Yef." I had to gasp air through my wounded mouth.

"Good," she said, lifting the shears again, and showing them to me, the hook-nosed blades now caked with blood. "Because I am only going to ask you eight more times . . ."

"No," I howled, screaming like a child, now too frantic even to spill my guts, stuttering, bubbling, squirming, and crying. Joel laughed uproariously. John snapped the shears like a hungry red beak before me. I shook my head and a pinky flew out. Joel guffawed even louder, pointing at me with glee. He noticed his arm was blue from wet sky. Looking down, he realized that he'd smeared his clothes with paint, smudging the mural behind him. He began to curse madly in Russian while John pointed at him and laughed merrily. Furious, he pointed his gun at me.

"Fuck you off, you fuck!"

I shook my head. He took careful aim at my face. I held my breath. Then his skull exploded. I heard the shot, breaking glass, and a whistle past my ear. His brain matter sprayed over the mural and, as John and I both stared, his eyes rolled up and he fell, revealing a back covered in a muddy rainbow of paint. As he hit the ground another shot rang out, chipping out a chunk of the bull's flank and revealing white plaster beneath it.

John reacted, diving like a swimmer across the room to the table where her gun lay and snatching it up as the table, cluttered with paints and brushes, collapsed beneath her. I twisted in my chair, unable to see the shooter behind me. As several more shots cracked the air, John sprang back up like a jack-in-the box, gun in hand, and unleashed an ear-splitting barrage. I tipped my chair violently sideways and went down as smoke and fire danced around the mouth of her gun. More glass shattered, I heard a grunt, and, like a deer, John dashed from the room.

I lay on my side in the sudden stillness, though I could hear voices and scattered shots beyond the walls. I craned my neck to see behind me. Uncle Coffee and Donuts lay dead in the patio door, eyes wide, chest soaked in red, a pistol still clenched in his fist. His upturned cowboy hat sat nearby, like an empty bowl. The fall had loosened the cord on my right leg and I could feel that the flimsy arm of the old chair was shaky too. Twisting myself as I never could in yoga, I managed to get my right foot on the floor and then to

stand, crouched low like an ancient hermit, the chair still strapped
to my back like a skeleton I was taking for a ride. I hobbled up to
the room's remaining table and leaned the chair's right arm (and
my own, still tied) against the table's edge. I took a deep breath, and
before I could reconsider, jumped up, bringing the chair down on
the rim of the table with all my weight. The chair's arm broke, loos-
ing the cord and freeing my own arm as it also freed a new spurt
of blood from my hand. Hissing through my teeth, I wriggled out
of my trap, undoing the cords from my left arm and leg. I felt like
shit, but even gimping around on numb, twisted legs and trailing
fat drops of blood from both missing pinkies, I was desperate to escape that room. Fear and adrenaline kept me moving. The pop and
boom of gunfire came from next door like the night's storm crackling over the sea. I picked up Joel's gun from where it lay alongside his paint-smeared body, clutching it awkwardly between my
crippled hands. The mural was cracked, as if the desert had broken
open, revealing the void beneath it. The bull was split down the
side. Mona had a bullet in her mouth. Ducking low, I crept up to the
door and peeked into the living room.

John and Billy, her other muscle boy, were crouched behind toppled furniture, firing out onto the patio through the holes that had
once been glass doors, while random shots from beyond blasted the
room to bits. In the midst of it was Nic, crouched in a corner like a
terrified animal, shaking like I'd seen mice and bunnies shake. Her
top was ripped and her breasts bare, but from what I could see her
nipples were intact. I leaned against the doorframe. Shock had really set in now, and I was in less pain, but numbness was spreading
through my hands. Finger by finger, they seemed to fan like fronds,
and the loss of blood was blurring my mind. The walls were swimming and the paintings swelled, images of Mona palpitating into life,
fattening and flattening, dancing and flowing along the edges of my
eyes. I struggled to aim the gun. My hands were trembling, slip-
pery with blood and oddly unbalanced without their pinkies. Nic

saw me and released a small choked cry, like a single swallow fluttering away. The muscle dude looked over first, saw me propping my gun up, weak legs bent, and he laughed, calling to John in Russian. She turned to me, smiled, and raised her gun.

I shot her. My aim wasn't much, and my hands shook, and the power of the gun threw me, but it didn't matter. I squeezed the trigger and the gun spat and a row of huge red tears opened in her flesh, belly, chest, face, and she fell back, dead. The boy went to fire but I squeezed my trigger again, wheeling in his general direction. This time I didn't aim at all and I was low, but the line of bullets cut across his thighs and he went down on his knees, firing his own gun up into the ceiling. He grunted—"Kafka," it sounded like—staring at me with big dark eyes. "Kafka," he coughed again, softly. By now my head was spinning and my ears rang. Steadying myself against the wall, I raised my gun carefully and shot again, a full burst right into his chest. He fell on his side. "Beckett," he whispered as blood flowed from his lips. The room was quiet. Nic and I both stayed where we were, she curled and staring, me against the wall, gun in both hands, leaking blood. I felt as though I were on the deck of a ship at sea, riding the high tide of my own wavering consciousness and feeling the house slide away beneath my feet. Ramón appeared in the doorway, holding his pistol. He rushed to Nic first, and checked her quickly. Blind Uncle stepped in, calm as ever, holding a rifle, which seemed to be pointed at me. Ramón called to him in Spanish, wrapping his jean jacket around Nic. Then he came to me.

"OK, amigo, it's over now." I nodded and let him take the gun. "We're going to bring you to the hospital."

"Glate," I said, my voice sounding surprisingly calm and yet odd, as if it were coming from someone else, another guy just off to my left. "I fink I'm gomma pass ow now."

"Good idea, go ahead," Ramón said.

"Pleab done forged my fingerth," I added, or imagined I added, as everything went dark.

81

I MISSED MOST OF THE NEXT twelve hours, so I will just report the high-lights as they were related to me. Ramón and the Blind Uncle some-how got me to the car, where they propped me in the back along with poor Uncle Coffee and Donuts, whom they hid under a blanket. Nic found my fingers. She dropped them in a ziplock bag and put that in a cup of ice, having heard somewhere that it was the thing to do. They rushed me to the closest large hospital, in Puerto Vallarta, and my fingers were reattached while my armed protectors sat out-side. Nic paid in cash. They brought in a dentist to patch up my tooth as well. When I awoke my fingers were like two small portions of cotton candy, wads of white cotton over gauze, held in place with tape. They told me to change the dressings daily and to see a doctor in LA right away. Nic told me she'd called Lonsky while I was out.

"Great. What did he say?"

"He said your injuries were unfortunate but that our overall con-duct was most suitable."

"That's it? Did you tell him about my wife?"

She patted my shoulder. "Of course. He said don't worry and that we would figure it all out together. Everything will be fine."

"Right. Just tell me what he really said."

She frowned. "He said interesting, but that he had to get off the line because his breakfast was ready."

"That fat bastard. What about Zed being alive? And the movie?"

"He just said return to America. He said to call your friend the cinephile, whoever that is, and see if he'll meet us with a projector."

"Milo? Lonsky wants him to come to the house?"

"No. We're picking Solar up and going right out to the desert to get the film from that bank. He said not to tarry."

"He's coming? To Twentynine Palms?"

"Yup."

"That is serious. We'd better get going." Determined, I pushed away the covers and stood up. My bare feet hit the linoleum. "Um, can you help me put on my pants?"

Ramón called a fellow taxi driver to take us to the airport and then returned to Tepic to organize another funeral for his uncle. The Blind Uncle gave us tight hugs. Ramón said he'd spoken to the owner of the white house, and the bodies we'd left behind would disappear. He shrugged.

"I am sorry to say that this is easily done in Mexico."

"Thank you," I said. "For everything. I don't know what I can do to repay you."

He smiled. "That is easy, *cabrón*. You can find the man who is responsible for my uncle, and my cousin too. And then you can kill him."

82

I HID MY HANDS under an airline blanket to avoid stares on the plane. "How's my tooth look?" I asked Nic.

"Fine. Just let it rest," she said, tucking me in and opening a magazine. We had not discussed the events of the previous night, except to ask each other, in an overly caring way, every time the flight attendant brought apple juice or we buckled our seat belts, Are you OK? But something between us had shifted. We sat close, shoulders and thighs touching, as if that were a normal thing. We lapsed into long silences and then picked up the strands of unfinished discussions. We were a couple. It was as if we had lived out a long, rocky relationship in a few days. And like many couples, we had a secret drama, those others who both joined and split us: Mona, a woman neither of us knew, but who had brought us together. And that other shadow, my wife, who had disappeared, only to return as a stranger, arriving out of a past grown so mysterious, it loomed before me now, imminent and impenetrable, like the future.

83

WE LANDED IN SAN DIEGO and picked up the car. Nic drove. As soon as my phone found a signal, I tried my wife's number. A recording told me that the subscriber was not accepting calls. And if she never did, how would I really feel? Hadn't some part of me wished for exactly this? I was free. I glanced at my blond companion coolly changing lanes. She noticed my stare and smiled.

"Why don't you try to nap?" she asked.

"I can't," I said and shut my eyes, certain I was too distraught to sleep. When I opened them I was outside the Lonsky residence and I felt almost normal.

Roz answered the door. Fine and snow-pure, her hair was like a halo, the pink of her skull shining through. She wore a powder-blue pantsuit, with nothing under the jacket but her bra.

"Oh, it's you. Nice tooth."

"What? Oh, is it noticeable?" I smiled and tested it with my tongue. "Thanks. It's from Mexico."

"Yeah, it looks Mexican."

"It does? Huh. And you can tell which one is new?"

Nic stepped between us. "Is Solar around?"

"Yeah," Roz said, lighting a 100. "And I hope you've come to talk him out of this nonsense. The fool hasn't been anywhere except the nuthouse in a decade."

"Kornberg! Kornberg!" I heard his bellow issue from the study and went in, trailed by Nic and Roz. The big man was dressing. He wore the pants and vest of a summer suit in white linen, a pale pink shirt, and black suspenders. He was knotting a deep blue tie, while his jacket enveloped the back of his chair. Mrs. Moon flustered about, adding items to a huge old leather suitcase that looked like something Charlie Chaplin might stow away inside.

"Ah, there you are," he said. "I'm almost ready to depart. Your friend Milo called and he obtained the projector. He's meeting us at the hotel." He slipped on his jacket and began to fold a silk hanky that matched the blue of his tie. "Nice tooth."

Nic shook her head. "Solar . . ." she began.

"You can tell too?" I said. "Funny, it doesn't hurt at all. I can't even remember which it is."

"Just remember it's the gold one," Lonksy suggested.

"Gold?" I asked. "What? Where's a mirror?"

"Next door." Solar waved a distracted hand.

"Wait . . ." Nic said. I rushed next door to the bathroom mirror. My upper left canine gleamed. Gold. Nic put her hand on my shoulder.

"I was going to tell you. I just wanted you to relax a bit first."

"I look ridiculous," I said, staring into my mouth.

"Not really. It looks kind of cool. Anyway, you can have it changed." She kissed my cheek. "It's sexy. I promise. Now let me change those dressings while we're here."

She opened her bag and began pulling out supplies. She looked in the medicine cabinet and found a small scissors, then shut it, causing my face to reappear. I practiced different expressions, trying to talk and smile without showing my tooth. Nic snipped away the tape and unwound the wrapping from my pinkies as if opening a prize. They were fat and turgid, like swollen tongues or blind purple grubs, stitched together with black thread.

"They look good," Nic said, not very convincingly. "I mean considering."

Lonsky loomed in the door. "We should leave," he said, finalizing his tie in the mirror. "I'm packed and ready, and I want to arrive before dinner. And by the way, you're pinkies are transposed."

"They're what?" I asked, holding them out like odd accessories I was considering returning to a store.

"Is that the word I want?" he said. "Reversed? They attached the severed appendages to the wrong stumps."

"No." I stared hard at them. "That's impossible. How do you know?"

"Because your right pinky, the old right, had a spot of psoriasis on the outside. And your left was a bit bent, perhaps from a childhood accident."

"What?" I remembered the psoriasis, and the jammed finger when I fell off my bike at twelve, my last bad injury till now. "Holy fuck, you're right. Jesus, what did those monsters do to me while I was unconscious?"

Nic patted my arm. "It looks fine, no one can tell."

"Fine? They maimed me. Weren't you watching?"

"I was in shock. That man was pinching my nipples. They're really sore."

"Yeah well, at least they're still attached. And to the right tits."

"Get a hold of yourself," Lonsky said. "They are merely pinkies after all. The least of the digits. Thumbs would be another matter. Or ears. Anyway, perhaps they can be corrected at a later date, but we really must go now if we're going to make dinner. I reserved a table."

"Solar," I said. "Fuck dinner." I slipped away from Nic and stood in the doorway, gauze trailing from my hands. "I want to know right now before we go anywhere. What do you know about my wife?"

"No more than you," he said, straightening his collar. "I don't even know the woman."

"I'm serious. I want to know what's going on. This can't be a coincidence."

He turned to regard me from his great eminence. He was as wide as the door. I felt I was staring up at a monument.

"No it cannot," he told me. "I have always said so. And now, if you indeed want to know the truth, which people rarely do, then I suggest we suspend debate, wrap your mismatched appendages, and proceed."

And with that Solar Lonsky proceeded, with a quiet dignity, out of his front door.

84

JOSHUA TREE IS MORE than just a great place to trip on mushrooms. It is a place created by the gods while they were tripping on mushrooms. It is the Land of the Lost. It is Bedrock, a Flintstones landscape of cartoon colors and morphing, melting shapes. Boulders the size of two-family homes are strewn like forgotten marbles across the horizon. There are drip castles and rock skulls, ice cream sundaes and sleeping dinosaurs all of stone and sand. There is a mountain made entirely of bowling balls. Then there are the namesake cacti, an army of scarecrows, pierced Gumbys beseeching the empty sky, crucified trees with pincushion hands and thorny heads that flame into white blossoms when the rain comes in the spring.

We took the Twentynine Palms Highway into the tiny sun-dazed town, low buildings and blank streets sparsely populated with an odd mix of spiritual hippies, desert rats, and Marines from the nearby base. We found the UPS franchise and Nic and I went in, leaving Lonsky stowed in the backseat, which he'd chosen for safety reasons. I'd been mulling the name question over during the drive, wondering what alias Zed would choose, and gave the clerk, a stout lady, redheaded and soap-pale in her glass room of frozen air, my best shot. Minutes later, she handed me a small express envelope addressed to B. Traven. It contained another plain white envelope, which in turn held a small key and a numerical code on a slip of paper: 12-15-22-5 6-18-15-13 8-1-4-5-19.

In the car, Lonsky glanced at the paper and chuckled. "Quite witty, really. He would have been a man worth meeting."

"You mean Zed?" I asked, craning my head. "Why?"

Lonsky scowled at me. "Surely you can solve a simple alphanumerical substitution code, Kornberg. They're for children." Nic grinned at this while she drove.

"Let's just say I don't feel like it."

"If one replaces the numbers with the corresponding letters, the message reads 'love from Hades.' No doubt Zed felt it was his own, and the real B. Traven's, most suitable return address."

At the bank, Nic said she was Mona Naught's daughter, and gave the code, which no one there chuckled at, and after a long delay, the young blond clerk returned.

"Oh my God," she warbled in her frank California accent. "No one's opened this box in ten years," as if ten were a thousand and we were unearthing a time capsule. She asked us if we wanted a private room, but she was clearly hoping not and it didn't seem likely that the box contained diamonds or a bomb. So she turned her key and I turned mine. She held her breath and widened her eyes. Nic grabbed my wrist under the counter. The lid stuck for a second and then I opened it with a pop. It contained two unlabeled film canisters. "Sixteen millimeter, I think," I said.

The clerk looked bummed. "Maybe you should open them and check," she suggested. We declined and returned to the car. While our backs were turned, evening had begun to creep in. The horizon darkened, and as evening approached, Lonsky's belly was growling.

"Well done," he said when I handed him the canisters. "We will watch these right after dinner."

"Do you really think we should wait?" I asked.

"I can't think on an empty stomach," Lonsky said petulantly.

"How about some nuts?" Nic asked. "Or chips and salsa?"

He didn't even stoop to a reply. Finally we compromised and pulled into a diner he somehow knew and picked up a couple of barbequed pork sandwiches and coleslaw sides to tide him over and keep his brain going. Then we went to the inn where he'd booked our rooms. Built on a palmy oasis, it was a pleasantly run-down cluster of bungalows surrounding a pool where a boy in goggles and a girl in a swim cap and nose plugs were seeing who could hold their breath the longest, and a restaurant, of which Lonsky approved as "homey and fulfilling." Like a bear leaving his winter cave, he emerged, blinking and grumbling, from the backseat and put on a panama hat.

Milo had already arrived with the projector and had set up in Lonksy's bungalow, which contained a rustic lounge. He'd hung a bedsheet on the wall and was extremely bored after hours of waiting with no TV or Internet.

"Jesus fucking Christ you kept me waiting long enough," he said as we entered. "Some emergency." Then noticing my hands, he brightened. "Holy shit, what happened to you? Hey!" He pointed cheerfully at my mouth, which I'd almost managed to forget for a minute. "You look like Eli Wallach in *The Good, the Bad, and the Ugly*. He's the ugly," he explained to Lonksy, in case he didn't know the film. Lonsky lowered himself onto a wicker love seat, which sighed tragically beneath him.

"Sandwiches," he commanded.

I handed him the paper bag and gave Milo the canisters. "Are you going to show this or not?"

Milo carefully pried open a canister. "The film gets brittle sitting so long and I don't want it to break." He slipped on white cotton gloves and took out a small film splicer and some black leader. While he worked, Lonksy munched thoughtfully. Nic offered to find cold drinks and ice.

"Do you need aspirin, for your hands?" she asked, stroking my arm.

"No thanks," I said, and she smiled, then sashayed out.

Milo turned to me, his voice low. "Are you doing her?"

"Yeah," I said. "Sort of. I guess."

"Nice work," he said, and I couldn't help feeling a surge of foolish pride. "I'm glad too," he went on, "because it makes it easier to break the news about me and MJ."

"What news?"

"We're going to have a baby."

"When? I've only been gone two days."

"Her and Margie want kids and they asked me to be the donor. We were worried you might be, you know, crushed emotionally, since you always had a thing for her and your wife just dumped you."

"But I don't have a thing."

"Whatever. It just seemed emotionally cleaner with me. Plus I'm extremely virile. My sperm count is unusually high. And my motility's off the charts."

"OK. Well, congratulations. That's . . . intense."

"They're talking turkey baster, but I'm pushing for direct insemination. You know. Penile. I think it's better for the kid."

"I thought you were gay?"

"What're you talking about? I'm so bi it's ridiculous. I watch straight porn all the time. I was watching *Sausage Fest Two* last night. Twenty naked dudes and this fat chick."

"If you say so."

He gave me an evil look and began to rewind the reel. "The point, hombre, is that MJ wants my sperm, not yours. OK? I'm going to breed with her and then while they raise the kid I will live temporarily in the guesthouse. Sorry if that's tough for you to accept. The guesthouse has its own little sauna."

"Congratulations, stud." I slapped his back. "I'm a proud uncle."

"Thanks." He grinned and slid a reel onto the arm of the projector. "I'm just glad you found a replacement for Lala. She kind of looks like her too."

"No she doesn't. She's blond and taller."

"Whatever. She's your type. The tragic femme fatale type."

"But she turned out not to be that at all," I said. "That was an act. She's more the hard-nosed chick with the soft heart. And besides, Lala's Mexican." I sighed. "At least that's one fact we established about her."

"I know. The big guy told me. Well, hang in there." He flipped a switch and the machine began to hum, throwing a white square onto the sheet. "Let's see what happens in the next reel. Go get your girl and your soda. It's showtime."

85

UNLIKE THE OTHER FILMS in the trilogy, *Ascension* was just uncut footage, shown as it was shot in the camera, so one could only guess at the themes and intended sequence. The movie was set in the desert, close to where we sat, among the crags and ridges of the park. The film stock gave it a brightly dated look, but the homemade, school-play-style costumes, and the timeless, epic, Biblical-Western scenery made it seem as if it could have been shot any time.

Two women in goddess gear (gauzy whatevers and body glitter, Venetian masks and peacock feathers) scamper over desert landmarks while a group of men in black suits, ties, and black masks pursues them. There were a lot of beauty shots: erect nipples silhouetted against the tangerine sun, firm buttocks rising between red rocks, a landscape of hips and hollows, soft focus sand-slopes and close-up beads of sweat. The damsels appear and disappear, with simple camera trickery, teasing and cajoling the men, who seem to be invoking them as muses or spirits, able to bestow the various gifts they demand: knowledge, power, money, glory, talent. A guy I knew was Zed, from his voice, stumbled around, sand in his hair, and shouted at the heavens, "Genius! Grant me genius, you goddess, you bitch, and I will give you all, my soul, my heart, my balls!" This drew snickers from Milo and Nic. Lonsky watched impassively, though I could hear his slow breathing back there, like an idling machine, like an enormous cat.

The second reel turns darker, in color and mood. The characters can be seen drinking from wine and whiskey bottles, smoking joints and taking what looks like acid, little white confetti flakes melting on the tongue. Behind them the sun begins its slow decline, and the desert light show turns on. There is sex, couples and groups, cavorting about the rocks and grappling in the dust, nude but for masks and climbing boots, as well as some gloves and capes. The women are unshaven, pits and groins.

"Wow, that's some serious bush," Milo called out, then turned to Nic, as if placating her, "I dig it."

"I don't," she said.

"No, me neither," he said. "I was just saying that to see if you shaved. And you do."

"Waxed, sucker."

"OK, shush," I said, smiling proudly at the way she'd handled him. "Check this out."

The women now stand triumphant-like, nude and with their arms spread, atop a narrow peak, crowned by the rays of the bloodred sun and calling for sacrifice. They keep sliding down the crumbling rock face and then clambering back up, raising their fists, and screaming, blood, blood, give us blood. Then one of the masked men, a schlubby guy with pale skin, a round belly and thin hairy legs, grabs Zed and pushes him over a cliff. A moment later someone yells cut, and he pops back up. As the camera wanders, we see that really he has only jumped down a few feet to a ridge. They reset and do it again. Again. The guy, the pusher, takes off his mask and wipes the grit and sweat from his eyes. Someone hands him a hanky. I recognized him from the other films, where he'd appeared as an ass kisser and a spear holder. Next they do a variation where he and Zed pretend to fight and both fall screaming, and then one where the pale guy just jumps. Zed looked pretty good naked, tan and lean with a big metal star on a chain around his neck. In the next shot Zed is alone, closer in, naked and unmasked, with a pistol. He holds it to his head, takes a deep breath, howls and then pulls the trigger. Nothing. He laughs and says, "How was that?" An offscreen voice says, "OK, but don't scream." He does it again, calmly. Someone yells, Bang! and he falls. He does it again. Again.

Now it is getting dark and they have a fire going. The third man, broad and strong, still masked and costumed, is kneeling behind the pale guy, pressing a dagger to his throat, and giggling. Their eyes are crazy in the flame light, gleaming dark and wet, pupils wide as saucers. We hear Zed offscreen, "OK, stop fucking around. We're going to lose the light in a second. Say the line."

"Hee, hee . . ." The masked fellow presses the blade. "You want clean shaven or mustache?"

"Cut!" Zed yells. "Fuck you. Seriously."

They do it again. The knife holder takes a deep breath, swallows his giggles, and booms: "I am the dark lord. I offer blood. I will rule here on earth and in hell."

"Good! Again!" They do it again.

"Good! Again!" They do it again.

"Good! Again!" He does it again. Then he cuts the schlubby guy's throat.

For a second no one else does anything. You can feel the shock. The victim himself looks confused, still smiling, as another red smile spreads across his neck. Then it flaps open like a busted lip and the blood pours. The killer laughs, high and fast. It sounded familiar.

"What the fuck!" Zed runs on camera, pushing the guy with the knife away, and tries to stanch the blood with a tie-dyed scarf. Both naked men are soaked. The women scream and scream. The killer's mask is knocked askew. He is still giggling. It is Buck Norman.

"See, I really am the dark king!" he chortles.

Zed pushes him back, screaming. "What did you fucking do? What did you fucking do?"

"See Zed, I really am!" Buck rambles on. "Not the king I mean, the dark prince! I really am." He grabs Zed, still waving the knife. "I rule! Not you! I rule!"

Zed flings the knife away and punches him in the face. The women rush over, crying, screaming. Their masks are off. The first girl I had not seen before, though she does look similar to the way Nic had: curvy, tan, dark-haired, green-eyed.

"Mona," Lonsky said, from the back. No one else spoke.

The next girl looks like she could be her cousin. She is maybe a bit younger and thinner than she would be now, but still I know her immediately. She is my wife.

86

THERE WAS A LONG silence, as in a real movie when the credits roll and everyone waits for the lights or music, as if for permission to get up. The film ran through the gate and started flapping. A white square like an empty window opened in the wall. A breeze rippled the sheet. Then I realized Nic was quietly crying. I wanted to take her hand but something held down my arm. Milo got up to stop the projector. The white window shut and it was dark. Lonksy turned on a lamp. A yellow umbrella spread. He said, "Kornberg, kindly get Mister Norman's man, Russ, I believe, on the phone for me, if you please."

I didn't move. "That was my wife, Solar."

"Yes, I know."

"You know?"

"Please, the phone first. Then we'll talk."

I got up. Now, in the soft lamplight, I could see that Nic was weeping into her palms but I dug in my pockets for my phone. I found Russ's number and pressed it.

"Here," I said. "It's ringing."

"Excuse me," Nic said and hurried out. I let her go.

Lonksy spoke into the phone. "Good evening. My name is Solar Lonsky. May I please speak to Mr. Buck Norman? It is regarding a film. Yes, I'll hold." He called after Nic: "We'll have dinner after this call," he said, "I booked a table," but she didn't turn. He frowned, then turned away as someone came on the phone. "Yes, Mr. Norman, good evening. Yes, I do, I just watched it. I don't know your other films, I admit, but your performance in this one is riveting. Yes. And the woman, Mona, she is alive? Put her on please." There was a pause. "Hello? Yes. Are you all right? I . . ." He frowned again. "Yes. Yes, I can get a map. Eight tomorrow then. No, I won't. Very good. Good night."

He turned off the phone and handed it back to me. "The exchange will be tomorrow on a high cliff a few miles inside the park, where it will be easy to see who's approaching, so we can't rely on the police. He put Mona on the phone, though of course all she said was yes. It could all be fakery. We will have to wait and hope. Milo, thank you, you've been most helpful indeed. We won't need you tomorrow but perhaps right now you could ask for a map in the office, then meet us in the dining room for dinner. I'd like a moment with Samuel."

"Sure." Milo put the film in the can, smiled sadly at me, and left.

"You said no cops," I told Lonsky. "But these people are killers. It will be very risky tomorrow."

"No doubt," he said. "You are walking proof of their ruthlessness. I've come prepared." He reached into his jacket and pulled a pistol from a shoulder holster. It was huge, a monstrous black Magnum.

"My God, don't wave that thing around."

"Don't worry, it's not loaded. Tomorrow it will be. It was my father's." He set it on the table. I didn't feel any safer.

I said, "Tell me about my wife."

"Please, sit," he said. I did, and he spoke, evenly and without pauses, as though he were reading from a book.

"A few months after I first met Mona in the hospital, she received a visit. I took special note, of course. I was in love with her already and fascinated with every aspect of her life, but also because she had never to my knowledge received a visitor, or for that matter any mail or phone calls at all. In fact, this was the one and only visit she ever had. Her guest was a young dark-haired woman, beautiful and very well dressed. They could have passed for cousins or even sisters, though of course the visitor looked healthier, stronger, and tanner than Mona, who'd been in a locked ward for six months. I don't know what they spoke about, they retired to Mona's room alone, but I pretended to nap in a chair in the lobby, and when the guest left, I noticed that she was crying. I peeked at the nurse's log. The visitor's name was Natalia Montes. Your wife to be.

"Since, as I said, she was the only visitor Mona ever had, the only connection to the outside world, I took an interest in Ms. Montes and kept track of her from a distance. I knew that she was from Mexico, that she worked at a local fashion shop, that she soon married and bought a house. I knew your name too and your address. Again these were mere facts in my file. I gave them no special attention, I was simply curious about anything to do with Mona. And so the years passed, until a week ago, when Dr. Parker called. Mona was missing, possibly in danger, and he asked for my help. Suddenly, I had a case. I needed an assistant of course, someone local to do the legwork, so I visited the jobseekers website and saw your résumé. Well you know how I feel about coincidences. There are none. I called you in immediately. When, during our initial meeting, I realized that your wife had left you, I knew my intuition was correct: the two events were somehow connected. And when you reported your wife's disappearance, I realized that by solving your own mystery, you would in the end help solve mine."

"Why didn't you tell me?"

"Tell you what? I had no answers to give. I had to let you lead me. But when Ms. Flynn called this morning with the information about your wife's photo, I understood, and now that theory has been confirmed: it seems your wife was Mona's Mexican friend, as mentioned by your informants, the third in the threesome with Zed, the other performer in the films. Probably your wife assisted the couple in their deception, the fake death, the escape, and then kept their secret safe all this time. Perhaps she even obtained that false ID to reenter the country safely. She met you, got married, went on with her own life. Then years later, when, Zed, realizing he was dying, attempted to reconnect with Mona, she was drawn back in. I am sorry to say this, but I think it is highly likely that she is dead, buried under another name in Mexico, and that Mr. Norman has used his great influence to cover his tracks and falsify the records. I have to surmise that it was her body all along, that it was she who was thrown from the balcony that night.

"My condolences. I know that due to my own psychological and emotional difficulties I do not process or demonstrate sentiment in

the culturally prescribed manner, and I am further emotionally insulated from my fellow humans by this excess of fat, but please accept my sympathies nevertheless."

"Thanks," I said. I hadn't moved. I didn't know what to do next.

"No doubt you are in shock. Would you like an alcoholic drink to
soothe your nerves? Or a whole roast chicken with new potatoes? I
find that helpful sometimes. They are juiciest when roasted whole."

"No thanks."

"I will leave you then, to grieve. It is nearly time for dinner. I'm
told the meeting spot is about twenty minutes' drive from here. Let's
convene for breakfast at seven."

He left for dinner. I grieved. Or I tried to. I stepped outside into
the soft dark and tried, but really I felt not much. Or to be honest,
nothing. But maybe that was right. That was it: the big nothing,
opening within me, vast as the nothing all around me. It was always
there, of course, but now I noticed it, felt it, sounded it, each thought
like an echo bouncing back to tell me of that emptiness, like a stone
dropped into a well. I took a last breath of sage-scented night and
went into the glowing cabin where Nic was waiting, to tell her my
wife was dead.

PART VII

ASCENSION

87

MY NAME IS EULALIA NATALIA Santoya de Marías de Montes, but I have
had other names. I was Ramona to my mother. And I became Mrs.
Mona Naught. But to you I was always Lala. Who knows which of
these names I will be remembered by, if any? None will be written
on my grave, because, my dear husband, if you are reading this,
then I am already dead. Do you miss me? Would you be sad if you
knew I had died? Do you hate me for leaving you? Or, worse yet,
have you already forgotten me, grown indifferent, moved on? Am I
just your ex-wife, your first wife, an old story? Do you even want to
know the truth anymore, or is it better if I just rest in peace, buried
along with my lies and secrets? Or would you hate me even more if
you knew who I really was, besides your Lala? I was born Ramona
Noon. Yes, I am one quarter Asian on my mother's side, Chinese
and Pacific Islander, her own mother was from Malaysia, and her father was Portuguese, though she was illegitimate and never knew
him, a tradition in my family. My father was white, they said, Black
Irish, and so my mixed colors, my tan skin, green eyes, black hair,
the standard human look, the look that to a white person especially
makes me seem vaguely from anywhere except the lands of blond
and blue. I could be Israeli or Arab, Greek or Turk, Ecuadorian or
Chilean or Argentine. Or Mexican. Sorry, darling. Another lie. I
never met my father, or rather my one meeting with him, a surprise
and gift-laden visit on my fifth birthday, was so steeped in misty
legend that it might as well have been a fairy tale. It sure felt like
one. He was a famous movie star, according to my mom, though

she was sworn to secrecy, supposedly because of his evil wife, whom he didn't really love, and the deadly effect that the scandal would have on his career. The story seems dubious now, I know, but as a little girl with no daddy getting teased at school, I was comforted by the thought that my father was a great actor, not a random one-night stand, or worse, maybe, a married sugar daddy. My mother was a glamorous, brave, but tragic beauty, or a frustrated artist who'd sacrificed it all for love, but definitely not a kept woman, or a lazy welfare mom, or a *puta* as the other kids suggested. I guess that's how I first fell in love with movies (and how I fell for you, my movie lover, those quadruple features under the covers when we first met, those long weekends cooking and fucking with Godard and Lynch and Hawks). My mother was addicted of course. On Saturdays she'd pack a lunch and take me to the multiplex, let me buy a coke, and then we'd sneak from movie to movie, spending six or eight hours in the air-conditioned darkness, a magical cave far from the glare of reality. At home we'd sit on the couch and cry or laugh in front of the TV, and she'd teach me, the way other parents taught religion or family history, about the trials and struggles, the marriages and divorces of the gods. Gary Cooper, Gregory Peck, Jimmy Stewart, Henry Fonda, each of these magical heroes appeared before me as a symbolic father, a fantasy that was only inflamed by my mother's coy denials: "No, Clint Eastwood is not your dad, though of course if he was I could never tell you." Ava Gardner, Elizabeth Taylor, Kate Hepburn, each was an idealized version of my mother, who spoke as if she were one of them. "See that lipstick Marilyn has on there, the deep pink? I used to use that exact shade." Who knows what the truth was? The money arrived from somewhere. God knows my mother never worked. It was a bohemian household I suppose. She had a lot of artsy friends who came and went. Dancers, male and female and undecided, came by in the morning to stretch and do yoga on our deck. Actors came for tea in the afternoon, to cry after auditions or to practice lines with my mom, whom they somehow considered an expert based on

nothing but her supposed affairs with famous men and, in one particularly scandalous case, a famous actress whose marriage to a secretly gay movie star was just a front. Painters came for the potluck
dinners. A guy with a huge belly and huge beard ran the grill, a
painter she knew named Gus who lived in a school bus that he
sometimes parked in our driveway. Others turned up, their torn
jeans covered in paint but driving shiny Mercedes convertibles with
bowls of salad in the back and heaps of pink hamburger wrapped in
brown paper from Chalet Gourmet, the fancy shop. Two gay boys
in matching red jumpsuits brought a case of beer. Then late at night
the musicians would arrive, after their gigs or recording sessions,
dressed in black, instrument cases slung over their shoulders, to
play old records and smoke pot and fall asleep on the couch or
sometimes slip off to bed, in silence, with my mom. I remember
meeting Tom Waits when he showed up at our house for a party
with a carful of people, though he didn't say much, just flipped
through our books and records. Once Leonard Cohen was sipping
tea with brandy on the porch. Another night Siouxsie Sioux rang
the doorbell, asking directions. She was at the wrong party but she
came in for a drink anyway. Johnny Rotten got into a big argument
in the kitchen over how to make a proper gazpacho. Lux and Ivy
from the Cramps came to a barbecue but instead of drinking and
dancing with the grown-ups in the yard, Lux ended up watching
TV with me, *Scooby-Doo* and *Thunderbirds Are Go*. Joseph Beuys
came with some art people and someone spilled ketchup on his
shirt and he sat just in his vest and hat while my mom washed it.
Dennis Hopper showed up late and wouldn't leave. He talked to my
mom all night until she crashed and was still there in the living
room watching movies when I got up for school and I made Pop-
Tarts for us both. Coppola and Scorsese had a long, passionate debate beside the fire, and now I wish I'd listened, but back then I
didn't know who they were, just two madmen with beards and
wild eyes, waving their arms and yelling. William Burroughs sat in
an armchair saying nothing and I was scared. Rich and powerful

men would come to see my mother or take her away for weekends when I'd be left with a series of sketchy teenage babysitters. Often I'd get a present when she returned, or new clothes. Sometimes her date would enter my room awkwardly, and while my mom watched in the doorway, he'd pat my head and stiffly, formally, hand me a toy, which I would confusedly thank him for, with only my mother seeming happy about it, all smiles. I wonder now if more than one of them thought he was my father. I remember the first time I ate a hash brownie, thinking it was just a desert and laughed hysterically and then freaked out and had nightmares and the old lady from next door, she was a retired TV writer, took care of me because my mom wasn't home and my babysitter who'd baked the brownies had panicked and split. My mom was furious at the sitter, but of course didn't feel responsible herself. I remember her all dressed up, in her high heels and jewelry and her hair piled high. Some tall man in a suit carried me upstairs and put me to bed. At nine I swiped pot from her underwear drawer and smoked it with a friend. At ten I got drunk for the first time, sneaking sips at a party. By twelve I was tagging along to shows to see bands. At thirteen I tried ecstasy and coke with school friends, girls and boys who lived in parentless mansions in Beverly Hills, getting wasted and playing in their pools, watching movies in their screening rooms while the maids made us food. At fourteen I lost my virginity in the back of a car to the drummer from Spork, a noise band that was passing through, after a show. At fifteen I was on the party circuit, beach houses in Malibu, downtown lofts, sometimes turning up with my date at the same parties where my mom was with hers. My mother wasn't embarrassed by this, though often our dates were, since they sometimes knew each other, mine too old for me, hers too young for her. It was at one of those parties that summer, at a movie producer's house in Benedict Canyon, that I met my husband. My first husband, that is. Zed Naught. He actually asked me to marry him that night right there in the hot tub. What a nut, I hadn't even seen his face in the light. I had no idea what he looked like. I turned him down, of course, but he got my attention, that's for sure. It was pretty romantic. A crazy artist. A glamorous European. Of course I gravitated toward older men, being dadless and all. But we didn't sleep with each other that night. He didn't even try. I think he was too nervous. He came over the next night and talked to my mom, then took me out. She was thrilled. I know that sounds weird, but from her point of view it was perfect. Since my birth, she'd been obsessed with turning me into an actress. I barely went to school, but she hauled me to ballet lessons, piano lessons, singing lessons, all of which I sucked at. She dragged me to auditions and actually got me in several commercials and ads. As a toddler there was one for baby powder where I run around the house with an open thing of powder, spraying it everywhere, until the mom follows the trail and finds me and laughs. Years later, she was still bitter about how she should have played the mom, but I think the residuals from that commercial bought her car. Then I was in a local bank commercial, pretending, with a boy and two grown-ups I didn't know, to be a family in our new house. I remember fantasizing about how this supernormal family and house really were mine, and that the curly haired actor with the kind eyes was my dad. Finally, I am standing around in the background in an episode of *T. J. Hooker* when they go to a school gym. You see why it was so easy for my mom to accept my future husband when we first met. A famous filmmaker, a director, an artist and intellectual who spoke several languages, had read all those books, who painted, wrote, knew a million people. He was handsome too. Long hair, fair skin, beautiful hands. I felt dizzy looking in his eyes. We drove out to the beach to eat and after dinner took our shoes off and walked and walked and talked. He kissed me. We went back to his place and spent the night. We saw each other every day after that. I pretty much moved right in. It was like another world, just around the corner. His house was full of books and he told me I didn't have to bother finishing high school if I just read, so I'd read all day by the pool. He had a ton of art books too and we went through those together, looking at the images, pulling down book after book from the shelves as one thing reminded him of another. Music too. We'd see punk shows at night and he loved slam dancing but he'd blast opera and classical at home. Not that life was fancy. Not at all. The house was at the top of a steep hill and the driveway was just dirt. You couldn't get up there without a four-wheel drive. The yard was a jungle. When it rained everything would flood and we walked around the property in boots along with our bathing suits. But it felt glamorous to me. I'd stomp out to the jeep with rubber boots under my dress, cruise into town, then change into high heels before we went into the restaurant. It was an education, just living there. I didn't miss out on sex ed either. At first, I was shy and inexperienced. But as soon as I felt comfortable, I started to do research. While he was out I'd watch all the porn flicks in the house and then when he came home I'd be like, let's try that or I want you to do that to me. He was thrilled, of course — who wouldn't be? A young cute girl saying I want to be tied up or spanked, coming home to find me in the sauna with another girl. We'd pick girls up at a club or whatever, they'd stay a night or two and move on. Boys too, Zed didn't mind, as long as they looked like girls. Other times it was just me and him alone in the house and yard together for days. We'd go around naked, eating, cooking, sleeping outside on a futon we'd drag out under the stars, swimming at night, waking up to hear him typing, reaching for a book and reading till breakfast. We got married. My mother had to sign a form. Then we drove to Vegas, just the two of us, with the top down on the jeep, at night. Passing through Death Valley was so black and still and hot it was like being inside an oven or driving through outer space. And then you see Vegas blazing up ahead, like a planet. Zed had never been before. It attracted and repelled him. The tourists freaked him out, that side of America he'd never seen. Even fatter than the Germans, he kept saying, but dressed like giant drunken kids. We got married and hit the casino, and won a bunch of money playing craps and blackjack. Little did I know that was the last time he'd win. He totally got bit by the gambling bug, would start driving to Vegas on weekends and also gambling at the underground clubs in Chinatown until he owed way too much. But that was later. That first night it was all just magic. Getting married then rolling dice in my white silk slip dress and his black vintage suit, outfits we'd bought in a thrift store, winning big. He bought me a ring in a pawn shop, a sapphire, and then we spent our wedding night in a cabin out in the desert alone, cooking steaks and lobsters on a grill over a campfire. My mother of course had assumed that Zed would turn me into a movie star in no time and we'd all be living in a huge mansion, but it didn't work out quite like that. In fact it was a difficult time for Zed. He'd come to LA enticed by offers from producers and agents but nothing ever worked out. Project after project would fall through and meanwhile whatever heat there was around him cooled off. We had money, or we seemed too. We lived like we did. He'd option scripts or get attached to projects and they'd pay something up front and we got by on that, but the big payoff never came. There was this sense of frustration building all the time, a manic depressive cycle with each project, where this was going to be the one and it was all going to be so great and Zed being Zed they were all so ambitious and there'd be scripts and drawings and models and renting office space and big meetings and dinners and then it would all fall apart and he'd be like totally shocked and devastated. He was naive that way. He still just thought, every time, this is it, my big shot, and then he'd be heartbroken. Then he'd go on a rampage, drinking and waving his gun around and threatening to kill them all, whoever. He'd shoot at bottles in the yard. Then he'd fall into depression and talk about killing himself. He'd researched it thoroughly, knew the best ways, the least pain, how he could rig a camera to film it. I was the one who talked him into doing the horror film. At first it didn't sound grandiose enough for Zed. But I was like, hey it's a job, and if you actually get a film made here, even low-budget, it will attract more investors and build confidence with money people, and a lot of cult movies and horror movies are better than the mainstream trash anyway, and what about all these European exiles who made the old B-movies? That grabbed him more than anything, I think. He liked thinking about Fritz Lang and all those guys, the one who made *Detour*. You and he could have talked about that all night. Still, he claimed he had no idea about horror movies, he'd never seen one, blah blah, so I offered to help him write it, like sit at the computer and type and so forth, and he finally agreed. I think that at first the idea of us working together intrigued him more than the script itself. That I was his muse. So all of a sudden just like that, we were collaborators. Now instead of being an actress, which I'd never really wanted anyway, I was going to be this genius writer. Of course I didn't stop to think that I'd simply switched from my mother's fantasy to his. But I liked writing at least. Honestly it didn't seem so hard to me, like it did to him or to you, all that misery and drama and hating yourself and ripping things up. You never really reminded me of him until that first time I came home and you were lying on the floor with torn paper all around you. I was like, uh-oh, here we go again. Another diva. You two were the real actresses. To me making up a story was fun. I liked the script. I didn't care if it was a masterpiece. I liked being behind the camera with Zed. I could tell people didn't really take me seriously of course, this seventeen-year-old girl, but Zed did. He'd make everyone wait while he took me in the corner and asked what I thought. Still, even though it was flattering and showed how highly he thought of me, I realize now that it signaled a shift in him, the first tremors of self-doubt. Looking to me for reassurance, trusting my taste, not his own. In any case, it didn't end well. Once again the suits fucked us over. The backers were shady and ran out of money. At one point Zed drove to Vegas with his cameraman and tried to raise the cash by playing blackjack. In the end the bank owned the movie. They took it away from Zed, had some hacks recut it, changed the title, and dumped it onto the video market. After that Zed vowed no more commercial Hollywood movies. But it didn't occur to him that it is hard to live a commercial Hollywood lifestyle without them. He assured me everything was just fine. What we needed was a new project, one of our own. That was when we started working on the trilogy. Of course the basic subject matter, the texts, the music, were all from Zed. But more and more, he seemed to turn to me, taking my ideas and fantasies and incorporating them into the films. The lines were blurring and he wanted to blur them even more, between art and life, between himself and me. When I woke up in the morning, he'd ask about my dreams and write them down in a notebook. We'd take ecstasy and he'd tape-record us talking. Then Maria joined us, and it got even more complicated. She was a Mexican girl we met at a salsa club and brought home with us, and somehow she just never left. Everyone thought it was Zed's fantasy, but really it was my idea. I was lonely. I had no friends of my own, I wasn't in school or working a job, I hung out at that house all day. Maria was my age and we actually looked similar. People used to think we were sisters, which amused us because it made us feel even more perverse. We had a room in the house that we painted all black, sealed the windows with tinfoil and heavy curtains, where she and I went to light black candles and read our black books, play around with spells and potions. It was silly, we were children, but dangerous, demented children, with money and drugs and freedom. We'd have a fantasy or read something in a book and act it out like an amateur theater troupe. Maria and I making love while Zed and his friends watched. Group scenes. Whips and masks and candles. Multiple men and me. I never wanted you to know all that or to think of me that way. I thought it would change the way you saw me, twist it, poison our love. Was I wrong? Could you be happy knowing your wife had been a crazy slut? Or that her first great love wasn't you? That's why I lied. I never wanted you to know Mona. I decided to bury that person in Mexico and forget her forever, and just be Lala, your wife. But the dead won't stay buried, not when they've been murdered and hidden away, then they won't rest in peace. Mona became my ghost. I dreamed as her and caught glimpses of her in mirrors. I'd see her in your eyes when we made love. She was always waiting and watching. Looking back now, it would be easy to blame Zed for everything. You'd say, he was older, the grown-up. He was rich, supposedly. He was a man who took advantage of a young girl, two young girls. And you'd be right. But at the same time, I knew just what I was up to. I knew how to work him and get whatever I wanted, how to exploit his fear of failure, his fear that I would leave. I had the killer instincts of a girl who grew up among hustlers and had to fend for herself around needy or predatory adults. I used to say that Maria and I were both raised by wolves, just different packs. No doubt, hers was tougher, harder. Her mom died young. Like me, she had no dad. She'd crossed into the US illegally when she was fifteen, fleeing a little town where there wasn't much hope for a poor girl born out of wedlock. She adored her grandma, who raised her, and grew up close to her cousins, but she still swore that she'd never go back. She fantasized about having a big house some-day and bringing her grandma up to live there. She was wild. She was hungrier than I was, for adventure, men, sex, money, glamour. She wanted to be a star. She dressed like me, wore her hair and makeup the same way, liked to snuggle in bed on one side of me with Zed spooning me on the other. Maybe she was in love with me a little, or with our lives, or maybe just desperate to become somebody else, rich, white, famous, American. Who knows? One thing is for sure, the whole mess was doomed from the start. The whole triangle. Maybe our whole lives. It was right around that time that Buck first showed up. Zed gave him that nickname. He was Bradley Norman, a trust fund kid from somewhere back east supposedly studying film at UCLA but really just getting high and sucking up to us. Zed used to tease him about his All-American kind of aw-shucks vibe and his rich-kid lameness, calling him Bor-ing Normal, Barely Human, and so forth. He didn't care, he fol-lowed Zed around like a dog, laughed at all his jokes, thought every idea was brilliant, supplied the drugs. Then late one night, one of those old black-and-white Buck Rogers shows was on and Zed thought he was just like the actor, a real Ken doll, started calling him Buck and that was it. He didn't even look like him, but it was the perfect kind of ultra-American nickname and it stuck. I couldn't stand him. He gave me the creeps, the way he was always staring at me, at Maria, at Zed. I wasn't sure who he had the hots for and I doubt he even knew himself, but a scene like that always attracts the freaks and psychos. We found out later that he already had a history—kicked out of his fancy boarding school for trying to burn the dorm down while his roommates were sleeping, then kicked out of the special farm school they sent him to for killing the cat. I think his rich family just paid him to stay away. Zed didn't really like him either. He just liked having followers, flatterers. What he really wanted was money. He hoped Buck would help support his films. What I think now is, Buck didn't really want to fuck any of us. He wanted to *be* us. To be Zed. Anyway, it all came to a head when we made those last movies, the trilogy. Maybe we jinxed ourselves messing around with that dark magical shit. I am not religious of course or even superstitious, but I do feel like when we foolishly unleash forces we don't understand the results can be tragic. Years later I took an anthropology class and this teacher said something that really rang true. Something like, true spirituality is about selflessness, it's surrender, giving up yourself to something higher, a greater good. But magic is an attempt to manipulate the world for personal gain, to increase your own power and like, swell up the self. Prayer should shrink it. Magic is selfish and selfishness creates pain, even for yourself. We shot the first two parts at our house. *Invitation* and *Consummation*. On the one hand it was a normal film shoot, or at least normal for us, low budget and artsy-fartsy, thrown together with help from friends and various oddballs. But under the surface was something else, a nightmare carnival aspect. Most of the performers and crew people were somehow in the scene, into rituals or kink or drugs. It was all real to them. To us, too. It was our private lives and fantasies being acted out in public for the world to see. After the second film, the

one with all that sex in it, Maria had a freak out and locked herself
in the bathroom for hours until Zed, who was worried she might
kill herself, axed down the door. Even then somebody filmed it. I
suggested canceling or postponing the last shoot after all that, but
Zed wouldn't hear of it. The money was in place. He was convinced
that the trilogy would finally get him established as an important
artist. Meanwhile, unknown to me, the gambling debts had
mounted, interest on the interest, way beyond anything we could
pay. That suddenly burst into the open too, Zed's dirty secret, like
an affair or a secret drinking problem would have been for regular
people. In our home drugs and random sex were normal, but not
the bank calling about past-due mortgage payments and all the
money he'd borrowed against the house. There were letters that
said Final Warning across the envelope in red. There were lawsuits
over the whole fiasco of *Succubi!* and now the lawyers themselves
were suing us for payment. And these were the legit, lawful bullies.
There were also the gangsters, Italians from Vegas and Chinese
from downtown, stopping by for a chat, always nicely dressed and
soft-spoken, but Zed pale and shook up when they left, sleeping
now in the guest room with his gun under the pillow while the big
bedroom with its king-size bed and mirrors was just for Maria and
me. Sex, which was now all about performance and ritual, took
place in the living room, where we entertained guests, or the black-
walled dungeon room, or outside. But no matter what, the shoot
was on. Zed overcame my misgivings, as did Maria, who bounced
back from her freak out and was all for it, though now she was high
all the time and never seemed to sleep or eat. And I guess I wanted
it too. I wanted to believe it would change things, get us out of the
corner we were in. Like magic. So we packed up and drove to the
desert. It was a tiny crew. Just me, Zed, Maria, Buck as DP, and our
friend Tommy, who took sound and had become a constant hanger-
on. I liked him though. He was the sweet and lost type, still going
to art school although he was almost as old as Zed, happy to come
over and help paint scenery or sew costumes or just get high and

watch TV with me. Technically he was gay but really he was just obliging. He had a thing for Zed, like everyone did, he was very magnetic in those days, but Tommy was kindhearted and sort of submissive and not creepy like Buck. We took the lightweight 16mm camera with the built-in mic, so that I could run it during the scenes where all the guys were on-screen. The shoot was a disaster from the get-go. Of course we got a late start and by the time we arrived in the desert the shops were closed. Zed said not to worry, we'd get groceries in the morning, but of course we overslept and the cabin we'd rented was way out in the middle of nowhere and he was frantic to shoot. So there we were, insufficient food and water, but more than sufficient booze and drugs, intense heat and light, hauling equipment up and down and dancing around naked on boulders. Drinking warm beer and whiskey to quench your thirst in hundred-degree heat isn't wise. Neither is taking acid and getting lost in the desert. By nightfall we were all out of our minds, half crazy, but I guess Buck was all crazy. What I now believe is that he is evil. Just a bad soul. Rotten. And real evil isn't big and monstrous, it's small and pathetic and mean and weak but capable of true hate and cruelty. The rest of us are just fucked up, messy people trying our best and screwing up all the time. That's what I like to think anyway. That's how I hope you will remember me. As someone who tried her best but fucked up. Someone who loved you but wasn't sure how to. How do we learn, people like us, except by practicing on each other? The sundown was gorgeous and Zed got some shots. We built a fire and tried to roast hot dogs and burgers but we were too wasted. They were part burned and part raw and we threw them away. Coyotes howled and I thought I saw wolves running, packs in formation in the shadows, but it was dusk and in the desert the dusk will play tricks on you. That's how I felt when Buck killed Tommy. Like I was seeing things. Like I was dreaming, until I got woken up by someone screaming and realized it was me. Zed tried to revive Tommy but there was no chance. He was gone. Then he attacked Buck and almost strangled him. I think he would have killed him but Maria and I begged him not to. I said to call the cops, to turn Buck in. Buck didn't even object. He just looked at me like the whole thing was out of his hands, like he wasn't even the one who did it, covered in Tommy's blood. It was Maria who was worried about the cops, who pointed out how much trouble we could all be in, with the drugs and weapons and so forth. Accessories, whatever. The whole night passed and at dawn we had a plan. By now Buck had come down to earth. He was desperate and willing to do anything if it meant he didn't have to go to prison. He claimed he couldn't remember what happened, that it was all a blackout from drugs. That was when we saw how this could solve a lot of problems for all of us. Zed and me with our debts. Maria with the INS. I felt sick about it, but nothing was going to bring Tommy back. First, Zed faked the suicide. He loaded his pistol with a real bullet, put the gun in Tommy's hand and blew his face off, then toppled him over the cliff. The damage from the fall made it hard to see the knife wound and he was unrecognizable anyway. Then Zed hid in the desert while the rest of us went back to town and reported it. We said it was Zed who'd killed himself. We pretended not to know exactly where we'd been so it took a few days to find the body and by then the coyotes were at it. We all gave statements and no one doubted it was Zed. Buck obtained a passport for him and an envelope full of cash for us and one for Maria. Zed held onto the film as insurance. Then Maria and I traded passports, agreeing that she would go to Europe using my name. As long as she left LA, it was easy. Everyone had always mixed us up and called us sisters, and over there, where we were only known by name or from our films, she could pass. People don't really look. They see what they expect to see. Zed and I got to escape a life in LA that was destroying us and disappear to Mexico like outlaws. Maria got to be the widow of a famous artist and an American. She got to be me and I got to stop being me. Perfect. Buck would use his trust fund to pay for it all, but it didn't feel like blackmail. More like we were helping a sick friend and being thanked for our trouble. He eagerly agreed.

He seemed totally stunned by what he'd done. He kept crying. I pretty much expected him to go mad or confess or take his own life. Imagine my shock a few years later when he directed a hit movie. I guess he got over it. He moved on like the sociopath he really is and after that his fame and wealth just grew. But we were safe. We had him by the balls and he knew it. The money went into our accounts, no questions asked. But I did feel sometimes, like maybe he really had sacrificed poor Tommy in exchange for fame and success, that he had sold his soul to the devil or been some demon in disguise all along, that he'd tricked us all and stolen our souls. When he struck the deal that bought his own success, he doomed the rest of us in the bargain. That's how I feel anyway, because while Buck went up and up, America's sweetheart, we all went down and down. Not at first. At first it seemed like we might just make it, get away with everything and start again together. I was twenty. We traveled around Mexico for a while, the jungle, the beach. It cleared your head out and made you feel clean. Then we got a house and settled in. We lived by the ocean in a small village full of smugglers where no one cared who we were and asking questions about the past or how you got your money was considered rude. I went surfing and learned Spanish. It was like college for me. I read all the books that other people read in school. I spoke some Spanish already, from growing up in LA, and Maria had taught me more, we'd speak it at home so Zed couldn't understand, but now in Mexico I got fluent, not enough to fool the Mexicans of course, but good enough to fool white people with my dark skin. I fooled you too, my love. And I took care of Zed. He set up a studio and started painting. Really I think he had talent, and if he had dedicated himself to it the way he had to film at the start, he could have had another whole career, as a reclusive Mexican painter. Anyway that's my opinion, but he didn't have it in him. I couldn't see it at the time, but he was done, burned out. He painted, but only in spurts and only pictures of me. Most days, he smoked weed instead, standing waist-deep in the pool. He went drinking with the locals, the

fishermen and smugglers and Indians, who would dump him off
drunk at our door. Five years went by. Zed's depression got worse.
He had a lot of guilt about Tommy. He felt like he was being pun-
ished, like he was cursed. He even went to the church and prayed,
though he was drunk at the time. He sought help from the Indians
and their healers. He would go on long rituals with them, out in the
jungle and in the desert, taking medicine and whipping his back to
chase out the demons. It didn't work. A shrink probably would have
helped more. Then he lost his sex drive, and though I tried to reas-
sure him, he felt like this too was a punishment. His talent and his
libido, the two engines that drove his life, both ran out on him.
Suddenly he was the old impotent fool with the sexy young wife he
was terrified of losing. And then at last I realized I really did have to
leave him. It was what he had always feared and predicted, but not
for the reasons he'd thought: not for new sexual or artistic adven-
tures, just the opposite. I was a twenty-five-year-old woman. I
wanted to go to school, to have a job, a life, maybe even a family
someday. I wanted to be single for a while, to be on my own, and
then I wanted another marriage maybe, with a real partner. I had
been Zed's lover, then his muse, his mistress, his caretaker, and at
last his nurse. Had I ever really been his wife? The other thing that
happened was my mother died. She'd become a big-time alcoholic
years before. She was in and out of rehab, Promises Malibu, Betty
Ford, only the best for her of course, but it never worked and finally
she smashed her car up on Mulholland Drive. I didn't go home for
the funeral, how could I, but I swore I was not going to watch Zed
do the same, drive off the cliff drunk or drown in our pool. Finally I
told him and he understood. He wasn't even mad. He said he'd help
me. With his shady local connections, we got a fake ID and a Mexican passport and then applied for a student visa under that name. I
packed and we spent a last night together, hugging and crying and
apologizing and thanking each other. Then in the morning, he
drove me into town to the airport and I left. I flew to New York and
spent a winter there, taking classes and working in a clothing shop,

then returned to LA. I suppose that might seem like a foolish choice. But there was no one left to recognize me, really. I never had normal friends, or any family besides my mom. Plus, Maria had come back, and she was in bad shape. She'd had some sort of breakdown in Europe and was in a psych ward in Pasadena. I went to see her, to see if I could help and also to find out what she was saying about us. It was a rough visit. After pretending to be me for so long, she finally believed it herself. In her mind, she was Mona, and I was her. So I just hugged her and went along with it. She would be Mona and I would be Eulalia Natalia, the new me. After that her doctor, this guy Parker, said it was better if I didn't come back, that seeing people from the past just upset her. But the trip home brought back good memories too. I missed the sun, the hills, the food. I just stayed. I got a job doing something I actually liked and was good at. I made friends. I got my own little studio apartment. And I met you. I want to say that no matter what, those next years with you were the best of my life and I will always be grateful for what you gave me. Real love, real happiness. You showed me what those were. But it didn't last, did it? Something happened. We wore each other down. We gave up on each other. Or maybe our expectations were wrong all along. In the end, you are not responsible for anyone else's unhappiness. And no one else can save you from your own. But I didn't know that and I got angry, so angry. I felt trapped in that house with you, like a cage. I felt like it was all wrong and it was all your fault. I felt like I had to make you change, or else be done. And then Zed wrote to me. I'd given him an email address when I left, for emergencies only, and honestly I'd forgotten about it, didn't even check it for months and months. But when I began to separate from you emotionally, to have secrets, it seemed natural to use that account and there it was, his note. He told me he was dying. He told me he was sending the film. It felt like a sign. It was like the old me, Mona, getting back in touch. Suddenly I had a way out. I could take that money and disappear again. I could be free. So I ran away from home, one more time. But of course I didn't get far.

Buck had been keeping tabs on us all along. He had people watching, in Mexico, in Europe, in LA. When Maria fell ill he made her a prisoner in that hospital. But he couldn't touch Zed or me because of the film. Then he found out about Zed's cancer, and he knew he had to make a move. He couldn't trust what a dying man would do, or leave the film floating out in the world. So he had his people snatch me up. Since then I've been here, alone, locked in this room. He says he will trade me to Zed for the film but I know he won't. He can't leave me alive. Once he has the movie, I am the only loose thread and he will cut me off. This is the end. I do feel some small comfort in knowing that by leaving I kept you out of this, that you are safe from Buck. I am glad that even though you will probably always hate me, you will never know the whole ugly truth. You won't even know my real name. Because you will never even read this, my good-bye letter. Because there is no letter. I am not writing it. There is no pen, no paper. I am handcuffed to a bed in a cabin in the desert, waiting for someone to come kill me, lying in the dark and talking to you. There is no one here to hear my voice when I talk. I am not even talking. It is silent. There are no words at all. Love always. Your Lala.

88

WE SET OUT THE NEXT morning after a breakfast that only Lonsky and Milo could eat. Nic and I were too nervous, just as we'd been too keyed up to sleep, lying together and talking all night. Lonksy had pancakes, eggs, bacon, ham, and biscuits. Milo had half that then went to rest by the pool. Lonsky wanted Nic to stay behind too, but she insisted, and we still needed her to drive.

It was only seven thirty and the air was still cool. Birds called to each other from out of sight. A jackrabbit looked us over then bounced into the scrub. We headed down the highway and turned in at the Joshua Tree National Park. No guard was on duty yet, but at Lonksy's insistence I stopped and paid, putting the cash into the envelope provided and sliding it into a slot. The park was empty and silent in the morning, the rocks and ridges shading and shining in the shifting light, changing form and color like the depths of the sea I'm told this once was, a fresh world where everything was still alive and aware, stone, sun, wind, a world free to start again from nothing. As she drove, Nic put her hand out and touched mine. I held it tight.

Lonsky, who held the map, told us where to turn and we began a steep climb, arriving at a lookout point atop a high cliff, a flat tablet overlooking the landscape. We parked. At first we were alone. We sat in silence, as if at a drive-in, too tense to speak.

"There," Lonsky said, just as Nic and I saw it too, a black sedan, tiny from this height, winding along the road like a bug. It vanished from view then reappeared over the far ridge. It made its way toward us, raising dust, windshield flaring in the light. We got out as it approached and stopped, facing us, about twenty yards away. The door opened. Buck emerged, holding a gun. His sunglasses flashed and his shirt flapped in the hot wind.

"I said come alone, Lonsky," he called.

"Preposterous," he answered. "I can't even drive."

"OK," Buck said. "Send the writer with the cans. The girl waits in the car."

"Show us the hostage first," Solar said.

Buck opened the back door and reached inside. He pulled out a woman, dressed in jeans and a white T-shirt. Her wrists were bound behind her and a white linen sack was tied around her head.

"Here she is. Now the film canisters."

"How do we know that's her?" I asked. "Mona!" I yelled. Her head perked up and she began to twist around. Buck yanked her close and pushed the gun to her head.

"How do I know there's film in those cans?" Buck answered.

"We'll just have to have faith, and if doesn't work out, kill each other later."

I glanced at Lonksy. He nodded.

"Sounds good," I called. Lonsky handed me the cans. "Be right back," I said to Nic. I realized there were tears in her eyes. She grabbed me tight.

"Be careful," she whispered.

"Hey, don't worry," I said. "I'll see you in a minute. Don't go soft on me now, hard ass." She sniffed, and I whispered in her ear. "I'm glad you turned out to be you and not anyone else."

She smiled. She kissed me.

"Let's go," Buck yelled. "It's getting hot out here."

Nic got back in the car. I held out the cans like a pizza I was delivering and started walking.

"Slow, slow, take it easy, writer," Buck said, holding Mona in front of him, gun on me now. "You know, I hate to disappoint you, but I don't think our film project is going to work out after all."

"I figured that," I said, stepping steadily, balancing the cans in my bandaged hands, trying not to tremble or let my voice break.

"I hope you don't mind," he went on, I was about a dozen yards away now, "I fed your manuscripts to my shredder. I'm a big recycler."

"No problem," I said. They were the only copies left. Three novels. A lifetime of labor. I shrugged.

"Let's face it," he said. "No one was ever going to read them. People need hope and comfort. Real stories that give them a sense of meaning. Boring books like yours just upset and confuse people. Life is already confusing and upsetting enough."

He had a point. There were a thousand, a hundred thousand great books already, sitting unvisited in libraries that were closing down every day, and what did it matter? Most would soon be forgotten, crumble to dust, and blow away. How many great masterpieces were already lost, written in languages no one read any longer, for people no one remembered?

Yet one had to do something to fill one's time on this planet. If by some chance I survived till lunchtime, what was I going to do? Paint houses? Sell cars? Cure cancer? Run for congress? Fuck it. I would really, really suck at all those things. I might as well write *Perineum*. Maybe if I was very lucky someday some heartbroken house painter or suicidal car salesman or lonely oncologist or congressman in an existential crisis, or even some angry poetry major, would come across something I wrote in a dusty, bankrupt used book shop, and recognize the message I left just for them, written in the secret tongue that you thought no one else spoke, that you almost forgot yourself, until you found it there, crushed like a whisper between the pages of a book.

"Sam, look out!" It was Nic, yelling. I turned. She was out of the car and running toward me, pointing and shouting. Russ had emerged from behind a boulder, aiming a rifle at me. I jumped as a bullet smacked the ground at my feet, throwing up a handful of dirt. Russ swerved and fired again, blowing a hole through Nic's chest. I rushed to her side, but she was already gone, a look of wonder on her face. What did she see? I hope not just dirt and a tire. I hope she saw some angel she would never stoop to believe in, or my face, at least. I hope she heard my voice, as I whispered, I love you, only then realizing it might be true.

"Down," Lonsky yelled, pushing me aside. He had that cannon in his hand. I dropped and he fired, one shot. The top of Russ's skull blew away. Lonsky whirled, gracefully, like a dancer, and aimed at Buck next, but it was too late. Buck fired and a red flower burst open on the meaty part of Lonksy's upper leg. He fell and his shot went wide, shattering the sky reflected in Buck's windshield.

"Run, Mona," I yelled and threw the cans at Buck, frisbeeing them toward his head. He ducked and the girl broke away, running blindly. I caught her in mid-flight and half-led, half-dragged her behind Buck's car. "Get down, get down," I said.

Peeking around under the car, I could see that one of the cans had popped open. Film was unspoiled in the dust, stirring like a snake in the wind. Buck picked up the other canister. I could see Lonsky crawling, dragging his huge body through the sand like a wounded monster, like a bloody bull, but he was on the wrong side of my car to take a clear shot. I knew I'd have to try and maneuver Buck into range. Mona sat up and Buck fired, shattering the side windows as her white, covered head popped into range like a target. I threw her down in the dirt and lay beside her.

"Get down, stay down," I told her, fumbling at the cord around her wrist. I loosened it a little. "Listen, Mona, you don't know me but I'm here to help. Get under the car, and don't come out till the shooting stops, OK?"

The white gauze head turned to me, like a ghost.

"Sam, is that you?"

"Lala?" I pulled the hood off. It was my wife. Alive. She screamed. Buck was there, over us, holding the film in one arm, pointing the gun with the other.

"Story over," he said. "You should thank me. Snobs like you hate happy endings."

I grabbed Lala's hand and she squeezed it. Buck smiled. Then I smiled back and he turned, just in time to see what I saw, Zed emerging from behind the scrub and running straight at him. Zed hit him hard, tackling him, and the two men stumbled, gripping each other, like boxers in a clutch or weary lovers, clinging together through one last dance. They went over the edge together with their film.

89

A HELICOPTER ARRIVED FIRST, and the medics patched up Lonsky, but decided it might be wiser not to try to airlift him. He agreed. "I assure you my vital arteries are well insulated. I will be fine." He was right, as usual. When the cops and ambulances showed up he was taken to a local hospital where the bullet was quickly removed with no major damage. He then had Milo drive him straight to another hospital, Green Haven, where he intended to take a very long rest.

"I'm sorry that you couldn't save your Mona," I told him as a team of rangers and medics loaded him.

"Yes," he said. "But we saved yours. And I suppose even I must be wrong once in my life." He blinked, and for a second I thought I saw a feeling flicker through him. Then he fixed his gaze on mine and shook my hand firmly. "Despite a few early missteps," he said, "your conduct throughout this case has been quite competent, generally speaking. You have the makings of a good detective."

"Thank you," I said. "That means a lot."

He nodded as they shut the door.

The bodies of Russ and Nic were bagged and removed. It took longer to recover Buck and Zed but when they did they found Zed had an empty bottle of morphine tablets. His cancer was far gone and he had to have been in great pain.

The news story that they eventually put out suggested that Buck Norman had died while scouting locations when he was attacked by bandits or would-be kidnappers who shot his bodyguard. Some suggested he'd even died trying to save his "unknown companion," the nameless blond woman who was also killed. Others said she was an actress whom he was about to transform into a star. America's storyteller would be remembered the way we knew him and everyone involved seemed happy to let it rest there. The film was damaged beyond repair, hung in a long, tattered strip down the side of the mountain.

90

FINALLY, AFTER THE QUESTIONS, the bandages, the hydration, the cops and ambulances, the promise to be reachable when needed, they finally told Lala and me that we too could go. Everyone cleared out and we found ourselves alone, standing in front of our old station wagon, in the middle of the desert, on top of a tower of rock. The sun beat down like a hammer on a nail head. The only sign of human life within sight was our car and the road beneath it.

"Well," I said. "Here we are. This is kind of awkward."

"Nice tooth," Lala said.

I smiled. "Thanks." Instinctively, I walked toward the driver's side and she to the passenger's, as we had every day for years.

"Wait," I said. "I can't drive." I held up my hands. We walked around, passing each other, and got in. I gave her the keys.

"What happened to your fingers, anyway?" she asked.

"It's a long story," I said. My eyes flicked down, then up to meet her eyes. I looked at her. "Actually I have a confession to make."

She looked back at me.

"So do I."

ACKNOWLEDGMENTS

I want to express my immense gratitude to my editor, Ed Park, for first adopting this book and then making it so much better, as well as to his entire championship team. I am also eternally grateful to Doug Stewart for continuing to make it all possible and to everyone at Sterling Lord Literistic, especially the amazing Madeleine Clark. I want to thank Eric Kosse and William Fitch for endless reading, encouragement and comfort; Rivka Galchen, my first and favorite responder; and Jennifer Martin for everything, always. I wish particularly to thank Irene Donoso for checking my Spanish. As usual, all errors of grammar, spelling, taste and judgment are my own. Lastly, I want to thank my family, who put up with the most for the longest, for their endless supply of patience and love.